Resounding praise for
ROBERT W. WALKER
and his first novel featuring
Inspector Alastair Ransom
CITY FOR RANSOM

"Robert W. Walker has enjoyed a solid reputation for his unique concoctions of twisted crimes, colorful characters, dark humor, and solid plotting. The Walker brew is as bubbly as ever in *City For Ransom*. . . . I can't wait for the second Ransom book—I'm hooked!"   Raymond Benson

"Lovers of historical thrillers will be shocked, stunned, beaten to hell, and, most importantly, riveted to this page-turner of peerless quality. Robert Walker is a master craftsman and this is the series he was born to create."
                              Jay Bonansinga, author of *Frozen*

"Vivid and passionate."   Barbara D'Amato

"*City For Ransom* is crime-noir at its finest. . . . In an era of high-tech crime-fighting, this novel is an old-fashioned but fresh surprise."
                    David W. Ellis, author of *In the Company of Liars*

"Walker writes . . . entertaining stories filled with surprises, clever twists, and wonderfully drawn characters."
                                 Daytona Beach News-Journal

"This is historical mystery with teeth, and Ransom is the best new hero in period fiction. I can't wait to be Ransomed again."
                                          J.A. Konrath

"*City for Ransom* is a superb, dark, skillful, hypnotic work. Calling it a mystery, or crime noir, or thriller, or work of suspense or horror would be short-changing this masterful creation. Yes, it's a gripping dark suspense-filled story but always, always, it's Chicago that marches proudly through these pages, breathing life into them as only a master like Robert W. Walker can accomplish."

Pat Mullan, author of *Blood Red Square*

"Walker has upped the bar for solid historical mysteries. With twists and turns galore, this is one story that earns its keep in the genre. Ransom is a character as smooth as Doyle's Holmes, as bold as Stout's Wolfe, and as vivid as Hammett's Charles. *City for Ransom* puts the reader right where they should be, in the thick of things. Outstanding!"

Alexis Hart, editor, publisher, and author of *Child of Hope*

"Key elements make the who-done-it intriguing but what comes alive from these components are insights into a by-gone era such as the early days of the science of criminology, and the role of women during an investigation . . . with a strong cast, especially Ransom and J. Phineas Tewes. Robert W. Walker is at his lofty best with this terrific historical mystery." *The Midwest Review of Books*

"Inspector Alastair Ransom's Chicago is brutal and violent, cloaking mysteries and intrigues in a façade of propriety as spectral and illusory as the grand and gleaming buildings of the vanished 'White City.' "

Richard Lindberg, author of *Chicago by Gaslight: A History of Chicago's Netherworld, 1880–1920*

Books by
Robert W. Walker

SHADOWS IN THE WHITE CITY
CITY FOR RANSOM

SHADOWS
IN THE
WHITE CITY

ROBERT W. WALKER

HARPER

An Imprint of HarperCollinsPublishers

This is a work of fiction. Names, characters, places, and incidents are products of the author's imagination or are used fictitiously and are not to be constructed as real. Any resemblance to actual events, locales, organizations, or persons, living or dead, is entirely coincidental.

HARPER

An Imprint of HarperCollins*Publishers*
10 East 53rd Street
New York, New York 10022-5299

Copyright © 2007 by Robert W. Walker
ISBN: 978-0-06-073996-6
ISBN-10: 0-06-073996-7

First Harper paperback printing: April 2007

HarperCollins® and Harper® are registered trademarks of HarperCollins Publishers.

Printed in the United States of America

Visit Harper paperbacks on the World Wide Web at
www.harpercollins .com

10 9 8 7 6 5 4 3 2 1

Shadows in the White City *is dedicated to my son,*
Stephen R. Walker,
who has loved me unconditionally from the day I met him.

SHADOWS
IN THE
WHITE CITY

CHAPTER 1

Chicago, Illinois, June 7, 1893 . . . 1 A.M.

PHANTOM OF THE FAIR STILL AT LARGE ARRESTS OF TWO SUSPECTS PROVE FALSE LEADS ARRESTING OFFICER RANSOM NEAR DEATH, UNDER INVESTIGATION

Chicago Herald exclusive by Thomas Carmichael

Despite two arrests in the case of the Phantom of the Fair (seven killings by garrote and incineration), both suspects are today free men, released due to lack of evidence against either man—one a photographer, the other a carriage driver.

Meanwhile, Inspector Alastair Ransom is credited with the most recent arrest in the case, now called a false arrest based upon conceit and harassment. In fact, if Mr. Ransom lives, he may well face charges of an extraordinary nature, not the least being incompetence.

In essence, police remain stymied by the

elusive Phantom, who no one doubts may strike again at any moment. The list of innocent lives lost to this fiend includes one unborn child, destroyed while in its mother's womb. When will public outrage over these crimes exceed our gratuitous fascination with murder? Masked as it is by the sheer growth of our great city. Masked as well by the commerce and the new skyscrapers rising up along our magnificent lakefront, and the marvels of modern invention and industry we see daily now at the World's Columbian Exposition.

At Cook County Hospital, Dr. Christian Fenger was a *god,* his word *law.* He also proved a capable showman. As faculty and doctors on staff taught medicine and surgery in connection with Rush Medical College, Cook County had a modest and typically adequate operating theater with well-worn equipment and staggered seating for just over seventy observers. The arena was a platformed, wooden-tiered wedding cake, so that from anywhere in the room, with good eyesight, anyone might look over Dr. Christian Fenger's shoulder. News had got out that he was performing emergency surgery on none other than the infamous Inspector Alastair Ransom of the Chicago Police Department, shot and mortally wounded. Despite the hour, the room bulged with the crowd.

Christian Fenger was, after all, known the country over as the best surgical mentor in the city. Watching him work to save a wounded copper with a hole the size of a woman's fan in his side proved fascinating and awe-inspiring. Indeed, such an opportunity proved irresistible to medical people—men and women. Indeed, it proved the best education a medical student could find in Chicago and all the Midwest.

It's a terrible thing what's happened to Ransom, thought

Dr. Jane Francis—dressed in the clothes and makeup of a male doctor people knew as Dr. James Phineas Tewes—*shot by my own daughter.*

Still, to see the operation so flawlessly done almost made it worth the experience. Certainly not for the patient, but for those who practiced surgery, and those like Jane who wanted to practice surgery, but could not. Christian was the penultimate surgeon. Watching him work again was, for Jane, like watching the miraculous before one's eyes. People spoke of how they wanted to see God's presence in things; if they only stopped to think of it—here it was, in the deft hands of one of His creations—Dr. Christian Fenger.

As these thoughts ebbed and flowed inside Jane's head while watching the master at work, she also realized that the man on the operating table was the man she'd fallen in love with all over again, and that he could as yet die—Dr. Fenger or no—of the trauma or infection. She privately admonished herself for "enjoying" the grand educational aspects of the moment. So far as surgery went, it was indeed remarkable. But it was also under circumstances that could end in the death of Alastair Ransom.

She had dragged her daughter, Gabrielle, into the theater to get a good position. But Gabby quickly became antsy watching Fenger perform surgery—not due to any squeamishness, as Gabby would one day be a skilled surgeon herself. Guilt had propelled her from the room. Guilt over having shot the patient. The *accident* with Ransom weighed too heavily on her heart, causing her inability to watch or to learn. Dr. Jane Francis—*the real Jane Francis below the makeup*—stood transfixed at the delicate operation that may or may not save Alastair for this world.

Even mesmerized at Christian's skill, Jane felt torn. She wanted to learn from Christian, but she wanted to rush out as well. Go behind her daughter and hold her and tell her it was not her fault—that all would be well. *To lie to her.* To fill her head with all the clichés of comfort necessary at such times; clichés seldom true. To tell her that things happened for a reason. That there is a purpose to all things great and small—regardless of one's limited perspective.

The city of Chicago itself had come about through either divine or satanic purpose, or perhaps both. The city could be seen as an enormous gift to cherish and nurture, or an enormous burden—a view that, if taken to extreme, might result in a desire to destroy it. Perhaps there was something of this dark emotion and purpose in the drive that sent a phantom night stalker scurrying about Chicago and the World's·Fair for victims to garrote and set aflame. Perhaps not. Throughout history men of science, philosophy, theology, literature, even military genius were studied, but mankind must also begin to understand the genesis of the maniac, the deviant, and the killer. To understand the workings of the perverted mind in order to, perhaps one day, correct it, possibly through surgery.

Jane's daughter, Gabby, too, was fascinated by the possibility of understanding root causes of murder, and more of the population in general seemed curious, reading such works as Bram Stoker's *The Snake's Pass,* Mary Shelley's *Frankenstein,* and going to see Robert Louis Stevenson's *The Strange Case of Dr. Jekyll and Mr. Hyde* performed live onstage.

"What's to understand?" Ransom had once doggedly asked Jane, when he knew her only as Dr. James Phineas Tewes. Speaking to Dr. Tewes, he'd added, "You don't need to understand the inner workings of a ratty ferret's brain to know that a bullet will end its career."

"We've got to understand the sort of prey you hunt, Ransom!"

"Understanding isn't apprehension."

"But it could lead to apprehension if we learn to think like them, to study the darker reaches of the mind."

"We all have our dark side."

"But a killer has given his soul over to it! Why? We must ask why."

"You ask why; I'll stick with when and how."

Ransom's stubbornness had infuriated her both as Tewes and as herself. *Yet that same stubbornness and iron will might yet save his life, if he holds on,* Jane now thought.

Jane continued to struggle with what to do about Gabby at this moment. *Should I stay to see a genius at work, or go in search of my inconsolable daughter?*

She chose to stay. *Gabrielle needs the alone time,* she rationalized; she'll understand: No one as interested in medicine as Jane must miss an opportunity to see Dr. Fenger doing what he did best. So Jane, in the garb of Dr. James Phineas Tewes, remained first at Christian's side and now in a niche of the operating theater, where young male interns from all over the city continued to arrive and crowd her.

She'd heard some remarks floating about the hospital that Ransom's regular doctor, a Dr. Caine McKinnette, a fellow rumored to be of low moral character, had arrived to look in on him and to consult with Dr. Fenger on the case. From all accounts, McKinnette was a pill-pushing quack who'd fed Alastair's drug habit; the man was known for replacing symptoms with euphoria. Jane had first recognized McKinnette as the man Fenger had cousulted before making his first cut. Christian had scolded McKinnette even as he interrogated the man about what chemical substances Alastair had been taking that might explain his breaking into Dr. James Phineas Tewes's home with a crazed drunken look and pointing a gun, crashing a tea party. "Hell I'd a shot 'im, too, if he'd come through my door like that!" Fenger had shouted when Jane told him the story.

Unlike the dapper Dr. Tewes—famed for dispensing magnetic therapy and phrenology—the aged Dr. McKinnette resembled Marley's raggle-taggle ghost as illustrated in Dickens's *A Christmas Carol.* McKinnette need post no bills, need make no claims, and need not one skill. On the other hand, Jane must post bills, make outrageous claims, and demonstrate extraordinary skills to survive as Dr.

James Phineas Tewes. In fact, she'd tacked up several of her posters just outside Cook County Hospital in an effort to gain patients. Her posters read,

Phrenological & Magnetic Examiner
at his residence, 2nd house north of the Episcopal Church

DR. TEWES

May be consulted in all cases of Nervous or Mental difficulty. Application of the remedies will enable relief or cure any case of Monomania, Insanity or Recent Madness wherein there is no Inflammation or destruction of the Mental Organs. Dr. Tewes's attention to diseases of the nervous system, such as St. Vitus's Dance and Spinal Afflictions has resulted in some remarkable cures. Having been engaged for the past ten years in teaching Mental Philosophy, Phrenology, together with numerous Phreno Magnetic Experiments enable Dr. Tewes to give correct and true delineations of Mental Dispositions of different persons. A visit to Dr. Tewes can be profitable to any and all who wish to better understand their own natures, and how best to apply their talents in the world at large.

Watching Dr. Fenger, Jane realized that allowing McKinnette to stand alongside him in the operating theater, although useless and in the way, left Jane to suspect that Christian Fenger was not above purchasing illegal drugs when circumstance called for it. This could be a nail in Christian's coffin, adding to abuses that could get him dismissed from Rush Medical and Cook County. His crown taken away. If information of this nature got into the wrong hands, it could also mean blackmail. Jane had enough information on Fenger to topple him if she chose to reveal what he'd confided in her at a time when he thought he was dealing with Dr. Tewes, while under magnetic and phrenological care.

Unable to continue the ruse with a man she so respected, Jane having been his student years before, had recently confessed her true identity to Dr. Fenger and had assured him that all his confidences remained safe within the purview of doctor-patient relations.

Christian had a lot of ghosts to deal with, but his hand was as steady today as it had been when Jane first came to his surgical classes ten years ago.

Still, Fenger had a habit, what people in her profession called *the doctor's curse*—morphine. Living daily with so much disease, suffering, and death, eventually it caught a man in its grip. No one staring into the abyss of human suffering as long as Dr. Fenger could possibly walk away unscathed.

She prayed his habit would not affect his handling of the blade over Alastair—a man for whom she felt deep affection. At one point, she'd debated whether to step in and protest, but she'd stopped short, seeing how in control Christian was. Then her faith was shaken anew at McKinnette's arrival. She didn't care for the degree of the palsied elder doctor's involvement in anesthetizing Alastair. The wrong dosage alone could kill him. Why this old fool McKinnette? Why not a younger man with more experience in this new field? She imagined that Caine McKinnette wanted to be on hand due to the notoriety this case must engender. Some measure of publicity for himself in the case, to improve his practice, to have some of the Fenger mystique rub off on him—a highly unlikely prospect. He'd even brought a newspaperman with him, same newsie who'd been at the train station the day Alastair had detached the loosely connected and incinerated head of a dead young man named Cliff Purvis and shoved it into Dr. Tewes's white cotton gloves and white linen suit. *Thom Carmichael for the* Herald, she thought now, no doubt also seeing Dr. McKinnette for medicinal needs, and no doubt here to report how Dr. McKinnette had helped save— or attempted his best to save—the life of the last hero of Haymarket, Inspector Alastair Ransom.

How wide a web did Dr. Caine McKinnette spin? She could not say, nor could she concern herself entirely with him at the moment. Instead she softly whispered a silent prayer for Ransom even as she watched, fascinated, at the procedure. Fenger's hands worked over his friend with a deft precision she'd never seen in any other man.

Ransom was in the hands of God, on the one hand, Dr. Fenger on the other. The result of this tug-of-war would not soon be known.

So all across Chicago, in circles of wealth and power, and in circles of poverty and despair, in barbershops and taverns, the odds makers took all bets. But few men who knew him personally would say there was any contest, for Ransom remained the last survivor of scars from the Haymarket Riot. Jane Francis thought about the impact the 1886 Haymarket Square Riot had had on the city. It'd established new laws governing the conduct of police officials, and was a turning point in public opinion regarding unionist workers and unions, and it ultimately brought the first labor laws into being. Illinois led in this political arena—far ahead of New York and other states. Little wonder, people still called Ransom a hero.

Few would bet against Ransom even now with the Grim Reaper hovering over the big man, although the urge to count him out had a strong appeal for men like Moose Muldoon, who skirted the law, and men like Chief Nathan Kohler—Ransom's immediate superior—who abused the law from a high position.

Ransom, on the operating table, erupted in voice, saying, "Tewes has cures for everything . . . even baldness." Ransom said these many words while under anesthetic. This sent up a wave of gasps and audible *awhs*.

"Confound it, Dr. McKinnette!" Fenger cried out in alarm. "More ether, now!"

"Right away!" And the anesthesiologist rushed to the job, attempting to put Alastair out again. How fitting a position for a man who dispensed dreams and euphoria.

As she witnessed the rest of the operation, Jane's heart stopped at the next words coming from Alastair's unconscious. He muttered in mournful fashion, "Like . . . ahhh beast . . ."

"What's he saying?" gasped a young intern.

". . . with horns . . . iii've torn . . ."

"What's it mean?" asked another internist.

". . . anyone who's reached out . . . to me . . ."

Finally, the ether did its work, and Alastair was silenced.

She wondered if it would be the last time she'd ever hear his voice again.

On street level, outside under the gas lamps lighting Cook County Hospital paced Dot'n'Carry—Henry Bosch—Ransom's peg-leg snitch. For him, news of the outcome, either way, live or die, meant cash. This information would sell.

CHAPTER 2

While Alastair lay on the operating table, Griffin Drimmer had work to do. He busied himself with processing the young, innocent-looking killer, but even as he filled out paperwork, he realized just how flimsy a case he and Ransom really had against Waldo Denton. Ninety percent of it lay in Alastair's head, and should he die . . .

Sure, they had the garrote, but even that had been rendered useless. Since the news stories of the Phantom—garrotes of all size and shape had been selling like proverbial hotcakes. Anyone might be carrying the deadly weapon, but what must be proven in court was *intent* and *use* issues; in short, that this *particular* garrote was, without doubt, the very one used on seven Chicago victims. As the diamond-shaped tattoo at the throat had been reported in some of the twenty-six Chicago newspapers, one underworld manufacturer of a line of garrotes now had incorporated this feature!

Did Denton intend to use the weapon as a weapon or as a mere tool, as he'd calmly explained. "I raise chickens on a rooftop, and when things become particularly bleak and there's no food, I'll kill a chicken."

"Using a garrote? On chickens?"

"It works wonderfully well—quick and painless. I cannot abide seeing an animal suffer."

Griff thought, *My God, if there's any truth in it, then we have no case.* Denton next quoted chapter and verse of the recently inaugurated law governing deadly intent and weapons use. If there could be shown any doubt whatsoever that Denton indeed used the garrote in the manner described, then the garrote found in his pocket—with what he claimed to be chicken blood adhering to it—was no longer a weapon but rather a tool used in a fowl business rather than a foul business, and must be treated as such. There was no science on earth that could separate and identify animal from human blood. Reasonable doubt had begun to spring up like so many freckles turning to boils.

Thus went the smoking evidence—the bloody garrote found on Waldo Denton.

A good lawyer like McCumbler would tear their case to shreds if Denton could afford him, but even with a court-appointed lawyer, the result might be the same. What did they have alongside the suspicions and assumptions held by Inspector Ransom? If asked to back Alastair Ransom a hundred percent, or if asked to swear to it in a court of law, Griff knew he'd have to do so, but that it would be at great peril to his job. However, it might never come to that. Sad as it might be, the law did not allow for tenuous connections made in the mind of a detective or policeman as evidence in a case—certainly not since Haymarket. There was a time—Alastair's time—when a cop's word alone could send a man to prison or to the gallows, but the "good old golden days," as many a cop called them, were long gone by 1893.

Already the city prosecutor's office disliked the "thinness" of the case, characterizing it as a "helluva stretch in credulity" to think that they must prosecute Denton—a mere boy without a criminal record, and without the least athletic appearance as a multiple killer. How could Denton possibly be the Phantom of the Fair? *To parade Denton before the*

*public as the infamous monster? This could turn them all
into laughingstocks, God forbid!* Given the lack of physical
evidence, and the lack of catching the killer in the act—
rather he was at tea with his *supposed* next victim—did not
help Ransom's cause. Still, Griffin tried as best he could to
stand in for Alastair and to argue Ransom's reasoning.

Unfortunately, by now Griff had little belief in it himself,
and this likely showed as Prosecutor Hiram Kehoe had
stopped at one point in his questioning of Griffin on the
particulars to ask point blank, "Inspector Drimmer, are *you*
convinced of the boy's guilt?"

"I . . . I well not at first, but . . ."

"Go on."

"—but Inspector Ransom has an uncanny ability at sniffing out the truth and tracking down felons—a thing proven
many times over."

"I'm not asking your opinion on Ransom. God knows we
all have an opinion on Ransom. I am asking for *your* conviction."

"The evidence points to Denton. He'd decoyed Inspector
Ransom, you see."

"Decoyed?" asked Kehoe.

"Ahhh . . . led him astray—to the lagoon in the park—
while Denton went straight for the Tewes's home."

"Led Ransom on a wild-goose chase? That could be con-
strued as a prank, a joke."

"Yes, sir, but, but—"

"Was anyone in the Tewes home harmed?"

"None but Alastair, no. But you see, Inspector Ransom's
emotions . . . ahhh . . . that is, as he has affections for Dr.
Tewes's sister and daughter, and fearing for their safety, he
rushed headlong—"

"Precisely . . . all this I've heard from the ladies and by-
standers nearly run over by the coach you two shared!"

"Haste was of the utmost—"

"The city is having to replace a Chinaman's hand lorry, a
vegetable kiosk, and a broken axle!"

"I am sorry for all inconven—"

"I think all concur," Kehoe stated while jotting notes in a small book he kept, "including you, from your words that Inspector Ransom acted rashly, foolishly!" He stopped to jot more notes on this. "Embarrassing not only himself but the Chicago Police Department. Being led astray on a prank amid the most horrific case the city has known . . . his emotions swaying in the proverbial wind . . . a fear gripping him—and he literally broke into the Tewes residence without a warrant, without provocation."

Griff kept his silence.

Kehoe finished the interview, saying, "I'll have to examine the case in light of all that Inspector Griffin has said."

A fear gripped Drimmer now. His words, meant to uphold Ransom had somehow permutated in Kehoe's hands, each becoming twisted around. *What've I said? What has Kehoe heard me say? Damn it, I'd meant everything in support of Ransom. Now I'll be leading the Ransom defense fund.*

Griffin did not want to be around when Alastair Ransom learned of all this. If they allowed Waldo Denton to go merrily on his way, and should Alastair survive his wound, the operation, and recuperation to one day sit up in his hospital bed, what would the inspector's rage do?

Cook County Hospital emergency surgery
recovery room, same night

Anesthetized Alastair Ransom dreams of being under Jane Francis's touch, once again, sitting in her curing chair below that pyramidal scaffold of "healing magnetized brass," which she designed herself in order to maximize the magnetic power of Earth to body.

"You're here about the case, aren't you?" asks Jane Francis, a ghostly apparition in Dr. Tewes's clothes.

"Brilliant deduction, Dr. Tewes," Alastair's dream self replies, as smug as his corporeal self, a certainty, a swagger, an arrogance that comes with confidence and skill.

"My God, Inspector, you must try to relax." Jane Francis's voice comes out of Tewes's now. "Allow the magnetism of my hands and the pyramid, and the magnetic rivers of your own arteries and veins to flow freely through you."

"I thought we'd agreed you'd call me Alastair."

"Concentrate on what is important." She's in a dress now.

"I really don't think this is going to work on me. I'm a . . . a . . ."

"Non-believer, I know. But your hat's off now, and you're in my hands. Relax. It won't hurt a bit, and who knows, you might actually learn something useful."

"Useful? About magnetic and phrenological practice?"

"God, man, relax. You're as stiff as the walls."

"I'd like to relax. I'd like my opium pipe!"

"Imagine you are elsewhere and not in the hands of a fraud." She's in her ladies' fineries now, her petticoat and bustier. She looks to him so touchable, so like a prize.

"A detective without an imagination is as useless as a bird without wings."

"Well, then, use it. Picture yourself in the most exotic, most pleasant place you've ever known."

Under Tewes's soothing guidance and hand, Ransom releases all his pent up anger, rage, and tension. He feels it draining from him, replaced by Jane's touch and a calm that Alastair has not known since before Haymarket. Ransom recalls an island at the northern tip of Michigan, a place called Mackinac across from Sault Ste. Marie and Canada. He'd gone there in his youth at a time when he'd thought working with his hands a good idea; perhaps the life of a fisherman on the Great Lakes. The life of a sailor held out great romantic possibilities.

He felt the warmth of a summer rain on his body, and he looked down to find himself nude and young and virile as he was before they nearly blew his leg off with a bomb. He felt the cool green grass of this place beneath him, and the bluest blue sky and the whitest white clouds overhead, and on a distant shore, he saw people fishing and laughing and lounging, picnicking and dancing. Lots of dancing. Among the partying throng, he saw himself. As if he belonged. As if in fact he were welcome and known, and it was all right that everyone knew his name. Then she was alongside him. Jane.

Jane reaches for both his hands. She no longer has underclothes on. Like him, her body is bathed in warm sunlight, warm rain, warm air, warmness of every kind. He feels as though he could never be cold again, not in his bones cold, not in his gut cold, not in his head. Neither cold nor evil could cross the warm waters here. Nothing untoward could get at them in his childhood hideaway.

Still, off in the distant shore, far from the warm lights and laughter and dancers, shadowed by the shadows of the dancers, something lurks. A kind of beastie . . . a bestial man, yes, low to the earth, near crawling, nearly on all fours, bearlike, it arms limp at its sides as if the thing's brain could get no message to limbs, while its paws and hairy legs carry its crooked body about with a godawful misshapen head likened only to a gargoyle that Ransom must study to determine the specifics of—bloody hell! He realizes how easily his cop's mind slips into being Inspector Alastair Ransom. He wants to fight it. He begins a torturous struggle to return to the peace and beauty and warmth, of what Jane offers on this long-ago shore among the willows, upon a carpet of grass.

"Damn you, Alastair Ransom. Stay with us . . . stay with *me*," he hears her say as if from afar, as if he were the beast across the water in the deepest shadow of this place, and she was looking at just how far away he'd gone. How out of reach her warm touch is. Yet somehow he feels her warmth, her touch, her breath, even her tears dropping on him. It feels real.

At the same time, he feels removed from all the dancers, the warm rain, and sunrays, the light, and the feel of

green and blue and white—all gone from this place so
deeply hidden within him. A place hidden from him, although he's carried it about in his head since boyhood.
The only new addition is Jane's and Gabby's features. Although there'd always been a woman in this place—in fact
a loving woman, and a daughter and son, all without definition. Still these people existed somewhere, people who
cared about him, and a lost part of Alastair had always re-
sided here in this place—hiding out. Jane now awaits him
on a well-lit, sparkling shore; waits for him to come for her
out of the darkness.

Is it clear? he asks. Is it Heaven?

Dr. Jane Francis had changed into the clothes of a proper
lady, an outfit that her daughter had secreted to her here at
the hospital. Should Alastair at any time regain consciousness, she did not want him to see her with mustache, ascot,
and men's clothing. She sat at his bedside, occasionally running her hand through his thinning hair, at times crying, at
times certain he must live, at times certain he would die like
so many dreams she'd lost in the past, but in all of her
thoughts and fears and hopes, she never stopped talking to
him as if he heard and could talk back, as if their invisible
dialogue—as he may well be talking back to her in his
head—might be the only lifeline left to Alastair.

Dr. Christian Fenger placed a hand on Jane's shoulder.
Fenger was one of a handful of people who knew that she
was James Phineas Tewes. "One hope Ransom has left."

Jane weighed Fenger's cryptic words. "And what is that,
Doctor?"

"The man's renown stubbornness, and he has unfinished
business."

"And should St. Peter challenge him at the gate?" She attempted humor.

"Then it's a difficult time for St. Peter, who may want to
postpone dealing with Ransom."

"I hadn't thought of it, but you're right. He indeed has unfinished business—much of it with me, so St. Peter'll just have to get in line."

Together they laughed at the image of Ransom deciding who to argue with—her or St. Peter. Christian then hugged her. "Good to see you—the real you again, Jane. If you will end this Tewes charade, I'll pull every string to get you on at Rush Medical."

"I can't think of that now."

Dr. Fenger then left her alone with the patient. Gabrielle stepped in with a cup of lukewarm coffee she'd scrounged from someplace in the hospital.

"You should get some sleep, Mother."

"There'll be time for sleep later. I don't want him alone when he comes round."

"Then I'm staying, too."

"You should go home . . . to your own bed."

"I'll not be in comfort and leave you alone here."

Cook County's cold institutional walls and bare room reflected Jane's mood as she watched Gabby curl up in a chair on the other side of Ransom's bed.

"Ok, sweetheart. Whatever you think best." Jane sensed her daughter simply didn't want to be alone, and Jane had felt alone until Gabby's arrival. She now sipped at the coffee, glad for the small offering.

She replaced one hand on Alastair's forehead. He'd survived the surgery; however, a high fever had set in, and infection, a killer of the ages held Ransom in its awful grasp.

Two days later

Ransom felt a surge of emotion welling up inside when he awoke to a room full of people, his best friends. Jane Francis as herself held his hand, Gabby sat in a chair where she'd fallen asleep. Griffin stood on the other side of the bed, nervously looking at the door as if about to make a break for it. Dr. Christian Fenger smiled down from the foot of his bed.

"Alastair, you've come back to us," Christian said, his normally sad eyes smiling now.

"Thank God! You'd slipped into a coma," Jane said, squeezing his hand.

Gabby awoke in a start amid the commotion. Tentative about speaking to the man she'd laid low, one eye still shut with sleepiness, she quietly said, "Mother never left your side, and she never gave up."

"Is-sat righ', Jane?" Alastair managed to croak, dry-mouthed.

"Nothing anyone else wouldn't do," Jane replied.

Gabby spoke for Jane. "She's talked to you in the last days more than she's talked to me in a month!"

"Welcome back to Chicago, Rance," added Griffin.

Ransom could hardly swallow, let alone speak, as his mouth felt stuffed with a combination of cotton and glue. Jane helped him with a glass of water. Finally, he could swallow, and he said, "Thank you all for . . . for being here. Either I'm in some sort of purgatory or this is Cook County?"

"You're going to take a few days to heal, Alastair," said a stern Christian Fenger. "Do you understand? No more of these acrobatics of yours."

"Yeah," agreed Gabby, "and certainly not in our parlor!"

"If you want acrobatics, go to the Chinese pavilion at the fair," agreed Griffin.

"I hear the French acrobats are on strike," Alastair replied with a smirk, recalling how he had literally dived— after being shot—to flatten Waldo Denton, and how he'd broken Jane's furniture.

"If there's a labor strike at the fair, you'd be the man to know it," teased Griff.

Everyone laughed at this.

"And Waldo Denton?" asked Alastair. "Will he be spending the rest of his miserable life behind bars, or will Kehoe go for a hanging? Perhaps they'll build a gallows for him at the bleeding fair! Or does Hiram think the poor unfortunate, misguided murdering youth far too sweet for a public hanging?"

Everyone had silenced at the mention of Denton. Griffin Drimmer had filled the others in on the recent decision to release the suspect, due to a lack of evidence against him.

Alastair looked queerly round the room, his eyes questioning. "What's become of Denton? Suicide? A cell-room drama? Did you have to shoot him? An escape attempt, Griff, what?"

"He's not, *ahhh* . . . Alastair . . . we failed to ahhh . . . that is Prosecutor Kehoe, that is to say that Hiram . . . he would not—"

"Confound it, man, spit it out!"

"Hiram refused to take it to a judge, and Denton was—"

"Released?" Alastair pulled himself up with every intention of getting out of bed, but Fenger and Drimmer sat on him, Christian calling for his attendants, Shanks and Gwinn, just outside the door, to help restrain Alastair, who kept repeating the single word, "Released? Released! But how? How in the world?"

When Gwinn and Shanks grabbed hold of Ransom, they did so with glee. Shoved away, the two women watched the attendants strap Alastair down. The big man on the bed hadn't a chance, but even so, he lashed out, kicked, and shouted, "Get your grubby, dirty grave-robbing ghouls off me, Christian! Christian!"

"You're damned determined to rip your stitches!" Fenger countered. "Now settle down or we'll have to keep those restraints on you!"

Alastair replied with his angry eyes that went from side to side, staring at his hands locked now in horse-hide straps. "You got me in one of your nutcase wards, Christian? Like I'm a candidate for your asylum?"

"Not at all, you fool! The restraints are on every bed in

emergency recovery. To keep you still, and to protect you from your worst enemy."

"Some friend you turned out to be. And you, Griffin! How could you let this happen? You and that idiot Kehoe? And just how much input came from Nathan Kohler? This has got to be another of his nasty games to make me look incompetent."

Griffin nervously said, "In fact, Alastair, they're holding hearings about your competence right now, and I stood up for you, gave you good marks!"

Ransom stared at his partner. "My *comeuppence* hearings, heh?"

"The jury's still out on you," he warned.

Alastair raged. "Do you hear it, Jane?"

Jane pleaded for calm. "Your stitches."

"Hang the stitches!"

"Your constitution, then, your stomach and peace of mind."

"Hang it all! I catch a multiple murderer, and they let him go so that Nathan can nail me to the cross? The bastard!"

"I'm sorry, Rance," countered Griff. "Did all I could, I tell you. I pleaded with Hiram Kehoe not to let Denton go, but in truth, there's very little to tie him to the killings save what is inside your head, Rance."

"Did you search him for the weapon? The garrote?"

"Yes, and one was found but—"

"But what? What else does Hiram want, damn it?"

"He said every criminal and prostitute in the city owns a garrote."

"But the angle of the cut, how small we thought the killer was according to the undeniable angle of the cut . . . all this we did not release to anyone—and the two handprints?"

"I made a comparison of the handprints to Denton's," said Fenger.

"And?"

"Inconclusive; couldn't say without a doubt that it was Denton's hand."

"Maybe you need a new microscope?"

"Damn it, man. There were too many variables even under magnification."

Griff added, "We can begin surveillance, build a case."

"But the garrote! We have a case!"

"You yourself said the diamond garrote is fairly easy to purchase," countered Griff. "Kehoe pulled forth three garroting wires, all three with double-wire crisscrossed centers. They're as easily had as pocketknives, cheap handguns, and opium."

Alastair's consternation showed in his strained features. "Are you saying that the prosecutor determined that Denton is more likely a prostitute than a murderer?"

"On having interviewed Denton, he came to the conclusion that he might well be a male prostitute, yes, and he is not choosy as to which sex so long as he is paid his price."

"Fast-talking weasel-bastard convinced Kehoe he's a harmless male prostitute?"

"My God," interjected Jane, "if that's true, then what must Mr. Kehoe think of our having him in for tea?"

Ransom ignored this and spoke to Griffin. "At least Griff here knows we had in hand—*had*—the right man before the fools turned him loose. May God blind me!"

"Well yes, I mean, hell yes . . ." sputtered Griff. ". . . did believe it firmly at the time when we . . . when—"

"Did? Did believe it *when*? And when did you change your mind, and why?"

"I believe that you believe it with all the sincerity of—"

"Get out!"

"What?"

"Get out of here and take your sincerity garbage with you, Griffin; and whatever else you do, put in for a change of partners!"

"I will not, Rance. I tell you, I'm standing by you. God only knows why, but I want to help prove your side of it, and I will."

"Do so, then, but do it *elsewhere*!" He yanked and fought

his restraints like a bull with its horns sheared to dull nubs.

Griffin, ever the shrewd one, sensed it time to leave, and he did so quietly and quickly. Shanks and Gwinn held vigil at the door like a pair of guards. "And you, Christian, how can you justify strapping me to a bed! If you won't untie me now, then take yourself and your two eunuchs off with you"—he paused to catch his breath—"and by damn, get the hell outta my sight."

Jane immediately leaned in over him, literally in his face. "That is enough, Alastair Ransom!" she shouted. "This man saved your life with his hands and his skill, so you will not address him in that tone!"

"Jane, the man has a right to his anger," countered Dr. Fenger. "After all, he's been hurt, along with his pride, shot and nearly killed in an effort to bring in a killer, and all for naught."

"Of course, but still—"

"Imagine it," continued Dr. Fenger, "if our friend here is correct about Denton? Then that foul-minded gargoyle is just biding his time before he *must* kill again to feed a satanic appetite."

"Then you grasp my point!" said Alastair.

"Grasp it, yes, but you fail to grasp mine!"

"Which is?"

"Yes, murder has become his addiction, his obsession, but what of you?"

"What of me?"

"What of your obsession? Will it drive you to kill yourself, literally, here and now? Bed rest and attention to your wounds! That is called for. That is what you need to obsess on right now."

"You can stop worrying about me. I'm fine!"

"Nonsense! If your wound were to go the way of gangrene—" Fenger stopped, sighing. "Alastair, at your age . . . well then, Shanks and Gwinn will happily see you to your grave this time for sure."

Ransom settled, no longer pulling at his restraints. "All right, remove these leather shackles of yours, Doctor, and you've my word."

"Your word?"

"That I'll *not* make any attempt at finding my clothes."

"I'm not so sure."

"We're friends. Would I lie to a friend, Christian?"

"I cannot imagine you lying there unrestrained with so much venom pumping through that fevered brain," replied Fenger, his eyes going from Ransom to Jane. "No, sorry, my friend. I'll not remove the restraints, not till I see a good measure more healing."

"It's a nasty wound, Alastair," added Jane.

"Come on, Christian!" he shouted at the doctor's back as Fenger goose-stepped from the room. "Christian! Live up to your bloody name! Christian! A little charity, if you will!"

Nothing. No turnaround, no slowing, no response.

"Jane, you'll listen to reason, won't you?"

"I am a reasonable person, and I think it time I took Gabrielle home. She's missed schooling over this, but first my daughter has something to say to you."

He looked into Gabby's eyes, filled now with tears. "I am so sorry I fired on you. It just all happened so fast and, and, and . . ."

"You frightened us to wit's end." Jane pulled wrinkles from the sheet covering him, tucking it here and there. "But I had thought the gun unloaded."

"I might've killed you," continued Gabby, gasping, "just when . . . just when I was beginning to like you."

"It's all right, child. As the bard says, 'All's well that ends well.' "

"But it hasn't ended well. You are seriously injured. You may have pain in your innards for the rest of your life due to this injury. You may walk with a limp."

"I already do."

"A more pronounced limp, then. Just please know that I am dreadfully, terribly, horribly sorry, and I did not mean to fire. It just went off."

"I understand. I suppose a bit more caution on entering was called for, after all. Like diving into a hot springs without knowing enough about it. Entirely my fault, Gabby, and none of your own."

She reached over and hugged him, still tearful. He did not know how to react, but said, "Had I the use of my arms, I'd hug you."

This made Gabby erupt, bawling.

"It's all right . . . it's all right . . . it's all right, Gabby, dear."

"You are a fine man, no matter the stories people tell," she replied.

He laughed lightly and this hurt too. "Tell no one! And, Gabby, will you be the one to loose my—"

"Do not ask it of her!" Jane's face flushed red with anger. "It is not fair to play on her guilt, and you well know it, Alastair Ransom."

"It's all right, Mother. I'm not about to go against Dr. Fenger's wishes." Do you take me for a fool?"

Jane reached out to Gabby, but Gabby rushed for the door.

"Whatever you do, steer clear of that Waldo Denton!" shouted Ransom to Gabby's back as she rushed out. He then glared at Jane. "Do you have any idea the danger Gabby is in so long as that maniac lunatic is walking free?"

"Alastair! Just stop it!"

"What?"

"I won't release you from this bed any more than Christian—not before it's time."

"But Jane, I must be—"

"You know very well more surgical patients die of infections afterward than from surgery!"

Jane's final stern comment acted as a signal to Christian's two ghouls, Shanks and Gwinn, who left the room now.

Alastair could hear their scratchy, crowlike mutterings and hyena laughter trailing after.

"I can't abide those two anymore than you," she confided.

"Yeah . . . they're like a pair of grim bookends. How could you allow them to put me into that meat wagon of theirs?"

"Speed was of the essence."

"Speed in the back of that thing can kill, trust me!" He realized his tone had hurt her. He softened, adding, "Hey . . . thanks."

"For what?"

"Saving my life."

"I had my daughter's future to think of."

"And perhaps ours?"

She blushed.

"Now undo these damnable straps."

"No."

"But—"

"End of argument, Inspector Ransom."

CHAPTER 3

The following day in Ransom's hospital room

"Now that we're alone and out of earshot of ev-eryone, Jane," Alastair whispered, "please, undo Christian's damned horse cinches." He pulled at the hospital bed restraints.

"Alastair . . . please."

"What do you say? I promise I'll not go for my clothes."

"Then you'd run out and down the avenue naked. I know you by now, Alastair Ransom."

"I'd never insinuate my nudity on the public."

"I'm sure."

"Jane, if ever you cared a wit about me, and since you have not left my side for a moment, from the opening cut till now—yes, I heard you there in the operating theater dressing down McKinnette for doing a botched job of the anesthetic."

"You were dreaming. No such thing happened."

"But it seemed so real."

She laughed. "Imagine a woman with no standing in the hospital or the college telling a Chicago doctor how to do his job! Horror of horrors!"

"You did so, as Dr. Tewes."

"Preposterous—a phrenologist telling an anesthesiologist what to do during an operation." *Uncanny,* she thought, as she'd wanted to do exactly that—had thought it—but she'd held herself in check.

"Are you of the same mind as Griff? Regarding Denton being the murderer?"

"Eye for eye, tooth for tooth, flesh for flesh? If we all lived by that rule of ancient times, where would civilization be now, Alastair?"

"Then you think I am drunk on vengeance?"

"It has crossed my mind. After all, Waldo Denton hardly looks capable of multiple murder of a hand-to-hand nature."

"Nonsense, Jane, even a petite woman like you could kill with a garrote, and it was no coincidence that Denton attacked and killed Gabby's boyfriend."

"You'll not terrify me into untying you."

"Then it'd be a useless exercise for me to again ask that you remove the restraints?"

"I'd say so, yes."

"You fear my pursuing Denton?"

"When you are healed and stronger, but not now . . . not in a weakened state of mind and body. Whatever you decide, it should be done when you're fully recovered, a hundred percent."

"I feel just fine now. Please, undo the straps."

She feared doing so, feared he'd come up like a shark, tearing at everyone in his path, and what would become of him in the bargain? She thought of the old fairytale of the beauty and the beast.

"Do it for me," he said.

She moved her hands to the strap closest to her.

"Undo it."

"Will you kill Denton when everyone thinks him your *mistake*?"

"Do you have an opinion of Waldo Denton? An impression?"

"The night he came to the house, the night you were shot, I . . . we talked, and I convinced him to sit for a phrenological examination."

"All while he had me chasing phantoms at the fair."

"Alastair, I've never touched a more quivering bundle of nervous energy in my entire practice."

"Which tells you what?"

"That he feared me—*ahhh,* actually Dr. Tewes."

"He thought you the doctor?"

"I was on my way out to a call, but then I didn't want to leave Gabby alone with him."

"Aha! So, you did think him a deviant!"

"Not deviant but troubled. The feeling I got from him was . . . I don't know . . . a mind that never stops planning, working, ticking?"

"You mean plotting, I think."

"A con artist, crossed my mind."

"Plotting your and Gabby's murder."

"I didn't get that, Alastair, no."

"But you said you got a . . . a confused mind. Suppose he is right this moment plotting your death or rather the death of Dr. Tewes? Suspicious and unnerved by your mind-reading act, that the great Tewes might unmask him?"

"That's just such a stretch."

"And Gabby? Take no chances. You must get her and yourself out of the city, unless you undo these bindings!"

"I got some anger during the reading, but murdering Gabby was not coming through."

"My God . . . then it is Tewes he's after! Don't you see?"

"Due to my readings of the earlier victim's skull? Well . . . at least someone 'believes'!"

"Yes, the last one you want to believe! Jane, it's so clear now. He's been sniffing about Gabby to test Tewes, to learn if you—Tewes—is a fraud or the genuine article, capable of seeing into the Invisible World and straight through his lies and secrets using your pseudoscience of phrenology."

"I—I did come away with some fear of the young man."

"Aha!"

"Not for myself but for Gabby. After, the sitting, I pulled her aside."

"Yes? Go on."

"And I made the mistake of asking her to get rid of him."

"And her response was to sit him down to tea?"

"I was in the process of talking him out the door when she guided him in for tea."

"She can be contrary."

"Moments after this, moments after, you charged in, Gabby shot you, and I feared Griffin might shoot her. By the way, you owe me for two kicked-in doors, two ruined locks, and a demoralized French parlor table." She paused, taking a deep breath, holding firm to his huge hand. "Frankly, I felt something strangely odd about that young man from the moment he walked in with Gabby's umbrella."

"Gabby's umbrella?"

"She'd left it in his cab."

"So he seized the opportunity."

"I'd seen him hanging about the house before, in that cab of his, but I'd thought nothing of it."

"He counts on his invisibility," replied Ransom, a grunt of pain escaping him. "And the gun that was so ready at hand? Would you care to explain that?"

"Yes . . . the gun that shot you."

"Guns do not in and of themselves shoot people."

"All right . . . OK. I had excused myself. Retrieved it, placed it on the table so that he could clearly see it."

"Then you did feel threatened by him?"

"Absolutely, but he'd done nothing overt to warrant my fears, and I did not want to alarm Gabby. I told them both there'd been a prowler at the back door."

"Don't tell me—Bosch?"

"Well, no. I lied."

"Then you came back as Jane with the gun because you suspected something dangerous about Denton?"

"Nothing I can put my finger on. Just eerie, creepy, odd,

awkward . . . nothing you could use in a court of law any-more than you might use phrenology or magnetism—or your cop's intuition for that matter."

"So it was you this time who hauled out the weapon and not Gabby?"

"Yes, but . . . but all the time, I thought it unloaded as usual. I hadn't the slightest idea, and had I known, I would've emptied it, and you . . . you wouldn't be on your back strapped down to this bed like a—"

"Like some sort of wild boar ready for the pit?"

"I was about to say like a prisoner."

"Aye, that too." He paused and with his left hand locked in the leather bracelet at her breast, Ransom's finger stretched to touch her there. She responded with a little gasp, then leaned in over him and they kissed.

He did not understand it, but being helpless and unable to put his arms around her while she passionately kissed him over many times, made him want her the more. "Lock the door," he whispered in her ear.

"What?"

"It's a private room Christian's given me."

"You want to test just how private?"

"Do it."

She went to the door, closed and locked it.

She made love to him while in the restraints, and it was the best lovemaking he'd ever known, as Jane Francis turned it into a sensuous dance, a dance of light and life and won-der. No woman had ever made him feel so unreservedly wanted before.

Their passion consumed them, blotting out all but their mutual caresses, although his were limited to lips and eyes. Their mutual kisses and movements seemed of one mind, one body. When she finished, Jane fell into him, sated, with-out ever removing her skirt.

After a moment's tidying up, her cheeks flushed, Jane became all business again—the doctor. She examined his bandages and found a good result. "You didn't break your stitches," she informed him. "Had you not been strapped down—"

"You'd have not found me so attractive? You do like taking control."

"There is that, but I was pointing out that you may well've broken your stitches and opened that horrid wound."

"I like you, Jane . . . I like your touch, the way you smell, your hair. The only thing I don't like about you is when you are that man Tewes!"

"Hey, that *man* feeds my family."

"All right, touché." He returned to his bonds. "Since you've determined rigorous exercise has not ripped my wound open, it can do no harm if you let me up from this *confounded* bed."

"But I like you *tied* to the bed."

"Jane, please."

"Why? So you can go shoot down Denton? Make it look like an accident?"

"Why do you think so ill of me that I would kill a man in bushwhack fashion?"

"Things I've heard all my life."

"All your life? About me?"

"You really don't remember me as a child, do you?"

"No. I am sorry, but I do not."

"But my father, Dr. Francis. He was well known even then."

"I'm sorry. As I said . . . my childhood was bitter . . . too bitter to store away as memory."

"That's so . . . so sad. And when you were out of your head with fever, you said something about a stillborn child."

"My twin at birth. One of us died, one lived."

"I am so terribly sorry."

"It's really quite all right now. I tell people my parents attempted to drown me at birth because I was not the other one." He lightly laughed at this. "Other times, I tell people that no one in the family knew which of us died in the womb, but it sure as hell wasn't me." He laughed again.

She realized his laughter and jokes covered his true feelings of guilt. She hugged him to her. "Do you ever . . ."

"Visit his grave?" He avoided her eyes.

"Yes."

"No . . . not since it was moved."

"The grave was moved?"

"Along with hundreds to make way for Lincoln Park."

"Still . . . perhaps you should make an effort. I'd go with."

Instead of answering, he whispered, "Undo me."

"I thought I had."

"I am speaking of the cuffs."

"All right, if you *promise* to do nothing foolish, and remember your promise to Dr. Fenger."

"You *were* on hand when he operated, weren't you?"

"I was." She loosed his left hand, and it went to her cheek, caressing her. They again kissed. A long, lazy, dreamy, indolent kiss, fully alive with passion on both sides. She was petite enough that he hefted her atop him again with one hand. But even as he held her, his left hand went about her waist to the second strap, and he undid himself while they continued kissing.

In an instant, she felt both his hands wrap round her and squeeze her into him. "It feels so good, so right.

"You feel good atop me." He smoothed her cheek with his hand.

"And you feel good below me."

"But I have to go now."

"Now?"

"Now."

"To work?"

"To work."

"Despite doctor's orders?"

"Despite, yes."

"You will be careful?"

"Yes . . . I will. I have a reason to take care now."

She kissed him again. "Yes, you do, so be careful and watch your back."

"Where Chief Kohler stands ever present?"

"I should say so."

"As you once said, he fears me."

"Passionately so. It is eating him alive."

"Which says he does indeed have something to hide."

"R-regarding the Haymarket bomb?"

He eased Jane over the edge of the bed now and stood her up like a child's toy. She acquiesced, sensing his need. He remained true to form. Like a bear, he might hibernate best in his own lair, and he felt most uncomfortable here. She kissed him good-bye with a slight admonition. "Do not— please do not overexert yourself, and please kill no one, and please, if for any unforeseen reason that something should happen, I had nothing whatsoever to do with loosening your bonds."

"A bargain it is."

"A bargain with Ransom, I fear, may be a bargain with the Devil."

"Then kiss the Devil once more."

She did so. "Promise me you will see me regularly to treat you."

"Absolutely. I promise."

Jane watched him dress, and she winced each time he gasped in pain. She knew he'd not heed any further warnings. With mixed feelings, she watched him disappear from the room, fearing she'd made a terrible mistake in allowing Alastair his freedom. But the man was, after all, all about freedom.

Two weeks later . . .

Alastair Ransom stood on the corner of Lincoln Avenue where it met Lake Michigan, where an entire cemetery had been uprooted and moved for the common good, to make way for the sprawling Lincoln Park, now a common green stretching out before the oceanlike vistas of Lake Michigan. In fact, Alastair stood very near to where his brother's grave had once been. Beyond the point where the rocks had been laid as a breaker, in the distance beyond, stood the world's largest lit-up amusement wheel—Mr. Ferris's wheel rising hundreds of feet into the night sky, a beacon and a marker for the northernmost section of the great fair where the crowds continued to flock daily and nightly. South along the lakefront stood the grand fairway running down the center of the World's Columbian Exposition like a concrete spine.

All trains, all carriages, all foot traffic—or very nearly all—made for the fair. All save a killer and the man who pursued him.

It had been two weeks since the operation, and Ransom felt and looked exhausted from his vigil to be on hand when Waldo Denton slipped up. Ransom's presence wherever Denton showed up had led the young killer to change his routes, to change his times, and now to change his main location with his hack and horse from the fair to here. No more deaths had occurred since the double murder at the lagoon inside the World's Fair grounds, and this had led some to speculate that the real Phantom of the Fair had left the area altogether, while it only led Ransom to a sense of vindication; instinct told him that he was correct about Denton. And he had the deaths of seven victims—one an unborn child—to avenge.

Alastair's driving new obsession, then, was Denton, and no one could dissuade him from his crusade. In fact, all attempts had failed. He'd tried without success to order Denton to come in to again test his hand against the two bloody handprints. This time with a print expert, Theopolis Harris.

Ransom's harassing of Denton now had continued daily. It might cost him his job, and it had already cost him friends and colleagues like Griffin Drimmer and even Dr. Fenger—the only family he had ever known. The chase had in fact eclipsed Ransom's previous obsession, his years-long search for the truth surrounding the mystery of who bombed Haymarket Square in 1886.

Philo Keane, police photographer, artist, and friend had come along with Ransom tonight, and now the two stood in a juniper thicket mid-park, shadowing a man Ransom believed to be a repeat killer. Philo had come for fear of leaving his friend Alastair alone, a strange feeling having gripped Philo. This faith and cocksureness Ransom felt in his own cunning in the matter of the Phantom overtook all else. They had argued about it only an hour earlier at Philo's studio, and Keane kept up his steady barrage of concern even now.

"Give this madness up, at least long enough to take some sleep, man, and remind yourself what is good in life! Look at you!"

"I won't rest until I have my hands around that punk's throat and can justifiably choke a confession out of him."

"Some people would call you cunning, a master detective, but not anymore. Here you are . . . on the verge of hallucination from fatigue. Come back to my place. Just lie down on my sofa to catch some rest. I'll wake you in an hour or two."

"Cunning . . . yes, I can be cunning, but this boy killer now he is *cunning*."

"To think him so near me all those weeks he apprenticed with me," began the pencil-thin Philo, his knitted brow twitching. "And he still has my Night Hawk, you know. Weird thing is . . . I never once considered him a threat of any sort, much less a camera thief and a murderer. Still, he did leave me with an uneasy feeling the time I caught him with his hands where they oughtn't've been."

"As when he dropped a victim's ring in your pocket just to frame you?"

"Ironic, I was in jail when Griffin drags him in. And Griff so damned sure at the time you two had your man. He even had the damn garrote in his hand; held it up to me as proof positive."

"Griff is like a reed in the wind. Whatever the prevailing winds."

"At least Chief Kohler didn't come back after me for the killings."

"Don't be so sure he won't."

"What've you heard?" Philo gasped.

"He's working closely with the city prosecutor to charge you again, while everyone else—including the mayor—is content to leave it alone."

"Leave it alone?"

"Glad simply that the killings've ended, and that their precious White City boondoggle continues without further stain."   .

"Then I say the mayor is a rational man."

"Quite."

"Afraid I can't say the same for you. Have you considered all that you've forfeited for this business with Denton? How others've distanced themselves from you? That woman I ran into at the hospital who sat at your bedside night and day, and her niece, is it?—whom you claim as your friend despite the fact it was she who shot you? And your partner, Griffin, to whom you refuse to speak. Not to mention Dr. Fenger? Who next will abandon you?"

"You. I am sure of it. So good-bye. Make haste!"

"I'll not leave you here in the darkness contemplating murder."

"You'll miss your booze."

Philo held up a flask of whiskey. "Portable. Have some! You need it more'n I."

Ransom's limp and need for the cane was now even more pronounced. His fatigue only added to his leaning on the new one, which Philo had gifted him at his hospital bed when he was still in a coma—and the steady thumping of that cane now felt like some sort of Chinese water torture to Philo.

"Why're we standing in the drizzle, Ransom?"

"Bosch got word on where Denton has relocated his carriage."

"How much did that bit cost you?"

"Denton's picked out a new killing ground, Lincoln Park. I'm sure of it."

"And you're going to catch him in the act?"

"I have my own flask to keep me company. You needn't've come, Philo."

"You've a strange sense of duty, Alastair. Duty to yourself."

"Duty to Polly, to Purvis, Trelaine, Chesley, all the victims, even that unborn child that Denton killed."

They had earlier climbed from a hansom cab a block away from the park's cabstand, and now cautiously approached, in a roundabout fashion, through the dense woods of Lincoln Park, named for the fallen president.

The park, Ransom said at one point, reminded him of a place he'd dreamed about while in the hospital fighting for his life. A place ever reminiscent of a somewhereland in Michigan where his parents had taken him as a child. "You're not going to get all maudlin on me, are you, Rance?"

"Just something about the two shores of the lagoon here . . . just like in the dream. Only in the dream, I was with a beautiful woman."

"Well, don't look for me to help you out there, old friend."

Again Philo Keane thought of the terrible price a man like Ransom paid to the public at large. This determination to catch the Phantom for the safety of all Chicagoans had become a personal affair, a single-minded obsession to be sure, and yet if he were to succeed, it benefited all of the city. Benefited the lowliest street person to the Potter Palmers and the Marshal Fields. But at what price to Ransom? To his peace of mind? To his sleep? It had already cost Ransom dearly in so many ways. Worst of all, it could eventually cost him Jane Francis and any opportunity along those lines. It had cost Alastair friends as well, but Philo understood obsessions, and he understood his friend's need for vengeance.

In fact, Philo guessed it'd been vengeance that kept him alive.

Philo wondered now if he and Alastair would be arrested at any moment for loitering and lurking, or worse if a copper came along and saw them amid the trees, two grown men playing hide-and-seek. Philo could ill-afford being arrested again. "If we're arrested for pandering," he complained, "it's on you, Alastair."

But Alastair's full concentration remained on the row of horse-drawn buggies and covered cabs at the cabstand, where Waldo Denton casually awaited the Lincoln Park strollers who weaved about the pathways, amid the greenery, locked in embrace, their eyes interested only in one another. Watching the strolling couples, Ransom realized how easily the Phantom of the Fair operated, using his hansom cab as central headquarters. He'd move about the paths of the park in his black uniform, strike like a shadow, murder with that garrote of his, set the body aflame, and be sitting atop his hack, an invisible man, all in a matter of minutes. Orchestrated murder.

The lakefront Lincoln Park was a killer's dream, a place where people allowed their common sense and justifiable fears and natural defenses to drop like stones one after another. A place to distract one from the horrors at one's shoulder. Unlike the fair, this place kissed the senses with solitude and privacy and peace, whereas the fair rang loud with the sound of multiple calliopes, the barkers, and the hawkers, amid which worked the street prostitutes. Here the noises were of nature, squirrels, and chipmunks chasing one another, birds chirping in the trees, leaves rustling a languid whisper.

"What the hell keeps you on your feet?" Philo whispered in Ransom's ear.

Ransom took a long pull on his flask of whiskey. "I've stayed off the opium and cut back on the Quinine. Feel like . . . like a . . . *ahhh* . . ."

"New man?"

"Feel like a man who's stepped out of Hell's furthest jaw."

"Why don't you ask more of life for Alastair Ransom?" Philo then drank.

"You ask enough for the both of us, Philo." Ransom tripped on his own shoe.

"Do you think you can keep your feet? You, my friend, are no longer making any g'damn sense."

Philo looked all about their surroundings, uneasy. Here was the newly created lagoon. The lovely grand lake ever in the eye, here in this park, which only a few years before had been the cemetery where Alastair's twin had reposed. The graves had long been relocated in the effort of city fathers to keep pristine all of the lakefront coastal property, purchasing it for the use of the common good—*common ground meant common green*. Denton had removed his theater of operations to here, thinking that perhaps Ransom could be outdone or outrun or outfoxed; thinking, at least for a night, he had ditched his constant new shadow, a shadow that accosted him with accusation at every turn. A shadow the size of a standing bear.

Some said Denton had gone to Chief Kohler and Prosecutor Kehoe to ask that they muzzle the big man's mouth, take his gun and badge away, and remove him from the Chicago Police Department.

Some rumors had it that the two men, chief and prosecutor, had hired Denton to continue on as normal, and to report any and all bad conduct of one Inspector Alastair Ransom directly to them. Ransom's snitch, Bosch, had informed him that "The powers that be're after you, Ransom; working up a case against you."

"Don't hold back, Bosch. Give me the full story," he'd said.

Stunted Henry Bosch screwed up his features until his face was a dried-up potato. "It's about that *poor* harassed citizen, Denton, wrongfully accused, wrongfully jailed, and wrongly hounded after being released for lack of evidence."

And so here they were, Ransom in full knowledge of this "trap" set for him, but like any dumb bear, he forged straight into the snare. They stood in the snare now, Philo and Ransom observing, watching, studying the hansom cabstand, staring across at the youngest cabbie in the group—Denton—listening to banter and laughter wafting over, under, and through the park leaves.

All the hansom drivers saw to their own stock, feeding bits of cabbage, carrots, and corn to their mares. All stood about a barrel they used for shucking corn and oysters, and for tossing bones and cigarette butts, and a second barrel used as a cooking fire. This pair of barrels created a fulcrum along with a newsstand for the *Herald,* the *Tribune,* and other papers—common ground for the common man. The cabbies busily discussed the rising cost of grain feed, cigarettes, beer, wine, coal oil, and whatever else came to mind from a broken horseshoe to a tear in a cloak. Some of them joked with Denton about being the infamous Phantom of the Fair, and he joked back—actually prancing about and using his garrote, making a mock attack on another driver's horse! Then in a chillingly ironic voice, Denton laughingly asked, "What'd you boys give to know where the Phantom can be found?"

"I hear that is what you asked Inspector Ransom the night he arrested you for the killer!" shouted another, and they all burst into laughter.

"You know the rumor now as to the killer being a prostitute," said Denton. "It might well be. I can tell you that with a garrote, a woman can take down that fat tub of lard, Ransom!"

"Is that true?" Philo asked Ransom where they stood in the bush.

"Manys-a-prostitute chooses the garrote over the blade. The great equalizer, a way to overpower someone twice your size," Alastair replied. "And manys-a-poor-bloke's had his penis sheared off by a whore's garrote."

"Ouch! That happens? Damn, but you see some awful things."

"Can you imagine waking up to your little head being garroted?"

"I can imagine . . . you've no idea how I can imagine." He protectively crossed his legs.

"Yes, same weapon as Denton carries."

"But what does Waldo get from . . . get out of . . ."

"Murder? It makes Denton feel our equal, Philo—"

"Our equal is it?"

"—you and me, and every man with a larger, ahhh, body, and a rank of some sort in Chicago."

The men at the cabstand got up an impromptu lottery on the question of whether the true Phantom, once caught, would prove male or female. Denton had named a name they all knew, the infamous Pekinese-faced Chicago madame, Laveeda Grimaldi. They laughed at the notion.

CHAPTER 4

At the World's Fair, the chaos of hundreds of thousands continued unabated as though nothing untoward had occurred in the least here, and the increased numbers of uniformed police stationed about the fair also went unnoticed, but for some the police presence was much appreciated, especially the monied men backing the fair and the merchants working it for all they might. In fact, the fair had its own private police force, partially reinforced by part-timers moonlighting from the CPD. The fair cops worked independently of city government, however, answering only to their private employers—Chicago's elite, and this smacked of the old days when private enforcers and police ran amuck in their zeal to please private business interests and put down any strike or talk of strike as in the days of Haymarket. The sense they'd taken two steps back in police enforcement with this untrained crew stuck in Griffin Drimmer's craw, aside from their namby-pamby uniforms.

In fitting with the fabulous White City, this specialized army wore a light gray uniform, approximating an off-white, with fake mother-of-pearl rather than copper-toned buttons, a far cry from the traditional blues. Even so, there were never enough of the "Pearly Gate coppers," as some called them, to cover the massive fairgrounds and huge pavilions, each of which looked in scale and appearance like Roman and Greek halls of learning where Euripides and Socrates might appear in heated debate at any moment amid the fountains and the boats and the columns. Each major exhibit hall looked from a distance like some giant dragon that crawled up out of Lake Michigan to curl up and go to sleep here.

Griffin Drimmer had been assigned here, but he'd gotten lucky. He must wear his old CPD uniform as the fair force had run out of grays. On the other hand, he'd been unlucky. He missed working real detective cases. This was, to be sure, his comeuppance for having, in the end, sided with Alastair and in helping clear Philo's good name, and for not further supporting Chief Nathan Kohler. Busted to rank of a footman is what must be on his horizon, unless . . . unless he himself could catch the Phantom.

Although he strolled amid the throngs of fairgoers, revisiting known areas where the killer had struck, he came up empty. Nothing doing.

He decided to make inquiries to determine where everyone had got off to. What was Ransom doing right this moment? Keane? Dr. Tewes? He located the same call box he and Ransom had used the night they were so cocksure they had Denton by the shorthairs. He called in to inquire if there'd been any calls for him at the station he worked out of. It took an interminably long time to get a reply. When he did, there was a message for him to call Dr. James Phineas Tewes.

He had additional difficulty getting the blasted dispatcher to make connections to Dr. Tewes's residence. Something made possible only recently. Still Griffin had to threaten the man with his job as the last dispatcher who caused Inspector Drimmer problems had been fired. He was finally put through.

The good doctor came on to static, a note of concern in his high-pitched voice. "Your friend and colleague is barely capable of remaining on his feet another hour, yet he's on a stake-outing at Lincoln Park."

"Do you mean stakeout, Doctor?"

"Whatever! Can you please get over there and relieve him? Please?"

"God, the whining doctor sounded like a woman in his concern for Alastair. "I'm on my way, Doctor, but whereabouts in Lincoln Park is he, and what is he staking out there? The lake?"

"The cabstand. He's shadowing Denton."

"*Ahhh . . .* of course. I hadn't seen Denton about the fair all day."

"He's removed himself from the fair traffic in an attempt to get clear of Ransom, and Ransom, fool that he is, has taken no sleep or rest for two days."

"Damn . . . look, I'll try to get him home."

"He'll only do so if you take over for him, Griff . . . *ahhh*, Inspector."

"I understand."

He rushed from the call box past the stone steps of the newly erected building exhibiting the sciences and industries that had carried America to the forefront of global production of food and manufactured goods. The exhibits here recognized the importance of such inventions as the Cotton Gin, the McCormick Reaper, and other marvels of modern farming, and the wonders of lighting a city, and the telephone, and the phonograph—all among other amazing new instruments, and the newly created machines housed inside the museum. The giant steam engines that powered a huge platform that descended and returned up a mock coal mine-shaft. The massive displays of ocean liners of the *White Star* and *Cunard* class, to mighty generators like those used at Cook County in the event of an electrical shut down, to the mighty train engines of America. All the marvels of mechanical science under one enormous roof.

There is only one problem. When does a working cop find the time? Where does he find the money it would take to spend a day at the fair? Lucinda kept demanding Griff give more time to her and their children.

The grotesque headless corpse of the beautiful Miss Mandor found burning in a boat here on the lagoon had dissuaded no one from attending the Chicago World's Fair. Odd as that seemed, Griffin imagined it went right along with human nature. A cynical Alastair would have plenty to say.

He pulled out a pipe like the one Alastair used, and as he found a cab to take him to Lincoln Park, he tamped in some tobacco and worked on lighting up. He looked closely at the cab driver of the dram he climbed into to be sure it was neither Denton nor the madman who'd opened up his horses at full gallop with Griff and Ransom on the cushions, bouncing about that night they'd busted into the Tewes's residence to ostensibly save Miss Jane Francis and Gabby Tewes from the clutches of the maniac that Alastair had identified as Waldo Denton.

Griff thought he'd die in a hansom cab accident that night long before arriving at the Tewes home. He now called out an address he knew a block off the park where Ransom must be. He'd disembark a block early; to go unnoticed.

Along with the rhythm of the cab ride, a flitting thought of a future victim struck him as an inevitability. He imagined some poor defenseless woman, her throat cut by the garrote, her body set aflame. When and where would it happen?

Then he gave a good deal more thought to why the killer liked fire. Then he thought of Ransom's history with fire, the awful rumors, the awful truth no doubt embedded there, and he wondered if this killer who seemed to have a penchant for Ransom's circle of friends, if he did not have a quite personal reason for terrorizing Ransom's life and city.

Then he wondered if Waldo Denton might not have an alias. Then he wondered if Waldo Denton *were* an alias. He had the cab stop at another call box, and he got Luther Noble, an able man, to run Denton's name as an alias. It was not found. Then try Campaneua. If anyone by the name of Campaneua has been arrested at any time in the city in the last say three years.

"That'll take time."

"Then take time. I'll call you back later."

"It is already later. I am headed out the door. But there is tomorrow."

"Tomorrow, then, and thanks."

"Oh hell, look . . . I will turn it over to our new intern."

"And does he have a name?"

"She . . . she has a name."

"She? A woman on the force?"

"Not yet. She has as yet to go through boot camp."

"Gotcha, so what do I call her when I call back?"

"Gabby."

"Gabrielle Tewes?"

"*Ahhh* . . . then you know her? A friend of yours, Detective?"

"I'd have never guessed her to be interested in police work."

"Wants to learn it all, she says."

"Damn surprise is all."

"Keep an open mind, Inspector."

"Is she good at it?"

"A natural."

Junior Inspector Griffin Drimmer stared across from his position behind a tree at Philo Keane and Ransom, disbelieving. "Ransom," he whispered, "what are you doing here?"

"More to the point, Griff, what're you doing here? Are you converted to my cause?"

"A call came in that you were about to make a public nuisance of yourself at this location."

"Really? And who made the call—prophetic as it was?"

"An anonymous caller," Griff lied.

"Denton, no doubt. One cheeky bastard."

"The complaint came from a woman. At least it sounded like a woman."

"Jane . . . Jane Francis?"

"Like I said, it came as an anonymous call."

"She's trying to protect you from yourself," suggested Philo.

"So I'm to thank her?"

"We are all worried about you, Rance," added Griffin.

"I should give her a piece of my mind."

"All right! It wasn't Miss Francis," said Griff.

"Then who?"

"Dr. Tewes. He's also concerned about you, though I can't understand why."

"Tewes and Jane, both concerned." Both Philo and Griffin had as yet to discover that Dr. James Tewes and Jane Francis were one and the same.

"And Gabby," added Griff.

"And everyone who cares about your hide," put in Philo.

"I've already given everyone a piece of my mind!" retaliated Ransom.

"All they want, you fool," said Philo, "is your mean heart. Go see Jane and smooth it over." Philo pulled at him.

"Leave off. Let go."

"Have you read a paper in the past week, Ransom?" Griffin sternly asked. "They're saying you're spirit possessed, that you fingered Waldo Denton through some sort of drunken occult spiritualism. Séances, they're saying! Even your old friend Carmichael has—"

"Bastard son of a bitch is on Kohler's bribe list?"

Philo and Griff exchanged a look of concern. Philo said, "You are beginning to sound like a raving lunatic, Ransom, and you don't even hear it."

"Indigestion . . . just indigestion," Ransom replied.

"And in the meantime, we wait until the monster strikes again?" complained Griffin.

"In the meantime, we have to rely on our instincts," countered Ransom. "And my instincts are still screaming that Waldo Denton kills people for the fun of it."

"Intuition is often all we have left in the last analysis," agreed Philo. "My own tells me that Denton shrewdly doctored the second photograph, making a comparison of the two handprints impossible."

"All the while you were whoring, he was doctoring the photo under your nose." Ransom gritted his teeth and glared.

"In fact, I, *ahhh* . . . taught him too well every process I know."

"Sounds like a willing learner, heh?" asked Griff, blinking.

"Crafty, cunning little prick is what he is." Ransom smothered a cough.

"After all, he was my apprentice." Philo looked sheepishly at the other two. "Well . . . think of it. He cops to the first bloody print due to mere clumsiness at the crime scene. Then he exposes the second in development just a bit too soon."

"Leaving us with nothing, and Fenger testifying on his behalf instead of ours."

"Galls me to think he himself took the second handprint photo with my Night Hawk, complained Philo. Used my materials and my studio, all while I sat behind bars, arrested as the Phantom! Me!"

Ransom held back a laugh. "As absurd as that Chinaman singing our national anthem at the fair in Chinese."

"Did you hear about that?" Griff's words dripped with disapproval.

But Ransom returned to the subject of Denton. "Then the weasel doctored the second one to make it inconclusive as evidence. So why can't we get him on evidence tampering?"

"Ransom, it can only be proven a bad job of processing. Even Christian Fenger couldn't testify that it was doctored and not simply fouled up."

"Fenger should've lied then; should've made it fit."

The other two remained silent, unsure what to say to

make Alastair feel better. Philo finally muttered, "It'll be a great ally some day—*science*—if you beefy-headed coppers'll ever open your eyes to it. And maybe learn to prize it and to protect scientific evidence."

"What's that supposed to mean?" Griffin's defenses had gone up.

"If you had a processing center kept under lock and key, for instance, Denton could not've handled that photo alone. There'd've been channels, proper procedures, all of it."

Ransom only grinned at his friend, while Griff firmly replied, "Now hold on, Inspector Ransom's the one got the CPD to go full force into fingerprint collections."

"And still no headway in that area! Dragging their feet. They don't trust it . . . don't trust anything new or scientific. You law enforcement types are the worst for it."

Dr. James Phineas Tewes stepped from nowhere it seemed, and said, "I suggest we have some ale and talk about it at length, sirs, at the nearest establishment for libations."

"Coffee perhaps," replied Griffin. "I think Inspector Ransom needs coffee or tea more so than alcohol."

Philo quickly put in, "Fact is, Griffin and I were just saying that Ransom here could use *your* cure, sir. I understand it worked well for him once before."

"That can certainly be arranged. My residence is only a few blocks away. Shall we, Inspector Ransom? I know my sister would be pleased beyond measure to see you again at our home."

"Did I ask for a committee meeting out here? Is everyone following me?" Ransom looked on the verge of collapse.

"You fellows are quite welcome to join us, of course," said Tewes, ignoring Alastair's complaint.

"Perhaps another time," said Philo. "I've much work awaiting." He secretly punched at Griffin's side. Griffin got the message that he needed an exit line.

"I . . . I too have a lot of paperwork back at the office."

"No, Griff, stay on Denton for me. Will you do that, Griff?" asked Ransom.

"I will, Ransom. You may rely on it."

"He is our man, so don't take your eyes off the monster."

"Aye, Inspector, I will not."

"I always knew you were a good lad, Griff." Ransom sounded drunk, fatigue slurring his words.

Tewes led a still weak Ransom off toward her and Gabby's home. Alastair asked, "Has Denton come around to the house? Have you seen him skulking about for glimpses of Gabrielle?"

"No, there's been no such trouble out of the young man, and while Waldo has pursued Gabby, she's utterly rejected his advances."

Philo turned from watching Tewes and Ransom walk off into a growing mist in the park, actually a low-hanging fog moving steadily in from the lake with unseasonably cool weather. In fact, a fog was beginning to envelope the entire city. In the gloom, he tried to get Griffin to come away with him, that Waldo Denton did not deserve the attention of a stakeout.

"Perhaps, but suppose it should turn out Ransom is right about Denton? What then?"

"Are you mad? You're going to stand round in this mucky weather on some off chance that Denton will show himself a murderer?"

Raindrops began falling. "I will do it for Ransom, yes. A promise is, after all—"

"A promise, yes, I know all that rubbish."

"You, sir, you need to spend less time in Bohemian taverns and more time deciding precisely what you do believe in."

"Hmmm . . . and I was about to suggest that you go home to your wife and kiddies, and allow me to stand guard over this criminal suspect."

"No . . . this calls for a badge. Go home, Mr. Keane."

"Do you imagine if it is Denton, and if he never kills again . . . do you imagine he will have gotten away with murder?"

"Neither Rance nor I will let that happen, not if it takes the rest of our careers."

"If it is Denton at all."

"Yes, well, why don't you have a close look at that Night Hawk shot that you suspect he doctored. That could go a long way to prove his guilt."

"Good idea. I will."

"A search of Denton's house turned up nothing in the way of additional stolen goods from the victims, like the ring found in your possession. Tell me, did Polly Pete give the ring to you as some sort of payment? You said so the night you were questioned."

"The night I was questioned, I would've said anything to be left in peace, man!"

"Yes . . . well that is the way of interrogation, sir."

"So I've learned."

"Good night, sir."

"Then I take it, you will keep vigil on Denton until he retires to whatever hole he sleeps?"

"A ramshackle place down on Halsted among the rows of shantytown there."

"Where he keeps a chicken coup atop the roof."

"Correct. I understand he is no longer in your employ."

"Damn straight, right-o," replied Philo. "And that scoundrel has yet to return my camera!"

"I could arrest him if you choose to swear out a warrant for theft."

"Tomorrow."

"Do it! It would get me into his private quarters, where I know I'll find items torn from his victims."

"First thing tomorrow." Philo Keane slowly, reluctantly walked off, going in a direction that would cause no curiosity from the cabbies or Denton. He curiously looked back at young Griffin Drimmer, and a twinge of eeriness came over him as Griff disappeared ghost-fashion on fog. Alastair had once himself suspected Griffin of the crimes, later confiding how foolish it'd been, but if it were not Denton, then who better to plant evidence than another copper?

From his vantage point, obscured now in a blanket of fog, Griffin watched the strange Philo Keane amble off, and when Philo had disappeared into the encroaching night, the young inspector felt a chill loneliness pass through him as if a spectral creature of dream walked over his grave. He took out a photo of his Lucinda, and next a photo of himself, Lucinda, and the children—all of whom he'd secretly moved to Portage, Indiana—far from harm's way, until the Phantom of the Fair should unequivocally be either jailed or killed.

The following morning at the Tewes residence

Everyone in Chicago was awakened by the shrill bells of emergency fire equipment and police wagons careening down the streets, going away from the city proper toward the fairgrounds of White City. The noise awakened Ransom, who was equally startled to find that he lay in his underwear alongside Jane Francis. He recalled nothing of the night before, except that he'd fallen asleep under her caressing fingers. He feared the worst with respect to their relationship. He feared he'd fallen asleep while in her embrace.

He rushed to the window and stared out.

"What is it, Rance?" she asked.

"I can't say, but whatever it is, it's big. Perhaps a fire's broke out at the fair. Best make a call. May I use your phone?"

"By all means, yes."

He quickly dressed and coming out of the room, he found himself face-to-face with Gabby, whose eyes informed the inspector that he needn't concern himself over her sensibilities.

"What do you suppose the uproar is about?" Gabby asked.

"Dunno . . . maybe someone's hurt, maybe an accident at the fair with that blasted wheel in the sky. See to your mother, Gabrielle."

Gabby did exactly that, going in to her mother. Behind him, he could hear their feminine whispers, no doubt about his being here and coming out of Jane's bedroom. He did hear Gabby jokingly say, "Mother, you must join the suffragettes! We need the scandalous among us so badly!"

He then heard Jane declare there was nothing scandalous about love.

This only served to set Gabby off further and the whisperings returned.

He grabbed up the phone and called into headquarters, getting a dispatcher named Llewyn on the line. The man stammered until Ransom yelled, "Settle down and just tell me what's happened at the fair, man!"

"Dead he is . . . hanging on the door like a ragdoll, they're saying."

"Who? Who is killed?"

"His head near severed by the garrote."

"The garrote!"

"Trussed up on the door like a pig—at the science and industry exhibit hall—hog-tied through the underarms was the way I got it."

"Who damn you! Who is dead?"

"Your young assistant, Inspector."

He went cold inside.

"Young Drimmer," said Llewyn.

"Griff . . . but it can't be."

"I'm sorry, Inspector."

"But we left him in Lincoln Park only hours ago."

"Yes, sir."

"He was fine when I last saw him."

"Sorry," continued the mantra. "So sorry, sir."

Behind him, the women wanted to know what'd happened.

News of a body hanging from the huge doors of the Science and Industry Pavilion spread fire fashion throughout the city, and the further news that it was the murdered body of a police inspector fueled fear and nonstop speculation. It was obvious that the Phantom of the Fair was back with a vengeance, and that, as always, he loved taunting the police. Now he had killed one of their own in the same hideous fashion as with previous victims.

No doubt Griffin's body had been left on public display to rub it into the collective face of authorities, and in particular, Alastair Ransom. The Phantom had returned to his ugly modus operandi to the letter, the pattern of his work vengefully intact and identical.

Ransom had raced to the scene, and he'd gone to his knees on seeing Griffin in the same state as the earlier victims. No one had dared touch the body, not until Alastair arrived. Now that he was here, he shouted, "For God's sake, cut him down, and do it with a care to the head!"

Ransom recognized Griffin's shoes, his argyle socks, and a few other elements of his clothing. The head and face and torso had been cruelly torched. "Neither his wife nor children'll recognize him," Ransom lamented to Philo, who'd just reached him. "It's as though this monster has it in for me personally."

"My God . . . I left him alone out there," muttered Philo. "He . . . Griff *insisted* I go. I should've insisted I stay."

"Then I'd be burying both of you. This little fiend kills like . . . like some sort of preternatural badger. Had you been out in that fog, you'd now be hanging here lifeless, your body burned, your throat severed."

"What'll you do now, Alastair?"

"Kill Denton my way, in my time."

"I never heard that."

"Good . . . keep it so."

"When will you strike him down?"

"Look there, in the crowd over your left shoulder and tell me what you see?"

Philo glanced over his shoulder to find Waldo Denton amid the milling crowd with his hansom hack and horse. Philo saw the slight little near imperceptible nod he threw in Ransom's direction, as if tossing down the gauntlet, as if Griff's death was just that—a taunt to further infuriate Ransom.

"Philo, I want you to plan a trip."

"A trip?"

"Perhaps go to Mackinaw City . . . maybe out to Mackinac Island."

"Where the deuce is that?"

"Michigan, top of the Great Lakes."

"Lovely there, I'm sure, but—"

"And I want you to escort Miss Gabrielle Tewes and her aunt there, to get them to a place of safety until I come for you or send a telegram. Is that understood?"

"But, Ransom."

"No buts. Just do it. This maniac is killing everyone who means anything to me, and Philo, you are my closest friend, and as for the women—"

"All right . . . I'll do it. I've never cast myself a hero."

"You will be if you take care of Jane and Gabby."

"What about Dr. Tewes and Christian Fenger? Do you imagine either or both in danger?"

"I'll talk to them, but neither man is likely to do as I say. Still, I'll warn each off and away from this madness."

"If Griff's body was transported in Denton's cab, there'll be blood in the coach. I could get photos."

"Forget about it."

"What? Why?"

"Denton's thorough."

"He'd have cleaned up by now, you mean?"

"Even if the cushions were soaked in blood, it wouldn't be proof enough for the likes of Kehoe and Kohler!"

"They'll say he was carving up chickens in the coach, heh?"

"The dirty bastard'll be handled in Chicago fashion."

Philo, a Canadian native, asked, "Chicago fashion by way of Galway? Belfast?"

"Waste no time and travel light as to stir no interest. Tell the women the same."

"When will you do it, Ransom, and what form will it take?"

"The least you know, the better."

"I suppose it's the only way now."

"I see no other way to combat this evil. This creep's convinced a willing cadre of my enemies that I've faked evidence against him—including the weapon and even his own handprint."

"Planted there by you, I've heard it said. As you've some unreasonable hatred of the poor boy. But, Rance, everyone in the city *will know* when they find Denton's body that *you* killed him."

"There are ways to dispose of a body in a city this size, trust me. No one will ever find Denton's remains."

He placed a hand on Alastair. "You will be careful?"

"As always, of course."

"Griffin was not a big man by any means, but he had forty pounds on Denton and he was a trained investigator with fight in him."

"Nothing saved him . . . I know." He stared again at Griff's corpse. "That unholy bastard Denton must've come up out of the fog, took him from behind like all the others."

"You should at least have the coach inspected for blood, Rance."

"For all the bloody good it'd do! He'll explain it as some fare who called for Cook County emergency, someone whose hand perhaps had been cut in a bar fight. He's twisted each piece of evidence to Kohler's liking and Kehoe's excusing of it—even the photograph of his handprint at two crime scenes—direct lies."

"Yes, the charming little fellow has convinced Kohler and Kehoe that handprints can be misread and flawed."

"Corroborated by Dr. Fenger's findings—inconclusive."

"A magic trick in the developing room," said Philo.

"I am convinced there's only one path now."

"Will you go down that path today?"

"No. Today I see to Griff's family, to his proper burial, to the scant policeman's fund his wife has coming, and in my private moments, I plot Denton's execution."

"I can imagine any number of fine executions you've dreamed up."

"Aye, but keep your voice down."

"Will you burn him alive?" whispered Philo, eyes dilated.

"It would be fitting."

"But first you'll wanna beat it from him as to *why* he's done this."

"Officially, we say *learn what possible motive set all this in motion.*"

"Good luck, my friend, but beware the truth."

Ransom reacted with a deep glare into Philo's eyes. "Waste no time putting distance between Chicago and the ladies. Off to Mackinaw, and tell no one your destination."

"Promise."

"And try . . . try to explain to Jane and Gabby for me, please."

"No one is likely to applaud your actions, Ransom."

"I want no applause, nor expect absolution afterward."

"How long then until we might expect to hear from you?"

"As long as it takes. Look . . . look at him, sitting atop his cab now, moving off as if . . . so damn smug."

"I suppose even if you could get the goods on him, it would take a long time to see justice done, and they'd likely give him a suite at Straight-jacket Academy."

"Cook County Asylum, where at everyone's expense Christian Fenger will be his keeper to study him like a zoological wonder."

"And what justice for the dead?"

The question hung in the air between the two men, both of whom had lost people they'd loved to the fiend.

"You naive wonder, Philo."

"Naive? How so?"

"Whenever have you seen real justice meted out?"

"I—I . . . dunno, really."

"You haven't. Few have! When does it happen? True justice found in this life?"

As he spoke, Ransom had watched Denton take on a new fare. The hansom cab carrying a new passenger from this section of the fair to another with Waldo Denton sitting taller, prouder atop it. Alastair then saw Chief Kohler closely watching Ransom's reaction to facing his dead partner. Kohler had been made curious of the whispers passing between Ransom and the former suspect, Philo Keane. *What scheme is Nathan now hatching?*

Philo asked, "What do you want, Rance?"

"What do I want?"

"Yes, in the best possible world?"

Ransom shook inside with what he wanted as an outcome. He walked in a small circle, contemplating the depth of his hatred for the so-called Phantom. His new wolf's-head cane tapped at the pavement like small-caliber fire.

Finally, Ransom answered his friend. "What do I want to see happen? Eye for eye, tooth for tooth. And it shall come to pass in a time of my choosing."

Just then Dr. Tewes himself stood alongside Ransom, pushing between him and Philo. She saw Griffin Drimmer's body being eased down by Shanks and Gwinn, and she saw Dr. Christian Fenger crossing himself where he stood alongside as the body was laid on a stretcher. Fenger leaned in so close, while the county prosecutor, Hiram Kehoe, stood off to one side, whispering in Nathan Kohler's ear. Carmichael, the *Herald* reporter, and a small army of others of his profession were crawling all over this new fresh kill, headlines in their eyes: THE PHANTOM RETURNS. A spectacular return it was, too, and obviously meant to strike at Ransom.

Something about the scene reminded Jane of a crucifixion and a sacrifice, as though it had been inevitable that young Griffin give up his life on the altar of these men's egos and their political wrangling, and to some degree she could not help but blame Alastair Ransom as well. The war between him and Nathan Kohler had brought this about, and young Griff had died a horrible death as a result of their petty differences and the hatred between Ransom and Kohler—which after all had contributed to Denton's release.

Her voice broke when she shouted, "This is all your faults! All of you!"

She pulled from Alastair's attempted touch meant to calm Dr. Tewes here in public. She saw that he wanted to console her, take her in his arms and hold her.

She rushed off after her own carriage, and he looked for Gabrielle to be hanging from the window, giving Ransom a slight wave of one hand, two fingers extended as was her habit, but Gabby did not appear. Perhaps young Gabby was the only one in the city who truly did not judge him . . . up till now. If she were with Jane, perhaps Gabby could not face him, knowing that Griffin had been killed just after taking *his* place.

"Follow Tewes, Philo. Convince him that he must get his women out of the city."

"You'd have me baby-sitting Dr. Tewes as well?"

"Tewes as well, yes! Tell Tewes that I confided in you everything. She will understand."

"You mean *he* will understand, don't you?"

"Philo, just do it."

"Of course. But how safe are you with those jackals there?" His eyes indicated Kehoe, Kohler, and Carmichael. "And when did Carmichael stop being a reporter and turn into a lackey?"

"Philo . . . go. Pack a few things and quietly get them down to the train station and out of harm's way. If I'm right, it could've been any one of you left disfigured and dangling here."

"But if you're right about Denton, and what you say about his infatuation with Gabrielle Tewes is correct, then—"

"No! I will not use her to bait this monster. Now do as I bloody well said!"

"All right, all right, calm down." Philo finally started off for his assignment.

"Use the girl for bait," Ransom muttered. The awful idea *had* crossed his mind but was at once instantly rejected. It'd be like using his own daughter to lure a fiend out of hiding. He would not place her in such jeopardy, and if left in the city much longer, she would likely come to think of doing just that on her own. No, he must relocate her and her mother to a far place.

Like a patient, all-knowing wolf, at the right moment he would pounce on Denton and tear him to pieces with his bare hands, his bear claws. He would send Denton out of this world and to the Hades from which he'd come, but first he would know why Denton killed as he did, and what possible personal connection they had—why the vendetta aimed at him from the beginning?

From the beginning he'd planned on killing his Polly-Merielle and of framing Philo Keane, the two people closest to Ransom—and now this. Killing young Griff and shoving it into Ransom's face. Public humiliation and private punishment for what wrongs, he could not know for certain, but he'd begun to approach a damned good guess.

He slid to the stones of the Science and Industry Pavilion, one of the few permanent structures built here at the fair, one that would remain forever as a marker and a reminder of the greatest fair the city had ever known. He knew he must sit now or else go to his knees, and he chose to allow no one to see him on his knees, not to this fiend—not a second time.

CHAPTER 5

Gabrielle was suddenly standing before the seated Inspector Ransom on the pavilion steps below an intense sun. Griffin's body had been hauled off, but the stain of where his remains had been defiled remained nearby. "Inspector Drimmer requested this information, sir, and learning that he . . . that he is . . . no longer among us . . . well, I know he was working in close tandem with you, Inspector."

"Gabby?" He looked up from where he sat on the hot steps of the museum pavilion. His face telegraphed how stunned he was to see her. "I thought you were in the carriage with your mother. I asked Philo to get the two of you out of the city for a few days while . . . until there's an end to this madness."

"I'm not going anywhere, and I *doubt* my mother would agree to it either. She called me at the Des Plaines station house—"

"Called for you at my station house?"

"Yes, I've a job there now." She handed him one manila file while holding back a second.

"Wait, hold on . . . what . . . Just what're you doing with an official police report?" He waved the papers she'd handed him. "And what're you doing here?"

"Look . . . look at the report, Inspector."

Ransom read the official police report. It was a list of aliases for a name he had hoped never to see again, *Campaneua*.

"Who put you up to this?" His voice startled her.

"I told you. Inspector Drimmer. He requested it last night over the phone."

"And since when do you take police calls and—"

"Chief Nathan Kohler hired me on the spot when I went to talk to him about working for the Chicago Police Department while I get my degree in pathology through Rush Medical College, working with Dr. Fenger. Dr. Fenger provided me with a wonderful recommendation."

"Christian sent you into that lair of Kohler's?"

"If you mean the man's office, yes. Dr. Fenger believes in me."

"OK, OK." He began studying the list. "There's an arrest here of a year ago of a Campaneua, just south of the city, Joliet, but he was sent on his way."

"To Chicago . . . or so he told Joliet authorities."

A gasp escaped Ransom. "The alias they have on him. Walter Dunston."

"Yes, not far from Waldo Denton."

"And if he is really a Campaneua, then he has come to kill me."

Gabby looked curiously at him when he said this. "If so, he's botched the job like a poor marksman."

"Agreed . . . killing everyone around me, purposefully missing me, dragging it out."

"He's decided you should suffer."

"Suffer long and hard *before* he kills me."

"It would appear so."

"Does Kohler know about this?" He indicated the police report.

"No."

"Anyone? Did you tell anyone of it?"

"No, but I will tell Mother. You know Jane and I share everything."

He nodded, understanding. "Get to her. Make her promise as you promise to me now that you tell no one of this. I will handle things from here."

"It—it has to do with Haymarket . . . has from the start, hasn't it?"

"I killed a man, or rather a number of us coppers killed a man named Campaneua while attempting to get information from him."

She looked stricken. "Then the rumors are true?"

"It was in order to save lives, I thought at the time."

"But if Denton is Campaneua's relative and out to get you . . . why'd he kill Cliffton Purvis, who had no connection to you . . . not to mention other victims with no connection to you? People you didn't even know. Why?"

Purvis had been Gabby's one-time boyfriend.

"The others were intended less to wound me personally than to wound my pride, my confidence, the public trust in my reputation."

"Yes, to . . . to wound you professionally."

"Denton has succeeded on both counts. And as for Purvis, I suspect it had to do with you, Gabby."

"Whatever do you mean?"

"He's pervertedly infatuated with you, and the Purvis boy showed an interest in you, Gabby."

Tears welled up unbidden as Gabby's eyes traced the topsail of a merchant ship out on Lake Michigan making its approach to the city. She swallowed hard. "I hardly knew Cliffton. We'd just met in fact, yet I feel some small measure of how you must be feeling right now. And it makes for more understanding of this report from France, the Sûreté police—your response to the measurements taken of one Dr. James Phineas Tewes, sir. The night you'd gotten mother intoxicated."

"I do apologize for the suspicion and chicanery on my

part, but with her Tewes part played so well, she brought suspicion on herself."

"But it took you to get her stewed!"

"Frankly, she managed to get herself stewed."

"The report details exactly who Dr. Tewes was."

"Was?" He took the report and began studying it.

"It details my father's crimes—a true con artist indeed—and his death in a prison. It's why Mother has hidden him from me all these years. Allain Tewes."

"I'm sorry, Gabrielle. I believed that . . . I thought it the right thing at the time."

"You have nothing to apologize for. You were onto a fraud, and you were right in a sense. You are a good detective, after all. Both my parents have now lived false lives."

She stood as if to go but lingered, awkwardly shaking.

He stood and held her to him. "It's all right," he muttered.

They held in a moment of silence. "I was so shocked to learn of Inspector Drimmer's murder."

"Think what is in Denton's mind now, Gabby. *You.* So you must leave the city. I am sending you and your mother to a safe place."

"I won't go."

"Yes, you will, young lady. You'll do as I say."

She smiled up at him.

"Think now as Denton is thinking, Gabby."

"Think like a killer?"

"Precisely, if you are to survive."

"Or if you are to catch him?"

"Now you have it."

"It's difficult . . . to think such dark thoughts."

"Denton means to celebrate when all this vengeance he's taken out on me is over, when finally it is my body burned and garroted and laid low in my grave."

"So this's been the plan hatched by the younger Campaneua—"

"Denton—he means to be with you, Gabby Tewes, to have you—possess you."

She shakily repeated it. "Possess me?"

"He has set his mind for you."

"The purpose of his returning my umbrella that night was to gain entry to our home?"

"You tell me, *Inspector* Tewes."

She sniffed and blew her nose and looked terribly young doing it.

"Gabrielle, you now have some idea how close you and your mother came to dying that night."

"And how you sacrificed for us."

He shrugged this off. "One slight, one offense can set a deviant like him off."

"All of this you know, and yet Denton freely roams the streets of Chicago right this moment."

"All of this the two of us know as a matter of a cop's innate intuition. We have that edge, and yet we can't touch the man, not legally at any rate."

"All this we know, yet a mystery remains. How a person like Denton can bring on himself so much black-hearted dementia in the first place?"

"And why? *Why*—the question all this time that I've been blind to comes clear at last. Why this sick boy holds such an enormous hatred for me. Jane was right on that score."

"It has to do with who you are, the stories about you, sir, your own black reputation."

"My stock and trade, but I'd thought the incident with Campaneua long buried."

"*Cremated perhaps.* Look, it has all to do with your being called the 'hero' of Haymarket. Mother held suspicions of it all along."

"You and your mother have formidable minds, young lady."

"*Ahhh* . . . thank you. Formidable . . ." Gabby giggled at the word no one had ever leveled at her before.

"Waldo Denton . . . an alias," Ransom mused. "And Griff was onto it."

"He was indeed."

"But Denton's entire bloody plan must've been hatched years ago, perhaps as a child."

"So now you're worried about Mother and me?"

"Gabby, if you value your life and your mother's life, you'll go to her now and with Philo Keane's help, convince her to leave Chicago until I send word. Until this is over."

She nodded. "I will follow your wishes, Inspector."

He hugged her once more, and together they felt a father-daughter concern that had evolved between them. Parting, he wished her hail and well-being, waving her off, adding, "Take every precaution!"

Surgeon and coroner, Dr. Christian Fenger, joined Ransom only after Gabby had gone. "What'll you do now, Alastair? Now that he's killed Drimmer?"

"Walk with me, Doctor."

They took a little-used footpath toward the lake. For a time, they remained in silence until Fenger said, "I want you to know something, Alastair."

"And that is?"

"My morgue is not a stone's throw from the stockyards where cattle and swine are kept and slaughtered."

"And this fact is of what importance?"

"It would not be a small matter, but Shanks and Gwinn have been known to dispose of a body there. Pigs are one of the few animals on earth that will eat human flesh in quantity, and while Waldo Denton is slight, I am sure they might enjoy a nice appetizer."

Ransom looked at the doctor as if he'd never seen him before. At one time the two of them had halfheartedly spoken of making Dr. Tewes disappear, when Ransom only knew James Phineas Tewes as a man, and that Tewes was blackmailing Fenger. Christian had backed off the idea, but here was no equivocation whatsoever. "I—I will take that under advisement, Christian."

"There also exists a pit where the hospital disposes of severed limbs."

"I will handle this my way, Doctor, and I do not want you or your hospital involved."

"To be sure, Denton has ransomed his body and soul to you. No pun intended."

"Griff would've enjoyed the pun."

"I realize you don't trust Shanks and Gwinn, but please, Alastair, you must trust me."

"One can't be too careful, but Christian, I know your heart."

"Good."

"And conspiracy to murder does not become you, Doctor. So let us just say that this particular execution is a one-man *operation*—and no pun intended."

"All the same, should you need 'em, I can put Shanks and Gwinn at your disposal."

"Daft idea! Neither of those maggot-eaters could keep their mouths shut for more'n a night. And which of the two sells information to Kohler do you guess?"

"All right, then, but like I said, I know some pigs need feeding."

Alastair looked deep into the doctor's eyes and found him dead serious.

Christian added, "I was quite fond of Griffin."

"As I. Fret not, Dr. Christian. Something will come of the ripple this monster has made in our pond. In the meantime, you sir, you should take a holiday."

"I see . . . for my health, say Springfield or Missouri?"

"Good choice, sir."

"All right, Ransom. Perhaps I will."

"Without delay."

"Then you intend on seeing to this little matter of the little man soon?"

"I will waste no more time."

"Careful of your back, then, Rance, as there is *so much of it back there!*" He tapped Ransom's shoulder. "You'd never see Denton coming."

"I am not so old and fat that I can't take care of myself in a fight."

"I'd've said the same of Griffin, before today." Fenger bid him good-bye and good luck. They'd come full circle, the path having led them back to the steps of the museum.

Fenger and Ransom watched Kehoe and Kohler approaching now—the men who'd allowed Denton his freedom while Alastair lay on his back in hospital. "Speaking of swine," said Dr. Fenger.

"The two men—other than myself—responsible for Griff's death," muttered Ransom, working hard to control his temper and to curb his tongue.

"Gentlemen," said Fenger to Kohler and Kehoe. "A brave new day and again the viper strikes—and this time at one of our own."

"All bets're come to this," began Ransom in icy voice. "What'll the papers make of it, Chief? Mr. Prosecutor?"

"People seem to be dying around you at every turn, Inspector Ransom," began Kohler. "That's what's to be made of it."

"You partnered me with the young man so that he might keep tabs on me, keep close to my investigation of Haymarket, and when he failed you, you failed him by—"

"I resent the accusation on its surface!" countered Chief Nathan Kohler. "I partnered him with you, so he might learn . . . so he could be all that he could be under your tutelage, Alastair. To learn from the best in the department."

"Kohler, you beset my life with one spy after another. Now you intend on using a young girl, Gabrielle Tewes. Do you have any notion the wrath you are going to stir up in her Aunt Jane Francis and her father, Dr. Tewes, when they learn of this? No, I suppose you don't have a clue."

Kohler stared long into Alastair's eyes. Each man silently told the other that Dr. Tewes's disguise as a man was known to them both. Still, Kohler affected a smug look that said "I mean to say nothing on the subject."

"Setting spies on me. You are so subtle, and your subtlety got Griff killed as surely as any factor in this horror. When our common enemy surfaced, you should've backed me, but I knew early on that you'd fail to draw ranks, even in the face of a multiple murderer."

Prosecutor Kehoe stood dumbfounded at this outburst. "Careful, man, or you will be up on libel charges, and I will happily stand witness."

"Screw you, Kehoe! What hole did you dig your head out of now that all hell's broke loose, thanks to the failure of your office in all this!"

"That's insulting!"

"Damn straight it is!" Alastair banged his cane on the pavilion steps. "But not so insulting as your order releasing a multiple murderer to the street."

"There's no proof of any such—"

"To again terrorize the city and make a mockery of your precious, grandiose fair!" Ransom clutched his cane until his knuckles bled white. His raised voice attracted media attention, while the boisterous, even rowdy crowds continued along the fairways as if it were just another day of jolliness and sunshine.

"Curb your bloody tongue, Ransom!" ordered Kohler.

"How could you let a killer go just to spite me, Nathan?"

Thom Carmichael had obviously been given special privileges, as he'd come in Kohler's company and was this side of the police barricade. The *Herald* reporter began furiously taking notes when Kohler said, "Thom, none of this sees light of day, understood?"

Other reporters had begun to take notes as well. "You getting this?" shouted Ransom to the hungry press, salivating for a scandal.

"This man's ranting nonsense, Carmichael." Kohler glared at Ransom. "Another word, and I'll have your badge, Inspector!"

"Is it my bloody badge you want, Kohler? Is that it?" Ransom shouted, raising his cane. "Is that why Griff is dead?"

Several of the gray-uniformed World's Fair cops moved in to take hold of Alastair, to pull him away. Their concern rested with returning the fair to its former peaceful atmosphere. But even in their grasp, Ransom kept up his rant: "Is that why you let a killer walk free? All to make me look incompetent?"

The fair brigade coppers tugged him farther, but he only raised his voice to reach across the chasm. "Like the stories you've supplied the press? Giving Carmichael an exclusive on my breakdown?" He snatched his inspector's badge from a breast pocket and threw it at Kohler's feet. "You've wanted this for so long and so badly that you got Griffin killed for it, so by God take it!"

The crowd close enough to hear all of this rose up in a single-minded cheer for Ransom's resigning. He could not be sure if they were for it, against it, or simply glad to see the Chief of Police shouted down and embarrassed in public.

Ransom then pulled free of the men holding him back. He went to where Shanks and Gwinn held the meat wagon for Dr. Christian, the stretcher with Griffin's mutilated body in the rear. "You two take extra care with this man. He was a good cop."

"Whatever you say, Inspector." Gwinn's tone was solemn, practiced.

"We'll be as gentle with 'im as me own mum," added Shanks.

Shanks's tongue itself is larcenous, Ransom thought. "You're to do better than your mum. Do you hear?"

"How so?" crowed Gwinn.

"We've harshly limited resources, Inspector," replied the second crow.

Ransom pushed a silver dollar into each attendant's hand. "Should I hear otherwise, I'll take that two dollars back, but I'll taken it outta your flesh, the both of you! Now, where is the man's wedding ring?"

"The killer, he must've got hol't of it."

"There were none," said the second crow.

"His wallet? His effects?"

"Every pocket emptied. Not so much as a watch." Gwinn's hands rose in unconscious supplication.

Shanks cranked his head from side to side, saying, "I swear, Inspector, on me dear departed—"

"All right, all right, take him to the morgue."

Fenger gave the two ghoulish characters the nod. Like two hungry men of one mind, they rushed to the rear, each slamming a door on Griffin's body. In a moment, they were trundling off with the body in tow, their converted meat wagon pulled by two unhealthy horses. The image of the interior of that filthy wagon stuck in Ransom's craw and brain. It hadn't been so long ago that he'd awakened locked inside this same so-called ambulance.

"Piece of work, those two," came a thick voice in his ear.

"No doubt, some day I'll be on their stretcher again, too," Ransom muttered to Thom Carmichael who'd joined him.

"That was rash, tossing your badge at Kohler."

"What do you want from me, Thom?"

"We're old poker buddies, you and I. I wanted you to know that I had little choice in presenting the news as I did, given the lack of evidence against Denton. Do you really think Denton murdered Griffin?"

"Who but?"

"So, the killer stays true to form in every aspect, doing precisely the same thing over and over. He has to know he leaves his mark."

"Like a rutting deer or a dog in heat, spraying his trail, leading to . . . to—"

"To Waldo Denton?"

"You know where I stand. What is it, Thom?"

"It's what Dr. Tewes's sister pointed out to me earlier, that the killer cannot seem to help but repeat his act in a kind of ritualistic fashion."

"We call it in police circles a pattern."

"A pattern crime—like leaving a byline?"

"Some call it his signature mark, yes—his modus operandi."

"*Ahhh* . . . method of operation. I get it. But, Rance, doing the same thing over an' over with the same result, is that not a definition of insanity?"

"It is."

"Then he is insane?"

"Insane with his obsessive needs, yes. But make no mistake, he knows right from wrong. He's not completely gone."

"Down to taking wallets, purses, pocket watches, rings, jewels, and necklaces."

"Yes, taking jewelry like some damned crow whose eye is caught by a shining bauble. Someplace that creep Denton has to have all those jewels he's pilfered from his victims, and now he adds Griff's wedding band."

"What will you do now, Alastair? Now as citizen Ransom?"

"Off the record?"

"Off the record."

"On or off, I can't tell you what I will do next. Frankly, it is not my problem any longer." The lie fell flat with Thom Carmichael. He knew Ransom too well.

"Come now, any problem for Chicago is a problem for Ransom. Goes hand in hand."

"No longer. No longer on the payroll. So as far as I'm concerned, it's over."

"You lie magnificently; it is what marks you as the consummate poker player, Alastair. I look forward, then, to reporting on the mysterious death or disappearance of one Waldo Denton."

"Have you now become convinced of his guilt? Or are you still working for Kohler? Trying to dirty my name any more is, at best, superfluous."

"Trust me. I can't stand Kohler, or Kehoe for that matter, and am done with them. For a reporter, being in the inner circle . . . given first crack at the story . . . well, there's always conditions."

"You mean it's not all that it's 'cracked up' to be?"

"Funny . . . but correct. I know of no reporter worth his salt who'd not take the gamble."

"But?" Ransom lit his pipe.

"But I know no reporter who's won against the house, the city in this case."

"So now you're on the outs with them *and* me, so save your confounded questions for someone who gives a damn. But I will ask *you* a question."

"Go right ahead."

"All right, just when did you decide that Denton was in fact the Phantom?"

"Last night."

"Last night?"

"I ran into Denton last night."

Alastair was instantly on this. "Was it late?"

"Quite. Coming from Muldoon's, I was."

"And he came out of the dark?"

"No . . . cloppin' alongside me atop his hack."

"Just like that?"

"Said he was looking for you."

"Really? In the fog?"

"Said he had a message for you."

"Really, now."

"I thought it all quite odd."

"Odd? Odd how?"

"Odd, Ransom, that he'd want anything whatever to do with you after all that's transpired between you two!"

"All this last night? In the fog? As you walked the curb?"

"I wasn't walking so well on the curb but in the roadway. Weavin' a bit, you might say."

"Put a scare into you, did he?"

"Some, yeah . . . I admit to it, knowing your suspicions of him, yes."

Where did he find you? Near Lincoln Park?"

"Yes, just off the park. I was making my way home . . . maybe round midnight. Just left the Red Lion."

"You said Muldoon's." Ransom knew the Red Lion as a favorite watering hole for reporters, down-and-out poets, writers, and artists.

"All right . . . I was between the two places."

Bar crawling, Ransom realized. "He flagged you down, or you him?"

"He was grinning like a madman, saying that *your day*— Ransom's time had come."

"What else did the ferret say?"

"Spoke of your stalking and shadowing tactics, of your harassing him. He talked nonstop even though I repeatedly asked my leave, albeit in a stupor. I was going in the same direction as he, and I fully expected him to ask if I should like a ride up on the seat with him—so's he might carry on about you to a reporter. But he let me walk off."

"What has this to do with . . . wait a moment. . . ."

"Yes, the cab was occupied."

"He had someone in the cab the whole time?"

"I saw the silhouette of a man."

"And?"

"I believe now it was Griffin Drimmer."

"Griffin?"

"Yes, stiff but sitting up, but not really moving the way a man does even asleep. Griffin—if it was him, and I am convinced of what I saw, but at the time, I took him for a drunk. When I finally realized it was Griffin, I got my voice, shouted after the disappearing cab—"

"But it was too late."

"A few hours later, like you, I learn of this shocking scene involving Drimmer."

"Of course. He'd used his cab to transport the body here to the museum to make a show of it. Philo was right—said as much."

"And to make matters even more suspicious and eerie, he was humming a tune."

"A tune?"

"Yes, the one they play to distraction at the beer gardens till you forget to hear it."

"What tune, man?"

" 'Comin' through the Rye,' and if I ne'er hear it again, I can die a happy—"

"Same as has been heard by our only witness, Saville."

"You'd confided as much, but had asked me to not publish it, recall? When it dawned on me, drunk as I was, I went cold to the bone."

Ransom had gone deep into thought.

Carmichael nudged Alastair, the odor of alcohol wafting off him still. "So what will you do next?"

"What indeed. I think that, sir, must remain between me and my Maker and—"

"I see."

"—and not between me and the *Herald*."

"Time to clean the city streets, you mean?"

"They have been gathering a great lot of dirt and blood of late."

"For too long, yes."

A deep silence fell over them where the lakeshore breeze lifted their hair, and the warm morning sun bathed them, making them blink. Nearby birds chased one another through the agricultural exhibit meant as an orchard and garden. By night, the modern miracle of electric lampposts lit the paved paths that snaked through the White City wonderland. So much of the fair stood at odds with what they spoke of— *murdering a murderer before he should murder again.*

"I want to express my deepest, sincerest apology, Alastair, about Griffin Drimmer."

"You already said that, my friend."

"All right damn you, then, I want to say I am in . . . that I'm sorry in general for ever doubting you."

"For doubt? It's the most natural of all human—"

"All right, then! Sorry for any libelous, felonious words I may've used against you."

"In print?"

"Or in the ale houses!"

"Just doing your bloody job. Dirt . . . it's your business. Words are weapons to a man like you."

Carmichael fell silent. He looked so contrite. "Aye, my business, and it cost me dearly. I wonder what might've occurred last eve had I opened that cab door?"

"You'd've lost your head along with Griffin, and we'd not be here having this conversation."

"Yes . . . difficult to speak if your throat's cut. Just that knowing who Denton was . . . knowing my own suspicions of him, and even sensing some unease in him as he spoke . . . I knew I'd not open that door for any reason, not even for a story, not on *any* account."

"Smart of you, Thom."

"Do you find me a coward, Alastair?"

"A coward? No . . . a man of words. No one expects more from you, Thom."

"But suppose . . . suppose Denton was alive in there, only stunned? Perhaps I could've done something to . . . to help him, you see, and—"

"Damn it, man! You do your battles with words. Your sword is language. You have nothing to feel ashamed of."

"And you? Your weapon of choice?"

"I can tell you it is not a garrote."

"Yes, I imagine if you used a blade, it'd be a full-blown guillotine."

"Do you know where I can find one?"

"Gotta be one somewhere at the fair. France's contributions to the world since Columbus discovered America, all that."

Ransom couldn't help but laugh at Thom's sardonic wit.

"Then you *are* off to outwit the Phantom once again?"

"I am his match, sir."

"But there is something you want from him first, something you must have or know? Before you kill him?"

"Keep your voice down."

"Well, is there? Something you want from him?"

"I want to know where the jewelry is kept."

"No . . . come along. You must confide in someone, trust someone."

"I *have* confided in someone."

"A person or God? The confessional?"

"A person, the only man I trust."

Ransom walked off, leaving Carmichael to ponder who it might be that had Alastair Ransom's complete confidence. He suspected Thom would guess it to be Philo Keane, so often seen with Ransom in bawdy houses and at the gambling table, but Thom was a bright fellow, and he'd likely soon dismiss the notion and instead go in search of Dr. Christian Fenger for the answer.

As he stormed off, Alastair heard his former chief, County Prosecutor Kehoe, laughing over some joke made by another man who'd come on scene, a man who created a sensation among the reporters and populace—Mayor Carter Harrison. Alastair did not look back as he stepped out of the circuslike atmosphere of White City and continued into *the real city*—cold-blooded murder on his mind.

Thom Carmichael went to see Dr. Christian Fenger at Cook County, and making it clear that he'd come as a friend of Ransom's and not as a reporter, he asked Fenger if he were the one man that Alastair had confided in. "I need to know, Doctor, please."

Christian Fenger poured Thom a drink. "I'd prescribe something more medicinal, but you'd never take it."

Carmichael took the offering, his hangover killing him. "What about my question?"

"Ransom did not lie, but I am not the man you seek."

"Then who? To whom does he confide?"

"One man."

"Yes? His name?"

"His name is Ransom."

"Yet he confides in you as well."

"On certain topics . . . at times."

"Then you know very well he intends to dispatch Denton to the cosmos, don't you?"

"I know nothing of the kind, and neither do you."

"But, Doctor—"

"Put it out of your mind, Carmichael, and I never want to see an inkling of it, not a whisper of it in that rag you call a newspaper."

"*Ahhh* . . . yes, of course, the bane of every reporter's existence, 'No one knows nothing.' "

"And if we are friends of Ransom, let's keep it that way." Dr. Fenger laughed heartily. Carmichael, after a hesitation, began laughing with the good doctor.

For the next twenty-four to forty-eight hours, the time period Ransom allowed to dispatch Waldo Denton, he'd designated himself the avenging wind that would rid the city of the ghost of Campaneua. He'd do it for his murdered partner, Griff, his murdered mistress, Merielle, the farm boy who wanted to be an architect, the young woman, Miss Mandor, to whom Philo had lost his heart, the officious bean counter, Trelaine, the already forgotten by public and press earliest victims, two defenseless women, and one unborn child.

But before *this* monster crushed the life of the other monster, Alastair Ransom would know why . . . why? He wanted to know what forged this collision, this coming together of forces bent on destruction, this seemingly inevitable, unalterable fate?

This he must know.

Must know if my instincts and what Griff and Gabby had uncovered is true or not.

The same instincts tore at him with talons of a great beast. He must know if it were true that this horror and death were all somehow his fault. He had to know if God had meant for it to be all laid at his doorstep for past indiscretions.

Even so, Waldo Denton would not spend a day in jail, or in an asylum. Nor would Denton face a quick and painless execution. Not if Ransom's justice rained down on him.

In Ransom's time and in his court, with him as judge, jury, and executioner. People would know, but he'd leave no evidence, not even Denton's body. It was good that people would know. Men like Muldoon, Kohler, Kehoe, Carmichael, the mob bosses, the Tong leaders, the Irish thugs, all the rats inhabiting Ransom's city would know to fear him— to fear his idea of retribution.

Denton hadn't the brains to fear him.

Had no idea what Alastair Ransom was capable of.

Alastair had only one fear of his *own* remaining: that, in his vengeance and what he perceived his duty, he'd leave Jane and Gabby and men like Philo also fearful of him.

"One hell of a price to pay for peace and payback," he muttered to himself. In the exchange, for loving and protecting Jane and Gabby, he'd teach them fear as well.

Others would wait and see.

Wait and see—and expect to read about it in tomorrow's *Tribune* or *Herald*.

CHAPTER 6

Alastair awaited the arrival of the hansom cab as it was due any moment now at the Chicago River wharf. Alastair knew who would alight from the cab and precisely what would happen when Chicago fire investigator Harry Stratemeyer climbed from that coach. All had been timed, but already the timing was off.

Harry Stratemeyer and Investigator Alastair Ransom had shared many a drink and brawl, and were usually on one another's side. Alastair had asked Harry for a favor earlier in the day, saying, "I need to take some garbage out, Harry."

"Garbage? And how far *out* are you talking?"

"The deep."

"Ahhh . . . I see."

"And I don't own a boat."

"It's been too long since we last cranked up the old fire boat."

"You're a good man, Harry."

"I consider it my duty—anything to heave out the stench." Harry had seen firsthand and close up the results of Denton's kill-spree.

Ransom now saw the cab turn onto Randolph and approach

the wharf, where he remained in deep shadow in a recessed warehouse doorway. It was not far from here that young Campaneua's cursed father had died amid the flames during that botched interrogation years ago. Now it was the kid's turn to die. He'd caused enough suffering.

Alastair patiently watched the cab halt before the wharves, Denton sitting high and blinking in the setting sun. Harry played his part well, slurring his words and stumbling about as he asked Waldo if he'd like to see the Chicago Fire Department's pride and joy, a diesel-powered tug that piped its way up and down the river in the event of a fire along the length of the Chicago River, the boat fully equipped with the latest in pumps and utilizing the river water itself to douse errant fires that might break out at warehouses or aboard ships harbored as far as the eye could see.

Waldo Denton—Campaneua—took the bait, wide-eyed and curious at the wondrous fire tug sitting at the end of the pier. He stepped aboard behind Stratemeyer, who waved at a couple of his lads already aboard. "I've another to take the tour, boys!" he proclaimed.

This was met with boredom from the two men aboard, both in suspenders and boots, a heat wave having descended over the city.

Waldo was well into the tour, being conducted about the fire-fighting tug and his head half in the barrel of the water cannon when Harry said, "And just to your left is Inspector Ransom."

Ransom and the two other firemen grabbed Denton, who was quickly overpowered and hog-tied. "Into the ice chest, now!" shouted Ransom even as Harry lifted the lid to the huge onboard ice chest, a leftover from a time when the fire tug had been a fishing trawler. It held nearly a ton of ice and Waldo Denton, tied and gagged, was dropped inside.

In a matter of a half hour, the fire boat was out over Lake Michigan, its crew, Harry and Ransom enjoying a Pabst—the beer that "Only Yesterday" won the blue ribbon at the World's Fair. Harry remained skeptical of the new beer, but said he wanted to give it a try. They toasted to a job well done.

Alastair added, "To my lovely Polly Pete, my Merielle. May she find the peace in death she sought in life."

"Here, here!" cheered the firemen, all of whom had been on hand the day Polly's blackened body and separated head had been discovered amid the ruins of a fire, the source of which had been her apartment. She'd been one of Denton's first victims.

"And to Griffin Drimmer," added Harry.

Alastair raised his bottle of Pabst and clinked it against the others. "A better-hearted young detective, and so dedicated, never lived."

"Nor died," agreed Harry as he and Ransom began feeling the effects of their third beer now. By now they'd taken the boat several nautical miles out over Lake Michigan.

All four men stared at the ice box, imagining its contents, now silent after much kicking and thrashing.

"You think he's froze to death, Alastair?" asked Harry as he gulped down his Pabst.

"We need to get back to the river and soon," said one of the fireboat men.

"Don't want anyone missing us," agreed the second boatman.

As if on cue, Denton kicked out at his ice coffin again. "Frankly, I want the bastard alive for the next shock to his system," replied Alastair. "Boys," he addressed the two younger firemen, "appears we are alone with the elements and the waves here, so let's get the bastard outta deep freeze for phase two."

The two younger men stared at one another.

Harry erupted, shouting, "Do as Inspector Ransom says, boys!"

Ransom explained, "So he's conscious of his fate. I want him to know he's to be cold beneath the lake for eternity."

They opened the chest to find Denton turned blue and near solid save for the shivering. "Took some doing packing all that ice into the old chest for you, Inspector," said Harry, "but there's not a one of us who didn't like Griff."

The younger men hauled Denton from the ice. They laid him on the deck and attached his hog-tied body to a wench and hauled him up over the deck, just high enough so Alastair could look him in the eye. Alastair pulled away the gag and said, "I'd suggest you say your prayers, but then . . . what sort of prayer does a hound of Hell send up?"

"Yeah," agreed Harry in back of Alastair, "pray to your dark savior in the underworld?"

"Tell me why? Why bloody hell did you do it? Did you like it?" Ransom struck him so hard blood spewed from his mouth despite his temperature.

He made an animal cry, unable to form words, his teeth chattering, blood dripping onto the deck.

"I'll have an answer! Why kill so many innocent people who had naught to do with your father, Campaneua? Answer me, you bastard!"

Denton attempted to spit on Alastair, but he could not manage it as his chattering teeth and thick tongue were in the way along with the blood he was swallowing. But he didn't deny the truth—the conclusion Alastair had come to understand.

"OK, then! Pray now to the bloody father who spawned you!" Alastair cried out, wrapping Denton's garrote about his own neck.

"You b-bastard, you—you killed my father!" he choked out.

"Know this, you gutless, heartless bastard, and take it to your grave: It wasn't my doing—your father's burning to death. Yes, I was there! But the torching was the work of your friend Nathan Kohler, you fool."

Denton, while thawing, remained too chilled to respond, but he made another feeble attempt to bring up phlegm to spit on Ransom, failing but obviously also failing to believe a word Alastair had imparted. He could not; it would obliterate a worldview, a customary mindset, a way of rationalizing all his actions.

"I say ice followed by fire," said Harry. "We are, after all, firemen, and this bastard was spawned in flame."

"Just drop him, now!" shouted Ransom.

And the block and tackle lifted him higher and the boom sent him out over the lake, dangling like a limp, gangly bird, legs flailing. For a moment, Alastair saw a human being inside this cretin, a child that never was, struggling to the surface. Denton began begging for his life. "Please, please! For God's sake! You have the wrong man!"

"End it! End it now!" Ransom ordered.

"Say your good-bye to this world, you son of a bitch!" shouted Stratemeyer at the moment the hook was released and Denton, still bound and gagged, was sent to the depths of the Great Lake like a parcel of trash.

"Finally . . . it's over," Alastair muttered as if to himself.

"An end to the Phantom of the Fair," added Harry.

"Fish food now," muttered one of the younger men.

"We can all sleep better tonight," added the other. "Knowing the mad garroter is gone at last."

"Take us home, boys!" ordered Harry. "And let's raise another cold Pabst."

"I know old man Pabst," said Alastair, "and I know he'd be thrilled to know to what purpose his beer was put today." This made his firemen friends laugh uproariously as they got back to work, guiding the boat back toward Ransom's city.

Alastair looked at Chicago's growing, sprawling skyline in the distance. It all looked so different from here—*no shadows, no crime, no poverty, no grime,* he mentally quipped . . . *only peace.* How could the same place have so many different faces? This one face, he must one day show to Jane. Take her on an outing here on the lake to view the sprawling row of skyscrapers. He sipped at his beer, and he tried to imagine how it might look in five years, in ten, in twenty, in the next century.

He'd felt not a single qualm about disposing of Denton in the manner he had, and every man aboard the fire tug named the *DuSable* had reason to keep their combined secret. Each had been touched by the horror brought to their city by this madman; each had known one or more of the victims. Each wanted payback, and Ransom must admit, it did feel not only like justice and vengeance but right in its every aspect save for one.

"I should've cut his bleeding head off with that garrote before we committed him to the deep," he complained as Harry handed him another beer.

"You shoulda made him walk the plank, sure, suffer more, but it's done now, and Chicago is again yours, Ransom."

"What's that supposed to mean?"

"Means that everyone will eventually know that you took care of this mess when Kohler and Kehoe and all others failed."

"That you took action," said another.

"Regardless of your new status as Citizen Ransom," finished Harry.

"Regardless of it, or due to it?" asked Ransom.

"We all take an oath on it boys, one and all!" shouted Harry, standing and raising his closed fist above his head.

"No one'll ever know," said one of the younger men.

The others joined hands, Alastair the last. "An oath," he repeated, "that no one ever know where Denton's body lies."

"Sure . . . everyone will look cross-eyed at you, Ransom, any time the name Denton is mentioned," began Harry, pointing to the depths of the lake, "but no one will ever find the cretin's remains."

"Denton can never harm anyone ever again," Ransom assured Jane Francis and her daughter, Gabby Tewes. He'd sent word to Philo that they might all safely return to Chicago only to get word that he was to instead come to them, to see the beauty of Mackinac Island as an adult.

Unable to say no, he took the train north and joined them.

Tonight they dined at the Mooseheide Lodge, and he quietly assured them that Denton was no longer a threat. He refused to go into any detail as to why this should be believed. Over dinner, Gabby and Jane began having fun with Philo Keane, who'd brought up the subject of bravery displayed by Dr. James Phineas Tewes, who had refused to leave Chicago, refused to step out of harm's way along with his family, citing patient responsibilities. After a time, with Alastair joining in the fun, Jane finally confessed to being Dr. James Tewes, and Gabby explained the reasons why.

Ransom spent the remainder of the weekend enjoying the fishing and hunting, in watching Philo take photographs, and in conversations and walks and horseback rides with Jane Francis, Gabby accompanying them at times.

The weekend was over all too abruptly and together, the four of them returned to Chicago via train. While on the train, Alastair revealed secrets to the others, sharing his compartment and a series of items laid out before them. Bracelets, a silk necktie, lipstick case, a makeup case, a gold locket—two pocket watches, a gold ring.

"What is all this, Alastair?" asked Jane.

"After his sudden disappearance, I had Mike . . . ahhh, a cop friend, impound and search Denton's cab . . . working on his unfortunate disappearance, you see."

"All of this hidden in his cab?" asked Gabby. "But where? I was in that cab! There is no place where—and besides, you had no badge!"

"Beneath the cushions," he explained. "As for the badge, well let's just say I have more friends in more places than I'd realized."

"What led you to suspect the carriage?" asked Philo.

"I did a break-in at his home and found nothing. Determined not to give up, I suppose an absolute stubbornness of will led me to . . . an epiphany."

"Which led you to search below the cushions," said Jane.

"Where I discovered all these items, all belonging to one or another of his victims. And I found this, Jane." He held up a silver clasped locket and popped it open. Staring back at them was a picture of Gabby."

"I'd thought it lost forever," Jane said.

"Either he pickpocketed it or you dropped it in his cab." Alastair handed the locket to her. "Proof positive that he was not only the Phantom but that he'd targeted Gabby."

Jane held the locket to her breast. "Tell me . . . did you find these items before or after Mr. Denton, *ahhh . . . left town*?"

"After. Not long after. Someone filed a missing persons report on Denton."

"Who filed the report?"

"Landlord. Seems he left quite an untidy mess and a sizable bill."

"And you thought a serious search of his cab might turn up something?" asked Gabby.

"So you searched his cab," commented Philo.

"Actually, as I was ordered to stay clear of Denton even before I tossed my badge at Kohler, it was not logged as my impound. Beat cop called in on the nonpayment complaint lodged against Denton, so I put Mike on it, and he called me soon as he got a hit."

"How well you obey your superiors, Alastair," Jane said, smirking.

"I thought it wise to let others search the cab."

"And who might that be?"

"I asked it of Dr. Fenger and any eyewitness of his choosing. He wanted you, Jane—well, Dr. Tewes, that is—but since Tewes proved unavailable, he chose another prominent person."

"Kohler?" she asked.

"Yes, Christian talked Nathan Kohler into being on hand."

"Then you've been vindicated?"

"Yes, and a wanted poster's gone out across the land with Denton's mug above the line WANTED DEAD OR ALIVE."

Philo saw the dark humor in this and said, "It might so easily've been me on that poster, Alastair."

"And you still couldn't level with Nathan?" asked Jane. "After all that's happened; after losing Griffin? After the truth's being dragged into the light?"

"Nathan has not changed his opinion of me, no."

"And the horse and hansom cab?" asked Gabby. "It was a horse needing relief and a pasture."

"Belongs to the company. Returned to them. Horse and cab consigned to a new driver. Fischer company reoutfitted the interior as the cushions had blood stains."

Jane only half heard this as she stared at the photo of Gabby in the recovered locket.

"It'll all have to be returned to evidence lockup," Ransom explained, gathering all the items up again.

"All but your ring—Polly's ring?" Jane asked.

"That and your locket. Keep it."

Jane understood the look in his eye; Alastair wanted to keep Gabby's name out of it altogether.

"What's the point of shutting all these items away in a box behind some locked door, Alastair?" asked Philo.

Gabby piped in with, "Against the day when Denton will be brought to justice of course. Evidence in the event it's called, in police parlance."

Jane frowned. "I still disapprove of this new position of yours, Gabby. You should be concentrating on your medical studies."

And so began a mother-daughter "discussion" that sent Philo and Alastair in search of the smoking car.

On arriving back in the city, before getting out of the station, Inspector Ransom was suddenly surrounded by news hounds, all barking questions at him about the story on page one. Jane wisely whisked Gabby off in another direction, going in search of a carriage, Philo Keane helping with their bags.

Insisting that Alastair pay attention, Thom Carmichael held up a copy of his *Herald* to Ransom's astonished eyes:
PHANTOM STRIKES AGAIN!

The headline screamed inside his head even louder than it did on the page. "No, this can't be!" he shouted.

"I tried to tell them it wasn't the work of the Phantom," began Carmichael, his tone clearly conspiratorial as he took Alastair aside, "but it's papers they want to sell, not truth. I'm on the verge of writing out my resignation again."

But Ransom was busy reading the details of this latest atrocity. "You're right about one thing, Thom."

"I know."

"But you'll never quit the *Herald*."

"Ohhh . . . watch me."

But Ransom continued scanning the story instead. The murder was indeed brutal and might live up to such billing as a result. By the same token, the missing Mr. Waldo Denton did not appear an item for discussion in the press or a concern of the other journalists.

Alastair gripped the copy of the *Herald* and made his way out of the station and into the night. September one and already a nip in the air. Fall was coming. Soon the followers of Burnham, the architect of White City, and the merchants of the World's Fair would have to concede an end to the biggest party the city had ever hosted. But it was not planned anytime soon. Likely only a brutal early frost might curtail the glorious problem that had half the Chicago Police force baby-sitting tourists here.

"Hint of an early winter, I'd say," said Philo, joining him and Carmichael. Philo had sent off Jane and Gabby.

"Yes, an early clipper outta Canada ought to settle us all in for a long winter," suggested Alastair.

Philo Keane nodded. "Might even cut down on crime."

"Still . . . highly unlikely that icy Chicago conditions will ever cool the passions, heh?"

"May I quote you on that?" asked Carmichael.

"You may." Alastair gave a fleeting thought to how he'd had the Phantom of the Fair frozen near to death before disposing of him in the deep. A wild, crazed notion flit behind this thought, that somehow Denton survived his drowning in Lake Michigan. But this was impossible.

"What's got you newsies all up in arms?" Philo asked Carmichael, snatching the copy of the *Herald* from Alastair's grip. They awaited a carriage as Philo got the gist of the article on page one. It read in part,

> An innocent dove of Chicago, a young girl of a mere fourteen, named Anne Chapman, has joined others now collectively being called "The Vanished"—victims of some fiendish butcher, possibly a man of the Yards, possibly a knacker. Young Chapman was found murdered and floating in the Chicago River near the Wabash Street Bridge, horribly disfigured. In fact, gutted like a slaughtered animal, her entrails taken off by her killer for what reason no one in authority can say. It was subsequently determined by Chicago Police investigators that Chapman is the granddaughter of Senator Harold J. Chapman and his wife, Anne Sr., who has undergone rigorous medical treatment since learning of young Annie's awful fate. The girl's parents grieve her passing and a closed casket wake is being held at Scrimlure's Funeral Emporium, 248 North Irving Park Road, 7 P.M. Tuesday evening, funeral to follow 9 A.M. Wednesday.

"How much bloody speculation and latitude do your editors give you, Carmichael?" asked Philo. "Do you know how many butchers work in this city?"

"They call us hog-butcher to the nation, so yeah . . . I got some notion."

Philo slammed the rolled newspaper into his palm. "You fools in the press're going to get someone hung before day's end."

"We don't create the news or mobs, Keane. We can only report the brewing storm. Nature and human nature in particular creates the storm."

"You fan the damn flames!"

Carmichael only shrugged, then added, "We sell papers. You know that."

"And this damnable, confounded headline calling it the work of the Phantom?" asked Ransom.

"Yeah," agreed Philo, poking a finger in Carmichael's chest. "The victim has her head intact and was not set aflame!"

"That's likely no comfort to her loved ones, Philo." Ransom got into a cab and Philo climbed in beside him.

"Share the cost?" asked Philo.

"Sure, but I'm going to the station house. Still have some contacts there, and these vanishings began some time ago. Need to check some missing persons reports."

"On other vanished people?"

"On other vanished children, Philo. These poor missing appear to've been snatched off the street at random. Possibly kept like animals until starved. According to cops working the case, the last one turned up like Chapman . . . dead and gutted. Her name was Millie Edeh, aged eleven."

"Another little girl?"

"If it is the same monster, he does not discriminate; several boys of the same or close age have also gone missing."

"Bloody hell, and the papers're just getting it now?"

"Yes, well who's story is it now? Senator Chapman's granddaughter's involved."

"Are you saying the Chicago press doesn't care if the victims are unknowns, say, homeless children?"

"What rock do you live under, Philo? It's not the press doesn't care if homeless children go away—by any means—but society's wish!"

This silenced Philo for a moment. "And have all these young victims gone missing their entrails?"

"Entrails, organs, fleshy protrusions, eyes—"

"Enough!" said Philo.

Ransom gritted his teeth and shrugged. "We may well have a cannibal-killer on our hands."

"A man eater?"

"A child eater."

"You think he's cooking up their entrails?"

"What else does a madman do with entrails than to boil 'em and consume 'em?"

"Like so much sausage?"

"Do you have another theory?"

"Perhaps he feeds his dogs thus."

"Yeah . . . there is that possibility."

"So how're you feeling now, Alastair, now that you've had time to reflect on events?"

"Events?"

"The end of the Phantom, of course. Taking out the garbage, I think you called it."

"*Ahhh* . . . you mean, how do I feel about myself?"

The carriage slowed to a standstill over the brick street outside the Des Plaines Street station house.

"Yes, now that you've set the scales right?"

"Set the scales right? I am the scales, Philo, in the end . . . setting myself up the avenger?"

"I suppose, yes. But you are evading my question: how do you feel?"

"How do I feel?"

"About yourself, my friend?"

"Philo, my father left me with little, but he often said the only material thing you can gain, lose, or possess that is of any consequence is how you feel about yourself."

"Wise man . . . and so?"

"In that regard, I've come a long way toward liking myself."

"A small miracle to hear you say it."

"Yes, something isn't it? Small miracle. Something to

thank myself for on this fine day. Nonetheless . . . it would seem that the ugliness of our species intends to keep me pacing if only I were employed."

"You'll land on your feet, somehow."

Alastair alighted the carriage and grabbed the copy of the *Herald*. "No doubt I'll be calling on your skills with that Night Hawk all too soon, heh?"

"Whatever are you saying, Rance?"

"Pinkerton Detective Agency has offered me a position as one of their operatives."

Alastair quickly made for the station-house steps as the carriage, carrying Philo off, pulled away. Philo hung from the window of the hansom, shouting, "Great news! And you've gotten my Night Hawk back?"

"Unofficially confiscated."

"Alastair, you're a magician and a gentleman, and my knight! I crown thee Sir Alastair Ransom of the Kingdom of Chicago!"

"Do I get a brandy with that?"

CHAPTER 7

From the outside, the old stone structure called the Des Plaines Police Headquarters looked as cool and peaceful as any mausoleum, bathed as it were in a blue halo of gaslight, its yellow brick exterior reflecting back like gold. Despite the horrors of untold crimes filling the files and murder books inside, the edifice could be taken for a church if only a steeple were added, Alastair thought, pushing through the door, making his way into the mayhem. Clutter and noise hit him. Two uniforms had a wild man on the floor, attempting to cuff the rowdy drunk. The desk sergeant pleaded, at wit's end with some woman, saying "I kin do naught-a-thing to solve yer outhouse plumbing problem, my dear lady—"

"Then what bloody good're you coppers and the taxes I pay?"

"—and had you any sense, you'd know that no one kin turn rock to running water, so without a description down to the length of his nose, or a bloody name'n'address, would you kindly be leavin' now?" Alastair instantly realized how much he'd missed his sour, old second home. Then he realized how little thought he'd actually given it other than the unusual weightlessness over his heart, where his badge used to be.

Other cops whisked from desk to desk, but everyone froze when Jed Logan shouted Alastair's name over the din. A sudden silence descended over the station house as word went around that Alastair had come home. Even the complaining woman at the front desk and the man in cuffs silenced.

Sergeant of the watch came down from his high seat and around his desk, braving any blow that might come his way, and as if seeing the pope, stepped up to Ransom to shake his hand.

"What's this?" asked Ransom. "What're ya all gone daft?"

"Hail, the conquering hero!" Ken Behan was one of two inspectors working on the rash of killings now making headlines.

"Welcome home, Rance!" Jedidiah Logan, Behan's partner, slapped Alastair on the back.

"What's it all for, boys?" Ransom did a clumsy pirouette, hands extended.

"You're a hero, Alastair."

"For what in the name of God?"

"Indeed."

Laughter erupted. "Does everyone in the city know?" he whispered to Behan.

"Know what? I know nothing. Logan, whataya know?"

"Nothing."

"We're as good as the old Know-Nothing party, aren't we boys?" shouted Behan and a roar went up, ending in laughter and a chorus of "naught nothings."

"See?" asked Behan amid the uproar over the mention of the anti-immigrant movement and party.

Suddenly Chief Nathan Kohler, standing on the second-floor landing, shouted over all, silencing the room with, "What goes on here?"

"Knock it off, all of you!" shouted Ransom. "Some hero. I've lost both my badge and my partner." He pointed to Drimmer's empty desk facing his own and a feeling of enormous, sick emptiness filled Alastair.

"He were a good man!" declared Sergeant Dolan, shaking his head.

"We raised more'n a pint to Griff's memory." Ken Behan lowered his head.

"And raised three hundred dollars for his family," added Logan.

Alastair continued cleaning out his desk. "He was a fine assistant inspector although he had some training yet, getting himself knicked like that."

"Remember the time we set his report on fire, Behan?" asked Jedidiah Logan.

"And that day someone stole his lunch from the icebox, and he couldn't detect who was behind it?"

They all broke out in good-natured laughter.

The laughs ended abruptly when Chief Nathan Kohler, again shouted, "Ransom! My office, now!"

"Shitty man," complained Logan under his breath.

"Go get 'im, Alastair," added Behan. "Now you no longer have to eat his shit."

"And remember," said Sergeant Dolan, a skeletal man who stood a head taller than Ransom, "we none of us know a thing, and it's an oath we've taken to your health, Inspector."

"*Ahhh* . . . well thanks, Dolan. I didn't know I had so many friends among ye."

"Aye, you do now."

Alastair imagined the story must have circulated throughout the force about his having quietly "taken out the garbage," but he wondered with whom the leak had begun and precisely when and maybe where and perhaps who was on hand. Harry or one of his men perhaps, during a drinking bout? He pondered the notion while making the stairs taking him up to Kohler's closed office.

He hesitated a moment at the turning of the knob, not wishing to get into turmoil with Nathan so soon back, but as he could hardly stand Kohler in the same room, he imagined there was no dodging it. He opened the door and pushed through.

Inside the semi-darkened office, he found Kohler was not alone. In one corner stood Dr. Christian Fenger, a man to whom Alastair owed deference, as Christian had saved his life now twice—once after Haymarket exploded and more recently when Gabby's gun had exploded.

Alastair did not recognize the seated figure who appeared doubled over, so far into himself did he lean. The stranger was white haired and white bearded, a Santa Claus figure, dumpy, doughy, and looking as if he'd slept in his suit. A gold watch fob and a diamond ring marked him as a wealthy man. When he looked up to see Ransom enter, Alastair saw that it was Senator Harold J. Chapman, the grandfather of the deceased girl. Chapman looked a shadow of himself, on the verge of death's endgame. The terrible tragedy had left him a tattered soul.

"Senator Chapman," began Kohler, "here is our best man for such an assignment. Along with Logan and Behan—introduced to you yesterday—Inspector Ransom here will hunt down this madman who's brought this horror on your family. I assure you that—"

"Shut up, Kohler!" ordered the old man, getting to his feet. He lifted his cane and placed it in Alastair's face. "You find this monster, Ransom, and you turn him over to me."

"What's this?" Alastair asked Kohler, confused.

"Talk to me," the senator said sternly. "Understand, this is what I want. You do this thing and the three of you, gentlemen, you will have my fortune. The paperwork is already complete at my lawyer's, all quite in order. All you need is to bring him to me out at my farm in Evanston alive for me to flay. I'll strip him of every inch of his bloody skin while he's yet alive. I want to hear him beg and scream and cry the entire—"

Unfortunately and all too often, Ransom had seen this kind of unrestrained, unconditional hatred born of unmitigated hurt, pain, and a sense of entitlement to justice and order in an unjust and disordered world. For men like Chapman, it amounted to an extreme insult. A shock to the com-

fortable existence of an otherwise honorable soul now
twisted and confused and filled with a sense of outrage that
reached back to an ancestral past: the old eye-for-eye vengeance legitimized by the man's bible. Still, Ransom felt
sorry for the man's terrifying loss; he empathized, and being in his position earlier, he, too, had resorted to the same
ancient code. But something felt different here, somehow.
Most men of Chapman's stature would never know a simple
truth: no execution, no amount of punishment, no amount
of justice could end the pain or quail the loss of an innocent
life.

"Have you agreed to this, Dr. Fenger?" asked Alastair,
amazed, lifting his own cane now.

"I have."

"How so. You, a man of high moral ethics? A surgeon?"

"I know you, of all people," interrupted the senator, "can
and will put a capper on this maniac, and so why not make
a bargain of it?" asked the senator, his gold tooth and gold
ring and gold watch all lighting him up like a Christmas
tree.

"I see my reputation precedes me."

"Alastair," said Dr. Fenger, "it means a new wing at Cook
County. You've no idea how much it's needed."

"And you, Chief Kohler?" asked Ransom. "The defender
of law in Chicago?"

"No one need know outside this room, Alastair."

"I see . . . given it much thought have you?"

"Look, man, we—you and I—civil servants . . . what becomes of us, Alastair?" Kohler asked. "When retirement
comes round? And hell, face it, we don't know from year to
year if we even have jobs! Do you stand on principle? We
are talking a fortune here." Nathan Kohler extended Ransom's badge to him.

But Alastair turned from Kohler to Senator Chapman.
"I . . . I have to tell you, sir, that even without your bribe and
your hatred, I would do all in my power to bring this fiend to
justice."

Chapman leapt even closer at him. "Justice? I want nothing of justice I haven't a hand in. Do you understand?"

"That much is clear, yes."

The old senator snatched the badge out of Kohler's hand and pushed it on Alastair. "Get it done. See to this, Kohler, or it *will* be your job!" The senator pushed past Alastair and was out the door, his cane beating a sad rhythm in his wake down the stairs and out the door.

"The old man believes the rumors, Alastair." Kohler actually grimaced.

"The rumors?"

"That you single-handedly caught and dispatched the Phantom," added Christian Fenger, who then turned to Kohler and said, "How 'bout we have a drink, the three of us, Nathan. Snatch out that bottle you keep in your desk."

Kohler did so, placing three small tumblers of whiskey between the others and himself. Fenger lifted and toasted, "To the end of the Phantom, and to a quick end to this new fiend making children vanish."

Kohler lifted his glass, about to accept the toast, when both men saw that Ransom had not taken hold of his drink. "Come now, Alastair," began Fenger. "You of all men, reservations? It wasn't so long ago you and I were plotting violence against Dr. Tewes."

"I'd like to sleep on it . . . give it some thought. A thing like this . . . well, it could ruin the three of us sooner than make us rich."

Fenger gulped his whiskey and slammed the glass down. He abruptly left.

Kohler and Alastair stared across at one another. "Are you trying to figure out a way to gain this treasure that's fallen in our laps all for yourself, Alastair?"

"Don't be a fool, Nathan. A thing like this gets out; people talk."

"People are already talking about you, Inspector, and some are speculating you had my blessing in murdering Waldo Denton."

"That's a bald-faced lie."

"That you had my blessing or that you did it? And how else to explain his sudden disappearance?"

"I don't know. I was in Michigan. I heard about it when I got back, like I am hearing about this mess with the grieving senator for the first time."

"The press is calling this madman Leather Apron."

"Why Leather Apron?"

"Who knows. Someone put forth the theory he is a knacker."

"A horse butcher?"

"Someone says they saw a knacker fellow in a leather apron in the area right before the Chapman girl's body was found."

"So we are going on hearsay now?"

"The press is."

"Is the body still at Fenger's morgue?"

"Unrecognizable if it were not for a birthmark. Did you know that some birthmarks go all the way down to the bone? I hadn't known that until Fenger educated me."

"The senator had to identify his granddaughter by a birthmark?"

"A bell-shaped mark, yes. I tell you, Alastair, the body was scavenged in the manner of . . . well of a deer carcass hanging from a tree is how Fenger put it."

Alastair took the drink now and downed it.

"Then you are with us?" asked Kohler, his long-time nemesis.

Alastair tried on the notion, looking at it from all angles, trying to see how Kohler could twist it to get at him. How might it backfire? In how many ways?

"I didn't say that," he announced.

"You drink my whiskey—a peace offering—and yet you stand against me?"

"I'll need that drink," he replied, "if I'm to have a look at this little girl's butchered carcass." Ransom left with his badge in hand as abruptly as had Fenger, hoping to catch

Christian on the street, to talk privately about this matter. He wanted to know how Christian could have gotten in so deep in so short a time.

But Alastair was stopped by Logan and Behan, who had assembled all their notes and files on the case, dumping them onto his desk. "Chief's idea," said Logan.

Behan added, "Told us we're taking our lead from you now, even before you arrived, Inspector Ransom."

"Here's a brief on the whole bloody matter." Logan slapped a file into his hands.

"Shit, boys! This is your case, not mine." He pushed the file back into Logan's hands. "I'm outta here."

Dr. Fenger moved far too fast for Alastair to catch him outside the Des Plaines house. He must see the body in the morgue anyway, so he would see Christian in private there to ferret out how he came to be in such a fix. Why did he need money? It couldn't just be that he wanted it for the hospital.

At Cook County, he followed the usual route into the bowels of this place where the morgue had been relegated, and as always the stench of death and chemicals proved only the first obstacle here in the basement facilities.

"They should tear down this place and start over," he muttered to himself. "Now that would require quite the sum."

The lift door opened on a long corridor that took Alastair to its terminus, Dr. Fenger's second domain here. There were several reasons they placed morgues below ground. The ease of transportation to and from the hospital, the general public's sensibilities, yes, even the coolness, although with crude ice box refrigeration units now in use, the primary concern remained odors. Although it must be fifty degrees down here, the odors cut into the nostrils and brain sharper than Fenger's scalpel.

Prevailing overall, the odor of decay. Hard to maintain any sort of religious fervency here as all seemed lost in this undeniable odor of putrefaction. Cook County Morgue was the largest in all the Midwest. Its shelves and cold unit were filled with the indigent and unclaimed John and Jane Does, suicides, homicides, twisted corpses of those who died freak deaths. He half expected to see the bloated, water-logged corpse of one Waldo Denton here someday, washed ashore. But for now the odor was the predominant matter. No amount of cleansing fluids or fans could overpower this stench.

Ransom moved onward toward the source.

Aboveground and in his operating theater, Dr. Christian Fenger reigned as the surgeon of the century, well regarded and respected, even canonized by everyone in the hospital—a hero in his own "home." But not belowground in his morgue. Here there was no heroic life-saving measures; here there was no life to save, and his surgical skills did not repair so much as they deconstructed the "patient" if he could be called a patient; certainly he was "patient" to a fault, the corpse.

Down in the depths of the morgue, then, Christian put on another hat, and he performed something closer to the butcher, meatball surgery it was called in some circles— the work of the pathologist who spent all his time "reading" the corpse of anyone who may have met with foul play, committed suicide, or was victim of a freak accident. Here Christian determined cause of death, an act at opposite poles from being the savior upstairs.

Acting as city coroner had to take its toll on a man, reasoned Alastair as he pushed through the double doors, his cane against the stone floor along the corridor having announced him before his barging in. Ransom was so often in and out of here that few paid any special attention to him. He'd come on the occasion of every victim of the Phantom. Dr. Fenger's medical assistants paid him no heed now, save a nod before going back to their various tasks.

"I thought I'd find Dr. Fenger here," he said to the room.

"He's had to see to Dr. Tewes," replied one of the men, his once white apron a rainbow of florid and dull colors.

"Tewes? Tewes was here?"

"They carried him out on a gurney," explained the man.

"Fell out like a girl when he looked at the Chapman child's corpse; the mutilation was that horrid."

"The child . . . her body."

"Have you come for a look yourself?" came the obvious question.

"I have, but what bloody business has Tewes in all this? Damn him!"

"I suspect he's just out to make a name for himself," came the reply as the attendant wheeled a death gurney before Alastair.

"Oh, he'll be talked about in the pubs tonight, he will," chimed in the other man from behind his mask. "How he fell out."

"Morgan, it's a normal reaction for most people!" shouted the first attendant. "Not everyone's got the constitution of a knacker." He then casually pulled away the sheet that had covered a misshapen lump of flesh beneath.

Alastair audibly gasped. Only the long flowing curling red tresses of her hair looked human. He had now laid eyes on every conceivable horror done a human being. Beheadings of the Phantom did not compare; fire victims did not compare. Nothing in all his career had prepared him for this. "It's . . . are you sure it's human?" he asked.

"Dr. Fenger and a team of us have determined not only is it human but that it is Senator Chapman's missing grandchild."

"There's no face left. No nose . . . ears . . . not even eyes."

"Nor cheek, nor forehead."

The birthmark alone they had said in Kohler's office. Ransom saw that whole chunks of flesh had been carved away. It brought to mind an evening at Berghoff's where the chef stood behind his roast or ham and carved off slices for your plate.

"Cover it . . . cover it now!" Alastair raced from the room.

Behind him, he heard the man called Morgan snicker and say, "And him the man of the hour."

"Shut up, Morgan," said the other.

Alastair went searching the building for Fenger and Jane Francis, who had said she would end Dr. Tewes's career in Chicago, and now this. She had come as Tewes to view the remains of the Chapman girl. Whatever possessed her to do so?

He went for Christian's surgery. From there he went to the surgeon's office, and here he cornered him. "I understand you allowed Jane in to see that awful mess your men are trying to put back together again."

The senator's already held a wake without a body; they— he—wants the funeral to come off tonight and the coffin into hallowed ground at the family's church tomorrow."

"Look, it's awful, the whole thing, but Christian, how did you get sucked into this business of accepting money from Chapman for your services? Think what might happen if it got out?"

"I have gambling debts about to eat me alive, Alastair, and . . . besides, we need a lot of things here at the hospital, and he mentioned a wing in her name."

"The Anne Chapman wing, heh?"

"Why not?"

"And a trust or a charitable fund set up?"

"Precisely."

"One that you alone will control?"

"Someone must administer the—" he paused, seeing Ransom's smirk. "Look, here! Someone's going to do it, so why shouldn't those funds come to Rush Medical and Cook County?"

"*Ahhh* . . . it comes down to your age-old rivalry with Northwestern, does it?"

"Regardless, Rance, why shouldn't something good come of this horror? Why shouldn't decent people benefit in some manner if we do our jobs right?"

"You have no qualms about it in the least?"

"None! Did you see that child's body?" Christian's eyes

and jaw were firmly set. "What I'd give for a retirement home and a volume of Kipling right now."

"Christian, when it comes time for us to deliver up this obvious lunatic to Senator Chapman, are you sure you'll have the stomach for it?"

"I'll happily light the fire that'll boil him alive, yes."

"And Jane—acting as Tewes again? Was that her idea or yours, coming down here to see this atrocity? Have you cut her in on the deal?"

"She has street contacts I don't have, contacts you should be cultivating right now instead of harassing me."

"Damn . . . then you did call her here."

"I told her the circumstances of the case, and I am asking her to do a . . . a psychological mock-up of what kind of mind could concoct such a fate for a child. Don't for a moment think this is the last of the Vanishings."

"I see . . . so you are just playing 'Catcher in the Rye' to save the future children from harm's way."

"Don't try to get all moral with me, Alastair. Not you!"

"Next you'll be marching out the bagpipes and singing verses from Robbie Burns, heh?"

"Bull! I know you too well for this, Rance."

"Or perhaps Kipling. Do a bit of flag-waving, trumpets, drums, all that?"

"You forget, I did the autopsy on what was left of Anne Chapman."

This stopped Ransom's joking, and he nodded to his old friend. "I know that must've been . . . must've been hell." Then he repeated, "I saw her remains just now."

"Butcher is too kind a word for this madman, but, Alastair, there is something else . . . something I have to share with you."

"What is it?"

"At the nape of the neck, right here," he indicated on himself, his hand going to the base of his neck at the back. "Where the vertebra meet the skull."

"Spit it out, man."

"She was kept for some time on a hook, dangling like . . . like a carcass, and there is some justification in believing . . . God . . . hard to even voice it."

"Say it, Doctor."

"The missing portions of her—cheeks, torso, appendages."

"Yes, yes?"

"They were taken from her over time."

"Over time?"

"This was not a single sit down."

"Whataya saying that—"

"Not a single one-time carving."

"Jesus—"

"Mary—"

"—and Joseph. These victims were carved on multiple times at different sittings?"

"Proven by each wound carefully examined. Each carving displays a different time frame."

"My God. You're saying she was spiked on a nail or a hook in some godforsaken place and carved on like a leg of lamb."

"Multiple blades used on her as well. Some well after death set in, obviously. Merciful shock will have killed her before the fiend or fiends could make that many stabs and slashes."

"Does Kohler know all this?"

"He does."

"And he informed Chapman of this?"

"He did, against my better judgment. I had to tell someone, and you weren't here. I could not keep absolutely silent on the matter."

"So you share with Kohler? And then Kohler rushes off to inform Chapman of these awful details better kept in-house to begin with? That's not standard procedure, Christian, and you know it."

"I agree but there's no fetching it back now."

Alastair shook his head in disdain. "This is what sent the senator over the edge, correct?"

"Afraid so."

"And now we're having to deal with—or *deal in*—an insane wealthy senator . . . and there's a fortune to be had. We could likely name our price, heh?"

"Alastair, will you please stop preaching to me? Christ!"

"I tell you, Christian, the whole thing smacks of evil wrapped in evil."

"I did not for a moment suspect Nathan Kohler would impart the details to Senator Chapman."

"But he did, and now we have this situation on our hands."

"And what can we do but make the best of a bad bargain, Alastair. That is all I am hoping for now."

"It's a bargain that will haunt you to your grave."

"Come now! What are we proposing? To see this bastard who did this desecration of a child get precisely what he gave out? At one time that was called *justice*."

"Rationalizing it does not change what it is, Christian, and if it got out, you can kiss your career and connection with Cook County and Rush Medical College good-bye."

"Northwestern could send us all packing, given their growth. Rush needs a major influx of funds."

"Get off it, man. I believe Christian Fenger needs funds far more than does Cook County or Rush."

He dropped his gaze. "All right, I need the money as well. Hell, Alastair, you need the money more than any of us."

"How much of it have you confided to Jane?"

"Not much . . . the sketchy details."

"Tell me she knows nothing of this devil's bargain you've struck with Nathan Kohler and Chapman."

"Nothing."

"Keep it that way if you wish to keep her respect. Where is she, by the way?"

"She's two doors down, resting . . . lying down. Look, Alastair—"

But he was gone, banging down the hallway with his cane, going in search of Jane, his anger at boiling point.

* * *

Alastair found Dr. Tewes—Jane incognito—in the room down the hall, recovering from a bruise to the head from when she'd fainted in the morgue. Given the circumstances, the usual odors of that place conspiring with the brutality done to young Anne Chapman, he little wondered that even a surgeon such as Jane could fall faint.

"Are you all right?" was his first question. She was sitting on the edge of the bed they'd placed Tewes in to regain himself. Jane looked out through those unmistakable eyes and from behind her mustache and makeup at Alastair.

"It's horrible what he did to her."

"And somehow Fenger thinks you should be involved in all this? Jane, I forbid it."

"What?"

"You are not to get involved. Not one whit."

"Hold on. Who do you think you're addressing?"

"I know who I am addressing."

"Apparently, you do not."

"Whatever he's paying you to do this psychology on this madman, Jane, I will double it if you drop it now."

"Look here, Alastair. We do not have the sort of relationship in which you order me around."

"I'm *asking* you, then."

"It's already too late. I've made promises to Christian, promises I intend to keep."

"Damn you for a stubborn woman!"

A nurse entered asking Dr. Tewes if he were feeling better. Jane replied in male voice, "I am fit. Shouldn't've accompanied Dr. Fenger into his morgue on a full stomach."

The nurse had Tewes sign a release form, and with this formality complete and the nurse gone, Jane got to her feet, readying to leave.

"Wait . . . you do not know the whole picture here, Jane. You must trust me."

"I see a man trying to protect me from unsavory business. It's the same sort of attitude that kept me out of medical school here . . . sent me overseas to finish my training." She was at the door now. "And frankly, Alastair, I had come to expect more from you."

"More *what* from me?"

"More . . . just that I expected better coming from you."

"But I tell you—"

"No more. You've disappointed me enough for one day."

She left him standing alone in the empty room.

Every time he got into a covered carriage now to get around Chicago, Alastair was reminded of how Waldo Denton had been in every frame of his existence during the entire hunt for the Phantom of the Fair—ever present yet invisible at once. How effective a tool it was to be cloaked in such mundane existence as to go about invisible even while in plain sight. Alastair vowed never to let this kind of blindness stand in his way again, and he began to ponder the invisibility of the so-called horse butcher in leather apron who might have abducted a number of young people from the fitful streets of Ransom's city, to jam them onto meat hooks, and to begin a steady filleting of their features and work over them until the entrails were gone. The papers had hinted at missing intestines, but according to the autopsy report that Alastair had perused as he stood over the latest victim's remains, *all* major organs had gone missing.

"Where're the parts . . . the evidence of his crimes? Where does he hide them if not in a refrigeration unit of some sort?"

Alastair heard the cry of a newsboy on the street, waving the latest *Tribune* and shouting, "The Vanishings! Read all about it! No arrest made!"

Alastair banged with his cane for the cabbie to stop and fetch a paper. The paper was deposited through the window and Alastair scanned it for the reasons he always scanned news accounts: to take the pulse of the people, to gauge the mood. He did not expect to find any evidence floating about the story. Nor did the *Tribune* disappoint him in this any more than the *Herald* had.

Rumors mostly. Eyewitness accounts to nothing. A source quoted as saying, "I saw ol' Leather Apron nab the lil' nicker, but I could see no face on the man."

Another "eyewitness" added, "It was pitch that night, but I heard a noise as I come out of O'Dhule's and of a sudden, I heard a scream like a little kid, but it was silenced soon as it sounded. I followed a shadow into the alleyway there, but he disappeared like smoke. Some others, a little family of homeless, stood there staring at me and swore they saw no one come that way."

Alastair cast the paper aside, its pages covering the floorboard. "Another invisible killer who turns into the very darkness surrounding him."

He wondered if in the future, if in the twentieth century, if there'd ever come a time when men like him would be an anachronism, a thing of the past, unnecessary, as science will have found a way to end the lives of men born into evil, born with the mark of Caine permanently on their foreheads.

For now, he wanted to go home. In the cab that he'd ordered to wait for him, his bag brought back from Mackinac remained. He wanted a shower, a shave, a moment's respite, and some time alone to sort things.

"As to the victim, a well-known, proper lady is her mother," Jed Logan had said back at the station.

"Lives at the Chapman family home, north shore, with her husband, a banker."

"How did they lose sight of the little girl?"

"Fourteen-year-old. You ever try keeping up with a kid that age, Ransom?" asked Behan. "I didn't think so."

"The mother and Anne were out for a day in the park when Anne went missing," added Logan, who took a moment to burp out a gas bubble. "Hell man, read the report."

Alastair did not know the details of how the girl had gone missing that day. It had gone to Logan and Behan as a missing-persons case for a week and a half before Dr. Fenger was called to the river at Wabash to identify remains there. Called to the scene by Logan and Behan, who'd been notified by uniformed police, who'd been aware that the detectives had been chasing down the missing grandchild of an important man.

How the first police on scene discerned that what they had was human at all, Alastair could not say. The mutilated body had been in the water for days, ropes clinging to the small bloated package of flesh. The ropes and its discovery clearly indicated that Anne's remains had been poorly weighted down.

"Whoever did it, dropped her into the river, we are guessing around the Michigan Avenue Bridge, given the current," Logan had added.

"We think likely in a weed patch just west of the bridge," Behan had said.

"Even so, we could not identify her as Anne. The mother refused to believe it and could not be made to really look at the remains."

"So the senator showed up to do the job," Alastair had said.

"Dr. Fenger was preparing to have the body buried in the Potter's Field as a little Jane Doe, as there was nothing identifying her, until he asked Chapman about the mark he'd found on the buttocks—which had also been carved into."

"The birthmark, I see."

"That and her lovely red curls."

Yes . . . red curls, he said to himself here in the back of the cab, *curls which curiously enough, appeared the only feature on her body that did not meet the knife.*

"You can't eat hair," Behan had commented.

"If you're hungry enough, you'll eat anything," countered Logan.

Ransom had replied, "But when you have flesh, why eat hair?"

CHAPTER 8

Ransom felt privileged to own one of the first indoor plumbing facilities in the city, where he could shower and shave in peace, as well as relieve himself without having to go down a flight of stairs to an outdoor privy.

After cleaning up, he listened to a Bach symphony on his phonograph while perusing the paperwork that he'd had a messenger bring to him from the station house.

He learned little from the information save that Logan and Behan had padded their murder book with a great deal of useless anecdotal testimony and a lot of pointing fingers, most of them pointing in the direction of the slaughterhouses along Market Street and farther south at the Chicago Stock Yards. There was no lack of suspicious characters in the bovine and hog-slaughtering business or among the horse knackers—all of whom wore the obligatory leather apron. Once a hue and cry had gone up that the killer was a leather-apron man, there was no stopping the flood of informers and invectives.

There also came the typical outcry against foreigners. At once fear the "other tribe," particularly the Jews among them. Arm in arm with accusation came the usual bigotry and outlandish charges that even seeped into the newspapers. It was well known that Jews routinely sacrificed children to their god, so why not abduct gentile children with red and blond curls and blue eyes and cut them to ribbons to appease a Jewish custom and to feed their sadistic cannibalistic needs? Yes, a Jewish knacker would do nicely . . . wouldn't raise an eyebrow. Alastair had heard it in many permutations and in every venue at every level of society since his return.

Actually anyone unable to succinctly speak English had become suspect to his neighbors. There had already been mob attacks on individuals who were thought to be the one and only Leather Apron. One hefty Austrian fellow had bloodied the noses and bruised the eyes of twenty men when he was attacked, but he was himself hospitalized with multiple contusions at Cook County before police could end the violence.

Another theory had it that a now dead—*killed*—horse butcher by the name of Timothy Crutcheon was the man behind the Vanishings. Crutcheon sold rags and bottles when he could not find a dead horse in need of butchering. Most knackers were independent, and if they did not work at the yards, then they must drum up their own business by finding someone wanting to rid the farm of a useless aged animal. A lot of locals suspected Crutcheon of many a local crime, especially when a horse came up lame or too suddenly off his feet. People suspected this particular Leather Apron of poisoning a horse in order to generate revenue. A knacker normally purchased a sick or aged animal for a scant price and butchered it for parts, hide, and flesh, which he then turned around and sold at a handy profit. It was grueling, cruel work indeed; not the sort of career path people wanted for their children.

Aside from his unfortunate profession, Crutcheon traded on his unfortunate looks, having boils all over his body and face. It was rumored he'd once been a sideshow attraction. People called him a cunning man, a male witch of the black arts, and to make a living, he traded on his notoriety. Possibly another offshoot victim of the real killer, Crutcheon had turned up dead. Logan and Behan had investigated and declared that old Crutcheon had died of multiple stab wounds with a pitchfork where he lay sleeping in a barn well within the city limits, a barn owning to a family with ten children afoot. The pitchfork also belonged to the farmer, and it'd somehow become buried in Crutcheon's chest, discovered when the eldest son had come out to feed stock and milk the family cow.

No one knew why Crutcheon chose this place to sleep; he'd come in the night, uninvited. Most likely, if pursued, the case of Crutcheon would unravel quickly and surround the fears a mother and father had for their children on seeing the boil-infested wizard waddle into their barn. Alastair imagined the man waking with a scream due to a sharp three-pronged pain in his aged chest.

Other such outbreaks of fear would continue citywide until the killer was caught and the Vanishings ended.

His phone rang. He'd finally taken the step to have one installed since the fiasco of being unable to contact Jane and Gabby at the moment they were in the most danger from the Phantom, the night he and Griff had had to navigate the city in a hansom cab going full tilt during a thunderstorm as the only means of getting to Jane's in time. He now lifted the phone to learn it was Nathan Kohler calling.

"You have had time to think it over. What do you say? Think of it as an opportunity for the two of us to work toward a common goal and to bury old hatchets, Alastair."

Alastair said nothing.

"Alastair?"

Since when has Nathan my best interest at heart?"

"Alastair?"

And when did I become Alastair instead of Inspector or simply Ransom to this man?

"Are you there?"

"I said I wanted to sleep on it."

"Make the right decision, man." Kohler hung up.

"Now that's the Nathan I know," he said to the silent phone.

* * *

"You can 'ave no kinna self-worth in such a business, even though it keeps bread on ye table," the horse knacker named Houston told Alastair as he kept moving about the Chicago Stock Yards, pulling on his leather gloves and apron, snatching for his tools. "Bloody truth of it is, even round here there's a hexarchy."

"What do you mean, Jack, a hexarchy?" Alastair, while not a friend knew Jack Houston from the pubs.

"Six levels of men atop you!"

"A pecking order?"

"Aye . . . even in the yards." He stopped in his tracks long enough to give a shake of the head, then launched into butchering a dead horse at his feet. "The ones doing beef, now they're at the top, then comes swine—the real money-makers, you see." He'd already removed the horse's head. "Then it trickles down to your lamb and chicken and veal, down to goat meat, you see, but horse meat . . ." He paused, lifting his bloody mallet-sized hatchet and using it to punctuate his words, blood dribbling from it as he did so. "Well, now you see horse meat's tough as hell, and it's not so savory nor wanted, and as most of the cutting we do ends in food for other animals—dogs, cats, and then there's the soap-makers buying a ton of it. You see, then, we knackers, we're the bottom of the rung 'round here, so I say again, you can't have no opinion of yourself in this business."

Ransom asked Jack if he knew anyone around the yards who was strange or eccentric, and he immediately knew it was a ridiculous question to ask under the circumstances.

"You mean someone capable of taking one of these"— he held up the cleaver this time—"to a human being?"

"Yes, I believe it's what I'm asking."

Jack thought long and hard about this as he continued to butcher the dead horse, working off the limbs one joint at a time. "There's old Hatch, maybe Quinn . . . even Sharkey, but I gotta tell you, even those fellows, bloody crazy as they are . . . even they'd have to be pushed to considerable limit to chop up a senator's lass."

Jack never stopped talking, even as Alastair started away, unable to take the stench of the yards any longer. Alastair understood Jack's excitement. It was most assuredly the first time anyone had ever come asking questions of his profession or the men in it.

Ransom could still hear Jack talking as he closed the last gate on the last stall he must pass through to get clear of this place. It would take a carriage ride of several blocks to get clear of the odors that daily hovered over the entire area of the Southside Stock Yards. Even so, the stench in his nostrils and throat remained.

He had the cabbie pull over at a neighborhood grocery and got out. He went inside and purchased a sarsaparilla to wash down the clinging odors in his throat. The label on the drink made amazing claims, that it could settle the mind and provide a mental state for making enormous sums of money among other things. The label had three paragraphs of text touting the wonderful properties of cocaine, which made up two thirds of the drink's marvelous ingredients, and the rest was sugar. But the label made no claim of effectiveness against horrid odors, and it did nothing for odors clinging to his clothes.

He stepped from the store, having drained half the bottle, when he saw a homeless street urchin, dirty and hungry-looking, staring up at him. The boy was missing his front teeth, and Ransom hoped this was due to natural causes. The boy appeared perhaps eight or nine—same age as some of the Vanished.

"Say, Mister, you got a penny?"

Alastair saw such children about the streets of Chicago every day; the number of homeless families and the growing population of children on the street like this boy represented a staggering problem that seemed without answer. The city fathers had begun talking about it, but no one had done anything about it.

"Mind drinking after me, son?" Alastair asked, handing him the remainder of his soft drink.

"No, sir! Thank you, sir!" The boy took hold of the bottle as if it were a lifeline, and before Ransom could ask his name, he'd scurried off with the drink as if to find a secret place to relax and enjoy its contents.

Alastair had intentionally gone to work on the Vanishings case by hitting the streets, in an effort to avoid going into the station house, to avoid another confrontation with Chief Kohler and to buy time. He'd earlier arranged to meet with his street snitch, and he did not have a long wait before Bosch—otherwise known as Dot 'n' Carry—showed up. They got into the cab, and the driver was told to drift about the area.

"It's the Vanishings, isn't it?" Bosch asked. "They put you onto the case, didn't they? I'm not surprised. Told me mates the other night they gotta put Ransom onto the case."

"Never mind butterin' me up, Bosch. What've you got?"

"Got?"

"Your ear's always to the ground. So, what've you got?" Alastair repeated.

"Sometimes an ear to the ground ain't enough."

Ransom pulled forth a dollar bill, dangling it before Bosch's sad eyes. "This help your ears out? What can you tell me about these disappearances?"

"I tell you true, *nothing.*"

"You don't get paid for *nothings,* old-timer. Tell me what you hear."

"I tell you, the street is moot. And oh, by the way, glad to hear that the Phantom is no more. I like to think I played a small part in it."

"Get me something, Bosch . . . get me something soon."

"I'll keep me eyes and ears open. You know that. In the meantime . . . you know how scarce money is for me now?"

"I'm not a charity, Bosch."

"All right, then I got something for you on Haymarket."

Ransom sat up straight. "Haymarket?"

"Someone who was on the other side."

"A worker?"

"One who was there, yes."

"I've interviewed every living survivor already, Bosch. This is old ground."

"Not this survivor."

"What's his name."

"*Her* name. She was a seamstress, but she got all balled up in the movement."

"What's her name?"

"Josephine Lister."

"Where do I find her?"

"Well . . . that's the problem. She's dead."

"Get outta my coach, Bosch."

"No, but you don't understand."

"Out!"

"Her daughter's got a diary Josephine kept."

"A diary?"

"And there's a section on the riot and the bomb."

"How do I get in touch with the daughter?"

"She wants to sell the diary to you, and I'm to broker the deal."

"I see. And how do I know it isn't pure fiction, Bosch?"

"Would I fabricate such a thing?"

"Yes, you would if you thought you could get away with it."

"You hurt a man to the quick, Inspector."

"I want to meet with the woman."

"But that cuts me outta the deal."

"If I find her credible, you'll be paid handsomely."

"Ten percent is what she agreed on."

"Agreed."

"Till then . . . what about an advance?" He snatched at the dollar bill, but Ransom was too fast, pulling it out of reach.

"Come on, man! How do you expect me to live?"

Frowning, Ransom put the bill away. As Bosch's features fell, Alastair reached deep into a coat pocket and dragged out his reluctance in the form of two bits.

"Thanks, Inspector." He said it sourly, but he knew better than to complain.

"Ten dollars if you bring me something I can use."

"Ten dollars? On the Haymarket deal, you mean?"

"Haymarket, yes, but also the Vanishings."

"Lor' blind me! Twenty dollars. Imagine what I could do with twenty? Have not had hold of that much money in forever."

"Now get out. My coach is beginning to take on your odor."

"Hmmm . . . smells of the stockyards to me." He sniffed the air like a rodent.

The cab had come full circle to the same corner drugstore. As the crooked, arthritic Henry Bosch climbed from the cab, Alastair saw the same little boy on the street panhandling someone else out front of the store. He called the boy over to the cab.

"Yes, sir?"

"Two dollars for you, son, if you learn anything about the Vanishings," he told the boy, handing him a nickel. "Any news at all that might help."

"You're a copper, sir?"

"You'd best hone your powers of observation, son, if you're going to work for Inspector Ransom."

The boy's eyes went wide. Everyone in Chicago knew the name Ransom. "Yes, sir. I will indeed, Inspector, sir."

"And your name, son?"

"Sam . . . Samuel, sir. Everybody knows me as Sam."

"All right, then, Sam. Put your ear to the ground, nose to the stone."

"Yes, sir!"

Ransom tapped the roof of the cab with his cane and the carriage was off. "To one-twenty-nine Des Plaines," he shouted to the driver.

As the carriage picked up the pace, he quietly said to himself, "I need a drink, and I know where I don't have to pay for it."

He'd go home, clean the stockyard stench from himself, send out his clothes to that Chinese place halfway down the block, and once these chores were accomplished, he'd stroll to Philo Keane's studio home on Kingsbury Lane. Perhaps he might just enjoy the feel of warm sunshine on his face, smell the last blossoms on the wind, watch birds chase one another amid the trees of a neighborhood park, think of Jane out of her Tewes getup, and get his mind off this horrid case . . . at least for a time.

The word went out and they found Ransom at Philo's where he was enjoying a brandy, a cigar, and Beethoven on Philo's phonograph. Philo was talking about a series of photos he'd begun taking of ordinary homeless people all across the city. Ransom was hardly hearing this, but Philo had grown animated and spoke of the possibilities of a montage of such photos, if only he could find a venue for them. He was saying that perhaps if he worked on whatever small conscience Thom Carmichael had left, that perhaps with Thom's help, he could get the photos placed in the *Herald* as a poignant exposé, as he called it. "Certainly could use the money."

"When couldn't you use extra green, Philo?"

"But, Rance, it's more than about the money this time."

Ransom didn't take this too seriously, and so he grunted at all the appropriate moments, but he really just wanted to drink and hear the music. Then when Philo insisted he listen and Philo repeated that it wasn't a job for money, Alastair capitulated. "All right, all right. Never known you to minimize the monetary aspects of a job, that's all."

But this peaceful time was interrupted when a messenger—a junior officer in uniform and a friend, Mike O'Malley, knocked, knowing he could find Alastair here. O'Malley had bad news to impart.

"Another child found dead?"

"Dead and butchered . . . like a bloody knacker got at her."

"Another girl?"

"Aye."

Philo joined Alastair, grabbing his Night Hawk for photos, and as an afterthought, he slipped a single photo into his breast pocket. Alastair saw this but said nothing. They had then rushed to the scene, as Mike had wisely commandeered transportation for them. Along the way, Philo recalled how Alastair had returned his Night Hawk, evidence of their friendship. Now the two friends traversed the city and soon stood staring over the carnage.

Ransom's knee-jerk reaction on seeing the dead child was to say, "She's a local girl."

"How can you know that?" asked Dr. Tewes, who had arrived on scene after Ransom and Philo. They had sent for Dr. Fenger to come as well to preside over the newly discovered remains; Tewes had come along with Dr. Fenger, apparently with him, when he had learned of the most recent find.

"Her clothing," Alastair replied to Jane dressed as Tewes.

"You mean the tatters hanging on her?"

"Yeah . . . what's left of the blue dress with the yellow buttons. She was wearing that when she vanished. It's in the missing-persons file."

"Expensive clothes for a young woman not yet out of her teens."

"All from Fields, including her shoes," added Alastair. "Besides, I have seen her on her rounds. She works and lives somewhere in my area, or did."

"She worked? At her age?"

"Don't be naive. Half the children in the city work."

"How can you be sure it's her? You can't possibly make out her features."

"What features?" asked Philo, snapping off another shot with his Night Hawk. "But Alastair is correct. It's Alice Cadin, all right."

"It's her, Cadin, Alice Cadin," Ransom repeated the name in a tone of eulogy.

Philo then pulled forth a photograph of the girl from his breast pocket. Fenger and Tewes studied the girl in the blue frock with yellow flowers. "I'd asked the family for it. Made duplicates. Takes good professional equipment, but I photographed the photograph, you see, since they had no negatives, and it worked fairly well. I mean from a professional point of view it is appalling and it's technically—"

"Shut up, Philo," Ransom put in.

"Did what I could."

"Don't be modest, Philo," said Alastair, who then spoke to Jane and Christian. "He spread the photo to every police district, every station house."

"She'd gone missing for over a week." Christian measured the depth of a wound over the heart as he spoke. "Others've gone missing as well.

Philo said, "Alice was a hard worker, her parents told me. She wasn't homeless, but she loved the lakefront and the park. The last time they saw her, she'd gone off with friends to the park. Darkness came on, and she didn't come home. They never saw her again."

"What of the friends she went off with?"

"They left her on the path for home, or so they tell it."

"Still . . . given the disfigurement, how can you be sure?" asked Tewes.

"The blond hair," Ransom replied.

"The flowered blue dress," Philo repeated. "The yellow buttons, the shoes."

"It all fits, down to her size," added Ransom.

"Now I must inform the parents." Fenger kept his steady hands at work over the corpse.

Philo, over his initial shock, continued taking photos from every angle.

Alastair stood looking out over the Chicago River, the killer's dumping ground of choice, pacing in a small circle with his cane, favoring a backache. He smelled Tewes's cologne behind him. "Drops them in the water like so much trash, the bastard."

"Why not?" she asked, equally angry. "The river's still seen as the city toilet. Everyone disregarding the law and health issues as if they mean nothing. So what might you expect from a child killer?"

"Turns my stomach what's happening."

"We're going to catch this monster, Alastair."

"We? Tell me, Dr. Tewes, by what magic do you propose to help this investigation? How do you propose to tell us what is in the mind of a man who would do this to a child—repeatedly so? Will your mind-reading, your phrenology, get us into his bloody mind?" Ransom's voice had raised more than he'd wanted, and everyone else looked to the pair only momentarily, realizing some things never changed. It was obvious to all that Ransom did not want Dr. Tewes anywhere near his case.

"How will I get into this madman's mind and help your investigation?" asked Jane as Tewes. "By the clues he leaves."

"There are none."

"Wrong," Jane countered.

"How so?"

"He is leaving observable patterns."

"All I observe is his butchery."

"Even his cuts have left patterns, Ransom."

"Whataya mean?"

"I've looked over the autopsies and either this fiend is ambidextrous and slashes and carves with both hands, or there are *two* of them cutting away at the body, if not more."

"You can tell that?"

"Christian will verify it; it was his discovery, but I agree."

Ransom sighed heavily and shook his head and looked out over the city from this perspective, a nearby garbage heap acting as a city for rats.

"Alastair, I am working closely with Christian, and we are prepared to make certain assumptions about the killer based on the very tools he uses and the cuts he has taken out of these . . . these poor children."

"Indeed. And how is that progressing? Are you sharing, or is this all for Senator Chapman's benefit?"

"Chapman? He's got nothing to do with our teaming up, if that's what you mean. Look, Alastair, there've been several different blades identified by Fenger and myself."

"Several different blades?"

"And all have varying sizes and lengths. One is more or less a cleaver. Others are smaller blades. One or two have definite large hilts that have left patterns against the skin, meaning some of the stab wounds were so furious as to drive the weapon to the hilt, fracturing bone beneath."

"This can all be deduced by measurement, I understand, but what does it say about the kind of mental state that can do this kind of turkey carving on children?"

"After the initial attack, the deep tissue stab wounds, Ransom, every cut is meticulous, thought out . . . and it may have—that is each cut may have some sort of ritualistic purpose or meaning for the killer."

"Do you mean to say each stab wound is symbolic?"

"No, not the stabbing, no. The carving up afterward. They are not all stab wounds."

"I got that. Hell, I can see that."

"In fact, none of the killings are what we traditionally call murder by stab wound," added Dr. Fenger, coming nearer, overhearing.

"What then are they, these killings?"

"We suspect a couple of things: a kind of barbaric ritual from the old world for one."

"Human sacrifice?"

"Something of that nature, yes."

"Each killing leads to something in the nature of a carving, and the areas carved from the bodies are . . . well . . . edible."

"Including the entrails?"

"Including the entrails."

All of them fell silent at the thoughts and images raised by this.

"So, Dr. Fenger, are you telling me now that these children were carved up for their meat, like a knacker does a horse, like a butcher slaughters a sow? Are you definitely confirming this?"

"That is what we are leaning toward, yes."

"Then you're saying none of the wounds on the Chapman girl were deadly in and of itself, that she died of multiple stab wounds and was then later, after death, carved up?"

"Evidence tells us that some of the carving up went on before the Chapman girl was completely dead."

"Like the taking of her nose, ears?"

"Correct."

"How can you know that?"

"It's a theory but it has to do with the coloration around the wounds," explained the medical genius, Fenger. "Blood in the living rises to meet the knife, but not in a corpse where we'd see no color. In most of the knife wounds found on Anne Chapman, the color isn't there."

"As a result," said Jane, "we theorize death ensued due to a blow to the head—before any of the major cuts."

"Earlier, I proved to myself that he dispatched them *before* he cleaved off their flesh," added Dr. Fenger.

"How then was the last victim killed? A blow to the head, strangulation? What?"

"Alice Cadin over there was stabbed to death."

"How was she lured into this?"

"Sorry . . . we haven't a clue as to that." Fenger tugged at his beard.

"No intoxication, no poison?"

"Poison is hard to determine without testing her fluids, and that takes time, but I have a fine man on it. Dr. Joseph Konrath."

Ransom and Jane both knew that Konrath was a rarity, a man who'd pursued the alliance of the study of poisons—toxicology—and crime fighting, a new direction begun in the 1840s with the breakthrough in the infamous Marie Lafarge case, breakthroughs shared by two men working independently of one another—Frenchman Dr. Mathieu Orfila and Englishman Dr. James Marsh, who invented the process that could detect gas arsine, produced when arsenic is heated to the correct temperature. Konrath carried on a fifty-year-old tradition nowadays of seeking out gases in any number of bodily tissues and fluids to determine if poisoning were present in the deceased.

"But such things as belladonna are easily accessed nowadays."

"There've been no sign of any narcotic or poison in earlier victims, Alastair."

"Whoever this so-called Leather Apron is, we suspect rampant cannibalism," said Jane. "I suspect most cannibals don't stop to use poison. Wouldn't want to spoil the . . . the meal."

"Why'd he take her eyes?"

"Usually the first to go . . . soft tissues, a delicacy for a cannibal," said Fenger.

Alastair began tamping his unlit pipe. "Christian, what do you know of cases of cannibalism?"

Fenger took in a deep breath and exhaled. "All right, you've found me out, Rance. I've not *ever* handled a case like this, but I am reading up on it, you can bet."

"Rampant cannibalism of children. God . . . what has the world come to?" asked Ransom, not expecting an answer.

"Actually, it was not so very long ago that Jonathan Swift wrote his answer to the problem of the homeless children of London," began Jane, "that the government should round them up and feed them to the populace."

"Swift was satirizing," said Christian, "to bring the problem to the attention of Parliament and the Crown."

"Well, the Vanishings is not satire," replied Alastair. "This is real."

Alastair asked again, "OK, so what do you think you know about this madman?"

She ticked off a number of beliefs. "He is ingratiating, charming, luring the victim; he lives in the city and knows every avenue and byway."

"He likely uses candy or a drink *possibly* laced with some narcotic we can't detect," added Fenger.

"That's any soft drink on the market," Ransom said, recalling the boy, Sam, who so easily gulped down the soft drink that he'd been offered.

Jane continued, stating the obvious. "As he uses multiple blades, he is either in a profession relying on blades or is a collector."

"That narrows it down for us," he chided. "Look, Jane, have you given thought to the notion that since there're multiple blades used, that there just might be a violent gang or nutty religious cult using cannibalism as a kind of badge of honor or an initiation, or both? Each gang or cultist with his own blade, racking up points with their leaders."

"I confess," began Fenger, "it has crossed our collective minds, yes. Haven't ruled anything out at this point."

"Then we are no closer to knowing the truth about Leather Apron or his possible followers, are we?"

Fenger looked tired, his emotion on his face. "What I earlier suggested, some sort of religious cult sacrificing these lambs; perhaps it's a collective mind at work here?"

"Like a very, very dark mob or lynching party?" asked Alastair, helping secure Tewes's mustache back into place. "Only this mob likes the blades and cleavers."

"It is as old as mankind, ritual sacrifice," said Jane, shivering, "and if it is symbolism you're out for . . . well, there you have it. Trust me, the phrase Blood of the Lamb predates Christ."

"These lambs—our Chicago lambs—are silent witnesses, if that is the case," replied Ransom. "But do you really think there's some ancient cult operating here in Chicago, drinking the blood and eating the flesh of these disappearing children?"

Jane fielded the question. "Some pagan cult, something out of Romania or Eastern Europe, Druids perhaps?"

Alastair breathed deeply of the night air. Lights had gone on all across the city and they stood beneath a gaslight at the bridge. The fire boat that'd taken Denton out to the depths tugged by beneath them. He stared back at the little weed patch far below at river's edge where Dr. Fenger's attendants finished up, readying to cart the pitiful remains to County Morgue. "I have people in the city working to find out and find out quickly. If there is a sick religious cult at work here, I'll soon know it, and we'll hang them all in a public square."

Even as he said it, he wondered how Kohler, Fenger, and he would deliver an entire religious sect to the senator's farm to be boiled in oil and skinned alive in the manner of butchering swine. The senator certainly had the equipment out there on that big farm of his, the cauldron, the oil, the tools, and the know-how.

But it had been Alastair's experience with religious cults that there were more than just men and women involved but whole families, children. He tried to imagine a cultist ritual involving drinking human blood and feeding human organs and chunks of flesh to children—items torn from other children.

He prayed they were all wrong.

He imagined Christian and Jane must also have problems wrapping their minds around the notion, but apparently, they had discussed it at length sometime earlier.

This new victim had not looked in any better shape than had the Chapman girl, but this one had not been in the water as long and more of her clothing had survived. It seemed someone had made a feeble attempt to dress her before laying her into her watery grave.

Dr. Fenger, his sad eyes downcast, grumbled, "I have to leave you two. Must give Shanks and Gwinn strict orders regarding transportation of the body."

"Do they take directions well, Christian?" Ransom held back a snicker.

"I'm sick to death of seeing attendant bruises and especially broken necks postmortem." Fenger rushed off on this odious duty. Ransom glanced at Shanks and Gwinn where they stood sharing a stogie.

"Well, Jane . . . Dr. Tewes," said Ransom, "have you eaten lately?"

"Don't think I could swallow a thing save some ale."

"Then you've taken a liking to red ale, have you?" He recalled the night he'd gotten her drunk on ale while investigating her alias, Dr. Tewes. How he'd had to carry her home to Gabby. The same night as he had become attached to Gabby, who was so fiercely protective of her "father," Dr. Tewes.

"Well, I think a pint would not hurt."

"I know a nearby place. Shall we?"

After the single pint, Dr. Tewes wanted a refill, but Jane held him to one. Instead she and Ransom enjoyed a horse-drawn cab ride through Lincoln Park and down tree-lined Clark Street. While passing the scenery, he dared ask, "Jane, I thought you finished with this Tewes act. I thought we agreed—*made a pact*—on the train back from Mackinaw City . . . remember Mackinac Island? Our getaway?"

"You agreed with yourself, Alastair. Look, first and foremost, I have Gabby to think of, and Tewes is beginning to rake in too much cash right now for me to simply drop the act."

"And besides, you like it, don't you? Playing police-adviser."

"I'm no longer on Nathan's payroll, if that's what you mean. I'm being paid by Christian through his Cook County budget."

"But Christian draws partial payment from the Chicago Police Department. So he actually still works for Nathan, and so then does Dr. J. P. Tewes."

She laughed lightly at this, her femininity showing through. "And who do you answer to directly at the end of the day?"

Alastair frowned and changed the subject in rapid fashion, asking, " You know what it will sound like among the men at the station house if it gets out I am having moonlight rides through the park with James Phineas Tewes?"

"Oh . . . please. It may soften your reputation a bit."

"Will you ever learn? I don't want some things softened . . . ever, and my reputation ranks high on that list."

"Kiss me, Alastair, and shut up."

He considered following her order but stopped short. "I
can't do it with that mustache on your face. You look too
much like my Uncle Fred."

"You are incorrigible. Take me home."

"If it is your wish, Doctor."

They traveled along in silence for a time save for the
hooves on bricks outside and the occasional row at a corner
tavern. Ransom peeked from behind the window sash and
mentally began counting the number of children he saw
wandering about so late. Where were the parents. Didn't
they read? Didn't they have ears? How could they not know
of the danger afoot in the city now, the danger lurking for
their children. He saw a smaller boy than the one he'd put on
his payroll panhandling at one pub. When he had gotten a
coin, he shuffled off to a black recessed doorway and handed
his beggings to a man, someone who then set him on his
mission for another coin, possibly his father or stepfather,
reasoned Ransom. Poor bloke was likely down on his luck
and had to use his kid to beg a pittance.

It had become brutally competitive to find the least job in
the city nowadays. Whole families had wandered in from
the various states all around, many from the Illinois prairie
land in a bad crop year. There had been destructive weather
all round the city and serious flooding in areas along the
Mississippi and the Ohio rivers, as well as the Kankakee.

It all conspired to swell the streets of the city with an out-
of-control transient population beyond the municipality's
capacity to cope. Chicago, the Gem of the Prairie, was like
a beacon to all comers. Stories of land speculation and endless work and new construction and a better life according
to advertisements in national magazines had brought about
a deluge until the population numbers outstripped any hope

of a newcomer making a living here. Many a family went straight to the few churches and shelters about, and many slept on the floor of City Hall, and many wound up in lock-ups all across Chicago. Meanwhile, the number of police remained woefully inadequate, and many on the force secretly worked for private companies—moonlighting—despite new laws enacted against this.

"Has Christian promised you any, *ahhh* . . . unusual bonus . . . or special remuneration for working on the Vanishings case with him?" Ransom finally asked the question burning inside.

"No . . . no more than normal."

"*Ahhh* . . . I see."

"See what?"

"I just mean that . . . *ahhh* . . ." Ransom did not want to tell her about Christian's meeting with Kohler and Chapman, and if Fenger hadn't offered to cut her in on the scheme, he certainly did not wish to spill it to her this way. "It's going to take some time, perhaps a lot of time, away from your—from Tewes's—practice, so a bit additional seems not out of line, you see."

"Perhaps I'll push him on it . . . next time."

They arrived at Jane's door, the sign still proclaiming it to be the clinic and residence of Dr. James Phineas Tewes. She climbed down, and he walked her to the door where, with a glance back at the bored cabbie who was digging out a pipe and feeding an apple to his horse, Alastair kissed her, mustache or no and said, "There . . . good afternoon and a pleasant good night, then, Doctor."

"You really know how to charm a girl," said Jane.

"Get some rest, and we'll put our heads together on this case tomorrow."

"Pray there's not another abducted child by then."

"Trust me, in some back rooms, Chicago oddsmakers are banking on it. And we both know the Vanishings won't stop until we put the mad dog down."

Another good-bye kiss, and Alastair returned to the cabbie, who'd given up on his pipe and had opted for chewing tobacco instead, remaining so intent on his tin that he remained completely oblivious to two kissing men on Tewes's porch, unlike Gabby at the window.

"Horrible thing, Inspector," said the cabbie when Alastair began to reboard.

Alastair did a double take, thinking that the man had witnessed him kissing Dr. Tewes after all, and Ransom's face flushed as red as a Santa Claus advertisement. "Horrible?" he repeated the single word.

"This Vanishing business," replied the cabbie, scratching his pockmarked face.

"Yes . . . yes it is horrendous indeed. Look here, you see a lot going about, hear a lot."

"I do . . . and am sure this is worse even than the Phantom, I say. I mean this madman's victims are mere lil' knickers."

Ransom pulled forth a five-dollar bill and held it up to the man.

"What's this?"

"Beyond your charge, Joseph is it?"

"Yes, 'tis my name, but what's the large tip for?"

"It's no tip."

"Then what be it?"

"You'll have more if you bring me any information you hear on the street regarding these murders."

"*Ahhh* . . . I see, and sure it's a deal. Where are you off to now?"

"Moose Muldoon's, just down the—"

"Aye, I know Muldoon's, Inspector."

"You've learned my habits. Watch the habits of others for me." Ransom climbed in for the short ride to Muldoon's, where he intended to drink until midnight to blot out the sight of Alice Cadin's body so that he might find sleep somewhere in the labyrinth of a horrible struggle going on inside his mind.

CHAPTER 9

Ransom had not been inside Moose Muldoon's since the night he had cracked its proprietor—Muldoon—in the head with his wolf's-head cane. Through the grapevine that snaked about Chicago's streets, Alastair had gotten word that Muldoon had forgiven him and all was square between them now that Alastair was a hero again, now that the Phantom had as mysteriously disappeared as he'd come on the scene. In fact, it was rumored that Muldoon had created an Inspector Ransom drink and had cordoned off a table now designated as the Inspector's, at which no other man could sit unless invited by Alastair himself.

It was too much to ignore.

Ransom felt moved to learn how much was true and how much embellishment. Among the riffraff that hung about Muldoon's, Ransom had spotted all levels of criminal and down-and-out, and he was grudgingly acknowledged as their best adversary. Where they called Muldoon the Moose, Ransom was the Bear to such fellows, and to this day they talked of the confrontation between Moose and Bear, their last exchange going to Ransom. Alastair knew the clientele wanted to see a return engagement, and he would not put it past the cursed bunch to have put out these lies just to entice him back into Muldoon's lair.

All the same, he was drawn to it—moth to flame. The place was, after all, a hotbed of information about what was afoot in the city. He rationalized a visit on these grounds alone. Besides, it was another diversion from taking a straight course into #13 Des Plaines to face off with Kohler.

As the cab stopped before Muldoon's tavern, the sign swaying in a breeze coming in off the lake, he admitted, "I'd rather face Moose than Nathan right now."

The idea of dispatching the Phantom to Lake Michigan without compunction was one fine notion and well accomplished, but this matter with the senator's bargain that Fenger and Kohler had gone into and wanted him to administer, this was an entirely different matter. In the case of the Phantom, no money had changed hands; no one paid him to kill Waldo Denton. It was just a thing needing to be done, no less true than Jack Houston must kill that horse before skinning and dismembering the carcass, as a matter of survival for himself and his family. Chicago was Ransom's only family, his job, all he knew. The Phantom had repeatedly harmed his family, and he'd threatened Ransom's life. The same could be said of the monster or monsters behind the Vanishings, except for the idea of special payment. Had it come in the legitimate way of a bonus, a raise, he would not balk, but this secret, closed-door deal smacked of its own kind of evil and left a stench no less than the yards in his craw. Perhaps if the senator had come to him alone, and they had really secretly worked out a deal, then perhaps he'd be more inclined to take it. However, a conspiracy of this size, involving three other men, all of whom were far more prominent and less expendable than he, simply was not the way Alastair cared to operate.

He could not definitively say why, but a good deal had to do with climbing into bed with the man he most hated in the city—Chief Nathan Kohler. A man who had worked tirelessly to get dirt on Ransom in an effort to discredit him, to see him off the force, and now a man bowing and scraping to a senator. Even in the way Nathan'd handed the senator's hat to him, dusting it off first, spoke volumes. Money motivated people in strange ways. Take the respectable Dr. Christian Fenger, he thought now. How he could climb into such a morass with Kohler was beyond Ransom's comprehension. Fenger was the most ethical and moralistic man Alastair had ever known . . . and now this. It felt like a betrayal, a blow to the chest, despite Christian's excuses of debt and desperation.

Music spilled out onto the street from inside Muldoon's when Alastair opened the door, a minstrel fellow strumming a banjo and singing about an Ohio steamboat called the *Glenn E. Burke* running down to New Orleans—*"When the* Glendie Burke *comes down again . . . bound to leave this town now . . . take my duds and throw 'em on my back . . . when the* Glendie Burke *come down again.* Banjo and harp made the bluesy lyrics as lively as a cockfight, and Ransom caught his toe tapping to the melody.

The music man playing both instruments at once did not slow for Ransom, as new to the city, he'd no idea who Alastair was. Muldoon's this time of night was, for the most part, just another den of losers and down-and-outs, most at the bar, on their feet, smoking and drinking and talking and thinking and planning and plotting—most with minds always in a state of disarray, confusion, and a mix of anger and fear. Anger at the world for having lost the race, fear at the world that it'd become too late to ever score big. The confusion came in the wonderment of how life had so quickly beaten them down. Some were no older than late twenties, early thirties. Yet they held longing, clinging memories for what might have been. To a man they were gamblers of one sort or another.

Those familiar to Muldoon's fell silent when they realized who'd walked in. Alastair represented a diversion from their sore, sordid lives, and to some he represented another hope. After all, hope dies hard, and hope has a place in a dreamer's heart, even a man who simply dreamed of betting for once on the right horse out at the racetrack.

The races proved a second home for most of these men, and each Sunday they went out to the course and laid their money on a horse in much better prime than the one Alastair had seen Jack Houston working over.

Alastair was given to a horse race himself on occasion, but it had not become the driving force in his life. Such a life is what Alastair Ransom feared, an end that left him daily standing before some bar and talking of past adventures to people he didn't like.

He momentarily thought of what Philo, his only true friend, would think of this new turn of events—him being enthroned at Muldoon's, if talk on the street were to be believed.

Due to his reputation and the rumors now abounding, he had indeed become a topic of interest in every bar in the growing prairie city. Stepping in from the light and finding himself striding toward the bar in the semi-darkness of this seedy place, Ransom realized that he was indeed an object of fascination for the regulars. Some had been on hand the night he'd smashed his cane into Muldoon's temple, knocking the owner senseless. How strange the turn of events now.

So when it became clear around the room that Inspector Ransom was indeed in their midst, the buzz went about the room, and all eyes turned on him.

Some few lifted their glasses, a salute to his having rid the city of the Phantom. When Moose Muldoon, busy behind the bar, realized that Ransom had come through the door, he set up a free beer—something Muldoon was not known for, giving beer away, waiving the usual five cents. "Look here, boys!" Muldoon shouted, his voice silencing the banjo man and every conversation remaining. "By God, it's our own Inspector Ransom it is, in Muldoon's, boys! I told you he and I were thick as brothers—hey, Inspector?"

"Muldoon . . . how've you been?" Alastair asked. "You're head clear these days on the drinking laws?"

"Aye, Inspector—Alastair—Rance, old friend. I've a special on for the whiskey-sarsaparillas concoction you like. Calling the drink a Whiskey Ransom. The boys here've taken to it, chasing it with ale and beer."

"So I hear on the street."

"And look there in the corner back booth," said Muldoon, pointing to a cordoned-off table. "Reserved for you alone, Inspector, so's you can conduct your own special business outta Muldoon's whenever you're moved to it."

"That's extremely generous of you, Pat—may I call you, Pat?"

"It's fine. Call me Paddy if you like."

"Then if it's OK with you, Paddy, I'll just take advantage now."

Ransom took his free beer to his special seat, wondering what was in it for Muldoon, sure he would soon learn. No doubt the man wanted a favor. Possibly protection from some heavies moving in on his action, demanding a cut for, what else, protection from other heavies wanting to move in on his action.

Ransom did not have to wait long to learn of Muldoon's purpose. In fact, the banjo player and songster was only halfway through his next song—a riotous tune about his mother's red cabbage and griddle cakes, the refrain being, *"Boil them cabbage down, my friend, boil them cabbage down!"*—and Alastair had only downed half his "free" beer when Muldoon joined him at the table. The two huge figures in the back booth seemed a pair of giants staring across at one another. "What's what, Paddy? Why're you being so lovely toward me?"

"It's not what you're thinking."

"Oh, and what am I thinking?"

"That I want some favor down at City Hall or with the aldermen, or that I want you to run someone off from seeing my sister."

"And you're saying it's none of those things?"

"Not in the least."

Alastair raised his glass in toast. "Then tell me why're we burying the ol' hatchet?"

"It's the business you did with the Phantom, and what I suspect you'll do with this bastard they're calling Leather Apron, the one causing the Vanishings. Awful . . . just awful . . . doing such to our poor innocent children, like so many defenseless chicks."

"Get to the point, Muldoon. I've business elsewhere."

"I only want you to *use* the place, this table, as *your* home away from home, so to speak."

"So to speak of what? Your point, Paddy?"

"Alastair, truly, as I've come to respect you so."

"I see."

"Then you'll accept my hospitality?"

"A free beer whenever I call for it?"

"*Ahhh* . . . one per day."

"One per visit?" dickered Ransom.

"*Ahhh* . . . all right, then."

"And the use of the table for long periods?"

"That's me gift to you for doing so much to keep Chicagoans safe, yes."

"I had a reputation *before* the Phantom's end, so why *now* Muldoon?"

"*Ahhh* . . . it's ever since we had that run-in, you and me. You have no idea how many people come here to see where you was standing when your cane come down across me head, and they want me to retell the story over and over, and then they bring in their friends and associates to hear it over again."

"And you're tired of telling it? Sounds as if business is good."

"Well . . . there attaches *some* embarrassment to the story in the first telling alone."

"I see, but there is more to this than our run-in."

"Like I'm telling you, people come through that door expecting to see you, some wanting to talk to you. I've spoke till I'm blue in the face that your headquarters are at number

13 Des Plaines, but they're normally not the type to go seeking out a policeman in a station house."

"I see." And finally it had come clear for Ransom. "You pay me off in free beer and my favorite table, and I become a sideshow freak for your bloody customers is it?"

"Now, don't get riled, Inspector," countered Muldoon. "It's not a bad bargain for either of us once word gets round that you've returned to your favorite old haunt, and that you and I've become *pals* again."

"Yes, the money motive. What drives Chicago."

"What is your answer. No . . . no, don't tell me now, Inspector. Give it time to sink in. Sleep on it. We'll talk again when you come back for your next one on me."

"And the Whiskey Ransom? Does it stay on the menu either way?"

"It does. Give you me word and me hand on it." Muldoon extended his huge paw.

"You're right. I'll need some time to think this proposition over."

"Any losers at cards, I can send your way, Alastair. There'll be easy pickings every day. You've no idea how many men hereabouts wanna say they played cards and lost to Inspector Ransom."

"Really now . . . you will sweeten the pot too much."

"I take a cut of course on each win."

"I would expect nothing less."

"Nothing less than ten percent."

"Like I said, Paddy, I'll have to give it serious thought."

"It could help you out after you retire from the force, Alastair. Think hard on it. Think of your future, man."

"I can see you now shouting it to the ceiling, Muldoon: Last man standing from the Haymarket Riot, infamous Inspector Alastair Ransom, come one, come all to hear the Phantom Slayer regale you with story 'pon story of his exploits!"

"And why not? I also know a publisher who'd pay handsome for your life story if we could, between us, write."

"Will you be setting me up with a tent over my table here, too?"

"I thought of a banner across the sign outside."

Ransom glared at Muldoon, gulped down the last of his beer, stood and walked out to the music of "Callie Rose" being played by the banjo man. "You're turning this place into a regular den of entertainment, Muldoon."

"I'll hold the table for you, old man!" Muldoon shouted over the banjo.

Standing in the thin gaslight, seeing clouds rolling in from over the lake, slowly turning the sky into a familiar black ash, Ransom could smell rain imminent. It was soon September, and August in Chicago always proved a bumpy ride where the weather was concerned. He glanced back at Muldoon's and asked, "Why're all mine enemies wanting to go into business with me all of a sudden?"

With cane in hand, not expecting an answer, he sauntered down the sidewalk back toward Des Plaines and the station house, at considerable distance, but he felt the need for air and time and exercise of his legs. He often walked the city streets too in order to feel in tune with his surroundings, but lately, at every street corner, he'd come upon another homeless person, male, female, adult, child. Chicago, always filled with scurrying rats, was now a breeding ground it seemed for the homeless. It had been coming on for a long time and nothing whatever had been done about it. The occasional politician shouted over the complacency of the merchants and aldermen and city fathers that something must be done about the problem, but as ever, nothing was done save in the private sector. Jane Addams's Hull House and a few churches offered space to sleep and a soup kitchen, and they worked diligently to find jobs, but there simply were none unless you belonged to a union gang and the Democratic party.

At the moment, Alastair's attention was taken off the homeless, drifting back to the singular idea of going into questionable partnership with Muldoon, making himself a kind of local attraction at the man's tavern. The proposal coming from Muldoon, however absurd, he respected more than that offered up by Senator Chapman, Chief Kohler, and Dr. Fenger. At least with Muldoon there were no surprises; in fact, the man was, as always—transparent. He had but one bone to gnaw on, one purpose in life, to make more money each week than he did the week before. Such motive was easy to gauge, but when a man like Kohler used the same argument, that he was purely interested in the money, Alastair knew better. Somewhere in back of that fevered brain of Nathan Kohler's, he had a plan, a plan to destroy Alastair even as he benefited from the outlawry he proposed. And make no mistake about it, Kohler, Fenger, Chapman, and Ransom would be engaging in illegal activity should they go through with this dark conspiracy to see Leather Apron turned over to the senator for his personal vengeance. It would be no less an act of outlawry as had been Alastair's conspiring with Harry Stratemeyer and his two men to abduct and kill that weasel that had gone about the World's Fair murdering innocent people in the vain hope of ultimately destroying Alastair Ransom.

No doubt remained in Alastair's mind now; Kohler, in some Machiavellian manner, meant to enter into this agreement only to nab Alastair at the precise moment of ultimate vulnerability—and most likely to bring down Dr. Fenger in the bargain as well—in order to install new people around him in both the department and at County Morgue. Why Christian could not see this was beyond Alastair, but the doctor must be made to see. It dawned on Ransom that he must thank Muldoon some time for helping him clarify his feelings and instincts on this matter, but of course neither Muldoon—nor anyone—could know about the Chapman proposal or Christian Fenger's part in it. Alastair wondered how he could counter whatever plot Kohler had in mind with his own and still keep Christian's name out of it.

Life and chaos in Chicago had not changed noticeably since his return.

* * *

"Remember Haymarket, Nathan?" Ransom dropped into the seat the other side of Kohler's desk. "If I am to agree to this deal you've struck with Chapman and Fenger, I want full access to all files on the riot at Haymarket turned over for my examination. Full disclosure."

"That's impossible, Alastair, and you know it."

"Then we have no deal." He stood to go, nothing to lose. At the door, he felt Kohler breathing down his neck and holding the door pinned against him.

"Wait."

"We have nothing further to discuss. I have thought this over thoroughly, and it is all that will calm my mind about either situation."

"Look . . . you are talking about sealed documents, locked away in places *I* have no access to. What in bloody hell do you expect to learn from digging up the dead past?"

"I won't know that until I see it, now will I?"

"Are you sure, Ransom, there is nothing else I . . . we can offer you?"

"Nothing whatever."

"Bastard."

Ransom pulled the door open, readying to leave. "Give it some thought; sleep on it as I did. Perhaps tomorrow, you may see it differently. Have a talk with your newfound friend, the senator. Hell, Prosecutor Kehoe. He is in a position to get his hands on those files."

"Hiram would lose his job as a result, along with all of us."

"Does the corruption go that high up?"

"Damn it, man, leave it in the grave!"

"My scars are not yet in the grave."

"They can be, Alastair," Kohler said with a curled smile. "There's an old proverb goes something like 'the scars of his past will determine his future,' but in your case, they may determine you have no future."

This stopped Ransom, whose stern eyes met Kohler's in a cold duel. "Is that a threat, Nathan?"

"Call it what you will. Chicago remains a dangerous place, and everyone knows you have more enemies than friends."

"Send my request on, Nathan. Send it on, and we'll talk about the future on the other side."

Kohler's tough features scrunched in consternation, attempting to mine the depths of Ransom's words. But Inspector Ransom walked away from his dumbfounded chief and closed the door behind him.

Kohler gnashed his teeth and muttered to his empty office, "Stubborn bastard's like a g'damn Jack Bull with his teeth sunk deep."

CHAPTER 10

Alastair found himself at his old wooden swivel desk chair and dropped into it with a heaviness that raised a resounding squeal. He sat for a moment, feeling extremely tired and as if every year of his life weighed heavy. He sat staring at the empty desk pushed against his own, Griffin's desk. While others in the department pretended busy work, he sensed them watching him now. No one could miss the subdued anger spilling out of Chief Kohler's office when Alastair had come down those steps.

Feeling like a bug here, Alastair located a pot of coffee kept on brew for Chicago's finest on skeleton crew. The grand World's Fair had siphoned off many a cop. Faithfuls were being asked to work double shifts, and why else hire on the first woman civilian in the department—Gabrielle Tewes?

Alastair was not about to give up his search for the truth surrounding what really happened that day at Haymarket, not for any avowed reason. The issue remained burning in his gut and in his heart; he couldn't let got so easily as others. He had lost six fellow officers and friends that day to a bomb no one had taken credit for. Historians already called it a defining moment in Illinois and U.S. labor-relations history, but it was also a defining moment in exactly who Alastair Ransom was. Perhaps he was chasing ghosts, phantom information that did not exist, but by the same token, he could not let any chance to get at the records on the subject go by. Too many good men had died for this, one having pulled Ransom to safety before keeling over with a severed femoral artery.

The riot was a benchmark for the establishment of new laws governing the conduct of police officials, a turning point in public opinion regarding unionist workers and unions, plus it forged the first labor laws with teeth. As a result, Illinois led the rest of the nation in this politically charged arena. The cost in human life was too great to ignore and a statue in a hidden cove outside a small police district was not enough for Ransom.

When he'd returned to his desk, coffee in hand, Ransom began cleaning away flyers and papers and files, only to discover an anonymous note printed in large letters, reading,

REMEMBER HAYMARKET

He took in the room. It could have been the sergeant who looked up at him, or Logan, or Behan, or any number of others. In a sense, Ransom's crusade to keep the memory of that day alive and fresh in every foot soldier's mind was perhaps sinking in with some of the lads. Still the prevailing winds kept saying, let the dead bury the dead.

Just then, coming through a doorway that led into the archives of dead cases and documents, came Gabrielle Tewes, Jane's daughter, her eyes wide, coming straight for Alastair. "I'm so glad I found you on duty and what a shock!"

"That I'm on duty?"

"Well, no . . . I'm referring to what I've uncovered."

"Which is?"

"A series of similar Vanishings in London, not five years ago."

"Really? Let me have a look."

Gabby spread the materials out for his perusal. She'd marked specific items from various police gazettes and reports.

"I had no idea you'd planned to continue working here."

"And why not?"

"I guess it was an assumption you would rush back to Northwestern and continue your studies in medicine there."

"A safe cozy plan indeed, one Mother wants for me. But, no. I love working with Dr. Fenger at Rush on my medical studies and on cases with Dr. Fenger. He put me to researching this one."

"You should share this with your mother."

"I may . . . when she settles into the notion that I am my own person and not a copy of her."

"I see." He really did not wish to get between mother and daughter on the issue, although it had been Alastair who had first encouraged her to pursue working with Christian Fenger in police medicine.

"Look, I have a meeting to get to," she informed him. "I'll leave this with you so you can get on the trail of this monster."

"A meeting?"

"Yes, a meeting."

"The drum-and-fife corps of ladies?"

"We are suffrage advocates and only want simple justice."

"You'll become a fine spokesperson for the cause."

"Well, I am terrible at marching, so perhaps I will brave the podium someday. For now, I am content to stand with my sisters in this noble cause."

"I wish you all the best."

"Persistence is the key according to our leaders. Do you know we are petitioning the president as we speak? Thousands and thousands have signed."

"Good luck, Gabby, but do be careful."

"I have a key to a police phone box now, and should I need you, I can call."

"Do not hesitate."

She left with a bounce in her step. He smiled after her, a strange concern coming over him. A fleeting emotion of fear should anything befall Gabby.

Logan leaned forward in his chair and said, "You act the part of father quite well, old chap."

"What're you fellows doing here so late?"

Behan laughed and Alastair shrugged it off, his attention going to the reports that Gabby had unearthed. Slowly Behan, followed by Logan, moved in and stood over each of Inspector Ransom's hefty shoulders.

The report he read in the London *Police Gazette* dated 1889 put forth yet another theory of the exact identity of Jack the Ripper, an American actor named Richard Mansfield, who'd terrified playgoers as Mr. Hyde, changing from Jekyll without makeup or leaving stage. The man sent ladies into a swoon and men running from the theater. But the story so riveting for these three Chicago cops was a tale of the Vanishings. It read in part:

> As near as this detective has ascertained, the Vanishings began in 1881 and continued until this past year of 1891, when they abruptly ended. The case represents for me, personally, the strangest case of my career, and the most frustrating and heart-rending, as I was called into each inquest to view the most horrid sights of my career—the remains of the victims, each barely of age. They began in Ham, and records are scarce, but I have pieced together a clear trail that leads from East and West Ham to London's East Side.

"Eerie, isn't it?" asked Behan over Alastair's right shoulder.

"Damned spooky, if you ask me," agreed Logan at his left.

Both men were smaller than Alastair. Compactly built like a prize fighter was Ken Behan, whereas the other was rail-thin and gaunt, his eyes sunken, yet Jedidiah Logan had hands as large as griddles. Pale as December snow, Logan looked as if death might claim him at any time. He smoked without end the strongest cigars made. Others joked that one day at the morgue, when Logan dozed against a wall, Dr. Fenger took him for an upright corpse and began shouting orders at his men about maltreatment of the dead.

The three inspectors next skimmed an account of an eleven-year-old girl who went missing after going out to plow a row in a field for her mother. Her name was Eliza Carter, and she simply vanished out of that field. Her yellow dress was found days later on the East Ham football field. No one ever saw her again. The Chicago detectives read on from the account of the London investigator. The next paragraph read:

> Charles Wagner, son of a West Ham butcher, vanished next, only a few weeks after the Carter girl. His body had been got at by animals, found seventy-five miles away at the bottom of a ravine at Ramsgate. The animals had got at him bad, tearing away all his face and much of his body. Oddly, neither the fall nor the drowning had caused death, according to the medical men. There was not one murderous abrasion or puncture mark that alone killed the boy but thirty-seven by count of the medical men.

Ransom stopped reading and said, "The work of multiple knifings? And as for cause of death . . . Fenger's determined our man uses a cleaver and a number of blades, and it's theorized there could be more than one madman doing the deed."

"Really? More than one doing the stabbing?" asked Logan.

"And carving, perhaps. And cannibalizing, perhaps."

Behan shivered at the idea.

Logan asked, "Rance, do you suspect one of these lunatic religious cults we've been seeing more and more of?"

"Maybe one begun in London, but moved to Chicago?" asked Behan.

"We've kicked over the thought, yes, of a cult sacrifice, but a London transport? No."

"Do you for a moment think our killer . . . or, *ahhh*, killers . . ." began Behan, "that he could be one and the same as in England?"

"Long way to come to harvest children," said Ransom, "especially when London's got plenty of her own."

"But then why not, Rance?" countered Logan. "Everyone else is coming to Chicago."

"Creepy is what it is," muttered Behan.

Ransom read on:

Next it was three girls in a row disappeared from West Ham all in January 1890. Only one of these dears was ever found, Amelia Jeffs, in West Ham Park. It's surmised that Amelia made a getaway as there were signs of a struggle, and she had been bruised over the right eye and stabbed through stomach and ribs multiple times.

In every case of the missing where there was anything in the way of eyewitness reports, all the girls involved had been seen talking to and in some cases walking off with a woman. A cautious coroner whispered in me ear that we are fools to think that women are less susceptible to the lowest forms of mania and sexual perversions.

What with the Ripper murders on London's East side in 1888 and '89, when new Vanishings began here in the city, they were overshadowed by the mutilations left behind by that fiend Jack. Six prostitutes in all that we know of. Meantime, dozens upon dozens of children going missing, and no one in authority or the press caring as they were focused on when the next Ripper letter might appear. The disappearances ended on the cusp of 1890 becoming '91. These Vanishings I speak of, and for ten years chased, to my disgrace, have never been solved.

Sincerely,
Inspector Kenan Heise, London, April 14, 1891

"So what do you make of it, lads?" asked Ransom of the other two inspectors.

"Are you asking our opinion of these circumstances?" asked Logan, hands gesturing with a wide swath. "Your eminence?"

"Cut out the foolishness."

Behan too was doing a bit of a pirouette before him, ending with a bow. "After all, it was our case before we became your dotes and gophers."

"Which am I," asked Logan, "dote or gopher?"

"Both!" announced Ransom. "Lads, we're working on equal footing here. We're a team."

"Like you and the kid?" asked Logan, indicating the empty desk across.

"That was different."

"Really?"

"How so?"

"He was young, green, and—" He stopped short of telling

them that Griffin Drimmer had been put on him by Kohler, not wishing to despoil Griff's memory.

"And . . . ?"

"And you fellows are old farts like myself, well versed in the ways of the detective," finished Ransom. "I suspect our combined years on the force *may* do better than this fellow Heise working alone in London."

"Do you think there is a link between his killer and ours?" asked Behan.

"Dunno. Interesting bit on perverted female suspects, heh?"

"Do you think there's a woman involved?" asked Logan.

"Dunno, but it's often true; you hear it in every lament and song—a woman made me do it."

"You think?"

"It's what we get paid for, to think."

Logan pulled at his beard. "Imagine if it's so . . . that the Vanishings is done by a woman."

"Women are more readily accepted by children, less threatening," Ransom suggested.

"Imagine it," repeated Logan.

"A lotta shell games are begun by a pretty woman," said Behan.

Logan laughed. "You well know it, too, don'tcha, lover?"

Alastair laughed at this. "We shouldn't discard the notion out of hand, Logan."

"True enough, we've all seen tough bitches in our time, but a cannibalizing woman? What're you thinking, Alastair?

"The Phantom went invisible because we didn't see him, and who is more invisible in our society than—"

"Than a woman!" It was Dr. James Phineas Tewes standing over his desk now, looking straight in his eye.

"And how, Dr. Tewes, did you arrive at this conclusion?"

"I interviewed a child who was nearly snatched by a woman."

"What child? What woman?"

"A rag-and-bottle lady who makes her rounds pretty regularly in the child's neighborhood."

He took Jane aside. "How did you come by this information in the first place?"

"I intercepted your man."

"What man?"

"Bosch."

"Bosch? He spilled information to you meant for me?"

"Says I pay better."

"The little weasel."

"He's rather cute when you get to know him."

"All right, tell me what he said."

"I can do better than that."

"How so?"

"I have the child at my home. Gabby is with her now."

"Why didn't you bring her with you?"

"To this place? It'd only terrify her, and she's plenty terrified enough as is."

"I see . . . but she has no fear of Dr. Tewes?"

"None whatever; I am, after all, a gentle soul and children—"

"Know a gentle soul, yes."

Ransom found his cane and pressed on his bowler hat, checked his pocket watch, and joined Tewes at the door, telling the other detectives, "I'm off lads to interview this child that Dr. Tewes feels may have some useful information."

"Meantime, what would you like us to do, boss?" asked Behan.

"I may've been put on as lead investigator, Ken, but I'm no one's boss. Let's be clear on that."

"But Ken's question still remains, boss," countered Logan. "Whataya expectin' us to do meanwhile?"

He thought to say, *Carry on as you were before I was thrust in on your case.* But he saw that this was not going to do. "Go down to the yards tomorrow and speak with a fellow named Jack Houston, and—"

"A butcher?"

"A knacker to be specific."

"A g'damn horse cutter?" Behan erupted.

"You know my constitution doesn't permit such odors," said Logan.

"Meanwhile," Alastair emphasized the word *meanwhile,* "you're to interview three others at the yards."

"Four? Conduct four interviews at the yards?" Behan sounded stupefied.

Alastair flipped open his notes and rattled off the names. "Hatch . . . Quinn . . . and Sharkey. Houston can point you to Hatch, then on and on."

"Butchers? Our killer's not likely a butcher, Ransom, and you know it."

"Still . . . we have to cover the bases, boys."

"Cover the what?" asked Behan.

Logan explained, "It's an expression, comes out of cricket, and now that new game people are betting on, base on balls."

"Gotta look at the usual suspects and any leads," Alastair added.

"What lead?"

"Houston says that these other three are queer fellows, even for butchers."

"And you believe him?"

"Houston'll tell you all about it when you get out to the knacker stalls."

Logan gave a last verbal balk. "Look here, we're interviewing people who live in the areas where the children've disappeared."

"Continue that as well. Don't let me stop you." As Alastair was about to turn and exit with Tewes, he and Jane noticed Nathan Kohler atop the stairwell, staring down at them, his features unreadable. Ransom gave him a little wave of the hand and said, "Night, Chief."

On arriving at the Tewes home on Belmont, Jane quickly explained to Ransom, "I've a temporary house guest, now being kept occupied by Gabby, "Someone you must meet. It could be crucial to our case," she was going on in that practiced whining male voice of Tewes's that always got on Alastair's last nerve. Jane also pointed toward Gabby's room where the door stood partially open. "She's in there with her now, giving her things. Old clothes, old dolls, whatever the child wants."

"You say she's a homeless child?"

"'Fraid so, yes. Her name's Audra. Sweetest face you ever saw." Alastair caught snatches of giggling and words between Gabrielle and her guest.

"She won't talk at all to Dr. Tewes. For some reason, this personae frightens her. I suspect men have used her badly."

"If she fears men and in particular you as a man, she will likely be terrified of me," Alastair reasoned.

"Not necessarily. Her father was a large man like yourself, who unfortunately died of yellow fever while nursing her mother through it. Both died, leaving her an orphan six years ago, according to records I dug up at Cook."

"She's been on the street since then?"

"Not entirely. In and out of foster homes until she went into hiding."

"Into hiding?"

"OK . . . into a gang, I gather. She now considers this street gang family."

Alastair frowned at this as she closed her bedroom door to go change and remove makeup and mustache, ascot and wig. She was a consummate actress as well as a phrenologist and surgeon. He got only a peek at her large makeup lights and mirror.

He heard the soft laughter of Audra and Gabby as he made his way back toward the front of the house. Unsure what to do with himself until she'd return and introduce him to the would-be witness to Leather Apron, or whoever might be behind the Vanishings, Alastair wandered into the parlor, the room where he had been accidentally shot by Gabby. He stood gazing at the room as if in a dream, the memory of that thunder-and-lightning night coming in flashes. What he recalled most was lying over the top of Waldo Denton—the man he believed the garroter—and bleeding over him where he was pinned below Ransom's 260 pounds.

He looked down at his girth and wondered just how much he weighed these days. He feared what a scale might say about it.

"I am ready to proceed," said Jane from behind him. "Are you prepared to meet Audra?"

"Where best to conduct the interview?"

"Anywhere but here. What about the kitchen. We've nothing but good memories there."

She led the way, adding, "I've prepared the child to meet you. Have shown her photographs. It's how I first learned of her father and mother, and besides, she knows of you . . . says she has seen you on the street, knows you as The Bear, she says."

"You have photographs of me?"

"From newspaper accounts, yes, and one I purchased from Mr. Keane."

"Hold on! Are you saying Philo charged you for a photo of me, and you were foolish enough to pay?"

"Well, it was a rather memorable photo. I am in it as well," she replied, smiling. "Imagine a photo of us together."

"At the fair? On the Ferris wheel? When?"

"At the train station when you snatched that boy's head off his garroted neck and pushed it into my hands."

"Tewes's hands, you mean."

"Yes, if you wish to get technical. It's how we met, all the same, isn't it."

"Blasted Philo."

She called for Gabby to bring Audra into the kitchen to meet Inspector Ransom. In a moment, the college-aged Gabby, maternally guiding and hovering about the little girl, stood smiling before them. Although scruffy-haired, Audra's eyes were constantly working, suspicious. Gabby had bathed the girl and had dressed her in hand-me-downs.

Audra held firm to her newly acquired doll in one hand and Gabby with the other. Gabby introduced her to Alastair, ending with, "And you know my Aunt Jane."

Alastair smiled his warmest, wanting to get on the child's good side.

"Are you a Zoroaster?" asked the small girl.

"A what?"

"I forgot to tell you, Alastair, she asks everyone if they are a Zoroaster, a devil."

"Hmmmf," he let out a sound. "Do I look like a devil?"

"*Ahhh* . . . yeah, you do," came the small reply half swallowed in Audra's throat. Jane had not exaggerated; she was a cute little blond thing indeed.

"Zoroaster is a deity, Alastair, one that Audra believes is running loose and unchecked here in Chicago, at work and behind the Vanishings—telling other individuals, according to Audra, to bring him sacrifices. She also says some strange old sick-in-the-head bird named Bloody Mary procures for Zoroaster."

"Oh, great . . . our killer is a deity, a supernatural being who talks to that old crone, Bloody Mary."

"You know her?" Jane's look was incredulity at its zenith.

"Not a cop in Chicago doesn't know Bloody Mary or has arrested her at one time or another. Frankly, Jane, this doesn't *feel* like a useful lead. More like a frightened girl's tale."

"Then you know where to find this so-called Bloody Mary, but you're not going to look into this allegation that she is somehow connected to the Vanishings?" asked Jane.

"Why not at least pick her up for questioning!" said an excited Gabby.

Alastair took Jane into the hallway and whispered, "Look, the old bat is out of her head. A complete loon. From day to day, she doesn't even know who she is, but I've known her for years. Can find her almost any night in the drunk tank."

"Perhaps she has graduated to more serious crime than public intoxication."

"No . . . no . . . you amateur detectives . . ."

"What's that supposed to mean?"

"It means, I think this is a dead end."

"No! Don't shut down on this just yet. Hear the girl out."

"Bloody Mary's a vagrant, a regular at the station house."

"And like the Phantom has remained invisible until you opened your eyes to him and proved him a fiend."

"Bloody Mary is hardly invisible. She's a public nuisance and a beggar."

"But she sounds like she has the habits of a weasel."

"More like a rat and smells it. Lice ridden . . . nobody wants to go near her."

"Just hear the girl out, Alastair."

"OK . . . OK . . ."

They returned to join Gabby and Audra. Gabby was in midsentence, "And besides, I did some research and Zoroaster is not *all* bad; in fact, he's a she and she's a he, Mother. Ironic, huh?"

"Whatever do you mean?" asked Jane, blinking.

"Zoroaster is both good and evil. I showed Audra where it says so in my book on mythology, and she's accepting us as all from the *good* Zoroaster."

"Sounds promising," replied Alastair. "Now listen, little girl," he said, "I have arrested this Bloody Mary on occasion, so don't go suspecting she's anything but human, and if she is in any way involved in carving up little kids, she will pay dearly once I have her in my jail again." He displayed his enormous handcuffs. "So stop your worrying. Just tell me what you've seen."

She looked, big-eyed, all about the room, from face to face, still reluctant to speak. Gabby tried to dispel the tension with a joke. "If you at any time feel it necessary, you can always shoot Inspector Ransom."

Jane and Ransom both glared at Gabrielle, who instantly gasped, realizing what she'd said was not at all funny as she'd intended. "I didn't really mean . . . I mean . . . no Audra, there's no shooting the inspector."

Ransom pulled forth a photo of Anne Chapman in her yellow print dress. "Look, child, did you ever see Anne Chapman—this girl"—he put the photo in her hand—"with Bloody Mary?"

"*Ahhh* . . . no, I didn't but—"

Already skeptical of learning anything from the child, Alastair placed another photo and another and another before her. All the remaining victims, some still missing. "Have you ever seen Bloody Mary kicking about with *any* of these children?"

"They aren't street kids like me. They all had homes."

"I am aware of that, but did you or didn't you see them with Bloody Mary?"

Like a little one-man judge and jury, Audra looked from the photos and up at Alastair, sizing him up, reevaluating him. "I think I ought to take you to my king," she blurted out.

"Your king?"

"Yes, Robin. He'll tell you; they'll all tell you who the killer is, that it's Bloody Mary and no one else."

"The same old beggar lady who sells stolen stuff from windowsills and clotheslines?" asked Ransom.

"That's her, all right. But her real job is butchering children like me."

"And you say you can back this up with others like this Robin fellow's testimony?"

"The whole lot of us know it's her. She's been after us for months."

"Well, then, Audra, dear," came Jane's soothing voice, "why don't you take us to your king and his court?"

"They'll beat me if they don't go for it, they will . . . but I told King Robin that we gotta trust somebody, and when Miss Jane was so kind to me . . . I began to tell. Trouble is . . . if you tell *everything,* the demons—the bad Zoroaster's people—they'll kill you for it."

"She told me the demons don't want adults to know they're here," Gabby added.

Audra clutched her doll tighter. "Zoroasters're afraid of adults."

"Why?" asked Jane.

"Be-because until adults see them, they stay, like, invisible."

Alastair sat on the edge of his chair at this last remark, so prophetic. It was almost word for word what he had said of Leather Apron and the Phantom. So long as they went unseen even in plain sight, they remained powerful and capable of what seemed damn near supernatural.

"Tomorrow, will you take me to this king of yours, Audra?" said Alastair.

Secretly, Alastair believed it a wild goose chase, and he expected this would be a monumental waste of time, but it would score points with Jane and with Gabby, he supposed. At the very least, he hoped to make more recruits of the homeless children, convert them into that many more eyes and ears for the police. But they'd have to give him a great deal more than the tattered old, addle-brained, lice-infested Bloody Mary to interest him.

CHAPTER 11

The following day

Below the train viaduct at Ravenswood and Og-den, the Southside of Chicago, as far from the gaiety of the White City as one could be, a ragtag king and court looked Gabby, Jane, and Alastair up and down, some making jokes, some making threats, one lifting Gabby's skirt with a crooked cane his scepter—and all of them painted with the dirt of Chicago back alleys. The tall, gaunt one with the wooden-crutch scepter was Robin the King, their avowed and respected leader. King Robin of Nightmare Alley, it would seem.

Robin glared at Audra while he spoke to the strangers in their midst, coolly saying, "What business 'ave you here, you pretty people?" He let Gabby's skirt fall into place, sat on a rickety orange crate, and raised his scepter overhead.

One shorter and dirtier boy, calling himself Noel, seemed fearless. "See that green sign over there?"

"Yes," replied Jane, following the pointed finger. "It's a little hard to miss."

"Angels love the color green, 'specially dark-as-grass green."

"And why do you suppose?" she asked Noel.

"It's the best color."

"Shut up, all of you!" ordered Robin, oldest in the family.

"No, blue is," countered a smaller girl. "Blue's the color of the Lady of the Lake."

Another said, "After night falls on the city is when the angels come out and argue the prettiest color."

"A-a-angels come out?" asked Gabby.

"En masse."

"To—to make war on the red armies, not to fuss over colors," said another girl.

"Red armies?" Alastair's tone reeked of skepticism.

"Armies of the devil Zoroaster," explained Noel.

King Robin tempered the others like a storyteller whose audience has gotten away from him. "But sometimes the angels just come out to play."

A half-Spanish boy named Hector parted the younger children. "Angels look down from the tallest building in the city," he began, adding, "always with green, pink, or a golden glow, and sometimes all three colors at the same time."

"They eat light so they can fly," eight-year-old Marty piped in.

"The angels use the Ward's building's lookout tower for their headquarters?" Ransom frowned at the notion.

Noel said it was so, as if discussing the price of eggs or the weather.

"You see, there's a whole great lotta killing going on in Chicago . . . just like New York, Boston, Philadelphia, you name it," added Hector. "Lotta kids getting killed all over."

Eleven-year-old Audra solemnly added, "The angels study their battle maps all day long in the tower before they dare go out and kill demons. Hector ought've told you that first."

"I see." Alastair had never heard of this strange mythology; apparently every street kid in his town knew it—chapter and verse.

Robin now said, "You want to fight, want to learn how to live, you got to learn the secret stories. Else, you don't stand a chance."

Hector added, "Yeah, then's when you disappear."

"Gotta be on your toes at all times," Noel said in a raspy whisper.

"You mean . . . or else you disappear like these kids the cops are finding dead?" Alastair asked.

"Sure . . . how else do you explain such things?" asked Robin.

A kid named Mickey added, "It's the Judge of Hell and his minions against the angels. Simple as that."

An older boy who had remained silent, sullen, wary suddenly piped up with, "Christmas night the year eighteen ninety-one, God ran away from Heaven."

"God ran away?" Gabby asked, realizing the significance of this to the runaways. Their god was a runaway, too.

"Yeah, to escape a huge demon attack," replied Noel. "Tell 'em Hector, Peter. Pete knows the whole story. He taught all'n us."

Peter was the sullen one whose eyes had never left the adult strangers. He quietly muttered, "It's a war . . . and the prize is Heaven."

"A celestial war," gasped Jane.

Peter continued. "Yeah, and it's filled me with caution . . . caution of everyone—including you people."

An excited Audra blurted out, "The demons smashed God's palace of beautiful blue-moon marble to dust and ashes."

"Audra! You're gonna shut up now!" ordered Robin.

"What're you afraid of, Robin?" asked Jane. "We're here to help you, not harm you."

He snorted in response. "Your damned newspapers, the *Herald,* the *Tribune,* they don't print a word of what really matters."

"You're right about that," said Alastair, thinking how little play the problem of the homeless got in the press.

"Th-they all keep it secret," added Noel. "Tell 'em, Robin. Tell 'em!"

"Shut up, Noel!" ordered Peter, who seemed Robin's second-in-command.

Robin stepped ever closer to Gabby, ending so close in fact that she became uncomfortable from his odors and body heat. "No one knows why God's left us and his own angels to defend this world, but it's what we gotta do."

The others cheered this.

Jane Francis, as a woman, a mother, and a doctor felt stunned at these revelations, that children so young were coping not only with the streets but with a war between Heaven and Hell, and they found themselves square on the battlefield—their little souls being tugged in both directions.

Alastair's thoughts proved similar. These homeless kids not only faced the horrors of the real world, but for some bizarre reason, they had created a mythological world of gods and demons at war over their heads, angels perched atop the Montgomery Ward Tower, riding the Ferris wheel at the fair, lighting on telegraph wires, riding atop trolleys. All this while demons emerged out of holes, sewers, broken windows, and mirrors.

"What do you make of all this?" Alastair whispered in Jane's ear.

She whispered back, "I suspect it is how they cope."

"With reality, you mean?"

"It allows them to understand the daily terror. If one of them disappears, he's accepted comfort and aid from the enemy. In this case, Satan."

Overhearing, Robin declared, "Temptations are everywhere, and so are the portals to Hell." Using his scepter, he pointed to an abandoned train car, its doors standing open like a giant maw. "The devils sometime offer us safety, a warm place to sleep, a scrap of food, and sometimes the angels don't have nothing to counter it with."

"We're not with Zoroaster," said Jane, "I assure you."

"Demons oft take a pleasant form." Robin glared at Jane.

"And they've taken control of the sewers and Ghost Town," blurted Noel.

"Ghost Town?" asked Gabby, who'd been absorbed, intent on every word.

"Street lingo for County Cemetery," explained Ransom.

Something in his tone caused a scowl in Robin. The others instantly felt his displeasure, and when he turned his back on Ransom, Jane, and Gabby, stepping off, scepter in hand, the others sheepishly followed after King Robin.

"Demons feed on darkness and ignorance," said Jane like an epitaph.

Gabby added, "Jealousy, conceit, hatred fear, prejudice, bigotry."

"Or any negative anything . . ." added Alastair as all three watched the children go.

"Like when you can't stand yourself," Jane said.

He looked at her realizing how much alike the two of them really were. "Or your own kind . . ."

"But you can't get away from who you are, now can you?" she asked.

Gabby suddenly rushed a few steps toward the retreating children. "Wait! You can change things!" This while the children continued disappearing before their eyes. She took a few more tentative steps toward them, seeing Audra lingering behind. "You can build on things, travel, learn, get an education!"

No one stopped to listen, and Gabby watched as Audra dropped the doll she'd given her. Audra didn't look back. The doll might be a trap, so she instead raced to catch up to King Robin and the tribe.

Jane went to Gabby, crouched and lifted the soiled doll, and handed it to her daughter. "Audra may be back for this some day."

"You think so, Mother?"

"There's always that hope."

Mother and daughter hugged, and Alastair saw Audra,

just before the tribe disappeared around a final corner, look back to see the embrace.

Slowly, reluctantly, Alastair, Jane, and Gabby picked their way over broken glass, discarded paint buckets, soiled bedding, cardboard boxes, boards, and brick to finally set foot on a clean street and out from under the viaduct.

Alastair grumbled, "They didn't say a bloody word about Bloody Mary."

"They're afraid to say her name out loud," replied Gabby.

"Then what makes Audra so brave?"

"Her father was a soldier in the war."

"An angel in the war between good and evil, you mean?" asked Ransom, trying to quash a grimace.

"No, the War Between the States."

Audra surprised them all when she showed up the following day and knocked at Jane's and Gabby's door. Ransom was having breakfast with Jane when the girl was ushered in by a smiling, elated Gabby. "I knew she'd come back to us!"

"We can meet with Danielle's coven," Audra informed them.

"Really?" asked Alastair.

"Danielle's coven?" Jane inquired.

"They stay close to the Salvation Army's emergency shelter. Can we have another carriage ride there?"

"First a bite to eat," suggested Gabby, seating Audra before a plate of warm pastries."

While Audra devoured her roll and juice, Gabby rushed out and returned with her doll. Audra and Gabby hugged at the three-way reunion, the doll squished between the young people. It made Jane laugh and Alastair smiled his approval.

They were soon on their way to meet Danielle's coven.

There came a point where the cab could go no farther, and they must walk through a gangway, so-called for the habit of gangs slipping from sight, usually after a robbery.

Audra led the way. Ransom gestured to the cabbie to hold for their return. To assure the man's allegiance, Ransom waved an extra large bill in the air.

Jane whispered, "Do you believe this? How these children live under such pressures. Amazingly, profoundly sad."

"Perhaps so, but how is it relevant to my case?"

"Our case," she corrected him.

A part of him wanted to burst her idyllic bubble about Dr. Fenger, tell her of the deal he and Kohler had cut with Senator Chapman, but he held off. Again he asked, "What's it to do with *our* case, then?"

"I'm not sure, but I have a feeling it is . . . somehow relevant."

They soon found Danielle's camp—its epicenter an abandoned old livery stable near a burned-down warehouse shell. A nearby drainpipe large enough to drive a horse dray through—part of a reservoir system—ran alongside this area.

Danielle looked like a youthful man instead of a woman, a sad weariness to her features, but she could not be much older than King Robin. She too held a large stick, cleaned of its bark and varnished, as a scepter, and she too barked at people in the language of muleskinners.

Once she decided that Alastair, Jane, and Gabby could be trusted, because she trusted Audra, she opened up. Her first words were, "I gotta disagree with King Robin and his followers. This war shouldn't be treated like some kinda secret holy society that keeps others out. I want converts!"

Alastair liked this girl's attitude. She meant to spread the word of the war between Heaven and Hell going on now in the Prairie City and across America.

As a result, Danielle quickly warmed to her topic.

"One demon working for Satan is the worst, and children

know her by her English name here, but she also has a Spanish name"

"Bloody Mary," said Audra.

Danielle whispered, "La Llorona."

"The Crying Woman," said Alastair, knowing a little Spanish.

This impressed the homeless children gathered about Danielle, several of whom were Spanish. Alastair raised his shoulders as if to say "what," when Jane and Gabby stared at him, sharing a look of surprise.

"The woman weeps blood," one child added.

"Blood," echoed another, "and sometimes black oil tears."

"From ghoulish empty sockets."

"And she feeds on a child's terror," added Danielle. "It's why you can't be scared, and why you can't be a child."

Why you can't be a child, the adults rolled over the comment in their minds, thinking how sad the words, when a sudden chorus of the homeless children began talking over one another.

Danielle silenced them all with her upraised scepter, a thin stick. "When a child is killed accidentally or murdered outright, La Llorona sings out in delight and joy."

"And if a child goes missing?" asked Ransom.

"She is feeding on him . . . or her."

"Ffff-feeding on a child?" asked Gabby.

"If you wake up at night and see La Llorona, and you hear her song," began Danielle, "you have to go with her, cause . . . just because . . ."

"—cause it's like being hypnotized," added a young black girl.

"You're chosen, you gotta go," Danielle grimly said.

A stunted boy with a withered arm said, "Bloody Mary's clothes'll be blowing back, even in a room where there's no wind."

"If you see her, you know she's marked you for death," explained Danielle.

"But you're not afraid to say her name," said Alastair. "I

thought if you said her name aloud, you brought her anger down on you? No?"

"Robin's a good leader, but he's wrong about this," she explained. "You show the demons any sign of fear . . . they even smell it, you're dead. That's how it really goes."

"What about the angel lady I heard about?" asked Alastair. "The Blue Lady of the Lake, is it? Tell me something about her."

All the children began jabbering at once, talking over one another, anxious to tell all they knew of this lady, one shouting, "She's like my mum was!"

"She's kinda like my mum," repeated one boy with a thick British accent. "Has aliases."

"But the Blue Lady's secret name?" Jane wanted to understand their thinking. "Nobody knows it? So her power is limited? Can you tell me any of the Blue Lady's aliases?"

"One is Alia," Audra blurted out, emboldened in her new role as emissary between Danielle and the strangers.

"Another is Elisyan," said one of the older boys.

Danielle added, "That's all we know."

Their secrets keep them safe, Alastair thought, *and they keep their secrets safe . . . almost. So much symbolism.*

Alastair began questioning Danielle about her life. Her parents had emigrated from France and had kicked around New York for years and had relocated to Chicago on the hope of finding work as tailors. Instead, her father abandoned them. Her mother now worked in a sweatshop in the garment district, and Danielle pretty much lived on the streets, "Hating the hole mum pays rent on," she finished.

Alastair elicited additional information from Queen Danielle. Her mother had gone through three attempts to get clear of an addiction to heroin, and was trying to get her life back in order. Danielle was French on her mother's side, Spanish on her father's side, which accounted for her jet black hair and exotic features.

Gabby asked, "So what is the Blue Lady's most secret name?"

The children erupted with answers again all at once: "That's for you to find out."

"It's useless if someone just tells you what it is."

"Even if they did know it."

"You gotta find out all on your own."

"Anyone says it out loud is turned into an angel for the war."

They began addressing one another now. They shared many beliefs with Robin's band.

Gabby cautiously asked, "Then if, say, for instance, that you and your friends are on a street corner when a carriage comes racing down on you and only one of you knows her secret true name and yells out this name, then only the one will live?"

"No ma'am," said Audra.

"You don't get it," said Danielle. "You see her and she whispers her real heavenly name, then you gotta go with her."

The tallest boy in the group added, "You're dead, yeah, but you got eternal life as one of hers and that's Heaven, see?"

"And it makes you superhuman," said another.

"So you can fight the Devil."

"Got it," said Gabby, fighting back a frown.

"It's a spell that takes your soul up," Audra further explained, "and it's very loving. She says: 'Hold on' a lot, meaning, things're going to get better for us."

A freight train rushing toward the center of commerce suddenly came up, its roar deafening, so close were they to the tracks. It shook the earth around them.

A blond six-year-old with a bruise above his eye, swollen huge as a ruby egg and laced with black stitches, nodded vigorously at this. "I've seen her. The Blue Lady," he murmured.

A rustle of whispered "me too"s rippled through the small circle of initiates.

Alastair thought, *They instinctively know to curry favor with Danielle; that to remain under her considerable protection, they need only agree with everything she says.* "And where is Leather Apron in all this? Is he Zoroaster?"

Danielle's features turned suddenly stony, and she glared at Audra as if she'd like to strangle the younger girl. "Damn you, Audra! How much of your guts did you spill to these outsiders?"

"We just want to understand," pleaded Jane, "to see the connections, the patterns. How the killer is related to Bloody Mary, for instance?"

"They are interconnected by mutual hatred and war," Danielle finally explained.

"What is Leather Apron to La Llorona?" pressed Jane. "We want to understand."

Again the initiates erupted with answers, ignoring Danielle's undisguised disdain for the way things had gone, as the younger children exploded with responses.

"They're lovers."

"Dirty lovers, though!"

"Evil . . . just evil."

"Evil, twisted lovers."

"Addicted to a hatred of children."

"They eat flesh when they make love."

"They make love when they eat kids."

Alastair lifted his blue gun from its shoulder holster. "This proves I am on the side of the Blue Lady," he announced.

All the children went wide-eyed at the blue burnished steel .38 Police Special. None had ever seen a blue gun before, despite the fact anyone with the money could purchase one from a Sears Roebuck or Montgomery Ward catalog.

The gun impressed even Danielle, who suggested it'd make a fine gift for her information, "As an offering, so to speak."

When Alastair flatly refused, saying, "It's out of the question," Danielle flew into a rage. "You wanna know about patterns, do you? It's hatred fed by the flesh and bone of children, and you high-and-mighty types comin' down slummin' among us act as if you're seeing things for the first time, but it's only because it's a senator's daughter now! Ain't it the truth?"

Alastair was unsure what they might do with the confusing information they'd collected or how to ferret out truth from fiction, fabrication from whole cloth. Elements of the stories rang as true as sun and moon and stars, while other elements rang a wholly different bell—one alien to them all. Ransom summed it up in a single sentence. "And here I thought I'd heard it all, and I thought I knew what was going on in Chicago."

Meanwhile, Danielle loudly cautioned the other children, "And once you go into the system, they take your picture and your measurements, and your name and information, and it all goes into Zoroaster's files, and so now you're in their files, and it's only a matter of time before they catch you! And if they don't torture and skin you alive, they do worse! They steal your soul for all time."

This frightful idea had silenced all argument, and the band of children began to disappear before their eyes.

"Déjà vu," muttered Jane.

Ransom didn't know the French term, but he imagined it a swear word. Then he noticed the discarded doll that Gabby'd twice now gifted over to Audra. Up till now, Audra had kept the doll hidden beneath her fresh petticoats, also a gift from Gabby. Too late to warn her, Alastair realized how terribly attached Gabby had become to the girl. Gabby again tearfully lifted the doll dropped amid the rubble. The petticoats would likely follow as yet another possible sign of weakness at having accepted gifts from demons and of having gone over to Zoroaster.

In the long and sad carriage ride back to their own lives, Ransom attempted to rest his eyes and mind, shut down, while Jane and Gabby talked of their feelings of empty hopelessness that had nearly overwhelmed them as each had listened to the "religion" of the street children.

Gabby had rushed after Audra, offering her a way out, to come live with her and her mother for a time, but Audra followed Queen Danielle and her "family" instead.

"They are all suspicious of any sort of authority," Alastair, eyes still closed, told Jane and Gabby. Still this did not lessen the heartbreaking moment for Gabby. Knowing Audra's decision and action amounted to a performance for Danielle and the others, so that she might continue to belong with her street family, didn't mitigate the pain. Ransom knew that Audra was a rare exception, belonging to two such street families. Even so, Gabby had been hurt by Audra's last words, shouted loudly for all to hear: "They fooled me! They seemed nice, gave me donuts and presents, but they could still be working for demons!"

As the cab passed into their part of the city, Gabby held the doll as she might an infant, cradled on her lap. Out one eye, Alastair watched her and Jane, sorry for their grief, sorry they'd had to go through this sort of thing, but he wondered what they'd expected. All the same, Alastair now tried another soothing word. "Look, Gabby, with these kids, myth and fear of authority has gotten all twisted and balled up, so that as far as establishing any sort of lasting bond of friendship with any of them . . . well, you can just *forget-about-it*."

"Isn't that largely the problem, Alastair?" Jane took instant issue. "Everyone would *like* to forget about it, put it back on the children's shoulders, as if they had a choice."

"They do have a choice. You just saw choice twice thrown in your face!"

"Makes it so much easier then for us to ignore it, doesn't it, *In-spec-tor*."

Alastair grimaced. He hated it when she used that tone when calling him *Inspector* sometimes adding *Ran-som* to drag it out.

She was on a tear now. "And perhaps, then, *Inspector Ran-som,* perhaps if enough of us ignore the problem, it will by damn disappear. Just poof! Gone. Impossible situation."

"They're just children," added Gabby, sniffing back tears. "How . . . how can you be so . . . so callous, you a professed defender and servant of the people?"

"Oh, dear God," moaned Alastair. "OK, I see, now the problem is on me? Impossible is right," continued Alastair in a clumsy attempt to minimize what they'd witnessed and now felt. "Impossible for people on the street, and especially children on the street, as nothing in their lives even remotely appears or feels like permanence—especially bonds."

Alastair knew from experience and reading police reports that a common rule among homeless parents was that everything a child owned must fit into a small brown grocery bag for fast packing. But during brief stays in shelters, children would meet and tell each other stories—often harrowing *true* stories. Somehow enough stories told and they became huge exaggerations woven into the fabric of a strange belief system that, while terrifyingly odd, resonated as real for these kids and, in many cases, had likely kept them alert to *real* dangers. This by way of embracing their fears, mistrust, and suspicions—an animal instinct that was the gift of nature.

Jane must be thinking the same, as she said, "Actually there's no calculating the lives these cautionary tales may've saved, aside from simply getting a child through the harshest of nights."

Ransom knew from his own heritage as the son of Celtic believers that folktales were usually an inheritance from family or homeland, and that the religions of others were considered cultural folklore by non-believers. But what of children enduring a continual, grueling, dangerous journey here amid the unforgiving streets of Chicago, where Christ himself would find no pity? No parent or adult in a uniform, or carrying an inspector's shield, could possibly steel such a child against the outcast's fate—the endless slurs and snubs, the threats, the terror.

So here in the silence reigning inside the moving carriage Jane said, "What these children do is remarkable."

"How so, Mother?" Gabby wiped at her eyes with a hanky.

"Think of it. They snatch dark and bright fragments of Halloween fables, newspaper and dime novel accounts, and candy-colored Bible-story leaflets from street-corner preachers and doomsayers—and like birds building a nest from scraps, they weave their own survival myths."

Gabby quietly agreed, as she'd been disturbed to her core. "Yes, and we just got a glimpse into their secret stories and guarded knowledge."

"Knowledge or ignorance?" asked Alastair.

"For them this is knowledge and knowledge is survival," countered Jane. "They graced us with information they do not commonly share with adults, not their parents for certain, nor the shelter people, or the priests."

Sniffling, Gabby added, "We were privileged, "thanks to Audra paving our way. They don't share, for fear of being ridiculed—or beaten for blasphemy."

Jane sighed heavily. "Heartbreaking, their account of an exiled God unable or unwilling to respond to human pleas even as His angels wage war with Hell."

Alastair nodded. "Must be—to shelter children—a plausible explanation for having no safe place, no home."

The carriage bumped along streets in serious need of repair, the landscape of urban distress the other side of the window sash.

"Their stories have the dual purpose of engaging them in something larger than themselves," added Jane, "and in making their lives meaningful—the purpose of any religion. An astute phrenologist and student of the mind could do a lot with these children, but it would take an army of us."

"An astute folklorist could do even more," countered Gabby.

"How so?" asked Jane, holding back her tears.

"A folklorist . . . could see traces of old legends in the new ones spawned by Chicago's shelter children."

Alastair silently wondered what the hell a folklorist might be.

"For example, Yemana, a Santería ocean goddess, resembles the Blue Lady; she is compassionate and robed in blue, though she is portrayed with white or tan skin in her worshippers's shrines. And for how many generations have we heard of a disease-carrying Bloody Mary going about humanity?"

"Every group has to have its revenants, spirits, and ghosts," Jane said.

"Yes, of course, Celtic tales of revenants," began Alastair, chewing on an unlit pipe, "vampiric zombies digging their bloodless bodies from graves, returning souls, visitors from the land of the dead sent to console or warn, harm, or help? Trust me, they all arrived in America centuries ago with the first Native American."

Jane stared for a moment. "Mock all you like, but it makes perfect sense to these children. It's all they have to hold onto. It perpetuates itself through their leaders."

"It's still all a matter of shoveling outrageous *bullshit*."

"No it's a pseudo-religion based on religious archetypes. And while you may disagree with their version of reality, Alastair, you have to remember our reality is an absolute three-hundred-sixty degrees from theirs."

"Theirs born of pain and experiences we can't conceive of," agreed Gabby.

"True, born of a fear that is as deep a wound in the mind as any I have ever encountered," Jane said, sighing. "So they make myths."

"Yes, so they make myths out of earlier myths that influence this . . . this shelter folklore," muttered Ransom.

"The frightful and bizarre stories of these homeless children are certainly unique and foreign to our ears, most assuredly," Gabby continued, deeply moved. "But they also have a validity, and you're right, Inspector. They resonate with the myths of African tribes, Asian tribes, Afghanistan tribes, hell . . . all the tribes."

Jane hugged her daughter to her. "It's the certainty and detail that gets to me."

"What about the predator—Leather Apron—the one we're after?" Alastair asked Jane point-blank. "How does he figure into this war of angels?"

"How do we know there is a connection, Alastair? What instinct are we drawing on? Ask yourself!"

"Just an old-fashioned cop's hunch, Jane. Nothing supernatural about it, nothing extraordinary . . . just a gut feeling."

"You and I acted on *our* belief system, given our experience, given our myths. Isn't it the same as the popular mind immediately pointing a finger at the knacker and the butcher?"

The carriage pulled up before the sign outside Jane's place, the sign that read Dr. James Phineas Tewes.

Staring at the sign as the ladies disembarked, Alastair replied, "I suppose we all create our own myths, just as Dr. Tewes has done."

"Phrenology may strike you as a myth or pseudoscience, Alastair, but Dr. Tewes is able to get people into his practice on that mythology, and once in his chair, he can diagnose a real medical problem."

"Too bad helping those homeless children can't be as simple, heh?" As his carriage pulled away, Alastair waved mother and daughter off, going for Philo's place on Kingsbury. He needed a safe place where he could just relax, listen to music, have a drink, and feel confident that he did not have to pay too close attention to reason or to entertain reality. This day had been filled, perhaps, with too much reality, despite the mythology.

"That man can be so infuriating at times," Jane said of Ransom as she got on the phone.

"Who're you calling, Mother?"

"Shhh . . . it's ringing."

Dr. Jane Francis put in a call to a very dear friend, the indefatigable Jane Addams, the founder of Hull House and the settlement movement in the city, a woman who'd devoted her life to helping overburdened women and children.

Jane related what she and Gabby had just gone through. Jane Addams listened attentively and took in every word with an occasional yes, an uh-uh, uh-huh here, a groan there.

"Can you give us any advice on how to help this girl, Audra?"

By this time, Gabby hung on her mother's every word, craning to hear Addams's reply. It came immediately.

"According to the city and county people I have fights with every day, Dr. Francis," Jane Addams began in a calm, motherly tone, "the very people whose job it is to keep track of numbers of indigent and homeless families, nearly two thousand homeless children are currently bounced like rubber balls between the privately run, and publicly run, and the overrun shelters and welfare agencies and the streets. Your concern for one of these two thousand is touching, but I really must be getting back to my duties here. I have several hundred of those two thousand clamoring for another meal, and I have a ward filled with sick ones. So . . . I wish you luck with finding Audra again and perhaps adopting her."

"The chances of me adopting are zero, Jane, and you know it."

"*Ahhh*, yes, a single woman. Another reason why your Gabby is right, and you are wrong about the suffragette movement. Do you know that any single man may adopt a child and turn him or her into his personal slave? Putting boys to work in his fields, putting girls to work in his kitchen, and all too often other rooms in the house?"

Jane Addams hung up.

Jane Francis reconsidered all that Alastair had to say on the subject; Gabby tearfully sought out her bedroom, her doll in hand, breaking down.

Jane went to Gabby with the express purpose of consoling her, but she stopped at her daughter's door. She realized she could do nothing for her, that her young one must deal with this in her own time. Jane turned and went to find her own privacy and a bit of comfort in a hot cup of tea. Somewhere in the back of her mind she wondered if reading tea leaves could help a mother at such a time as this. She so hoped and prayed for Gabby's future. *Séances, spiritualism, phrenology, magnetic healing but not tea leaves, not yet anyway,* she thought. *But if I thought it could help Gabby . . .*

CHAPTER 12

Dr. Jane Francis had fully recovered and had even managed to help with the cooking tonight. She now looked across the dinner table at her daughter, Gabrielle, whose sullen and somber mood over Audra and the other street children had only deepened. She barely touched her meal, and the mother in Dr. Francis could not help mentally comparing her daughter's sheltered life to that of the homeless children of the streets, unable to do otherwise.

She theorized that in many ways the homeless children wore safer shields against evil than those who'd grown up like Gabby, under constant protection. The homeless, as sad as their plight was, were, in effect, more cautious and suspicious of others than those not living on the street, and this perhaps could keep them, at some distance from such predators as Leather Apron. But for how long?

As curiously logical as this theory was, Jane Francis wondered what this might portend. Was it just that the street kids were alert, more capable of smelling danger before it got hold of them? Perhaps. Again the fleeting thought, *But for how long?*

Jane studied the fine, graceful lines of her daughter's countenance, so angelic, so lovely, so perfect in its French and Irish refinement. Like one of those dolls sold at the World's Fair. For one so young and so Americanized as Gabby, she carried herself with a haughty self-esteem and an arrogance born of confidence, born of knowing who she was and what strengths she possessed and how intelligent she was and how sure of her future she felt—and most important that she was loved. Perhaps all her strength of character, indeed all her strengths, derived from this sure knowledge of unconditional and unequivocal love, showered on her daily. And yet she could be such a little brooder, as now, and a spoiler as when she was on the picket line with those insufferable suffragettes, shouting for equality for women. Yes, Gabby had been so sure of herself before, but today, the experience with Audra, seeing how other children lived, perhaps the nobler cause was beneath her nose all along and getting the vote seemed somehow less important to doing something for the homeless children in the overcrowded shelters. Then again, if women ever got the vote, would they use it for reform or for the same reasons men did? It was nearing thirty years now since American slaves had been given the right by legislators who saw a quick, dirty, and expedient use for a "black vote" during the Carpet Bagger years after the war. Would women only succeed in getting the vote if one or other of the National Parties deemed their numbers a way to gain the White House?

Jane felt she'd given Gabby all the advantages that a caring single mother could possibly provide in this so-called democracy that repressed the "weaker" sex on all fronts dealing with decision-making in law and government and business and medicine and education. Jane believed she'd done all in her power to shield Gabby from such realities. As a result, Gabby didn't accept being boxed in by this man's world. Now Gabby had seen children small, frail, and innocent in hopeless plight. How could Gabrielle Tewes share their pathos and their folklore with her colleagues at Rush Medical College, at Cook County, and on the suffragette front? What could a woman in American society in 1893 do about a damn thing? Then again . . . if women had the vote and enough trumpeted the cause of the indigent, homeless, and illiterate, perhaps one day women could effect sweeping changes in political priorities. Perhaps 1900 would see the suffragettes win equal rights for every woman. *Now, that surely would be a Second Coming, now wouldn't it,* she thought, a sad half smile gracing her features now.

"I know what you're thinking," said Gabby, who'd smelled the rich tea and joined Jane.

"You do? Surprise me, regale me with your powers, my sweet."

"You're thinking that you ought to've kept me from going with you down into the ghetto today; that you ought to've sheltered me from that, but Mother, I'm doing rounds at Cook County now on Dr. Fenger's surgical staff, and in his morgue. I've seen terrible human suffering there. Amputees, TB, bursting hearts, swollen bodies. Why, I've even seen two victims of the Vanishings."

"My God . . . what is Christian exposing you to?"

"Life . . . well, death . . . *reality* . . . whatever one care's call it, it's there at Cook County every day, every hour."

"As I am well aware." Jane drew in a deep breath and pushed her empty teacup aside. "Gabby, just know that I love you so much."

Gabby reached a hand across and squeezed her mother's. "I never realized just how protected and in luxury we are, able to afford the rent on this place, thinking of purchasing now that Dr. Tewes is raking in so much . . . but I do *now*. I also appreciate all that you and your Dr. Tewes have done for me, Mother."

"Children shouldn't have to spend a single night with hunger, cold, and discomfort gnawing at them, or have to create mythological underpinnings out of fear, need, and self-preservation, both physical and mental."

"I wish there were something we could do for the children."

"Perhaps we can start a fund . . . raise awareness. You could make it an offshoot of what the suffragettes do, maybe?"

"I will certainly propose it at our next meeting."

Jane had long ago given up any opposition to Gabby's participation in the suffragette cause, accepting her daughter's wishes and opinions on the matter, rethinking it altogether again after today.

"Look, dear, we can't allow a sense of guilt at our own comfort to overtake us either."

"As we sit here eating a sumptuous meal in the warm glow of a fire and candle-lit table with music on the phonograph?" asked Gabby. "What have we to feel guilty about? Isn't it the Chicago way? Every man, woman, and child for himself? And money is our religion?"

"Please, Gabby, I pray you'll not become bitter and angry over this."

"Frankly, I'd like to see the herd get a little bitter and angry over this."

"The herd?"

"All of us, Mother, including the big shots, the politicians and the merchants, the mayor, the city councilmen. Why are such matters considered unworthy of serious attention by the men running this city?"

"They are rather busy making money, I am afraid."

"It's the dark underbelly of this place no one wants to take a hard look at, isn't it?"

"Are you going to start a campaign? If you don't, Gabby, who will? Jane Addams and other reformers like her need more people, but you have your studies, and now your rounds, and time in at the morgue, and atop that, you've taken a civilian job with the Chicago Police Department as some sort of researcher. So . . . when do you find time to interview with the likes of Jane Addams?"

"The woman is a saint, and perhaps I am not," replied Gabby.

"Oh, but you are, dear, in your own way. You do so much

good every day. Christian tells me he is so pleased to have you working with him."

This was met by silence from Gabrielle Tewes.

A single word of mirth from my daughter, a half-smile please, Jane thought.

Gabby dropped her gaze; still said nothing. Finally, sobbing, she erupted, "It's so . . . so sad . . . so strange but also so sad and . . . and awful."

"It is sad and awful."

They sat in silence, pouring more tea, sipping.

"How do you think things are going between you and Inspector Ransom?" Gabby asked, surprising Jane with such a departure.

"How indeed is that your business?" Jane smilingly replied.

"Well, it is conceivable, is it not, that one day I may be calling him Dah . . . or Daddy . . . or Father."

"Wait up now! I might have something to say in all this, and I for one am not contemplating a holy union with the notorious Inspector Ransom."

Gabby laughed. "Then some juicy unholy union is in mind?"

"Stop that this minute, young woman!"

The laughter spilling from the Tewes dining room wafted gently out over the evening breeze. In the gaslight glow below a streetlamp, young Audra stared at the Tewes home for only a moment longer before she turned and started away. Opposite side of the street, coming in her direction was none other than Bloody Mary. Audra darted ratlike from sight down a narrow passageway and through an alley. She located the deepest black recess and hid in shadow. Slinking to the ground, Audra grabbed some rosary beads given her by Danielle and she chanted, as in a mantra, one name. "Blue Lady, Blue Lady, Blue Lady keep me safe."

* * *

Once finished relating to Philo Keane what Danielle, Robin, Audra, and the other children had imparted, Ransom downed the brandy that Philo had poured for him. Philo explained that the brandy manufacturer had hired him to do some photography for their advertisements of the product, and as partial payment, he had been given a case of the stuff—a suspect brew from another overnight company, this one calling itself Gray Jack Distillery, makers of fine sour mash whiskey right here in Chicago. Philo had been attracted by the terrible labeling job and advertising.

"What is it, like two days old?" asked Ransom after choking. "I predict it'll win zero ribbons at the fair."

"I'm unsure how long they've aged it, but it's a modern miracle—mass produced to keep the price down for quick sale."

"I'm sure, and violating between six and ten laws."

Philo added, "I don't expect them to remain in business long."

"There oughta be a law against vile-tasting liquor," Ransom said, wincing as he drank up. "So what do you think of my story of the children?"

"Dreadful . . . disgraceful. . . . As I recall, it tore William Stead up to see the little beggars about the streets when he was here writing his book."

" 'Buggars,' he called 'em. Any news on when that exposé of his will be published, if at all?"

"Who has the guts to publish a work so explosive? The very title itself—*If Christ Came to Chicago* is—"

"Intended to raise awareness," finished Ransom. "And he was toying with a subtitle . . ."

"Really?"

"A Cold Day in Hell." Alastair laughed. "Said Chicago was colder'n Russian Siberia so far as social consciousness was concerned."

"I just know he spent a lot of time on the homeless and indigent problems we 'natives' ignored here for too long."

"Still, you've skirted my question."

"Which was?" asked Philo.

Alastair shifted in his seat. "In all of the discussion with the homeless children, what've I to show for my case?"

The two men were surrounded by leather, wood, and books, Philo's phonograph softly playing a Viennese waltz. "I've a good mind to make you take me among these street urchins."

"You?"

"Yes, to photograph them in their natural habitat."

"Photograph them? What possible good could come of it? Certainly no one I know would pay you for—"

"You miss the point. It'd be for art not money, and maybe . . . perhaps, if I could get a showing at a gallery downtown, who knows . . . perhaps we can get Thom Carmichael to cover the gallery showing. Shed light on the problem."

"I doubt it could happen. Not here."

"You doubt everything, Rance. Even your own feelings about Jane Francis."

"Look, now that you've heard it, tell me what you think. Do you think there could possibly be a connection between the street myths and the killer?"

Philo shook his head. "That's right—change the subject."

"You, sir, changed the subject! Now, back on track, please."

"I couldn't say for a certainty either way."

"I need input on this damned Vanishings thing." Again, if Dr. Fenger were not one of the conspirators, he'd have told Philo in a heartbeat about Kohler and Senator Chapman's deal.

Philo finally settled into a chair opposite Ransom. His eyes narrowed, his face pinched, he took a long moment to respond, his hands opening and closing.

Alastair laughed. "Damn it, man, if I were interrogating you, I'd have to assume you are hiding something or guilty over some matter. Why so uncomfortable?"

"I find this so . . . so strangely coincidental."

"How so, my friend?"

"A group of us artists in the city *have* recently discussed this very phenomena. Allandale Wolfson, in fact, has gathered some numbers."

"The painter?"

"Yes, and as a result, I have formed some opinions, and these street religions you speak of are no surprise to me. Wolfson calls it polygenesis."

"Poly-genesis as in many a Genesis?" Alastair asked.

"Precisely. Those few people in little cubby-holes inside colleges and universities who study folklore use the term for the simultaneous appearance of vivid, similar tales in far-flung locales."

Alastair chewed on his lower lip and asked, "Are you referring, Professor Philo, to the similar themes running through all these homeless shelter stories?"

"Professor! That's funny, Rance. However, it's not *similar* but rather *identical themes;* and, yes, you're correct."

"Hmmm . . ." Ransom scratched at his chin. "The same overarching themes."

"Each linking the myths of thirty-five homeless children in Cook County facilities alone; facilities operated by the Salvation Army. And we suspect other U.S. and Canadian city shelters also spawn like religions."

"I'm impressed, professor."

"These children . . . they range in age from six to twelve, and when asked what stories, if any, they believe about heaven and God, it's nothing they've learned in formal religion or in any church."

"So you are chronicling the folklore?"

"Most of these kids don't write or don't know how to write, so they are asked to draw pictures for their stories with chalk and slate."

"I noticed they used the term spirit a lot."

"It's a biblical term for revenants, and they seldom to rarely use 'ghost.' "

"Why is that?"

"Ghosts are for little kids, babies, not tough guys. Ghosts are not real to them. Not like spirits. Spirits are real and dangerous."

"I see," replied Alastair, digesting all of this.

"In their lexicon, they always use *demon* to denote wicked spirits."

Alastair took a long moment to sip his refill of bad brandy, and to allow these facts to sink in. "Their folklore appears to cast them as comrades-in-arms, regardless of ethnicity."

Philo stared long into Ransom's Irish green eyes. "You are a quick student, Inspector, and I am amazed that you somehow made these skittish street kids comfortable enough to share their most guarded, secret stories with you. That is in itself no small feat, remarkable in fact."

"Thank you, but it was Gabby and Jane who accomplished it."

"Most people can get nothing from them without a significant bribe."

"Sure . . . this is Chicago, and kids learn from adults."

"For these kids, the secret stories do more than explain the mystifying universe."

"I see."

"Do you? They impose meaning upon the world in the telling and retelling of the stories."

"Story has power, always has," Ransom mused. "And this gives purpose to their lives."

"You've got it."

"I do?"

"As you've learned, this unusual belief system is cherished by white, black, Ukrainian, Polish, Portuguese, and Latin children, for the homeless youngsters see themselves as outgunned allies of the valiant angels in their battle against shared spiritual adversaries."

"Not too terribly different from African-American folklore and songs, created right through the horrors of slavery, heh?" suggested Alastair.

"Now you catch on."

"Bravo to the student."

Philo grew serious again. "Folktales are the only work of beauty a displaced people can keep," he explained. "And their power transcends class and race lines, because they address emotional questions."

"What kind of questions?" asked Ransom.

"Questions like . . . well . . . like, why side with good—or even God—when evil—or this Zoroaster, that is, Satan—is winning—"

"—or willing to reward you immediately—this moment?"

"Preee-cisely, Detective."

"Yeah . . . I see what you mean. Our own lifestyles might be examples." Ransom had lost his parents at an early age to an epidemic, and Philo had never known his father and had lost his mother to pneumonia.

Philo then shrugged and sipped at his drink. "Here is what the children of the street think, Alastair, if you wish to know."

"I do. Go on."

"If I'm homeless, and I am killed, how then can I make my life resonate beyond the grave?"

"You make it sound like a sense of mission," countered Ransom.

"Damn it, it is a mission for them!"

"Some would say that is ridiculous. These kids know what's what. They know they're making up shit as they go."

"This shit, as you call it, keeps them anchored, Inspector Ransom. You're likely familiar with Cajun beliefs, right? Superstitions out of Barbados? Haiti? West Virginia coal mines? Alastair, a belief system and a culture is necessary to well-being. It provides a sense of *mission*."

"I agree but I am also reminded daily of reality—what our own religious leaders push along with the merchants and money men of this city."

"Fools. Look at it this way, these kids have nothing but their beliefs, and their beliefs may explain why some children in crisis—and perhaps the adults they become—are brave, decent, and imaginative, while others more privileged"— Philo thought of someone he knew—"can be callous, mean-spirited, and mediocre, and lacking any sense of mission."

Alastair only now realized that Philo spoke from experience, and in a moment of realization, Philo saw that Alastair knew this. Alastair said, "I grew up here in inner-city Chicago, Philo, and let me tell you, there was very little sign of God on the landscape then as now."

"Same in Montreal where I grew up, but I wish I'd had half what these kids had in the way of a spiritual leaning or anchor."

Alastair nodded. "I begin to see." A series of words flashed through his mind: *homeless, violence, death, commonplace.* "Often highly advantageous to grovel before the powerful and shun the weak, and where adult rescuers are no place to be found."

"Ahhh," countered Philo Keane, "but the ability to grasp onto ideals larger than oneself and exert influence for good—*a sense of mission*—is nurtured in these eerie, beautiful, shelter folktales as sure as they were in *Beowulf,* which tales were encouragement to men to go out and slay dragons, giants, and beasts."

Ransom sat silent a moment, his cane at his side. "I'm sorry, professor, but regardless of any good intentions you or I or our friends may have for the homeless, their numbers are just too great for us alone to make much of a dent, wouldn't you say?"

Philo dismissed this, saying, "In any group that generates its own legends—whether in a business office, a police department, an agency like the Salvation Army, or a remote Amazonian village—the most articulate member becomes the semi-official keeper of the secrets. The same thing happens in homeless shelters. You've done well to gain even a temporary hold on these kids."

"So this is what I was actually being told by the street children, that their secret stories lay down the rules of spiritual behavior."

"The most verbally skilled children—such as this Robin and Danielle, and this Audra you describe—impart the secret stories to new arrivals. Ensuring that their truths survive regardless of their own fate. It's a duty felt deeply by these children, including one ten-year-old chap I met named Myles. After confiding and illustrating secret stories on a slate for me, Myles created a self-portrait for me."

"Really?"

"A gray charcoal drawn gravestone, meticulously and carefully rendered, inscribed with his own name and the year nineteen-o-six—thirteen years hence."

"How sad. . . . Listen you must never relate this to Jane or to Gabby."

Philo ignored this. "There is something more . . . something far more disturbing coming out of our few shelters, Alastair." Philo absently knocked over his now empty glass.

"And what is that?"

"Well . . . simply put," he began, righting the empty glass, "the children may have trusted you and Jane and Gabby, but only up to a point where they draw the line on first meetings."

"I got that loud and clear."

Philo raised a hand to silence his friend. "The bottom line in their theocracy, Alastair, is quite strange and disturbing."

"Trust me. All of us have been disturbed by all this, especially young Gabby."

"They did not get that far with you, so trust me! You've not yet heard the real disturbing stuff coming outta these kids."

"Tell me, then."

"As . . . as happens, there are Bloody Mary and the mother of Christ, Mary, but in essence they are one and the same."

"One and the same? What are you saying?"

"Mary laid down with Satan to beget *another* child—"

"How blasphemous do you intend being, Keane?"

"Hold on! Don't scream at the messenger! I'm only passing along the facts of reality according to the general belief of the shelter child."

"Sorry . . . go on."

"It's become a tenet of their faith, Rance, that Satan's child, born of Mary . . . not some stand-in but Mary Mother of God will carry on Zoroaster's evil plans throughout eternity."

"Such a horrid worldview."

"Agreed, yet there is more and worse."

"Worse than Mary pregnant with the Devil's seed?"

"Worse, yes, since it was Mary herself who killed her son."

Somewhere in the back of his head, Ransom seemed to recall how Bloody Mary in a drunk tank screamed out at him that she'd killed babies. "Killed Christ, you mean?"

"To replace him on the throne with Satan's son, the Anti-Christ."

"Damn . . ."

"And Mary abandoned God on His throne. In fact, it's as always, that woman Eve did it—this woman betrayed not Adam but all of Heaven itself, showing and leading the way for Satan's minions to overthrow God's throne. A kind of Joan of Arc for the dark side, so to speak."

"We didn't hear *any* of this from the children, and it is so outlandish, Philo, that quite frankly, I'm not at all sure I believe you."

"This is their secret of secrets. They trust no one in authority because of this; they know that no one wants to believe it! That no one will believe them. This is what they hold back. I can show you my documentation of this belief." He began rummaging through a brown valise lying in a pile on a nearby table. "I have it all right here."

Ransom examined Philo's notes and looked closely at the boy in the photographs who had purportedly told Philo the secret of secrets among the homeless and shelter children. The smiling, grimy face looked familiar. It was Samuel, the boy who Ransom had paid to keep his eyes and ears open.

"It's all such a perversion of Christianity."

"I know. It's the reason I've not shared it with anyone else, not Dr. Fenger, not Dr. Francis. It's difficult for men like you and I to swallow, men of the world, so to speak, but a lady?"

Ransom took another drink and lit his pipe.

"Thought you were getting off tobacco—that cough of yours."

"Tomorrow. I'll quit again tomorrow."

Philo returned to his subject, adding, "What this means to the average homeless child out there," Philo paused and pointed out the window, "is that the forces traditionally in Heaven, all the powers of God's throne overhead, are now under Satan's hand. That we are in the midst of an apocalyptic war, and our angels are not only on the run and bedraggled but losing, and losing badly, and why are they losing? Largely because they are abandoned. Abandoned by an embittered God who has seen His son killed by his mother, who has slept with Satan to spawn—"

"The Anit-Christ, I see."

"Sounds like enough to put God off His throne, but it also comes off as unbelievable balderdash."

"Claptrap, drivel, tripe? Not to someone facing death on the streets in a daily battle to survive, and at the same time, remain good and pure."

Shaken, Alastair returned the pages and photos offered up as evidence. "Philo, thank you for discussing this with me so openly."

"Not at all. I am pleased someone is showing an interest in the shelter children."

"You mean someone not wanting anything from them—especially their hides?"

"Someone in authority, you."

"Haven't seen you worked up over any cause ever, my friend. Have to tell you this takes me by surprise."

"One can sink his teeth into this cause and get attached by the jaw," replied Philo, his eyes alight with fervor.

Alastair instantly knew that Philo would one day create the photo array of the homeless he spoke of, but he wondered if anyone owning a gallery would support such a showing. He doubted it but would say nothing to quench Philo's thirst for his plan. Not even William Stead with all of his contacts and influence as a correspondent for the London *Times* had made a dent, unable to get his book into print, so far as Alastair knew.

"Do what you can to end this predator's life—the one they're calling Leather Apron, will you, Alastair?"

"Count on it."

"And I will do what I can to expose the city's disgrace in all this."

"It's a pact."

Ransom still felt that this mythology of the street children had little to nothing to do with his investigation, and now it'd interfered with his drink, his smoke, and his relaxation.

As if reading his thoughts, Philo said, "You always trust your first instinct, Alastair. What does it tell you?"

"Aye, I do trust myself . . . my intuition. Sometimes with your back to the wall, it's all you have, and there is a bit of naggin' about this Bloody Mary."

"And in matters of the heart? How goes it with Jane? Has she put your back to the wall, yet?"

"Police investigation is easy compared to mysteries of the heart."

"Perhaps, Alastair, you could remedy that."

"Oh? And how's that?"

"If you'd just tell Jane exactly how you feel about her, old man."

Bosch got word to Ransom through Muldoon that the meeting between Ransom and the daughter of the seamstress, who'd been on hand during the Haymarket Riot, was set. The inspector must go to the lady. Bosch supplied the time and place, an address in the worst part of the city, a place infested with the flotsam of human life here in Chicago. There were more homeless and destitute on the streets in Hair Trigger Alley than in all the rest of the city combined. Oddly, it would seem to be the easiest and best hunting grounds for

Leather Apron or anyone wishing to abduct a child, but this
had not been the case; in fact, this was the only area in the
city where children suspected of being victims of this maniac had remained untouched. *Something to be said for street
smarts and street myths,* Ransom thought.

As Ransom moved among the crowds here, as he took
one alleyway to gain another while searching out the address, he theorized that homeless people—especially those
on the street for any length of time—had developed street
savvy: the intuition and instinct to respect their own first
impulse, to pay heed to their first fear. As a result, in a
sense, such people, men, women, and children, knew who
was and who was not violent, who was and who was not
dangerous, who was and who was not conning them. Like
an evolved animal in the wild, an "evolved" street-smart
person's intuition and experience might well have kept a
whole segment of the city safe from Leather Apron.

Ransom's cane announced his approach, when another
cane tapped out a familiar rhythm as well, its noise in syn-
copation with his own. It was Henry Bosch's wooden peg
leg—the reason others rudely called him Dot 'n' Carry. But
what was the old fool doing here, now, in the dark court-
yard?

"Bosch? What're you—"

"Get out of here!" Bosch shouted across to Ransom. "It's
all a setup!"

"Setup?"

"Just go, quickly!"

Ransom instead grabbed Bosch by his lapels. "What's really going on here, Bosch!"

"Kohler!"

The single name said it all. Kohler had set him up for an
assassin's bullet. Ransom pulled out his gun and somehow
managed to hold on to the squirming Bosch, who pleaded to
let him go. Bosch added, "Soon as I figured it a hoax, I came
rushin' to warn you!"

"How much did Kohler pay you, Bosch?"

"All right, I took money from him, but only to keep tabs on you, Inspector. I never knew he meant to cut you down!"

A shot rang out, the bullet ripping a hole in Alastair's coat where it flapped in a sudden breeze. A second shot followed immediately, and its thunderous result came so close to Alastair's ear that he dropped to the dirty unpaved alleyway, letting go of Bosch in the process. He looked to his right to find Henry Bosch's form disappearing over a fence, and it made him wonder how agile the old veteran was, peg leg, cane, and all.

Alastair lay in a mud puddle, imagining dying here in Hair Trigger Alley, a perfect cover for Kohler's plot, for if he were to die here as the result of a gunshot, any number of scenarios could be brought to bear as to why. What was Inspector Ransom doing here alone and without backup? Without telling his superiors of his purpose in a known danger zone? How many enemies did Inspector Ransom have in Chicago? How many secret deals had Alastair Ransom brokered? Had one come back to bite him in the ass? These theories of his assassination would go on unsolved forever, or until Chicago simply forgot the existence of one Alastair Ransom.

Such thoughts fueled his anger, but the notion that Nathan Kohler would live on and benefit from his disappearance truly fueled his desire to see this night out, and to see Nathan Kohler again at his earliest convenience. While all he had to go on was Henry Bosch's word that Kohler had set him up for murder this night, Ransom did not doubt it.

Another bullet pierced the earth in front of his eyes, and too late he turned his head away. Eyes stinging with dirt, unable to see clearly into the deep shadows and recesses of doorways and stairways and wooden fire escapes, Alastair could locate no one, and mysteriously, the entire area in all directions had become deserted. Three shots had come so suddenly that he'd not seen the source or direction, but from the result, each hitting so close, he surmised the approximate direction. He rolled over and crawled to prop himself against a trash can, paper and debris raining round him. Another second and a fourth bullet hit the can, opening a hole beside him.

"Damn it!" he cursed, lifted and fired into a black hole ahead of him, then dropped behind cover again. Alastair knew it'd be the height of luck to actually hit someone, but as luck would have it, his single shot resulted in a cry. Someone was hit.

Alastair carefully inched his way to a standing position. There could well be two assassins as one, and the one he hit could still be alert enough to fire again. Alastair called out, "Chicago Police! Drop your weapon or I fire again!" As he did so, he walked, cane in one hand, gun in the other, searching the blackness of the hole into which the man he'd shot had fallen.

When he got within inches, he saw the man's hand reaching for the revolver he'd used, his fingers twitching, slithering still toward the weapon, still wanting only one thing—to kill Alastair Ransom. Ransom's eyes had adjusted to the darkness here, and people had begun materializing all around him, some shouting for police. Several uniformed cops rushed in with handheld lanterns, but even before the light hit the assassin, Ransom knew who he was: *Elias Jervis*. The slimy snake bastard.

Elias Jervis was Polly "Merielle" Pete's former boyfriend and, when the need arose, pimp. Watching the bottom-feeder die brought back images of the spoiled dove, whom Alastair had for a time loved. He'd desperately tried to clean her up after he'd cheated and "won" her in a card game during which he goaded Jervis to wager her "contract." After "winning her over," he'd made a show of burning the contract before witnesses, and his bravado intrigued Polly, a vivacious and wild woman. Alastair had then set himself the task of helping her get clean and clearheaded, so she might make something of herself. Meanwhile, he used her and she used him until he lost her to the murdering Phantom—that weasel, Denton.

Alastair now wondered if Jervis's motive for taking Ransom's life had to do with jealousy and Polly, or that Elias harbored the belief that Alastair's dangerous lifestyle had created a target of her, that Ransom had gotten her killed—and perhaps this was closer to the truth than Ranson wanted to admit. Or perhaps Elias Jervis acted true to form here, working as a paid assassin. Bosch had shouted the single name, Kohler. Had Kohler financed Elias? Was Jervis's motive a combination of all his pent up anger pushed to the edge by the right sum?

Ransom bodily lifted the wounded Jervis and began shaking it from him, causing two burly uniformed cops to pull Alastair off. Elias Jervis fell back like an empty gunnysack into the black hole painted now with his blood, looking purple in the CPD lantern light.

"Bastard took three or four shots at me before I laid him out!" shouted Ransom, tearing away from the cops holding him back. "An ambush! I was set up for a killing!" Alastair rushed Jervis's prone body and kicked it several times before he was again pulled away and advised to cool down. The man giving him the advice was his young friend, Mike O'Malley, with whom he'd lifted many a pint of ale. It was good to see a friendly face among this district's cops, someone he felt he could trust.

"Mikey, when did you get sent to this shithole to work?"

"I asked for it."

"Asked to work Hair Trigger?"

"I asked for it by getting smart with Chief Kohler."

"*Ahhh* . . . I see. You weren't by chance defending me at the time, were you?"

"You are such a great detective, Rance."

"And you? When do you take your exams?"

"I have, but since I was disciplined . . . well, that's by the wayside for now."

"That bastard, Kohler. One day . . ."

"Careful what you say. He has friends among these lads." O'Malley indicated the others in uniform. "And down here your name's poison, Rance."

"He just set me up for murder. I won't stand quiet for that! Search that bastard Jervis, and you'll find a wad of cash payment, you will."

"Everyone knows Elias Jervis had it in for you, Inspector," said another uniformed cop. "This looks like a personal matter to me."

"It's personal, all right!" Alastair stormed off but was stopped by a pair of brawny coppers standing in his way.

"Your gun, sir! We'll need it," said the cop who appeared in charge.

"What's your name, Officer?"

"Tenny, sir. Dane Tenny."

"You think you can take my gun, Tenny?"

Mike stepped in. "Rance, it's standard procedure now in a police shooting down here in the Alley."

"Your boss doesn't want my gun, Tenn," replied Alastair. "He wants my badge and my hide. Isn't that right, Mike?"

"Whatever your suspicions, Inspector," said Tenny, standing in military pose, feet set for a fight, "my job's to do the right thing here." Tenny held out his hand for the gun, one eye warily awaiting Ransom's cane coming up. Once again, Alastair's reputation preceded him.

Frowning, with a nod to Mike, he lifted his blue gun out and handed it to O'Malley. Alastair then started off. He had a houseful of guns at home, including another exactly like the one confiscated.

While all of this was transpiring, Ransom had also swallowed the fact that there never was any daughter of the riot with a mother's diary, that this was vintage baiting. Next Ransom became angry with himself for being so easily led into a trap that almost cost him his life here in this mudhole.

"I'm aware that there'll be a review of the shooting," Ransom said. "Let me know when and where, will you, Mike?" He refused to acknowledge Tenny.

"Sure . . . sure, Rance. You go on home, get cleaned up. You smell of mud and slop."

"Thanks . . . I think."

Ransom made his way out of the alley and onto the street where he hailed a hansom cab. All the way home, he sat angry as hell with himself, with Bosch, with Jervis for being such an easy mark, but he reserved his lethal hatred for Chief Nathan Kohler, and the incident only increased his suspicion that Kohler had a hand in all that had gone wrong in 1886 during the Haymarket Riot.

"And one day, by God, I'll prove it and put the bastard on trial for it."

The cabbie thought he'd barked some new order, and he shouted through the slot, "Sir? Another destination, sir?"

"No! One twenty-nine Des Plaines!"

Shaken from just having killed a man, and angry over circumstances that'd led him into a trap, Ransom felt the fool—Nathan Kohler's fool. A stronger emotion gripped him however. One he could not fend off. Alastair felt a cold grim vulnerability overtaking him, and he realized this naked raw feeling had all to do with his empty shoulder holster. It was brought on by his confiscated blue gun, which normally pressed against his heart.

The following night

"Yes, spirits appear as you remember them," Dr. James Phineas Tewes was saying when Ransom quietly entered Jane Francis's parlor, and as quietly stood in the entry, listening to the spiel of this new con. He felt a disappointment not so much in Tewes but in Jane, and it felt like a lump of calcified stone in his gut.

Jane as Tewes in trance was unaware of Gabby's having answered the doorbell. Tewes was saying, "Yes, the dearly departed come to us just as they looked when alive, even wearing favorite clothes, but they are surrounded by faint, colored light. And while the newly dead speak, it is difficult to make out. While the spirit's lips move, no sound is heard. But I have perfected the art of reading lips, you see."

The séance was in full swing when Alastair rested on his cane, thinking, *Jane's got to've heard the doorbell ring, must know the law is on hand, and that everyone else in the room had begun to fidget—séance-interruptis.*

Dr. Tewes had advertised that he could contact the dead, and this "new assertion" in all of Dr. Tewes's most recent flyers, was bringing in business and money for Dr. Tewes's bank account. Alastair wondered when and how Jane planned to empty Tewes's account and put it into her name. While women did not have the vote, and while most married women had no bank account whatsoever, some businesswomen and independent singles held bank accounts. Banks would take anyone's money regardless of sex, unless a husband forbade it.

Ransom had seen the new flyer tacked to a police phone box, and had read the new promises of contacting a loved one from the other side. The notion alone would typically outrage Alastair, but he'd not think of raiding such a party of fools who deserved what they got. Still, this being Jane in her getup as Tewes proved a double disappointment.

He'd come to demand to know what was going on in her head to make such outrageous claims in the name of Tewes or anyone else.

When Gabby had cautiously answered the door, her fingers to her lips, he'd allowed her to guide him by the hand into the darkened parlor.

Once in the darkened room, Ransom had immediately begun studying the faces to ID the family members sitting about a rippling candle throwing off shadows across the center table. Jane's bejeweled glass chandelier dangled low over this same center, creating a mesmerizing effect like none Ransom had ever seen.

Meanwhile, Dr. James Phineas Tewes held court. In gruff voice, "he" pontificated on the nature of the dead, launched into a sprig of philosophy followed by theology. Before Alastair had arrived, Tewes had undoubtedly insisted that everyone join hands in harmony and unity, so as together they might create a bridge and a bond with the other side, and so that Tewes had the energy to ask help of "his" spirit guide—a lost and wandering soul named Mariah, who had nothing better to do than make continued contact with Dr. Tewes. And today, this moment in fact, Mariah was going to bring Grandfather Nichodemus Pelham to his assembled heirs and assigns.

They were chanting this request of Mariah in no time at all.

Jane did not acknowledge Alastair as she was in a trance—or rather wanted the others to believe Dr. Tewes was in a deep trancelike state.

Alastair remained standing beside Gabby, his stare a study in disbelief. At the same instant that Alastair cleared his throat, one of the ladies in the group around the table swooned and said, "That's him! I'd know that snort anywhere. He was a tobacco man, you know. Chewed Red Man."

Jane as Tewes now said, "The spirits must learn to speak across the chasm between the living and the dead. Grunts, snorts . . . coughing is a simple matter for them, but words . . . words are as difficult for them as for any animal."

"Grandfather spoke in grunts and snorts; he never used words," said a young fellow at the table. "It's him, all right."

"Spirits have a unique function," Dr. Tewes informed his guests. "They provide dispatches from the other side. In fact, I met one once who was a fighting angel in a war for God and his throne. And like demons, once spirits have seen your face, they can always find you. So beware . . . be careful, vigilant at all times."

"That's precisely what the old bastard said he'd do," chimed in the older man at the table. "That he'd haunt me from the grave."

"But he is at peace now and holds no animosity toward anyone," said Tewes.

"He said that?" asked the elder son.

"He wants you all to be at peace as he is at peace."

"You mean dead?" asked the younger man.

"You've got it all wrong Tewes," said the elder son. "What he's saying is he'd as soon see us all dead as to find that will of his!"

"Charles! You'll frighten his spirit off!" chastised the woman.

"I'm afraid it is too late," announced Tewes, breaking the chain of hands and standing. "I have lost his presence. He is gone."

"Gone?"

"Just like that?"

"Afraid we will have to try again, perhaps at another time," said Tewes as Gabby lit a gas lamp, and the disgruntled family began leaving, accusing one another of lousing up the reading and getting them nowhere.

Some of the family members recognized Ransom as they filed out, one asking if he were here to arrest "that charlatan Tewes."

"Oh, but we can appeal to the spirits again, Mr. Pelham, Mrs. Pelham?" said Dr. Tewes to his clients. "Do not despair. Call again."

With a good deal of grumbling, the Pelhams were gone. Jane dropped back into the cushioned chair and let out a long breath of air as she pulled away her mustache, ascot, and wig.

"Are you mad?" Alastair asked her.

"Whatever do you mean?"

"Jane . . . spiritualism? Atop phrenology and magnetic healing?"

"Hey, my therapy worked on you, didn't it?"

"Don't change the subject. You seem bent on getting yourself thrown into jail or shot as a flimflam artist."

"Oh, please! You can be as dramatic as Mrs. Pelham!"

"And how long do you think your disguise would fool anyone behind bars? Ever hear of a strip search?"

"Tewes serves a purpose, Alastair, both for me and the community."

"Yes, to line your pockets while revealing lost wills of testament for ingrates."

"I don't know that they are ingrates, or that they won't use newfound wealth to, say, contribute to Hull House or the Salvation Army, now do I?"

"Either way Tewes gets his fee?"

"Yes, and why not? He performs a service."

"It's fraud, Jane, pure and simple."

"I don't see it that way."

"Are you a mentalist now, a medium, a gifted who speaks to the dead? No, you are a highly educated woman taking advantage of the less educated."

Gabby had vacated the moment voices were raised, but now she'd returned with steeping hot tea. "There's no arguing with her, Inspector. I've tired of trying." Gabby poured tea into cups as she spoke. "She means to have the capital at all cost."

"It's the only way to see you through Rush, young lady. They don't give women scholarship funds, I assure you."

"All I have . . . all you've given me, Mother, since . . . well, since meeting Audra and her street family, I feel guilty."

"For what?"

"For all we have, and all they will never have."

"And it is my avowed purpose in life, Gabrielle Tewes, to make sure you never become one of them! Do you understand? Do both of you understand?"

"Noble reasons for duping others out of their money, Jane."

"I carefully screen my clients in the séance end of things, Alastair, and those who get this far, as you saw, deserve a good fleecing."

"Then you admit to fraud?"

"What merchant in the city isn't a fraud? Have you seen the costs of medical insurance recently?"

"Call it what you will, it appears very bad."

"We are at a crossroads, and we're not to discuss it since none of us will agree," said Jane. "Besides, I'm exhausted."

"I'm sure after a long day, and now this business with Grandfather Pelham."

Gabby piped in. "It takes a great deal out of one to hold a séance, results or no."

They sipped at tea in silence, each lost in thought.

"I've spoken to Philo Keane about what we learned from the street children," Ransom said to the ladies between sips.

"Oh? And did he find it amusing?" Jane asked.

"On the contrary. He is and has been planning an unusual move with regard to the sheltered and homeless children. Contemplating it for some time, in fact."

"Would you care to give us some details?" Jane asked.

"Yes, do," added Gabby, curious.

Alastair related all that had transpired between Philo Keane and himself on the subject. The ladies were duly impressed with Keane's insights and his desire to help the children through his art.

"It's this sort of thing that restores my faith in the human heart," said Jane. She then stood and began pacing before turning to the others. "All right, I have a confession to make regarding the séances."

"What is it, Mother?"

"Go on, Jane."

"I'm setting aside all proceeds from Dr. Tewes's forays into the supernatural for a sizable donation, I hope, to Jane Addams's settlement community."

Gabby smiled wide. "For the shelter children, oh, Mother, how wonderful."

Ransom dropped his head and shook it from side to side as Gabby embraced her mother. "Isn't she wonderful, Alastair?" Gabby said.

"Aye, she is that and bravo, Jane. I'll have to come in and have you contact my uncle Faraday sometime so's I can contribute."

"Do that, Alastair. You do that." She toasted his health with an upraised teacup.

CHAPTER 13

The following day

A phone call awakened Alastair after a long night
of drinking and swapping stories with others on the police
force and a few hangers-on at Muldoon's where Ransom
held court at *his* back booth. Alastair had decided to take
Muldoon up on his "generous" offer. After all, there was
nothing in Chicago that was not for sale, not even a man's
reputation. Part of his decision had to do with his having
had no effect on changing Jane's decision to continue to
work as Dr. Tewes and to her having added séances to the
doctor's repertoire of diagnostic tools. If a highly educated
surgeon could behave in such a manner, then why not a Chicago police inspector—if it were for a good and righteous
cause? Why not bank on his infamy and reputation if it was
for *another* means to an end—a way to help kids like Audra,
Sam, and countless others? But no one must know.

As a result, people had bought him beer and whiskey
shots all night. As added result, this A.M. ringing phone
sounded like a fire alarm in his head. He rolled from bed
and had to cross the room and go out into the front room to
get the phone. It felt like a journey to India by foot.

Each time the phone rang, his headache throbbed at a lower decimal. He finally clutched the receiver in his paw and growled, "What is it?"

Alastair was stunned at what Inspector Logan conveyed. He'd hoped with the news of Thomas Crutcheon's death by pitchfork that the Leather Apron killings had ended. Even if Crutcheon wasn't the butcher, Ransom hoped the killer would take this opportunity to become "Crutcheon" to end his murderous attacks. Not so, as Logan related the fact of another child's body turning up. This time in an alleyway back of Loomis and Jackson, an area infested with tinder-box clapboard one-room shacks in which whole families lived atop one another. The entire area was slated for clearing and rebuilding—a thing they called beautifying in political speeches and in higher circles.

"I'm on my way."

"Sorry to bring such news, Alastair, but there it is. I've sent a police wagon for you."

"Well done, Logan. I'll be as quick as I can be."

Alastair drank down a concoction of juices and whiskey to fight the hangover, swallowed some pills that Jane'd prescribed for headache, and dressed at once. He was soon going across the city in an official horse-drawn police carriage. When he arrived at the scene, a large, ugly crowd had already gathered. A threatening atmosphere was evident, palpable. The police proved an easy target to the people's collective fear and frustration.

Alastair waved his cane and shouted over the jeers, "What've ya in mind here, people? Are you going to hang me to a tree and burn me in effigy?"

"Not you, Ransom!" shouted one.

"Hang 'em all!" shouted another.

"Do you have enough fellas to lift me?" replied Alastair, drawing a laugh and defusing the anger somewhat. "And can you afford enough petro to burn me?" His last words sent up more laughter among the crowd.

Logan and Behan signaled for him to join them. Alastair

had to pick his way through the overbearing crowd. More uniformed cops arrived to hold the concerned neighbors at bay so that the inspectors could do their job.

Alastair also had to pick his way through a minefield of discarded trash, bottles, castoff bedsprings, mattresses, boards, and scattered debris. Among all the trash one child's body, whole strips of flesh torn away from the fleshiest sections. Nude, the child had gone an ashen bluish color under the elements.

"Despite the butchering, Rance," began a jittery Behan, "the bastard who did this left her face pretty much intact and didn't take the eyes this time. Not sure why. . . ."

Logan added, "She's not been dead so long as the others, Alastair."

"Is that right?" he asked.

"Dr. Fenger's come and gone, leaving his opinion," added Logan, a cigar hanging from his mouth. Using the cigar to point, he indicated the meat wagon and Dr. Fenger's body snatchers, as some called Shanks and Gwinn. Ransom openly gritted his teeth at the two death mongers. While they filled a need, transporting the dead, they did so with an enthusiasm far outdistancing their professional acumen. Dr. Fenger, for some odd, unknown reason kept them on as a kind of pet project, as he had bailed them out of jail when under suspicion of actual body-snatching to sell bodies unearthed from cemeteries to local medical schools. Alastair never quite understood Fenger's involvement, but the appearance was not good—bailing out two men accused of such a heinous crime and making them legitimate ambulance attendants while they awaited the fury of Judge Grimes. Then the charges just dissipated, became watered down, and Grimes had turned the pair of ghouls over to Dr. Fenger's care to keep them on at Cook County Hospital and its adjacent asylum, and to keep them *out* of Cook County cemeteries, where they had been nabbed in the first place. They claimed not to be unearthing a body at the time but burying some beloved dog named Cecil. As outrageous as it all was, something going on behind the scenes, even in the judge's chambers, between Dr. Fenger and Grimes—two men normally thought of as enjoying the highest moral character—had agreed on the new state of affairs with regard to Shanks and Gwinn.

No matter, Alastair could not stand the pair, and not because they were homosexuals but because they undoubtedly scavenged bodies for jewelry and tickets and cash and coin and any shiny object, like a pair of vultures. Dr. Fenger insisted that he had broken the two of any such habits, and that he had trained them well, and that Cook County paid them a good wage, so they need not rob bodies they were put in charge of.

Alastair still had nightmares about when he'd been thrown unconscious into that stench-filled hell-hole they called an ambulance—*literally* a meat wagon. The whitewash given the old dram had not completely obscured the old Oscar Mayer Meat Company sign along each side.

Alastair put aside such thoughts and kneeled close in on the dead child, guessing from the size of the girl that she was about the age of young Audra or slightly older. Ransom lifted the broken neck, wondering if it'd been broken before or after death, or during some horrendous torture or struggle. "Didja fight the devil, lass?" he asked the small corpse.

Ransom then looked at the girl's features, and despite chunks of flesh slit from her cheeks, the face and eyes shocked him. He let the face drop away, gasping. "It's Danielle . . . Queen Danielle . . ."

"You know the victim, Alastair?" asked Logan, eyes wide.

Behan came closer, saying, "Keep it down. We don't need any more agitation from this crowd."

Logan whispered in his ear. "How do you know this Danielle?"

"I . . . I interviewed her just two days ago regarding . . . about what the word on the street was with regards to the case."

"Do you think it a coincidence then she's dead?"

"She becomes a victim immediately after my interviewing her?

"And the bastard left the eyes and face so's to be recognized." Behan swallowed hard and wiped his brow.

"I've never trusted coincidence, lads."

"So why start now?" Logan patted Ransom on the back.

"It mayn't be prudent to inform press or public of your connection with the girl, Ransom," suggested Behan.

Ransom looked Inspector Ken Behan in the eye. "I merely talked with her about the case, not even the case, really. About how she and other shelter and homeless children view the world, and who they fear, and why. I was looking for any kind of lead."

"Like any cop, you put your ear to the street." The thin-faced Logan swiped at a shock of unruly hair.

"Yeah . . . basic information gathering," agreed Behan, "but people don't know that. They only know what they wanna know."

"On the ground information gathering, Behan," Alastair said, "exactly."

"All the same, people can twist things, so keep it quiet, your connection to the victim," Behan continued to caution.

Alastair now glared openly at Behan, and then his glare took in Logan. "I did not say I slept with the child!"

Behan shushed him. "We . . . I didn't mean to imply—"

But Alastair loudly proclaimed, "Those two ghouls over there with their meat wagon won't get their hands on Danielle."

"Alastair! What're you doing?"

Ransom lifted her up into his arms. "No one cared for her in life, not anyone. In death, she'll be cared for." With that he carried Danielle's brutalized and butchered body to the police dram that had brought him here.

Shanks and Gwinn started to rush in, demanding to know what Ransom was doing. Cook County Morgue paid Shanks and Gwinn only for the numbers of bodies they brought in. Logan and Behan stepped in, running interference for Ransom, backing Shanks and Gwinn off.

"Sorry, boys, but the CPD has this one," said Logan.

"Back off," added Behan.

Ransom laid the body in the police carriage and ordered the uniformed driver to take him and Danielle's remains to the morgue. As the driver pulled away with Ransom and the unusual cargo, Alastair heard Shanks spit out a curse under his breath, while Gwinn toyed with a six-inch blade, cleaning his dirty nails. Both of the reputed resurrection men had sternly eye-balled Inspector Ransom as he'd closed the carriage door on himself and the body.

"Never seen a grown man cry," Behan muttered to his partner.

Logan looked from the retreating carriage to the ambulance men. "Yeah . . . just look at the vultures."

"I meant Rance."

"Rance? I saw no tears."

"Look a little deeper next time."

"They get paid by the number of bodies transported to County, Alastair, and those fellows, no matter what you think of them, have a right to a living as anyone," Dr. Fenger chastised him on learning that Ransom was in his morgue with the young woman's body. Fenger had guessed her age at thirteen, perhaps fourteen.

"Damn Shanks and Gwinn, Christian! I talk to this girl and two days later she's brutally murdered!"

"You knew the child?"

"Not really, no. I was following a lead . . . a lead that began with Jane and a young girl now in as much danger, a street urchin named Audra, who led us to Danielle."

"I have coffee in my office. Come, let's talk."

It was not long before Alastair downed his second cup of Irish coffee and had explained the religion of the street children he had run into. Fenger had listened with awe at the revelations both from the children and from Philo Keane.

"I had not known Philo was an orphan as a child."

"He had it pretty rough in Montreal."

"You know, Alastair . . . not that it has anything to do with Philo, but some people who grow up on the streets like that . . . as adults or older children, they begin bullying others, and it is not unusual for some to escalate to violence. Some escalating to murder of the very thing that reminds them of their past."

"Are you saying—"

"Just theorizing."

"Are you theorizing that the bastard behind these butcherings and vanishings was once a street child?"

"Was and perhaps still is—even if older!"

"Gone over to the dark side of that religion they preach, yes," agreed Ransom with himself. "Of course. Acting on the belief in this war between Heaven and Hell, and doing Satan's bidding."

"A strong possibility, yes."

"There're literally thousands of homeless here."

"And more flooding into the city every day."

Alastair declined a third cup of the potent, bourbon-spiked coffee. He stared, glassy-eyed, at Fenger's wall of degrees and awards.

"So what will you do now, Alastair?"

"I'm gonna hunt this predator down like the animal he is."

"And when you catch him?"

Inspector and doctor stared at one another for a long moment. Finally, Alastair said, "Nathan has surely informed you by now that I refuse to be a pawn in Senator Chapman's plan of vengeance."

"And nothing will dissuade you?"

"Even I have my standards, Doctor."

"We all must find the line we're unwilling to cross."

"Look, climbing into this pact with Kohler is a sure step toward hell; you can only regret it in the end, Christian."

"I'm sure you're right. Desperate times call for desperate measures."

"There has to be another way. With your reputation, you should be capable of naming your loan."

"I'm afraid not . . . not anymore. Have borrowed from all of 'em."

"I don't understand it, Christian. You don't gamble any-more than Philo or I, so where is all this money going?"

"I can't say."

"Secrets. Everybody's got secrets."

"This could ruin me."

Alastair shook his head. "Nothing you could do, old friend, could possibly ruin you in my eyes, unless you turn out to be the madman going about butchering children."

"Some in the press are saying he is a medical man."

"That's ridiculous."

"Saying Leather Apron makes incisions, makes surgical cuts. Damn fools. I made Carmichael sit through the last au-topsy, and I showed him the difference between butchery and surgery."

"Did it take? Did he get it?"

"Like the fools in London who called Jack the Ripper's twenty-nine or thirty insane slashes precision, and why? Because he ripped out a woman's uterus and other organs?" Fenger had stood and was now pacing, angry at the thought of it. "Damn fools. Sometimes I feel we are surrounded on all sides by imbeciles."

"Any copper can see these cuts have no similarity to sur-gery," agreed Ransom. "But it does not rule out that the killer could be a cagey medical fellow who wants it to *look like* anything but precision."

"Oh, please, not you, too."

"Doctor, I don't have the luxury of ruling out whole classes of people; I am in the business of suspecting every-one until they are cleared."

"Guilty till proven innocent?"

" 'Fraid so. How else do you expect me to operate?"

"Alastair . . . my instincts tell me this man has had no training whatsoever, and this latest of his kills is some sort of message."

"Message?"

"Either to you or to those street children you spoke of."

"Hmmm . . . I've said as much to Behan and Logan."

"So again, I ask," began Frenger, "what will your next move be?"

"It's back to the streets, and I must find a way to get word to every child in this city, because this maniac doesn't care if you have a home or not, are monied or poor, black or white, parentless or the child of a senator."

"He appears to have only one thing in mind."

"He wants your flesh."

"Yes," agreed Fenger, "a flesh vampire, who feeds off the carcass over time, generally, but with your last victim, he did not continue feeding but rather left the body in a well-traveled area, where cops routinely patrol, to be found early . . . *soon*—like now."

"Sending a message."

"Using a child's body to send a message, yes."

"Perhaps due to me."

"We don't know that, Alastair . . . not for certain."

"I should've bloody well stayed on Mackinac Island and not come back," Alastair said on his way out the door. "Fiends and monsters—I attract fiends and monsters."

Fenger shouted down the hall after him. "We don't know that the message is directed at you! Don't be so self-serving even in this, Ransom! Suppose the message is being sent to the other children?"

Ransom stopped and wheeled and lifted his cane at Fenger. "And that message is to dare not speak to me!" Ransom then stalked from the hospital morgue, finding the stone stairwell up to the first floor, sorely in need of feeling sunshine on his face, a breeze against his skin, and air enough to swell his lungs with anything other than formaldehyde and death.

Ransom wondered how he could break the news of Dani-elle's murder to Jane and Gabby, but he knew he wanted to get to them before they saw it in the *Herald* or *Tribune*.

While none of them had actually known Danielle beyond that first meeting, everyone nonetheless had bonded with Audra, and Audra was connected to Danielle and all those little kids they'd met two days before. Some of them so small and young as to look the part of those stuffed animals won by fairgoers.

Traveling across the city from Cook County Hospital to Jane's northside home, Alastairs's cab seemed the only one going away from the great fair. Cab after cab rushed past his, all making for the opposite direction. He had the feel of the only fish going upstream as the throngs flooded toward the lake and the sound of merriment.

Gabby met him at the door, smiling, happy, telling him she'd had a wonderful day, and that the suffragettes had made a dent. She held up a local neighborhood newspaper called the *Polishka Polityka*. While the story was in Polish, it supported the right of all women to vote.

"It's a coup, Alastair! We're making headway!"

"Congratulations, Gabby. You ladies deserve all the press and success you can get. Now, is your mother at home?"

Gabby immediately felt his cool abruptness. "She's in the clinic but as Dr. Tewes."

He frowned at this.

"Gabby pulled him into an alcove and conspiratorially whispered, "We must band together to get her to put an end to Tewes, and to these séances and phrenology. It's too much."

"I am your man."

"Despite her wrapping it all in a cloak of nobility, Mother'd be so much happier being herself."

"I know . . . yes, who she is, agreed, Gabby, but for the moment, I'm afraid I have some bad news to impart."

Her face turned grim in the half-light. "Please not another vanishing?"

" 'Fraid it's worse than that, and it's come close to home."

"Close to home?" she asked, a little gasp escaping her.

He absently asked, "Have you seen any more of Audra since we visited her street family?"

"Oh, God, tell me she's not gone the way of the Vanished, please!"

"No, no! Not Audra. I am hoping to speak to her again. To warn her and the others."

"Something dreadful has happened, hasn't it?"

"I'm afraid so."

"Mother's going to want to know. Come."

They found Jane in Tewes's clinic, and while busy, the good doctor left a patient in the chair beneath the brass pipe pyramid. In fact, the patient was snoring, asleep under Tewes's touch during his phrenological exam. *What a perfect scam,* Alastair thought, *cloaked as it was in the respectability of "science" and medication and this thing Jane called magnetic healing. And how many massage parlors are there in this town, he silently asked himself. Still her "exam" worked on me.*

Jane reacted immediately to the look on Gabby's face. She followed them into the kitchen where Alastair began to explain, "You're going to want to sit for this, both of you."

Due the tone of his voice, the ladies sat at the table. Alastair said, "Our latest victim is Danielle, the girl we met through Audra. She's . . . she is at Fenger's morgue now."

They sat stunned, silence filling the room. After a long pause, Alastair began providing some details as to where Queen Danielle was found, how she had been left in a trash heap, ending with, "It was unlike all the other killings."

"H-h-how so?" Jane's lip quivered with each word.

"In that she was left recognizable."

Gabby openly cried. Jane held her. "What else've you come to tell us, Alastair? I know there's more."

"You are intuitive. I give you that."

Gabby wiped away tears on a handkerchief he offered her. "Is she . . . is her body being taken care of?"

"Yes. I've seen to it."

"What else, Alastair?"

"Christian and I discussed the case, and we are of a mind that the killer may have targeted Danielle as a lesson to the other homeless children."

"A lesson?" asked Jane.

"Because she talked to us?" asked Gabby.

"We surmise because she talked to me," he countered. "You are blameless in this."

"This is awful . . . terrible," said Gabby, the tears returning.

"We need to protect those remaining somehow," said Jane.

"That's a highly unlikely proposition."

"What do you mean?"

"This news will spread like wildfire among the street people."

"Yes, those kids have lost their leader," began Gabby. "Chaos in the tribe. They'll be scattered, and likely impossible to find."

"Perhaps Audra will try to contact you again, Gabby, but finding the others? No."

"Through Audra," said Jane, eyes wide, "we could convince them to stay close to the shelters."

"I suppose, but you have to first find Audra."

"We must try. I'll call for a carriage."

"We can try the area where we last saw her," suggested Gabby.

Alastair hadn't the heart to tell them they would likely waste the evening finding no one, especially in the haunts the children had been frequenting. He was about to excuse himself when the patient from the clinic chair appeared in the doorway, asking, "Dr. Tewes? Is my session over?"

"Yes, it is definitely ended, and I am called away, Mr. Moritz."

Alastair took this moment to slip from the kitchen and the house.

The cool evening air felt good on his brow. He felt a sense of guilt that the ladies had not immediately laid it on his doorstep that Danielle's death was in fact a direct result of her having dared entertain Alastair Ransom in her court. Still, he worried, for if this were the case, King Robin could easily be next.

Alastair went in search of his snitch, Bosch, and to see if he could find Samuel, the street boy he'd put on his payroll, in hope of turning up something—*anything*—on Leather Apron, but he knew that Bosch might well have taken leave of Chicago altogether if he were smart. But then this was Bosch, and Ransom had known few snitches, indeed few criminals as well, who were smart enough, or confident enough, to start over elsewhere. The familiar terrain of his very own city, the criminal mind told itself, gave him an advantage; told itself that it knew every nook and cranny better than either the coppers or natives like Alastair. In fact, it was a foolish but recurrent habit of criminals to haunt the same places over and over; furthermore, Alastair knew it a matter of human nature. People held a map of their small, comfortable, manageable universe in their heads, and the older they became, the more trapped and mired were they within that terrain. For this reason, few men who committed crimes could long stay away from family, friends, old haunts. How many times had he shadowed men released from prison who'd returned to their childhood "maps" only to commit some new outrage, only to be rearrested and again incarcerated.

Still, Henry Bosch was a cut above the usual criminal turned snitch. Alastair had first made Bosch a snitch out of some pity for his story of how he'd become a cripple and *thus* a destitute man, and *thus* a desperate man, and the final *thus: a thief.* Ransom and other cops saw him routinely arrested and after serving time released, and each go-around, Bosch regaled the cops with his Civil War stories and opinions on General and later President Grant, with whom he claimed to have had personal contact on the battlefield, claiming they shared a bottle of whiskey in a firefight. Ransom only doubted half the story—the half that Bosch was in. However, as with all the police gathered about the peg-leg vet, Ransom found his storytelling amusing as hell. Ransom had urged him to come to work as his snitch.

"Me? A groundhog, a copper penny, a ferret, a rat?"

"You've all the talent for it, and it'll put your considerable mind and experience and knowledge of the streets to good use," Ransom had encouraged.

Bosch thought about it for several days, then suddenly agreed but only if an advance of twenty dollars was made.

Alastair quickly located a carriage and was soon west of the city. He found Bosch where he knew Bosch would be—at the racetrack—losing whatever money the leprechaun managed to gain from the ill-fated incident that almost got Ransom killed. After all, it was Sunday so the races were in full swing. With the beer garden open and ale mugs filled to spilling over, the crowd was as jovial as if at the World's Fair. The numbers looked to be in the upper hundreds, perhaps a thousand, all in high spirits, save for the recent losers, who could be picked out at a glance. Bosch was not hard to find within this congregation; one need only listen for the familiar dot 'n' carry sound of his peg leg and cane as he pushed along.

"Canya advance me, Inspector?" Bosch immediately asked, astonishing Ransom with his sheer nerve.

Ransom yanked him into the recessed area between two ticket booths not being used. Somewhere through a bullhorn speaker, a minstrel song played, the lyrics wafting over the track: *"Dance boatman dance, dance all night till the broad daylight, go home with a gal in the morning. Dance boatman dance, dance boatman dance."*

"You damn near got me killed, you gimp fool!"

"Oh, that. Now, Rance . . . it tweren't my fault in the least, you see—"

"Dance boatman dance . . ."

"It was Kohler set me up, wasn't it?"

"I only shouted that cause . . . cause I knew you'd jump."

"Dance boatman dance . . ."

"Lying little weasel! I know it was Nathan Kohler, and you're going to say so in a court of law."

He laughed at this. Ransom grabbed him roughly by the throat. A passing pair of friends in frock coats and bowler hats noticed the ruckus, but they quickly glanced away and moved off elsewhere to place their bets.

"You think this is funny, Bosch? You see me laughing?"

"I only laugh," he choked out, "cause I'm sick with nerves

at the thought. Me in a courta law. Imagine anyone believing me on a stack-a-Bibles!"

"Are you saying Elias Jervis acted on his own? That Jervis himself paid you?"

"Yes, but what would you've done at that instant if I'd've yelled out Jervis's name instead of Kohler, you see? Human nature, see. I am a student of it."

"Dance boatman dance . . ."

Ransom had not removed his hand from Bosch's scrawny neck.

"I saved your life, Inspector."

"And collected from both sides," added Ransom.

"Well *ahhh* yeah . . . I did collect both sides on the deal, but that's the mark of a good businessman now, isn't it?"

"Bosch, I ought to crack your head open."

"H-hey, at first, I didn't know anymore than you did."

"No?" Ransom had to remember this man weaved with words.

"Elias was wantin' to set up shop again in Chicago."

"Still buying and selling women?"

"Still dealin' women, like your Polly Pete once."

"Leave Polly to her grave, old man!"

"But Jervis, he sent a woman to stand in as this young lady with a diary, knowing that I was your, *ahhh* . . . associate, see? I was fooled for a time, too, so you needn't feel as if you were the only one made a fool of, Inspector."

"That's a real comfort to me, Bosch." Ransom released his hold on his "associate."

"If you've got something for me, you know, like a bonus for saving your hide, young man!" said Bosch as he straightened his clothes, his hand out. "I could use some wagerin' capital."

"Something for *you*?" Ransome laughed now, thinking it weird someone calling him "young man." "Damn it, Bosch, where've you been? Do you know another child's been killed?"

"Ohhh . . . it's a horror, what's happening on the streets, isn't it? I mean children! I know, but it's a stone-cold mystery, and nobody seems to know nothing whatsoever, but there is something in the wind." Bosch looked about to be certain no one was near enough to overhear this. "Still, I can't vouch for its validity, you see, only that it's blowin' 'bout."

Then Bosch heard the race begin, and he looked out longingly toward the gate, salivating. Ransom pushed him out of the booth area for the racetrack, following the old man as he ambled toward the free spectator's area, his cane and wooden leg silent on the turf.

They soon found a section of fence and Bosch's horse came thundering by in a neck-to-neck with another animal. Bosch leapt onto the fence, disregarding his handicap, slapping the inside of the fence with his cane, shouting, "Come on! Damn you, nag! Come on!" A note of desperation created an edge to his screaming at the dumb animal he'd bet on. Only Ransom was close enough to hear his excitement over the noise of the crowd. He'd never seen Bosch truly happy at any time in their "association" until now, watching him cry out to "his" horse, and for the first time in his life, Ransom realized that for the duration of the race, a guy like Bosch "owned" a piece of that racehorse.

"Do ya think the horse hears your prayers, Bosch?" Alastair asked.

Bosch's horse won.

"Damn straight he heard that one!" shouted Bosch, jubilant, dropping from the fence and doing a jig to the delight of people all round them, drawing too much attention so far as Alastair was concerned.

"All right, Bosch, so *tell* me now, what's in the wind?"

"I've got me winnings to pick up at the window, and that was a long shot. Twenty to one, Inspector. Twenty to one!"

"Damn it Bosch, next week you will be looking for cash again, so tell me now what it is you've heard on the bloody wind!"

"I am hearing the killer . . . well . . . he ain't no he. He's a she, and that it's Bloody Mary gone so far off her rocker as to do this thing."

"Bloody Mary, heh? You're a day late and a dollar short as usual," he replied, slapping two singles into Bosch's hands. "Get me something credible, will you? I know Bloody Mary. She's quite incapable of being Leather Apron."

"The old battle-ax is daft!" Bosch's frown shrank his entire face. "Makes her capable of anything."

"Half the population is daft, including you! Should I arrest you for being daft?"

Bosch's scrunched face now looked sour. "I didn't say it was Bloody Mary what done it."

"That's what you inferred for money, Bosch."

"You asked for what's being touted 'bout the street. I only told you what is going round, what people're whispering."

"All right, but it's no use, man."

"Didn't promise no great revelations, now did I?" He pouted.

"Nor have you given any. Look, Bosch, I heard it was Mary from the homeless kids on the street days ago, and I put no more stock in it now as then."

"And I hear you're paying homeless kids and cabbies to do my job! And I'm here to tell you that's a waste of money. You won't get no straight answer from a snot-nosed shelter kid or a lorry driver."

"Go claim your winnings, Bosch," Alastair replied, taking in a deep breath of air. "I'm done with you."

"Done with me?" Bosch stood his ground, stunned, silent, a look of disbelief coming over his features like a cloud moving in from over the lake.

"For the moment, man! Done for now, so please, just go—outta my sight!"

Bosch smiled at this. "*Ahhh* . . . then our association is still intact?" Bosch grabbed his hand and pumped it.

"Get the hell off."

"I'll keep working on it, Inspector. I'll get you something other than the nonsense about Mary."

"Do that! And in the meantime, work a little harder to keep us both from being killed. You think you can manage that?" he shouted as Bosch disappeared into the crowd, going for the payout window.

The music had resumed somewhere overhead. *"Dance boatman dance . . ."*

Alastair made his way back into the city streets, his carriage ride solemn. He ordered the driver to take him down to the Levy district. It was time to confront Bloody Mary and possibly arrest her before the mob took it into its collective mind to hang her as Leather Apron. In fact, the madwoman might decide to tout this newly acquired reputation—Ransom would not put it past the crone to revel in the notoriety—to even go about in a leather apron. If so, she'd be ripped apart before the mob hung her by the heels and set her aflame.

Alastair knew her as a dirty, lice-infested lunatic, addled and belonging in Cook County Asylum, but she'd proven even too much for officials there, who did not want her back, as she caused serious problems and upset other inmates due to her raw language and actions. She'd once created a riot there during which the inmates demanded better care and better food and better materials such as paper and wax crayons.

Alone now in the back of the carriage, Alastair felt a great weight on his shoulders and chest as if some nightmare gargoyle or incubus had perched atop him, and he felt a great sadness for young Danielle and her orphaned little band. He tightened his grip on his wolf's-head cane, and he said a silent prayer for help. A growing sense of urgency to locate the monster or monsters behind the Vanishings welled up and filled him with bile and hatred for Leather Apron and any others who conspired with him or her. Her . . .

The notion it could be a woman recalled the caution of the London detective, Heise, who'd chased a similar killer for a decade to no avail. Alastair must consider the possibility, remote as it was, that Leather Apron could as well be Bloody Mary and that a woman could, as well as any man, butcher and consume the flesh of children.

CHAPTER 14

Instead of finding Bloody Mary in the Levy sec-tion, he found Samuel, the boy he'd paid for any information floating about regarding the vanishings. "I got some news for you, Inspector," the boy informed him. "But you're not going to believe it unless Sara tells it."

"Sara?"

"She's a friend of mine."

"Who is Sara, Sam?"

"She's got a place in the park."

"She's a homeless?"

"Yes."

They found the little black girl named Sara Victoria Meghan Walters in a five foot clearing amid thick brush in Lake Park. Sam guided Alastair to sit on the grass here, and he introduced the Chicago Police inspector. Sara, unlike Robin or Danielle, had no qualms about talking to an adult and a police inspector. She sounded like a grown-up, but Alastair guessed her age at perhaps fifteen, possibly sixteen. She had eyes that looked through people. She said, "I hate what is happening . . . children going missing and found cut apart."

"Do you know something about these happenings? Can you help us put an end to it?" Alastair asked.

"First, let me tell you that Satan wears ratty human clothes that he finds in the trash, so he can go among us unseen or unnoticed."

"I see." Alastair felt an instant disappointment. He hadn't expected this to be about demons and angels, but rather about human forces. He had heard enough about celestial wars and God and Evil in battle. He so wanted to put a human face to the monster behind Leather Apron.

"He uses his supernatural powers to make any human shirt, coat, or pants fit him. His clothes always fit him, or one of his little demons."

"Little demons?"

"Satan likes to make babies."

"*Ahhh* . . . yes, yes, so I've heard."

"And the clothes for the little ones, it all helps the demons just fit right in. Who's going to know?"

"Smokes cigars, drinks brandy, he does," said Sam.

"None of you people in authority with all your money and power, none of you know how close he is, and how he wants to end the world come nineteen hundred."

"Really? Can you tell me where I can find him?"

She laughed. "Can I? He's dug a tunnel, and he's found a big hole right here in Chicago."

She sounded on the one hand like a lunatic, but something about her conviction and those eyes kept Ransom wondering. Was there some sort of twisted truth to what she had to say? "Where," he asked. "Where is this place?"

"Under your feet most of the day."

"What do you mean?"

"Under the street . . . in the sewers."

"They like the sewers," added Sam.

"Lives there with his wife and children," said Sara. "The bad spirits come walking into our world right out of the tunnels below us."

"How do you recognize them?"

"You don't! That's the problem. But they recognize you!"

"They're living off human flesh. They're using knives

forged in Hell and cutting off the flesh and cooking it with their fire-breathing, and then they eat it—eating little kids."

"*Ahhh* . . . but they cook it first." Ransom didn't mask his sarcasm.

What Sara was saying harkened back to what Jane had said about Jonathan Swift's sarcastic essay on how to rid London of the homeless. Could it be that someone had set out to do just that in real life and not simply in a book? Here and now in Chicago?

"How does Bloody Mary figure in all this?" Alastair asked, wanting to bring odd Mary into the discussion before Sara did.

"She shows the demons where we sleep, where to best grab children."

"She's procuring for the demons?"

"They're like a family or a gang," Sara clarified. "They only protect one another and feed one another. They hate everyone else, especially people who still pray to God and the angels for help."

"There's no helping it," Alastair said aloud. "I've got to locate Bloody Mary and take her in for questioning."

"She'll give you a fight," said Sara.

"A big fight," agreed Sam.

"Come on, Sam, I'm a lot bigger than Bloody Mary."

"Yeah . . . you're the Bear."

"The Bear?"

"That's what all the kids're calling you."

"Do they think me a demon?"

"Some do . . . but most don't. Most think you're a good Bear."

"So you think I can take down Bloody Mary?"

"I'd like to see it."

"Then help me find her. I suspect she's somewhere close."

"She naps in the sewer," said Sara. "She could be there."

"Do you know exactly where she goes? Can you show me?"

Sara visibly shook at the suggestion. "I do but I won't go there."

"Draw me a map, then."

"She'll know it was me."

"I'll take you," said Sam. "I ain't afraid of no one, not so long as I'm with you, sir."

Alastair smiled at the boy, recalling the picture Philo had taken of him. "All right. Perhaps tomorrow, during the day, huh? You can lead the way then."

Alastair looked from Sara to Sam and then out into the night-blackened lake nearby. He spied a handful of people moving about the lanes here in the park where everything was slowly being engulfed in fog. Trees in the distance began disappearing as had anyone on a stroll along the lakefront. Soon the fog had even blotted out the gigantean lake only thirty or forty yards away.

Alastair realized the full weight of his situation. Leather Apron and any followers of the madman or his cult might be as large as this now invisible lake, and he would not see it; he would miss it. He'd taken this overwhelming weight onto his shoulders alone, and he wanted some semblance of normalcy back, returned to his city. And he wanted to help them all—the Sams and Saras, the Audras and the Robins, and whole families like the one he'd just glimpsed out there in the gloom. But he could hardly do it alone. It would take a huge influx of money and effort put to a cause no one in this city wanted to even acknowledge much less set up a trust fund for unless. . . . Unless some profit could be had. Unless some scam motivated it—as had happened in 1871 with all those bogus charitable organizations collecting for the displaced victims of the Great Chicago Fire. It seemed only hoax and crookery worked here. Perhaps Jane Francis understood this even more than Alastair with her boundless optimism for change, and her James Phineas Tewes routine.

Sara had gone silent as had Sam, and each had been watching the fog-bound family out on the edge of the lake.

Sara, protective of her little hideaway, now asked that they leave by another direction. She had no more to impart.

Alastair saw Samuel slip a few coins to Sara. *The boy learns fast,* he thought.

Samuel then led Alastair out along the north side of the thicket. In the distance, they could see the masts and lights of private boats owned by Chicago's elite in Belmont Harbor. Alastair handed Samuel a five-dollar bill, and Sam stared at it as if he'd handed him the key to the city.

"What's it for? I've not found Leather Apron for you."

"You've done your best, and you'll continue doing your best."

"Thank you, sir."

"Are you familiar with Henry Bosch, Sam?"

"Bosch? No. Can't say as I am, sir."

"Goes by Dot 'n' Carry."

"*Ahhh* . . . yes, everyone knows 'im."

"He's, *ahhh* . . . well . . ."

"Says he's your associate, he does. Is he a copper?"

"Sam, steer clear of Bosch. He sees you as competition. He'll see payment to you as coming outta his pocket, so be wary of him, all right?"

"Will do, sir."

They had casually walked back toward the lights of the city when Alastair got the distinct impression they were being watched, followed even, perhaps stalked. He remained calm and sent Samuel off, back in the direction of the city. Seeing that Sam was safely away, Ransom spied a distant cabstand, and he made a show of a leisurely stroll toward it, half expecting some fool to attempt to mug a cop. But nothing happened.

At the carriage, he stopped and scanned the park. Little rustling noises larger than those of squirrels or rats came to his ears. It was almost as if Sara had followed them to see where they might end up, stalking amid the brush. Definitely sounds of small feet scurrying about. Then all went silent. *Nothing.*

"Something amiss, sir?" asked the coachman, looking out over the park and the lake beyond, as if to see what Alastair could not see.

"No, nothing," Ransom replied and climbed into the cab, giving the driver his destination—home to Des Plaines. He sat back in the cushions and parted the window sash just as several dirty little animals scurried off northward in the direction Samuel had gone. It was not so much that these homeless looked dirtier and poorer than most that attracted his attention and worried him, but that they moved so low to the ground, like a hunting pack—three in all that he could see, one a female from her more catlike pose. Were they playing at war games? Something in their stealth, something in the way they stopped and started, such wolf packlike crouching and darting of heads, the directing of their eyes, and something he could not put his finger on said these toughs were a nasty bit of a gang bent on robbing Samuel of the money that had changed hands. No doubt, they had seen the transaction.

Alastair's cane shot up and with the knocking, the driver peered down through the message slot and asked after the disturbance. Alastair said, "Never mind Des Plaines for now. Go slowly northward. I am looking for a boy about eight, maybe nine."

"Oh, indeed, sir, and will there be a tip in it for me?"

"What? G'damn you, man! The boy is *working* for me."

"Yes, sir . . . I am sure, sir."

"Pull your mind from the gutter and search for him!"

"'Tis hard seein' anyone on a night like this, sir."

"I just left him. He may be in danger!"

The confused cabbie decided he'd best remain silent on the subject. Ransom pushed up the window and scanned for any sign of Samuel, but the boy had disappeared into the night as effectively as had the family of homeless.

It appeared Samuel knew how to make a quick exit and how to take care of himself. *Needlessly worrying,* Ransom told himself.

The following night

The train yards in Chicago lay out in broad mass across a large portion of the South Levy district, some said like the spinal column of the city. Others called the yards at least as great a blight on the South Lakefront area as the stockyards they fed. But it was money hand over fist, as a thousand trains entered or left the city every day.

Getting a late start, Inspector Alastair Ransom, along with his latest investment, young Samuel, started out for the deepest, darkest depths of the Levy district, moving toward the train tracks, where yet another man had only this morning been killed by a passing freighter. Those who kept records on such accidents informed the press that Joseph Adair, a part Indian, on an early drunk, had not seen the train when he'd driven a mule lorry loaded with Hall's Bitterroot Cider kegs across the expanse of track; he'd just let one train pass when he slapped his reins and sent himself and the animal into the path of a train going in the opposite direction. Theory had it that he thought the sound of the second train was the echo of the retreating first. It proved a fatal assessment.

Adair represented the sixty-fourth victim of a train in the Chicagoland area this year, and once again the debate to force train companies or municipalities to foot the bill for crossings and alarms raged. But "civic improvements," railroad tycoons argued were the purview of civic leaders, not railroad barons. They all gave lip service to safety provisions, agreeing to the dangers inherent in speeding trains flying through, but it remained a loggerhead. *Just not at our expense . . . a "local" problem requiring a local tax measure that must be dealt with by each community the railroads served.* Meanwhile, the city council considered it an expense that ought to be borne by the railroad companies, which they "allowed" to flourish within their boundaries. Lost in all this were the over six hundred killed in the United States through train mishaps.

Beyond the giant washboard of tracks laid side by side over a hundred yard width, Alastair was joined by Sam. Together they passed into a fenced-off area that meant to keep people out of Chicago's intricate underground tunnels, blasted out years before. A train ran below ground on one level, but even farther down were tunnels and retired tracks. Samuel led him down and down.

Alastair began to feel like he'd found Dante's Inferno below the city. The walls here were alive with dampness and reflected light—as torches lined the area. All around them were homeless people huddled in groups, fearful of the well-dressed intruder who obviously did not belong.

"I'd heard rumors the homeless were using the underground, but I had no idea it'd become so widespread."

"This is nothing," began Sam. "Since the Vanishings began, a lotta people've had enough and they've left the tunnels and some have left the city. Gone westward."

This kid's got a future, Alastair thought, *so long as he doesn't vanish.*

Alastair attempted asking questions of the inhabitants here. Most were living in cardboard boxes, a few lucky ones had wooden crates. One man said to Alastair, "This is my place! This is my crate, and I will fight you to the death for it."

"I don't want your crate, sir."

"Sir?" He laughed. "No one calls me sir. Did you hear that, Mother?" he asked a sleeping woman behind him. The wife only grunted and turned over.

"I am looking for Bloody Mary; have you seen her?"

"Have not."

"Does she come here?"

"Seldom."

"When is seldom?"

"Seldom is seldom."

"Seldom in daylight or seldom at night?"

"I tell you, she has not been round here since . . . well since the vanishings began, I'd say."

Alastair noted several children clinging to the man and his wife. "Are you not fearful for your children, sir?"

"There he goes again, Mother . . . calling me sir."

"Well? Have you fear for your children?" persisted Ransom.

"My true children have abandoned us, mother and father. These little ones you see here have adopted us, so to speak."

"Adopted you?"

"They elect to stay close."

It did appear the children were here voluntarily and held no fear of this couple. "Still, sir, tell me, what is your name?" asked Alastair.

"Crusoe . . . Robinson Crusoe."

Obviously, the man was educated, well-read, and enjoyed verbal jousting. "Well, Mr. *Crusooo* . . . have you any opinion of the Vanishings?"

"I have my suspicions, yes."

"And what are these?"

He held out his palm for money. Alastair filled it with a dollar bill. "I have recently come across a horrid fellow, a man who is Anti-Christ if I am human."

"Anti-Christ?"

"The Anti-Christ."

"Who is this man, the same as the children call Zoroaster?"

"I suspect so. I've seen him slaughter small animals, skin 'em and eat 'em uncooked. Says I to him once, why not build a fire and fry that meat?"

"And his reply?"

"He asked back, 'Ever e't raw meat?' "

"Then what?"

"Then I decided to let it go."

"And what makes you think him evil other than eating the flesh of animals?"

"It did not stop at his eating uncooked animal flesh."

"Go on."

"He fed it to his children."

"Indeed!"

"Indeed . . . and his woman."

"The whole family is eating dog flesh?"

"Times are hard. Dog, rat, cat, and I fear *children* now."

"It is too crushing to believe it."

"Didn't someone say the bodies are carved up? Like grandma's holiday turkey?"

"Yes, this is true. All the same . . . what you propose, Mr. Crusoe, is beyond the kin of all but wolves."

"Wolves're kinder. Several knives of varying blades are used so I read." He held up a tattered *Herald*.

"You are well informed, but the general feeling is that the butcher uses several knives."

The decrepit man shook his head. "Reverse that thought. Several butchers, some large, some small, trained on a separate blade—all carving on the carcass."

"A horrible notion."

"Hard to swallow, you mean!" He laughed at the bad joke until the laugh turned into a coughing jag. "But it's what I told the other man who came asking."

"The other man? What other man?"

"Why the doctor. It's what I told the doctor."

"What doctor? Please tell me it wasn't Dr. James Phineas Tewes."

"No, not 'im. The surgeon, Dr. Fenger. He called himself Dr. Josephs, but I read the papers . . . maybe a week late, but I read 'em when folks throws 'em away, you see." He warmed to his subject, waving his soiled paper. "I've spied his picture in the paper more'n once."

"Fenger came down here and talked to you?"

"Yes."

"When?"

"A day ago now."

"And this butchering family . . . these cannibals? Did you point them out to Dr. Fenger?"

"Point them out? No. They've relocated by all accounts, so there was no chance."

"Where did they relocate to?"

"Dunno."

"And this is what you told Dr. Fenger?"

"I never let on I knew who he was."

"But you informed him as you did me? No deviation?"

"I did, and he paid me a damn sight better'n you."

"Was anyone with him?"

"Yes, that big-shot guy."

"Big shot?"

"*Ahhh* . . . fellow they call Chief in the papers."

Kohler and Fenger here, tracking down this cannibalistic family twenty-four hours ago, *and Christian knowing this even as he autopsied Danielle, yet he'd said nothing of it, confided nothing of it. It could only mean one thing.*

"Tell me . . . when'd you last see the Anti-Christ and his family?"

"Not for days now."

"Does the Anti-Christ go by a man's name? I understand he goes about in men's clothing."

"He calls himself Jones, Smith, and sometimes Dobbins."

"Dobbins?"

"Donald P. Dobbins."

Ransom wondered if the man made it up as he went. He decided this was the case to some degree. "Dobbins, I see. Can you show me where Dobbins and his family can be found? Where they sleep when here?"

"Aye . . . for another buck."

Alastair yanked out another bill and laid it in Robinson Crusoe's hand. "What about me?" asked Sam beside him. Ransom frowned at the boy but gave in, handing him his last single.

As they followed Crusoe down the maze of the sewer, tramping through turgid black water part of the way, Alastair gave thanks that it'd been a dry month.

They passed others who'd taken up residence here below the city—desertlike expressions on their faces like so many zombies. One gaunt, weather-beaten old woman loudly tsk-tsked at their passing and shook her head and loudly announced, "I told ya all . . . predicted this. My daughter told me so. They've come to root us out."

"I'm not here to harm you, old mother," Ransom assured her.

"The angels will catch him some day. Leave him to the angles. They'll destroy him," said the addled woman.

"In Chicago, we're not much for leaving justice to angels or to another life, my lady."

She twittered at his calling her "my lady." She came alongside Ransom with a small vial of water, splashing it over him, calling it holy water to protect him. "If you're that stubborn bent on it, you'll need protection," she finished. "Besides, the Anti-Christ hates holy water. Burns his soul like acid."

He imagined the old woman had stolen the water from one of a hundred churches in the city.

The old man shooed her off, while Sam said, "Holy water makes his skin dissolve and turn to steam . . . weakens him. But tainted holy water don't bother him in the least."

"Right, son," replied Alastair, tired of hearing this kind of nonsense.

But Sam kept on. "You know, like sewer water and like tap water'll do for 'im. That he can even drink and it don't bother him, but not blessed holy water. I know a priest sells it outta the back of St. Alexis shelter for the homeless."

"I'll bet you do." Alastair took a moment to jot down the priest's name, as he wanted a talk with this man.

Just then Alastair saw a large figure rise in the distance here, a strange steam coming off him. The figure appeared flanked on two sides. On one side, a woman, on the other a child. Then another child, then another. They seemed to curl up from out of the ground like smoke. Alastair heard the song sung in the streets by children replaying in his head:

> *On a night so dark,*
> *Amid a sky so blue,*
> *Down through the alley*
> *Satan flew*

It's here each night
he sends his Bloody Mary,
who looks such a fright
but flies like a fairy
and eats the flesh
of live snakes, drakes, and hakes—
Skins and eats kids too . . .
You may ask till blue
Answer is in the rhyme
That many ne'er see in time
That her secret name is true . . .
So call out Mary, Mother of God!
Else she carves you as a calf
and feeds you to her devil half.

Alastair looked from Sam and back to the homeless family shrouded in gloom here, below ground. They looked back with vacant eyes: This motley group, not so deadly as pathetic, recalled a family in one of Philo's photos.

Ransom spent a few moments with the father—a man calling himself Gideon Tell—commiserating about his inability to find work. Ransom made a few suggestions, people to speak to, an alderman in the district, telling him to use his name to break the ice as a kind of letter of introduction. "There is the chance in this to feed your family," finished Alastair. "You, too, Crusoe, but you'll have to supply your real name."

Crusoe grunted. "That'd be Robert Louis Stevenson."

CHAPTER 15

Across town at the same time

Jane and Gabby had not been able to sit idle all this time and had gone in search of Audra. They located her on a street corner in the company of others, including King Robin. All of the children had undoubtedly heard of Danielle's fate, and most of them scattered on seeing Jane and Gabby, but Audra, Robin, and a handful held their ground.

Jane convinced those remaining to accept a carriage ride to Hull House where she had friends who would take care of them. "At least until the police catch this madman who killed Danielle," she pleaded.

"No one can catch the Devil," countered Robin, even as he urged his followers to climb into the carriage. None of them had ever been in a cab before, and they took it as a great opportunity that would not come again. It quickly became a free-for-all.

In fact, the ride to Hull House was boisterous and fun for all, but as they neared their destination, Gabby began interrogating Audra, asking when she had last seen Danielle and who might have been with her when she'd disappeared. "Why was she alone? Where were the other children in her gang?"

"Danny . . . she sometimes went off on her own," said Robin.

"Said she needed thinking time." Audra began sobbing. None of the other children could add to this.

Robin explained that the two bands mutually supported one another, and that everyone liked Danny as they affectionately called her. After this, Robin opened up, telling Jane and Gabby a story about himself and his mother. "One night last year, we made a bed out of a large freight box, newspapers, and some brush in the park by the lake, the place where a lotta drunks gather after all the bars are closed. And it was my turn to stand guard against the "screamers.""

"Screamers?" Jane asked, making all of Robin's followers laugh.

"Packs of roaming addicts—screamers."

"What sort of addicts?"

"All sorts. Booze, heroin, opium. Anyhow, while mama slept, I guarded her. That's when all of a sudden Charlie was standing before me, dressed in his army uniform."

"And Charlie is?"

"My dead brother. Died in the Indian Wars out West."

"I'm so sorry Robin," Jane replied, placing a hand over his, but he quickly withdrew.

Robin then gnashed his teeth, gulped, and teared up but kept on with his story, pretending some lint had flown into his eye. "My brother's spirit, says he, 'The Devil got loose from under the river!'"

"The river?"

"The Chicago River. He found a hole under Lake Michigan and came up through the river is what Charlie was saying out of his dead mouth. Then he said, 'The rich people didn't stop him!' And then he says, 'The angels need soldiers.'"

"So he was warning you, your brother?"

"That's what I'm telling you. He's close by, watching us *right now*."

Gabby piped in. "One of the good angels, heh?"

"Where is your brother now?"

Robin opened the window sash on the carriage and looked about. Seeing nothing, he stuck his head out farther and returned his head with a smile. "He's atop the coach, beside the driver, enjoying the ride."

"He's perched on the coach seat?"

"Yes ma'am."

Gabby asked, "Is he, you know, stuck on this plane of existence, this realm?"

"Charlie's spirit thinks he is needed in the war."

"The war?" Gabby repeated just as the coach hit a huge pothole, jarring her but making the children cheer.

"War of angels, the one you've been told about."

"He's lingering here so he can fight back?" asked Jane.

"Now he has the power, yes."

"So where now is your mother, Robin?"

Robin looked about the cab at all the expectant faces. It was a secret he had not told anyone; he informed them now, prefacing what he wanted to unload. "Mum is in county hospital."

"Cook County?" asked Gabby.

"Sick . . . sick she is . . . up here." Robin pointed to his head.

A chubby Polish boy piped in, his name Stanley. "My dead cousin told me that as soon as water touches the Devil's skin, it turns deep burgundy and . . . and horns, they grow from his head. The river itself turns into blood; spirit screams and the bones of murdered children float on the water."

"And just when the angels think they've convinced *Good Streets*—people like us—that they are in as much danger as *Bad Streets,* Satan vanishes through a secret gateway beneath the river, or lake, or pond, or ocean depending where you are."

"I see," said Jane, her heart silently sobbing for these children.

"Now he's coming your way," Audra warned.

Robin quicky added, "You'll need to learn how to fight."

"Teach me," replied Jane.

At the same time Gabby asked Stanley why he was carrying a ratty old school book that'd been torn and beaten.

"I can't go to school," replied Stanley.

"But you carry school books?"

"Only cause Robin got them for me. He ought to grow up to be a teacher."

"Perhaps he will."

Stanley dropped his wide-eyed gaze in a gesture of sadness.

"'Study hard,' Robin tells us all," said another of the children.

"Stay strong and smart so's you count on yourself, no one else, is what he always says," added Audra.

"And he taught us to never stop watching out for one another," added little Stanley, his blond hair wispy and wild.

"To watch our backs," said Audra.

"For Bloody Mary, you mean?" asked Gabby.

"And Satan?" added Jane. "Zoroaster?"

"I tell them what I'm telling you now, ladies," Robin said, his voice ominous. "Bloody Mary is coming with Satan. And she's seen your face. She's picked you out for a no good end."

Jane placed a hand on Gabby's shoulder at this warning.

"What about this predator, the one the police and the press are after, the child killer?" Jane asked Robin point-blank. "How does he figure into this war of angels and with Bloody Mary?"

"How do you know that Leather Apron is a he?" Robin asked in return.

"Guess I've assumed it a statistical probability."

"I think Bloody Mary is Leather Apron," replied Robin.

"What makes you say so?"

"At least, she is directing his movements."

"Why do you say so?" asked Jane.

"I saw her with Danny a couple of times lately."

"Why do you think Danny'd go off with Bloody Mary, if she feared her so?" asked Gabby.

"Nothing goes on here on the streets without Bloody Mary having a hand in it," added the sullen Noel.

Jane's frustration filtered through in her voice. "Zoroaster, Satan . . . and the Blue Lady?"

"God, she works for God."

"And where are God and the Angel Warriors and the Blue Lady?"

"Hiding out. Lickin' their wounds . . ."

"Hiding out where?"

"Hiding out in plain sight. In hospitals, banks, schools. Here on the street. Danielle was an angel, and for all I know, you and your daughter, you could be warrior angels."

"That's sweet of you to say."

"It's not sweet. It's instinct." Robin then looked her hard in the eye and added, "You . . . you remind me of my mother before . . . before she got sick."

She reached across the carriage to hug him, but Robin pulled back, saying, "Look . . . I have nothing to give you beyond the facts of life on the street, but soon maybe . . . maybe I will know something. I have my eyes open and my ears to the ground. If you two are willing to pay in goods or coin."

"We're budgeted to pay for information that leads to this killer, sure."

"All right, then you're going to hear from me again . . . soon."

"No, not if it places you in danger, Robin—any of you," insisted Jane.

The carriage had pulled to a stop at Chicago's famous Hull House, where Jane Addams herself stood on the steps awaiting their arrival. Dr. Jane Francis had contacted her long-time friend and confidant, asking her to help out and offering a generous check for Hull House in the bargain. Jane had thought about the homeless children since the first day Audra had introduced them, and she'd sat down and asked herself a series of questions: Who would care to know about the homeless children? Who would want to create a program of hope for them? Who would already know that kids need love and perhaps pets as well as books and schooling to help save them from everyday fears and horrors, traumas and the exigencies of life on the street, life without a daily routine, life without a bed and a roof and four walls and a lock on the door?

Who indeed. The revelation coming in at her felt so horrible, so distasteful that she wanted to scream out its impossibility even as it formed in her mind. Chicago, her city, had helped greatly a madman by letting these children down. The Vanishings were nothing new; in a quieter but just as awful way, kids had been vanishing before their eyes since the city's inception.

Jane Addams had become the fulcrum for the settlement movement that preached for shelter communities in every neighborhood. She was always at the center of anything dealing with destitute women and children. If there were a program in place to put homeless children in physical touch with orphaned and impounded puppies, to give them a warm meal and a place to lay their heads at night, this was the place. If there was any chance whatsoever of finding good foster care for such as Robin, Audra, Stanley, and the others, it was Hull House, as Jane Addams had a sixth sense about people.

Dr. Jane Francis realized that Alastair had a job to do, and must end this slaughtering of the innocent, but it was increasingly clear to her that these children were not a direct path to the killer. They were the lure but could not be used as the bait.

It was possible, yes, that the killer had knowledge of the morbid "religion" professed by the homeless, and used its precepts against them along with enticements, no doubt—food, money, toys, the promise of a pet . . . or immortality as a follower of Zoroaster!

It was a wild, anxiety-ridden bird of a notion, which now fluttered insanely inside Jane's brain, and perhaps ought to remain there. She saw herself trying to sit astride the back of this "fowl" idea that had invaded her mind. The idea that

Dr. Christian Fenger, Nathan Kohler, and she—as she had entered into a deal with the others—might benefit from all of this horror by delivering up the killer to Senator Chapman's idea of justice.

Christian had told her of the secret only the day before. She'd been told that Alastair had flatly declined Senator Chapman's "kind and generous offer," and she respected him for taking the higher, moral ground, but to her mind there was a difference in her own notions of getting hold of a share of this treasure. How much good it could do in the hands of the caretakers of Hull House to feed and clothe these children. Still, she remained removed from any direct connection even as she'd quietly provided Christian with information gleaned from Audra and the other children.

Jane had not been comfortable with the role that Christian had placed her in, but unlike Alastair, she had no compunction about *how* this monster they called Leather Apron would meet justice, so long as he did! And if she could cash out a dramatic winner thanks to Chapman's deep pockets, so be it. Like Christian and Kohler, she could use the money, but now she'd begun thinking any such funds must go to these homeless—these daily survivors.

Still the godawful gnawing at the pit of her stomach and around the edges of her soul about this deal continued inexorably to erode away sane notions and to taunt her. So often good things were done in the name of humanity, religion, love, brotherly concern, fatherly passion, a mother's love, for god and country, and this for a grandfather's vengeance. But so often it proved a complete lie, a fabrication, a distortion, an illusion. It was one of life's tragic comedies, and largely due to her experience and training—she must pay close heed to her instincts and suspicions.

She watched the children line up at the order given them by a stern Jane Addams, whose very tone, icy and firm, the children seemed to welcome, even Robin, as though he would gladly relinquish his crown if someone else, an adult, would please take it.

Jane and Gabby climbed last from the carriage, waving at the heavyset woman on the steps with the unforgettable smile and commanding presence. At the same time, Jane Francis glanced at the topmost coach seat for Robin's brother, imagining him just there.

"What'd you make of Robin's story about his dead brother?" Gabby asked in her ear as if reading her thoughts. "You think it true?"

"I've no doubt that soldiers, who die a traumatic, violent, and sudden death often are left in limbo. They sometimes send out messages—confusing and vexing and conflicting images, yes, but images nonetheless."

Gabby and Jane helped settle the children in at Hull House, and once this was accomplished, Jane Addams gave them the full tour and a brief history of her work here. As she listened to the indefatigable Miss Addams, Dr. Jane Francis offered up her services as a physician to bring health care on a regular basis to Hull House.

Miss Addams stared for a moment at Jane Francis, a single tear appearing in the older woman's eye. The tear swelled and slipped down her cheek. Addams brushed it away. "So good of you, Dr. Francis."

The following night

Alastair was on a crawl tonight, but not a pub crawl—rather an information-gathering crawl in search of Bosch. Ransom the Bear was afoot, exercising his feet and hips and sweating off some pounds and getting nowhere.

Police work was like that. Hours upon hours of simple hard work leading to nothing, and sitting idle, and making rounds, and asking question after question with little result, and then came the explosion in the face. Some event or happening bursting on the scene to give a shock to the system.

Thus far no shock had come, only an interminable bore amid a lot of filth.

"Where the hell is Bosch?" he must have repeated the question a hundred times in a hundred permutations in a hundred venues tonight.

"'Ave ya seen Bosch?" he addressed the drunks in one alley.

"Seen that gimp, Bosch, tonight?" he inquired at Muldoon's.

"Heard Dot 'n' Carry comin' or goin' tonight?" he asked at the Red Lion.

"If you fellas see or hear that peg leg, tell 'im I'm looking for him."

No one had seen him. No one knew where he might be. He failed to appear at any of his normal haunts. It spelled only one thing: *fear.*

The tune from the racetrack played in Ransom's brain: *Dance boatman dance . . . dance boatman dance.*

Henry Bosch had gone into hiding like a frightened animal, and his brief stint at the track was a bid for much needed cash. Now that he had money, he'd become difficult to find. Normally, he showed up like a bad penny and Alastair did not have to go looking, but the game pieces on the board had changed significantly. With Jervis being shot dead by Alastair Ransom in an old-time gun battle in Hair Trigger Alley—despite a ruling of self-defense—rumors abounded. Rumors surrounding various notions having to do with Ransom's idea of vengeance; it was a vengeance that'd gone too far, spilled over the brim as it were, and next the rumors had Alastair drunk at the time (drunk with vengeance), despite his requiring a single shot to take down his man. Still, some felt that he had taken down the department with his street hooliganism. A lot of people suddenly liked Elias Jervis as next in line for sainthood. Perhaps Ransom ought be more than reprimanded; perhaps he should be made an example and stripped of his badge and placed on trial for murder.

Another rumor, this one circulating among authorities and whispered in his ear by both Behan and Logan had

County Prosecutor Kehoe working late nights to put a case against Alastair on the docket.

Should this occur, a sheared, declawed Ransom would be a prized sight for a lot of Chicagoans, and it would be a large feather in Nathan Kohler's cap. Sadly, if it should ever come, Ransom had but one witness, and a lousy one at that, Henry T. Bosch. How else might he prove a setup? How else might he cast a dark light on Nathan Kohler, should authorities above the police review board call for Ransom's head?

So far as Alastair was concerned, it'd been a conspiracy that definitely involved Nathan Kohler, a dangerous man indeed. The circumstances and his inability to turn up Bosch again since the racetrack made Ransom wonder if Bosch hadn't simply taken his winnings and made for Indianapolis or Davenport or Kankakee, if not farther from Chicago and Ransom. And it all made Ransom doubly suspicious that the wily old Civil War veteran indeed harbored damning information that Alastair could use against Nathan Kohler. Still, Bosch was correct about his sitting in a witness box. The image sent up red flags. Nonetheless, the more he stewed about it, the more Alastair meant to at least privately know everything. To this end, he meant to drag or beat the facts from Bosch. The sawed-off gimp knew what really happened the night Ransom was nearly killed by Elias Jervis.

Perhaps if he'd agreed with Kohler and Fenger, to throw in with their plan to turn over this Leather Apron killer to Senator Harold J. Chapman, then perhaps he'd not have Kohler on his back now. Kohler had to be sweating Ransom's decision to remain aloof from the money and the corruption suggested by Senator Chapman. Kohler surely saw it as yet another threat to his power base.

While Bosch failed to find Ransom, young Samuel did not, and Sam, eager to earn more money, offered to guide Ransom to a location where he suspected the Leather Apron gang might be hiding out.

"Leather Apron gang?" he asked Sam where they stood back of Muldoon's.

"Talk on the street is that there's more than one, maybe a gang of 'em."

"Where are you hearing this, Sam, from whom?"

"Sara for one, the girl you met the other night? She said the lot of them were following us that night, that they went right past her. She counted, like, sixteen of 'em."

"Sixteen?" Alastair was skeptical.

"Yes, sir . . . according to Sara."

"All right, do we need a carriage to get to this location?"

"*Ahhh* . . . I don't but it's pretty far for an old man."

"Thanks, Sam, for thinking of me. Let's go."

They were soon approaching Michigan Avenue, and it recalled to mind that the senator's granddaughter had been abducted not far from here. Sam announced that they needed to exit the cab and go on foot from here, the corner of Michigan at Wacker, and Ransom checked his weapon, seeing that it was loaded. Then he climbed out behind Samuel.

They were soon making their way down a series of ladders taking them into underground Chicago, passageways below Michigan Avenue and Wacker, an area used primarily by delivery wagons and drams coming and going, loading and unloading on docks built at the basement level—block upon block of businesses stretching from here to State Street.

The area was dirty, the roads here unpaved, cow paths originally to move beef on the hoof from railhead to slaughterhouse to market outlets, and finally to such establishments as Delmonico's and The Palmer House. The underground network of roads here were nowadays used by any number of downtown businesses for deliveries and intakes. Workmen used the roads as a trash heap, it seemed. The wind blew through here like a monstrous force, sending up dirt devils and trash in small tornadoes. "There's nothing down here," complained Ransom. "Sam, are you just yanking my chain?"

"You gotta go deeper, sir."

Ransom began to hear the tune again in the back of his head: *Dance boatman dance . . . Is this kid playing me for a fool,* he wondered.

After going down yet another level, finding an underground cavern, Ransom heard human voices ahead of them in the darkness. "We shoulda brought a lantern," said Ransom.

"No, a lantern would only warn the Leather Aprons, and they'd be running off like rats in every direction."

There was no need of a lantern because fires were burned in barrels ahead of them. They moved toward the light.

Samuel's shadow crept ahead of them, and Ransom's huge shadow foretold his coming, and it did appear a horror moving along the wall toward those huddled around the fire down here. They all began shouting at once:

"It's Bloody Mary!"

"Zoroaster!"

"Satan's come!"

Samuel shouted, "No! It's Inspector Ransom! He's come to kill the Aprons!"

"Please! Help me!" shouted one of the children in the grainy darkness where Alastair and Sam had stopped.

"I know Bloody Mary got Danielle, and I know I'm next!" shouted another.

This child was joined by the others. "You've got to hide me! Hide me!"

Alastair's companion, Sam, shouted, "Don't be fooled! Some of the Aprons have pretended to be like the rest of us, but they're pimps, luring kids to Zoroaster, and then they all jump 'em and stab 'em all at once."

"Sam's right!" shouted King Robin, who'd asserted his authority and had recently led any of his band willing to follow him from the safety of Hull House to this so-called hiding place. "But we don't know who's the traitor."

"But this time Zoroaster is dealing with me and not some child," countered Alastair.

"They're their own gang. There're a lot of 'em," warned Robin.

"Where're they hiding? Where, Robin?" implored Ransom. "Tell me! Tell me now, Robin!"

"Deeper in," he indicated the blackness of this underground passage.

Ransom was immediately suspicious, his near assassination still fresh in his mind. "Why, then, are all of you here? Why would you set up hiding so close to these Aprons?"

"We came to draw straws," said Robin.

"Draw straws?"

"Give Zoroaster a sacrifice."

The facts hit Ransom between the eyes like a blow from Muldoon's sap. "Are you kids crazy?"

"If our gang gives up one member," said Robin, "then . . . well then Zoroaster and Bloody Mary will leave us alone."

Pagan shit, Ransom thought but said, "I see, and this was your idea, King Robin?"

"Actually it was Audra's idea. I just put it in motion."

"Hmmm . . . and where is Audra?"

"She's a crybaby, so I sent her away."

"Banished her? Isn't that kinda like a death sentence these days?"

"She's always moping around and crying; got on everyone's nerves."

Ransom considered this. Any show of weakness and you were reprimanded, and if it persisted, you were cut loose by King and Court. He dropped it, asking, "So who drew the short straw?"

"I did," said Samuel, holding it up to the light.

"What? Wait . . . hold on. I didn't know you belonged to this band, Sam."

"I joined for safety. Just two days ago."

"Hmmm . . . some irony, then, the newest member of the group drawing that straw." Ransom knew the truth of it. They recruited Sam for this purpose, and Robin had seen to it that Sam got the short straw. It was about that time that Samuel had somehow bought some time and gone hunting for Alastair.

"OK, Sam, let's go meet your fate, the two of us together along with Blue."

"Blue?" asked Sam.

Alastair displayed his blue steel weapon. "I got it from the Blue Lady," he lied.

Alastair pushed ahead of Sam and Robin's band, telling them to hang back. As he moved from the fire, the darkness ahead of Alastair was near complete, only a small slither of light filtering from somewhere above at street level.

"Blood Mary's coming for us!" shouted one of the kids in blackness.

"You gotta hide me, copper! Else I'm dead like Danielle!" shouted Noel in tears. King Robin was also now blubbering, terrified and hanging back near the fire. He'd seen what they'd done to Danielle, so Ransom could hardly blame him for blubbering, but arranging for Sam to go in as his goat, this was indefensible. "Zoroaster is gonna do me next!" Robin shouted.

The youngest of them, his face streaked with tears, shouted out now. "Don't let Bloody Mary get us!"

The lanky, older boy named Hector added, "She's killing us one by one until there are no more children left in the world, so all humankind will die off! That's her plan."

Alastair rushed toward the end of the tunnel where the so-called Apron gang were supposedly this moment assembled, awaiting the sacrificial lamb—Samuel. They would get Ransom instead.

Alastair half expected to be set upon by this gang awaiting him, and he pictured the poor abducted ones who'd vanished as having been attacked by a knife-wielding gang of murderous cultists. This made sense and fit with what Dr. Christian Fenger's autopsy had supported. This could well be the end of the investigation. He knew these killers, whatever age, to be dangerous and well trained in wielding cleavers and knives. He recalled the "animals" he'd seen in the park after talking to Sara.

"Hang back, Sam," he told the boy, but Samuel now displayed a bowie knife all his own, almost the size of his leg. The thing shone like ice in the darkness here, and in a mo-

ment of fright, Alastair wondered if the boy might not be
one of *them*—one of the killing gang.

"I'll not go down without a fight," Sam whispered, "and
I'll not let you go it alone, Inspector."

Ransom looked anew at the boy, studying Sam's eyes and
finding truth there; a feeling of pride for the boy welled up.
"If ever had I a son, Sam . . . I'd have wanted him to be as
brave as you."

Sam choked out, "Thank you, sir."

They moved on, inching forward.

Knives could come flying at them at any moment from
any number of directions. Ransom extended his blue burnished .38 and was about to fire on seeing a large figure of a
man in a group ahead bathed in weak light. Alastair's night
vision had cleared, and he recognized faces. The faces of
Danielle's followers, the one's who'd gone into hiding on
learning of her murder. None of them were holding knives
so far as Alastair could see.

Some eleven children had followed the paths to here in
their effort to locate a safe place in the city. Learning it'd
been their leader—their queen—who'd been brutally murdered, they hadn't time to grieve when fear had gripped
them.

He put his gun away, making a show of it, realizing the
large shadow he'd seen earlier had merely been a projection
of the huddled group. "I've come to find you all," he lied.
"Come to take you to a safe house."

One of the children grabbed hold of his huge leg and held
on, and Alastair could feel the shivering little body against
him. Like a modern retelling of the Pied Piper, all the others, like so many mice, scampered to the Bear and hung on.
Sam stood back, put his knife away, and shook his head.

Alastair began guiding them from the underworld with
a mantra: "I gotcha . . . you're going to be all right . . . all
right . . . all right."

* * *

Alastair felt like Moses at having led the children and frightened young adults who wished to follow from the underground area around Wacker and Michigan. It had taken him another twenty-four hours to find places for them all. Most every shelter in the city was full to capacity. No one wanted to be on the streets with this madman on the loose, including homeless adults. So the Salvation Army and what few shelters existed bulged and were turning people away. Ransom had learned that Robin had led his followers out of Hull House, but these kids before him now had been Danielle's followers. Without a leader, they'd stay put.

Ransom wound up accommodating his more adult charges like Robin at the Des Plaines lockup, called the Bridewell, an old English term meaning that the man locked up here was well shackled to this bride. The jails were, as usual, jam-packed as well, every inch of stone floor covered in a sea of bodies where they slept, but there were the stairwells and hallways. Even City Hall was full with the indigent, the homeless, and the runaways.

Once he had settled all his charges, he realized that Samuel had simply disappeared again and no telling where. No one had seen him go.

Later, arriving home, Alastair found Sam on his doorstep, tearful and pleading to be taken in.

Alastair could not turn the boy away, and so he found a pillow and blanket and put him on his settee for the night. Sam's information had been wrong, and it had almost cost lives, had almost ended horribly in fact, had Alastair used his weapon down in that dungeon. Such an accident, involving the death of children, would most assuredly have given Chief Nathan Kohler all the ammunition he needed to end Alastair's career in Chicago. Sure it was an error, a serious one for a paid informant to make, but Sam was, after all, just a boy. Alastair had forgiven him, but the boy fell asleep blubbering apologies.

Asleep, he looked the angel indeed, Alastair thought, and his cherubic features made Alastair wonder anew over the various interpretations of the "Angels' War" and the where-abouts of little Audra about now.

The following morning, Sam had gone before Alastair rose from bed. "Vanished of his own accord," Alastair mumbled when someone banged loudly at his door.

He stumbled to the source and opened it wide, shading his eyes from a bright sunlit morning. Philo stormed past and into the room.

"Alastair, they've made an arrest in the Leather Apron killings."

"When will people stop calling it that? And who have they arrested?"

"That old crone, Bloody Mary!"

"Indeed . . . does not surprise me. In fact, it follows . . . as inevitable as the sun coming up and the moon going down."

"But in either case, the sun does not actually come up and the moon does not actually go down; science has *us* going up and down, or rather around, spinning through the cosmos, so it only looks to our limited perspective—"

"All right, I get it." Ransom covered his ears in a mocking gesture.

"Still, your point is well taken. Bloody Mary may well be a scapegoat in all this."

"To be sure, she may know *something,* but she's batty, and besides that, she has been here since the first brick was laid so—"

"So why now does she suddenly become a menace? Good question, one I'm sure that Chief Kohler is *not* asking."

"Kohler is behind the arrest?" Alastair was instantly alert.

"Well . . . actually it was your friends, Logan and Behan, who dragged her in kicking and screaming, I'm told."

"I don't envy them their duty, and I know those men well . . . well enough to realize it was not their idea."

"A smokescreen? A bone to throw press and public?"

"To make it appear we are hot on the trail of Leather Apron, would be my guess."

"What will you do, Alastair? How can you stop this maniac with so many obstacles thrown in your path, and . . . and with your hands continually tied behind your back by bureaucratic fools like—"

"Please, Philo!" he stopped him with an upraised hand. "Allow me to dress. Sit, listen to music, be patient."

"Of course, of course."

Alastair felt an attack coming on and tried to determine which sort of attack it might be; it felt more like panic than pain, so he decided it was withdrawal pains as he had abstained from any morphine or opium for the past two days while chasing leads, and with the boy in his home the night before, he'd opted to remain sober, although he'd dosed himself the night before with quinine and antimony to fend off a threatening fever.

"While I dress," he called over his shoulder, "tell me, how is your photographic study of the street children coming along?"

"Not well!" Philo's pent up energy kept pace with Alastair, and he stood at his bedroom door now. "Too many paying jobs ahead of it, I'm afraid. Matter of finding time. But Alastair, there is something I brought to show you. It struck me anew when I'd returned to the notion of doing such an exhibit."

"Oh? And what is that?" Alastair had reemerged with most of his clothes intact but buttons yet in need of latching, tie dangling over his shoulder, shoes in hand.

"Well, have a look." Philo laid out a large photo that was grim and peculiar, and beautifully rendered.

Ransom gasped at the sight of a family in a smoky fog standing in an alley entranceway—all sullen-eyed, sunken-featured, gaunt, and looking like a family of starved wolves. It was a heart-wrenching shot, this "cut" of Keane's, tearing at the soul until you looked more closely.

Mother held an infant in her arms while three others,

ranging in ages that appeared between four and eleven, hung on to her dress, save the older boy who stood opposite, alongside his father. The older boy held a dead cat by the tail, a curled smile on his lips. In his other hand, he held a deboning knife. On closer inspection, the father, too had a blade in a scabbard protruding from beneath his moth-eaten coat.

"The happy family," said Philo in dark jest. "Something about the whole picture is horribly disturbing, in light of developments."

"Funny thing is . . . last night, I was stalking what I have become convinced is our killer—a family described to me just like this—but a family of cannibalistic butchers."

"Too hideous to contemplate."

"And so long as it is not contemplated, evil triumphs, Philo."

"Agreed. And so it goes among us invisible, as the Phantom so recently proved."

"Invisibility is effective."

Philo nodded. "Requiring only our complacency."

"Look, I must get down to the station house, see what Logan and Behan are up to, and if I feel I can trust them, I'll share your photo and my new theory with them, and we can all proceed from there."

"Understood. The photo is yours to do with as needed, my friend."

Alastair snapped the last of his shoe buttons in place, stood and made for the door, where he grabbed his cane. "Good day, Philo."

"Alastair!" The tone of Philo's voice stopped him at the door.

"What is it?"

"Be . . . be careful out there!"

Alastair breathed deeply, tipped his hat, and replied, "Always . . . always," as he ushered Philo out and bid him a final adieu.

CHAPTER 16

Alastair made all due haste to the Des Plaines station house where he assumed Bloody Mary was being held, but once there, he learned that she was already being arraigned before Judge Grimes. He spoke to the desk sergeant, discovering that Logan and Behan were at the arraignment. He rushed to join them.

A large crowd had gathered outside the courthouse downtown, and feelings were running high. Most assuredly, the old crone was being thrown to the proverbial dogs, Alastair reasoned, as Chief Kohler *most assuredly* would've secreted her off to Senator Chapman's farmstead outside the city for the reward if he *really* thought her in any way guilty or implicated in the death of Anne Chapman.

Hooting and cheers and "atta-boy"'s trailed Alastair all the way up the steps through the crowd. On the inside, he went for Judge Grimes's courtroom. He quietly pushed through a door on hearing Bloody Mary cursing at the beefy, morose Judge Grimes.

Ransom immediately recognized the tall, stoop-shouldered, scraggly-haired, wild-eyed, feral looking woman who could easily pass for a stevedore down at the wharves. Bloody Mary was being gaveled down by the judge, and she suddenly fell silent, her curses on judge and court at an abrupt end; and so fascinated had she become with the judge's pounding gavel, which sounded like a series of angry gunshots. Grunting and cursing under her breath in animal fashion, her gaze taking in everything while in a pretense of blindness, drool came over her lips in globs that fell to the floor or splatted onto her curled, aged shoes.

Alastair noticed Behan and Logan sitting up front. The two looked as if they'd had a rough night's sleep, their clothes filthy, hair wild, but Alastair knew the cause: transporting Mary.

Alastair found a wall and leaned against it, watching, listening, and realizing here was a woman who represented everything that the city leaders and merchants most loathed and feared. She was a walking billboard for the underbelly of the city, and she lived by instinct alone.

Bloody Mary, under the harsh courtroom lights, was as out of place as any fish tossed ashore or any bird with a hole in its wing.

Ransom felt a wave of empathy and sadness wash over him for the ugly old woman—the penultimate outcast—the social excommunicant.

The judge held a handkerchief over his nose, so rancid was the odor rising off Mary. Keeping a safe distance from the accused, Grimes asked his bailiff to escort her to Room 148.

Her hands were cuffed to chains attached to ankle bracelets, all of it rattling like ship's rigging as she stomped, heavy footed, from the room, head slumped forward like some new species of captive animal with a strange curve to its spine, a species yet to be given a name. As she filed past, Alastair's eyes met hers, but there was no light and no recognition there. Only an emptiness.

Her chains rattled along the floor all the way through the door, the sound like sandpaper over the spine.

"It may well be a dead end," said Behan who, on seeing Alastair enter, had joined him at the rear.

Logan came next, adding, "But we won't know that till we get'er talking and to trust us—now will we?"

"I got an instinct about her," Ransom replied.

"We all know she's addled in the head."

"Exactly, so . . ."

"So what, Rance?"

"Damn it, man, so how can we trust a word she tells us?"

Behan raised his hands. "We'll never know unless she opens up."

"So I say we 'open' her head for her," joked Logan, deadpan.

Behan put in, "You can wait outside if you wish."

"I'm in the room for as long as I can stand it," Ransom said.

They located 148.

"We hadda wrestle her in cuffs and chains, and I can tell you," said Behan, "it was no fun."

"The woman needs a good delousing and bathing," said Logan.

"You two can draws straws, but I'm outta that one," said Ransom.

A light laugh accompanied the three of them into 148. Once inside, and with the bailiff stepping out, Behan sat across the table from Bloody Mary. He introduced himself with his title, and added, "And you know Inspector Logan and everyone knows Inspector Ransom."

Ransom remained standing and imposing nearby, nodding perfunctorily when introduced.

"Aye, the Big Bear they call 'im these days."

"Mary and me," began Ransom, "we go way back, don't we, my lovely girl?"

"I need my medicines," the woman replied. "Did yous two bring me my mendications? I got a magic blanket, you know, one I can spread out on command and ask it to fly. A flying carpet. Give it to you for some medicines. You want my magic blanket?"

"Mary, we're not interested in magic or bloody flying

carpets." Alastair held a handkerchief over his nose. "We've come to ask you questions." The odor exuding off the woman was preternaturally powerful. Something akin to a fetid over-ripe melon. If there was such a thing, Bloody Mary seemed a walking candidate for spontaneous human combustion.

"Finally, somebody wants me for something," she pathetically replied.

Behan stalwartly held his own against the assault on his senses from this homeless wretch. The judge had been right. Even cleaned up, her skin appeared dusky and covered with a gray patina. She appeared Spanish or Black or a mix of both, but it was impossible to say with any certainty. Her accent sounded Mexican.

"Let's make a deal." A mantra for her. "Let's make a deal. Anything you want," she toothlessly muttered and spread her legs as far as her ankle chains allowed. "Let's deal. I'll take care-a-all three of yous!"

Obviously, she'd fallen back on her usual method of relating to men. "Look at her teeth," said Ransom.

"God save us," muttered Behan.

Logan joked, "You want some time alone with her, Ken?"

"Let's make a deal," she repeated.

"Mary . . . we *do not* want a magic carpet ride," Ransom assured her.

"What teeth are you talking about, Rance?" asked Behan, talking over him. "She's got none."

"That's just the point. If she did barter with this Leather Apron devil in these vanishings, what did he pay her? She have any cash on her?"

"Not a nickel."

"And boys, I tell ya, she wasn't tearing at human flesh, not with her gums, so what motive has she?"

Twenty minutes and they learned nothing from Mary. She kept wanting to talk about an amusement park and a ride she had once taken, presumably as a child, deep in the bowels of a haunted castle. Then she slipped back into barter mode, her eyes lighting up with a cackling laugh. All her words came out of her toothless, cryptlike mouth along with spittle and froth that both sickened and amazed the three Chicago inspectors.

Finally, unable to take her voice—like a nail through the head, or her stench—like a spike of sewage through each nostril, or her frothy mouth—like a rabid dog—Behan pleaded that Alastair take over.

"There's nothing but mayhem inside your head, right, Mary? You don't know why you're here, do you, Mary?" asked Alastair, replacing Behan at the "front." "If she knows anything at all," he said to Logan and Behan, "about the Vanishings, she's likely forgotten it. Or it's locked away in her sponge." Alastair indicated his head.

But Mary exploded at the word Vanishings. "It's the work of the Anti-Christ himself! Nothing I had a hand in; nothing I could do anything about."

"Where do I find this Anti-Christ, Mary? Where?"

"Under the water . . . under the lake, under the fair."

"Under the fire?"

"Fair . . . I said fair! Under the bleedin' fair!"

"Now we know for sure she's batty," said Logan.

"I already knew that before you two nabbed her." Alastair turned his attention back to Mary. "Is there anything else you wish to tell us, Mary?"

"No."

"Nothing you wish to say in your defense?"

"No."

"What's your real name, Mary?"

She stared at him but said nothing.

"Your secret name?"

"I'll not tell."

"Is it full of Grace, as in Hail Mary, full of Grace?"

"I am full of Grace. My name . . . my real name is Grace. Grace Sheffield, originally from Shrewsbury, England."

Ransom jotted this down. He'd recalled it from arrests ten years prior.

"Whatya doing with that?" she asked, fixated on the moving pen over the notepad.

"Just going to check to see if it's true."

"Ohhh . . .'tis true enough."

Alastair stood and slipped from the room, the other two inspectors doing likewise. Outside, they began a group coughing-sneezing-hacking-snorting jag, filling their white handkerchiefs with the result of their combined interrogation.

Alastair said, "I believe she's a dead end, and that we're railroading a mindless old crone."

Behan shrugged, his mustache bobbing with his tie. "We're just following orders."

Frustrated, Logan blurted out, "We oughta take a g'damn club to the old witch and beat it outta her."

"That kinda talk in the face of what you just saw in there? Now, I can just imagine where the orders came from, but fellas, this old girl . . . she's got nothing but loose marbles and bird fodder for brains."

From where they stood out in the hallway, they heard Mary being Bloody Mary, shouting lunacies at some invisible demons in her head and inside Room 148. "My goddamn real name is Grace! You know 'cause I have a friend who digs earthworms in the cemetery! She ties 'em tail to head, head to tail and makes jewelry outta worms—living worms! Living jewelry! Says it's eatable jewels and the idea will sell in the thousands! Won't make her any less mad, but it will make her rich and mad! But she damn well ate 'em all! Now that's sick! Her name is Grace, but she's got none! Same as me. I had an accident with her, an accident with Grace . . . just like she had an accident with me. Her accident with Grace was with me!"

"The woman is battling the DTs," declared Ransom. "She's sick in too many ways to count—not unlike the charge brought against her."

Even as he said this, Alastair thought, *How fitting that she, like the Mother of God—according to the street children—had fallen so far from "Grace"* . . . Perhaps there was some small truth in the street beliefs after all. But it all seemed so tenuous.

Behan and Logan reluctantly followed Alastair back into 148, returning to the scolding Bloody Mary in her chains. Alastair asked, "When you were Grace, Mary, did you ever have a child?"

"Yes . . . yes, several."

"Whatever happened to your children?"

"Dead, all dead."

"All dead?"

"Cruel world."

"Not one survived?"

"Well . . . all that I knew of."

"Meaning?"

She began crying. " 'Cept one I left with the sisters."

"The sisters? What sisters?"

"The Sisters of the Holy Cross Convent."

"On South Michigan Avenue?"

"Yes, but Grace was just a child then."

"And how old would your son be today if alive?"

"I dunno. How should I know? Can't keep my head round numbers."

"Take a wild guess then."

" 'B-bout your age, I suspect."

"*Ahhh* . . . and have you seen him, Mary Grace, recently?"

She thought long and hard on this. "No . . . not 'im . . . that could not be *him*. Not that evil thing!"

"The street children say that you're the mother of Zoroaster's child. Any truth to it, Mary Grace?"

She smiled wide at this. "If I spawned a demon from me womb . . . I'm penitent sorry." A smirk on her face said otherwise. "And I've asked God's blessin' and forgiveness at the church's back door, 'cause the likes of *you* won't have me come through the *front*! And as I've God's forgiveness, I don't need none from murderers like *you*!"

"Well now, Mary, now we know where you stand," Logan said and chuckled.

"Don't hold back," added Behan.

But Alastair was intrigued by this and the image of her at the back door of a church, perhaps the same as Samuel had said where holy water was being sold; he imagined the same fellow could sell forgiveness to a fallen angel such as Mary Grace for the right price as well. He'd filed this away for a time when he could visit St. Alexis. Have a chat with the priests there. But for now, he wondered what connection Bloody Mary had with this man the children called Zoroaster—or the son of Zoroaster—and whether he was her son or not, and then she'd have motive . . . *if* she believed Leather Apron was indeed her son.

Alastair needed a clear idea who this mystery man and his mystery family might be, and what proof he'd used to convince Mary that he was in fact her evil spawn. Or was it all a fiction from her addled mind, a cunning one to create and build her own dangerous reputation, to ward off evil befalling her? Who in his right mind, man, woman or child would attack Satan's mother?

Alastair now manipulated the other two inspectors from the room without the least difficulty before he showed Mary the photo that he'd been given by Philo Keane that morning. He must assume either Behan or Logan or both were working in consort with Nathan Kohler.

When he laid the photo before Bloody Mary, she gasped and said, "How? How did you get the demon and his demon brood and his damned wife in a picture?"

"Have you seen your grandchildren, Mary Grace?"

"I . . . he said he was my son . . . that he'd been born of Satan, and that his offspring were the grandsons of Satan, and that I laid with Satan to begin the bloodline between human and Devil."

"And you've told children this?"

"They need to know. It's the truth. Only the strongest survive."

"And this man in the photograph, is he familiar to you?"

She near gasped and her eyes widened, but she immediately controlled herself. "Who is he?"

"Mary Grace, if he is Leather Apron, he is the one behind the Vanishings?"

"What do I get if I tell you?"

He promised her a warm, dry place with daily meals and a bed. He made it sound heavenly.

Finally, she said, "He is my lost son, yes, but he's not the only Leather Apron."

"Who then is his accomplice?"

She pointed at the woman in the photo and said, "She— his wifey."

"Really?"

"And them others."

"Others?"

"In the picture. The children. They're all Aprons, all meat eaters, trained to it. The Devil's own child and grandchildren're this brood, and I pleaded with Danielle to stay away from 'em."

"Where are they now, Mary Grace?"

"Like I told you, under the parks and under the water! They come up through the ground and sometimes through the bloody lake and the river."

He gave up, calling in Behan and Logan to take her to Cook County and turn her over to Christian Fenger.

"But what'll Chief Kohler say?" asked Logan.

"Put it on me, boys. The woman is too far gone to organize a single planned abduction and murder, much less a series of disappearances and butcherings."

Logan and Behan looked from Alastair to one another again. Finally, Ransom said, "Concentrate on it, boys. Mull it over as you make your way to Cook County, where this woman's to be committed."

"You know what a pain in the ass it was to get her here?"

Behan added, "What about Judge Grimes?"

"He will bless you. Now find a phone and call for Shanks

and Gwinn to come get her. Those boys know how to deal with troublesome types." Alastair laughed. "Hell, they transported me once in that meat wagon of theirs."

"Yeah, when you were half dead." The three laughed together.

"Fools rush in where wise men . . . well the truly wise would not go near that old bat," said Behan.

"For a price, Shanks and Gwinn will get her to the asylum."

"You think she'll be better off in that snake pit?"

"No, but she will be off the streets, and there are far more people living on the streets in needless fear of her than you can count, among them children. And if returned to the street, she'll wind up another Timothy Crutcheon or worse."

"Do you think her in any way complicit in the murders, Rance?" asked Logan.

"Something strange connects her to all this, to the children, to the killings, to the killer, I suspect, but exactly what . . . who can say?" lied Ransom.

"Yeah, just can't put a finger on it, right?" Logan winked as if a conspirator.

"But it's inside her, right?" added Behan.

Alastair thought about this long. "Yes, but so deeply locked away inside that lunatic brain, inside one of her personalities, that it's useless, lads."

"I got no sense of that whatsoever," Logan sarcastically replied. "Guess that's what makes you Alastair Ransom, heh?"

Behan agreed, "Yeah, all I got was a morass of meaningless gibberish going on at all times."

"Yeah . . . kinda sad, really," agreed Logan. "Hell, at some time she might've been someone's mum and maybe human."

Ransom nodded. "Some sort of odd continuous parade of lost memories and a head full of confusing voices, lads. She definitely marches to a different drum."

"Surprise is she's not marched off into Lake Michigan to end it all," said Behan.

"'Nough bodies out that way already, heh, Alastair?" Logan's remark was meant to say that he knew where at least one body was buried.

Alastair ignored the remark, however, saying, "Let's do the right thing by Grace, gentlemen."

"And that would be to shoot her?" asked Logan, causing Behan to erupt in laughter.

"No, that being treat her as you might your own mum if she were out of her head."

Behan frowned and nodded, while Logan said, "That'll never come to pass. My mother's as sharp as tacks."

Ransom gave them a cold stare. It was enough to send them off in search of a government phone to call in Shanks and Gwinn.

The following day

Jane Francis had come to Cook County in search of Dr. Fenger, and she had not come as Dr. Tewes but herself. She had come to learn his feeling about something she'd discovered only this morning, that the woman arrested as Leather Apron—Bloody Mary—had been sent to Cook County Asylum, where she supposedly had been admitted against her will. From what Jane could piece together, the lunatic fought her "captors" the entire way and that she had bitten one of the ambulance men, Shanks, in his shank, and that she'd somehow, while yet shackled, bloodied Gwinn's nose. She'd screamed that they had attempted to rape and kill her. Shanks and Gwinn denied they did anything whatsoever untoward, but rather had to restrain her, and in that attempt, she became even more violent.

Jane believed that Alastair, from his account of having faced down Bloody Mary at the courthouse, had been premature in shipping her off to a cell at the asylum. She believed that with careful probing—after winning the confidence of the woman—the aged woman might lead them to some clues to the Vanishings.

For this reason she'd not come as a man, as Dr. Tewes, but rather as Dr. Jane Francis, to ask her good friend and confidant, Dr. Fenger, if she could interview the so-called madwoman. All of the children spoke of Bloody Mary's being an accomplice, somehow connected to these horrendous crimes, that she perhaps procured for the killer, and yet Alastair had shrugged off any part she might play in this horrific opera, having made a medieval diagnosis about her sanity. "Insane people can be as immoral and as wicked as sane people, Alastair!" she had shouted at him when he made the ridiculous statement that the woman was too mad to be of any real danger. "And since when did you become a medical expert?"

Alastair had telephoned her from his home the night before, telling her of his day, and she'd informed him of how she and Gabby had gone again among the shelter children to gather more information. He'd then pleaded with her to not place herself and Gabby in danger, and next he mentioned the arrest and release of Bloody Mary as an afterthought. His cavalier remarks about having made the decision to institutionalize the suspect had set her off.

So now here she was, hoping that Christian Fenger would allow her an audience with the woman. Perhaps she could speak to this Bloody Mary woman-to-woman, to appeal to whatever motherly and natural impulses and instincts might be buried below her outward appearance and behavior.

Jane now rushed down the corridor, going for the stairwell and Christian—no doubt in his morgue below—when she heard the irritating voice of Dr. Caine McKinnette, whose reputation, so far as Jane believed, was unfounded. McKinnette represented the old guard who still believed in bleeding his patients, and still believed that all disease rested in the bloodstream. She heard McKinnette tell a nurse to call him when his patient died so that he could fill out the death certificate and in essence be done with the woman in the bed before him.

Unlike Christian Fenger, Dr. McKinnette did not know Jane; he only knew Dr. James Phineas Tewes, with whom McKinnette had shared ale and spoke on occasion. They had both been involved to some degree in saving Alastair Ransom's life from a bullet wound. McKinnette seemed to have somehow weaseled his way into Cook County as something other than an anesthesiologist and pill pusher, so that he was now overseeing the last breath of a dying patient. *How unfortunate for the patient,* Jane thought.

Jane knew she should leave it alone and go on her way. After all, she had her hands full as it were. But on seeing McKinnette disappear down the hall, something made her turn and walk into the patient's room. She entered quietly and nodded to the nurse, who hand-cranked the dying woman's bed to flatten it. The nurse assumed Jane to be a relative, so she ducked out to give Jane a moment with her loved one. No words passed between them.

Jane immediately checked the woman's medical chart, and she took a pulse at the throat. Yes, the patient was dying. But Jane felt a hand grasp hers as she took the pulse. The woman on the bed, a gray wire-haired lady with a face ashen as stone and etched with wrinkles named Eloise Howe, was desperate to communicate. Jane saw it in her weak eyes, and she felt it in Eloise's weak but persistent grip.

The strength in her touch told Jane that while she was weak, Eloise wanted a fight; she was not ready to give up, and Jane believed with proper treatment, Eloise could be turned around.

Jane pulled forth one of Dr. Tewes's cigars from her bag, lit it, and used it to burn off the leeches that Dr. McKinnette had placed on Eloise at incisions he had made in the woman. She began to administer other means to help the woman. She did so quietly and as nurses changed bed sheets and replaced water, she engaged them and found that the nurses disagreed in whispering voices with Dr. McKinnette and his care of this woman from the beginning. In fact, one went so far as to say that she felt the old doctor had caused more harm than good, saying that the woman had declined rapidly once he'd taken over her case.

"She was found on the street, passed out, brought in a week ago. She had fainted from lack of nourishment. Dr. McKinnette began treating her immediately as a dying cause."

Two days later and Jane had still not gotten around to Bloody Mary, but as the woman was in the asylum ward, she was going nowhere, and Jane had come to believe she could save a life here at Cook County.

Still, the nurses, assumed Jane a family member or dear friend, and she did not dissuade the notion. Two days and no more response but rather a comatose state had come over the elderly patient.

McKinnette did not once check his own steps, even down to a look at his damnable leeches. He claimed that his patient's mind was gone, that she was brain dead and would never recover herself again. He spoke of it as a matter of time, and he remarked that had he a race horse or a pet in the same condition, that he would put it out of its misery. It was an undisguised invitation to any nurse who wanted to do both patient and doctor a favor to "take action" on behalf of mercy.

Meanwhile, Dr. McKinnette was told that Jane had sat with the supposed brain dead, had talked nonstop to the patient, holding her hand. Jane's instinct told her this woman was not ready to go, that she had unfinished business, and Jane always went with her first instinct. After much frustration even with Christian Fenger, who Jane had brought to Eloise to show him that she was not only out of coma, but lucid—talking and touching Jane—and that Eloise had started to open her eyes and was trying to focus on Jane when Dr. Fenger had entered in the room. Christian, who'd been monitoring the situation and who'd had a shouting match with McKinnette in his office over his arcane practices, his esoteric handwriting, and his ill-treatment of this patient, was amazed at what Jane had accomplished. After a lot of aggressive therapies and ideas, Jane had talked them into pulling McKinnette off the case and allowing Dr. Tewes to come in and work with Eloise, calling Tewes a homeopathic healer as well as a phrenologist and magnetic healer.

Jane as Tewes combated dangerous infection created by McKinnette's sloppiness. Tewes was soon credited with what Jane had accomplished, getting Eloise's breathing to slow with thirty-minute hourly suctioning. When Jane as Tewes left Eloise, the elderly woman insisted on a hug, and she squeezed her with some strength in her arms, and she could keep her eyes open for a long period, and her gag reflex was good, and she responded well to Tewes's voice. She also exhibited a normal pain response. She wanted to know where that sweet woman—a nurse, she believed—had disappeared to. Dr. Fenger was amazed at the stark difference between McKinnette's patient and Jane's patient at this point. He walked with her outside and in the hallway, he shook her hand and praised her skills, drawing stares.

"So fire the quack and hire Dr. Jane Francis, then, Christian."

"I am going to work on it."

"And how long will that take?"

"There are bridges yet to build, but I am going to build them."

They stood staring at one another, she in men's clothing, he in his smeared white frock. Around them Cook County hospital was alive with activity.

"You saved that woman from a certain death."

"I've seen this before—too often—but I had a feeling from the first touch between us that I could help Eloise far, far better than Caine McKinnette."

"But how did you know you could bring the woman back?"

"Initially, I didn't, but I knew that I wouldn't turn over my dog to McKinnette and his leeches." She thought a moment. "But honestly, I had hope and she knew that, and so together she and I guided Eloise back."

"You should go home. Get some rest."

"No . . . not just yet, Christian. I want to talk to that woman they call Bloody Mary who's here in your asylum, but I want to do it as a woman, not as Tewes. Can I change in your office?"

"Jane, Bloody Mary is no longer here."

"No longer here?"

"She was discharged."

"I don't understand. How?"

"She has been in before, Jane, and no one . . . no one here can deal with her."

"Meaning?"

"She literally bites, kicks, and fistfights the staff and other patients. Furthermore, she refuses help and thinks we're trying to poison her."

"Isn't that what an asylum is for? People with delusions?"

"There is no cure for her madness, and I refuse to operate on the insane. It's against my principles."

"Agreed. Enough experimental surgery on the insane." She paced. "So you simply release a so-called lunatic and murder suspect to the streets?"

"She was not charged with any crime. Besides, according to her primary physician, she refused help, she attacked other inmates, and she made a habit of biting everyone."

"Let me guess—McKinnette!"

"Yes, you have me there."

"Damn, damn, damn, Christian, what hold does that man have on you?"

"I don't know what you're talking about, hold. He works for the hospital."

"Only so long as you suffer him! When is Cook County going to get it right?"

"Easy now, Jane!"

"I'd bite that man, myself! It's ridiculous to put such a

man in the care of the mentally diseased. Why not hire some good people in pathological conditions of the mind."

"Like you?"

"Yes, like me!" Jane let out a gasp. "I cannot believe you released that woman back onto the streets."

"She was put on a train bound for family we found in Iowa."

"Really?" Jane watched his eyes and body for any sign of chicanery, unhappy that they had arrived at this juncture. "Please tell me you didn't turn her over to Kohler and Chapman, Christian."

"I did nothing of the kind. I opted out of the whole entire business days ago. Afraid I still have a conscience."

She saw no reason to doubt him. "You're the better man for it, dear Christian."

"Yes, really very little call for that sort of thing nowadays, however . . ."

Jane decided there was no help for it. She went home with a splitting headache to be with Gabby and to find some corner of peace. Once home, Gabby found her agitated, and she became worried in turn, making her mother undress and go to bed to fend off any worse headache.

The following morning

"Hold on! Are you telling me that Christian just let her go?" asked Alastair at the kitchen table where this morning he'd joined Jane and Gabby for breakfast. "I tell you, the woman is absolutely daft and belongs in a place where she can do no harm either to herself or others."

"Apparently, she does only that—harm others," countered Jane. "Besides, you didn't charge her with any crime," countered Jane. As Christian wasn't here to defend himself, Jane took his side.

"She sounds perfectly dreadful," added Gabby, pouring more coffee into each cup.

Alastair's expression changed from one of surprise at Christian's letting the woman walk to one of shock, horror even. "My God, he's turned her over to Kohler, who has in turn—"

"Whatever do you mean?" asked Jane, confused. "No, no, you see Christian assured me that he'd have no part in this business between Nathan Kohler and Chapman, Alastair."

"So he's told you, and you believe him?"

"I do."

"She's been put on a train according to records. Bound for Iowa."

"Not simply turned back out on the streets, as I was told by Shanks and Gwinn when I went asking?"

"No, nor given over to Chief Kohler, Alastair."

"Is that what you fear?" asked Gabby.

Alastair rushed from the room as best he could with his stiff leg and cane, fighting to exit the door, the ladies on his heels. He was stopped when Jane shouted for him to explain.

"I must go and go now!" he replied, tearing the door from her hand and clamoring out onto the porch in the morning sunlight. He immediately shouted for a passing cab with a frightened couple inside as this bear of a man descended on their carriage. The man inside shouted for the driver to pull off and do it immediately even as Alastair waved down the driver. "Halt in the name of the law!"

The hansom coach stopped, the two horses lifting on hindlegs, fearful. As Ransom ordered everyone out, saying the cab was commandeered in the name of the Chicago Police Department, Jane shouted, "I am going with you, Alastair!"

"This will not be pleasant, Jane," he firmly said, shaking his head.

"Since when did you begin treating me as if I am some shrinking violet?"

"I haven't time to argue with her, Gabby! You do it!" he

was half in the cab, half out on the running board when he shouted to the driver, "The Chapman estate north of the city, my good man, and make haste!"

"Haste, sir?"

"All due haste, yes! Time is of the essence!"

The smile on the face of the horseman presaged his pleasure at opening up his team of horses from here to Evanston, Illinois.

Jane leapt in after Ransom and from the window, she shouted to Gabby, "Don't forget the roast I put in the oven, dear!"

Gabby stared after the dust cloud crafted of debris as the hansom lifted a whirlwind in its wake, the pair of horses pulling it thundering down the dust-laden street for the northern farms region where the wealthy Chapman family lived.

Inside the cab, Jane clung to Alastair where he sat braced with his cane as the coach squealed, its shocks bouncing, wheels revolving below them at an alarming rate, whip snapping, horses crying out in hysteria and bolting along, controlled only by the skill of the hackman.

Alastair pulled Jane Francis close to him and held her firmly against the mad rocking carriage interior.

"You could have at least warned me!" she shouted over the roar, deafening inside the cab, of frenetic hooves over stone. "My God, Alastair! Even on the Ferris wheel at the fair they're smart enough to give you a bar to hold on to."

"There wasn't time and is no time now, Jane! Christ, I should've seen this coming! Fool! But I know where they've taken Mary Grace, and it is not to a good end!"

"What're you saying?"

"Chapman will kill her if she does not talk."

"Chapman? Kill? Talk?"

"Chapman will gouge it out of her one way or another who Leather Apron "could be," and she will confess after a little pain, and for all I know, they've cornered a suspect and have drawn and quartered him by now."

"Who are *they*?"

"Chapman, Kohler, Fenger."

"Fenger? No! He would not be party to such—"

"Barbarity?"

"Yes, barbarity."

"Perhaps he has no idea the extent to which men like Kohler and Chapman will go to get what they want out of a suspect or a material witness."

"I've heard that you've interrogated suspects into the grave."

This momentarily silenced him. "Not you, too, and not now."

"Will you then please tell me what you know of this conspiracy between Christian and the other two. The details?" She wanted to hear it from him.

"If you've the stomach for it."

"I have."

He told her the whole sordid tale of how Kohler and Christian had cornered him in Nathan's office with Chapman, and how much money was involved, and how Christian saw it as his last chance to end his debts and his talk of a new wing on the hospital. The story fit with what Christian had relayed earlier.

"When he asked for my help, Christian didn't tell me the entire truth, and together, we led them to Bloody Mary, didn't we?"

"None of this is your fault, Jane. Truth be told, Christian is, while shrewd in his field, naive about men."

"Naive like me? Naive in what way?"

"In how men of power operate. Jane, I once witnessed Nathan Kohler burn a man alive while the poor devil was strapped to a chair."

"I've heard the same story told of you, Alastair."

"Which story is the more comfortable fit? I was there. I couldn't stop it, but I didn't throw the match. Nathan did."

"Jane shivered at these revelations. All well and true, I'm sure of the other two, but I can't believe it of Christian."

"He rammed his shiny new wolf's-head cane into the top of the cab, beating out a code to the driver that said, "Faster, faster, faster!" He then looked into her eyes.

She returned his gaze as much as possible for one who was so bounced about. "What?" she asked.

"I fear we may be too late."

The carriage now jostled and quaked over a rough, yet-to-be unpaved road. "Why? Why risk their reputations, their careers?"

"Money is a great motivator, Jane, and who knows that better than Dr. Tewes?"

She glared at him but said, "It's hardly the same."

"Do you think for a moment Christian and Nathan haven't rationalized their crimes down to misdemeanors as well?"

"Damn it, Alastair, I've harmed no one, and this is torture and perhaps murder. How do they hope to keep it hushed up?"

"For the same reason men post trunks to Canada under assumed names."

"Habeas corpus." She said the Latin legalese for what he meant.

"Last time I looked, if there's no body . . . there's no crime, and therefore, no prosecutor will touch it." Ransom squeezed her hand. "God only knows what's gone on out there at the Chapman estate the past few days. Wish you'd told me about Bloody Mary's being removed before this, Jane."

"But if you knew that she'd be taken, why'd you send her to Cook County Asylum to begin with?"

"I never would've believed it of Christian, that he could do such a thing." Ransom again pounded with his cane.

"Perhaps not . . . perhaps it was McKinnette, Shanks and Gwinn surely . . ."

"Caine would take a payoff sure as that pair of ghouls."

"Perhaps the Christian is innocent of this?"

"We'll know for sure if and when a Chapman wing is added to Cook County."

"It will never happen. Christian could not go through with such nefarious actions, not him, not if he knew."

"That's just it. He does not know the level of desperation and the lengths Chapman and Kohler will go to." Alastair squeezed her to him. "It may be you are correct, and I hope so for all our sakes; there are too few men today with the character to say no to Mammon."

"Money is not what Christian lives for . . . nor . . . nor do I, Alastair. Nor do I."

"But he does live to gamble and to practice medicine, and while owing a few sharks some hundreds, maybe a thousand in cash, he has also gambled large on Rush College and its connection to Cook County. I have a suspicion that even Christian Fenger would look the other way if he thought it would make his chances of beating out Northwestern Medical School for improvements and medical care."

"I can't believe it of him."

"Fine . . . don't. I am the last man on earth who wishes to defame Christian. No finer surgeon has ever graced this city, but as for his motives, they are cloaked in who he is and what he means for Cook County and Rush."

She grabbed his cane and pounded the cab roof beneath where the driver sat. Outside the window, the city streets had vanished behind them, giving way to a dirt road leading north toward Evanston, just outside Chicago. They skirted the massive Lake Michigan, placid and blue this morning as it winked between the forest trees. The expanse of lakefront property here remained pristine; while sold off by developers, it had not as yet been denuded. Sunlight and shadow played tiddledywinks as their coach careened along Chicago's northern regions and past the quiet little settlement of Evanston and out onto the other side until they turned into a massive estate created by Senator Harold J. Chapman.

Alastair stuck his head out the coach window, staring about as they approached the buildings here. His face framed in sashes, Ransom trusted that nothing of a criminal nature ending in blood would be permitted in the mansion itself. He shouted to the coachman to make for the outbuildings, the stables in particular.

When he again looked into Jane's eyes, he said, "I can almost smell it from here."

"Smell what?" she dared ask.

"The carnage."

CHAPTER 17

The carriage pulled up to the stables, and the hansom cab horses *did* literally smell the carnage, it seemed, as they balked and rose as in fear, whinnying discontent. Alastair leapt from the cab, holding out some thread of hope, but doubtful at once. Behind him Jane climbed from the cab. He turned and signaled for her to stay back and wait. The cab driver, curious, his horses ears and noses flaring, jumped down to soothe his animals.

Alastair moved ahead, cautious, pulling his blue-burnished steel firearm, holding it ahead of him in one hand, his cane in the other. The driver, sensing danger, located a safe spot behind the cab, inviting Jane to do likewise. Instead, she shakily moved toward the stables behind Ransom, staring at his massive back while attempting to peek around him.

His complete attention focused on the double doors to the forty-yard long stables, Ransom remained unaware that she was behind him. It felt as silent as it sounded in there. No sounds of horses, that was certain. In a nearby fenced pasture, six or seven horses nibbled at grass below box elder trees, some looking up at the disturbance at the stable.

Ransom put his cane against one of two swinging doors and forced it open; it swung on silent hinges, opening

incrementally with its own weight creating momentum
that built as it widened. Now Jane, too, could smell the
blood odors that wafted out through the doors like a fetid
spirit seeking freedom. Jane covered her nostrils but could
not get the stench of death out of her brain.

Ransom shook his head at the sight filling his eyes, but
Jane could not see around him. When he realized she had
followed him, he turned and firmly said, "This is no sight
for a lady, Jane. Please, go back to the cab."

"I am no lady, Alastair. I am a doctor. So stand aside!"

"Please, Jane!" He held her by both shoulders, his cane
pressing into her right arm.

"I've dealt with death and corpses before, Alastair."

"Not like this!"

She pulled from his grasp and stepped past him to see
what he had already seen and choked on.

In the rafters, hanging from tinder hooks, two upside
down animal carcasses hung, dripping decaying fluids and
blood into a floor matted with the sweet scent of hay. At
first, she believed them to be deer skinned and filleted like
fish, gutted, their intestines nowhere to be seen. Organs had
been eviscerated but again not in sight. The carcasses now
came into focus as not animal but human.

"My worst fear," muttered Ransom.

"How can men do such a thing?" She made out the one as
a hefty woman from her bloodied, skin-stripped breasts, the
crotch, and the long gray matted hair like a tangled mop
head, the strands touching the ground. From here Bloody
Mary looked the part of a cow that had been removed of its
hide. The second destroyed body hanging from the rafters
was male. Whoever he was, he had not been spared Bloody
Mary's fate.

His privates were also missing.

Arms gone, lobbed off.

Bloody stumps.

Head gone.

Internal organs—all gone.

Eye sockets turned to empty black holes.

"Nice of them to take the horses out to the pasture so they wouldn't witness this," Ransom said. "Shows concern for the sensibilities of an animal."

"What kind of sickness could motivate this? Christian can't possibly be a part of this anymore than . . . than you or I, Alastair."

"You forget, however, that you were negotiating to get in on this . . . this deal . . . through Christian."

"I was never in for this, and neither is Christian, damn you!"

"The senator is obviously gone mad with grief for his granddaughter. No sane man could do this. So what is Nathan Kohler's excuse or rationalization?" he wondered aloud.

"What do you suppose they've done with the organs and the missing parts?"

At the other end of the stables, beyond the opposite doors, the only noise they had heard since arriving rose and fell— the stuttering grunts of pigs.

Ransom could not help but recall Christian's suggestion when discussing the disappearance of Waldo Denton—to feed him to the hogs at the slaughter yards. Still, like Jane, he could not believe that Christian would have any part in such butchery.

He went toward the sound of hogs and found the pigsty. Leaning in over the rail, finding their stench easier to take than the odor of death inside the stable, Ransom saw the scattered, trampled, half-buried bones. "Obviously human," he said, pointing them out to Jane.

Alastair tried to imagine what had gone on here. They'd obviously conspired to get Bloody Mary here. Chapman had long before prepared the stable as his inquisition chamber. He had the old crone stripped and hauled up by her ankles, likely with the help of brawny hands who worked for the senator. Some of whom appeared on their way down the hill from the main house now, having spotted the commotion at the murder scene, for this was murder, pure and simple.

"These fellows coming toward us could prove dangerous given the situation," he told Jane, who was staring at the bones being tamped into the pigsty mud.

"Should we make a run for the coach?" she asked.

"We'd never make it."

"What, then?"

"I start making arrests, I suppose."

"But this is a U.S. senator, and given what's occurred here and that we're potential witnesses . . . perhaps we'd better find cover."

"Yes, a man who's killed two people in his stable won't balk at dispatching us unless—"

"How will we manage it, Alastair?"

"Listen carefully, if you don't want to wind up fodder for Chapman's hogs."

"Whatever you say."

"Just follow my lead, then."

"Talk? You're going to talk your way out of this?"

"I suspect it is our only way. I see two armed men with long-barreled rifles coming up from the river. We're cut off."

"But can you do it? Talk your way and mine out of this?" When Alastair did not readily reply, she said, "I know. I've got it."

"Got what?"

"Tell them we've bloody well come for our share of the loot."

"Cute." He stared at her.

"But it could work if they thought we had a hand in getting Bloody Mary turned over, and you did arrange to put her into a place where they waltzed her out and to her death. You are entitled to compensation, by the rules of fair play."

He laughed in her face. "Let me do the talking."

"Just do it," she said, getting the last word in, when voices from behind them broke out.

Wheeling for a look, Alastair cursed, "Damn! It's Kohler and Chapman with the rifles coming up the rise from the river. A fitting end to my career . . ." Ransom's lament had her turn about to see the men with guns. Ransom added, "We're surrounded by killers."

"But no sign of Christian."

"Keep still and play the dutiful girl without a brain, Doctor, as *my woman,* do you understand? As for how I will manage these fellows, just watch me. Stand clear and watch me."

"Have you an extra gun at least?" she asked.

"My ankle . . . in a holster under my pants-leg, but it has a hair trigger. Do not go for it."

"Then why tell me about it?"

"You've my permission if they kill me."

"*Ahhh* . . . thank you."

Ransom stood like a wall between three approaching farm-hands, who'd obviously had a hand in the killings in the stable—their overalls painted in the brown burnished color of dried blood. Varnish stains they'd tell a judge and jury, and no way to refute it.

Jane's only thoughts went to Gabrielle and what her daughter's life would be like without her mother; wondered how Gabby would cope on her own; wondered if she'd have to drop out of Rush Medical College; wondered if Dr. Christian Fenger would take her under wing, to see that she stretch to her full potential; finally, Jane wondered if dying here and now would be painful or quick.

Alastair had but one thought: *save Jane.*

The carriage driver had seen the approaching men as well, and he leapt to his seat, turned the cab round and attempted to make a dash for it when one of the farmers threw a heavy harness into his face, sending him over the side. He lay in the dust, unconscious, his carriage and horses startled but caught by a second brawny fellow.

Then, as if the two men had come up from a nearby turkey shoot down at the river, Senator Chapman and Chief Nathan Kohler, guns in hand, materialized at Jane's and Ransom's back.

"Wonderful time of year, don't you agree, Inspector Ransom?" asked Chapman, all smiles. "Love to go out on a hunt just after finishing a *prickly* job."

"Nathan," said Alastair, his hand white-knuckled around his blue gun, which he'd rested along his leg.

"Fancy seeing you here, Alastair," replied Kohler, "and with Miss Francis is it?"

"I came for my share."

Nathan laughed. "I'm sure you did. Smart move getting the old witch committed. With Christian being uncooperative, it was up to us, Alastair."

"I have a hefty check made out to you, Inspector Ransom," began the senator, a grim smile on his face as he narrowed the distance between them. "One you will be pleased with."

"Check?" asked Jane, her eyes going from Chapman and Kohler to Ransom who glared at her to be silent.

"Yes, Jane, a check," said Alastair, "one that will keep me from the poor house in my old age. Thank you, Senator Chapman."

"You knew about this? Then you were part of it all along?" Jane asked.

"I know how this must look to you, Jane," said Kohler, his hands extended in a gesture that swept her eyes back to the business in the barn. "But it does save the lives of countless children in our city, now doesn't it? You can't argue with that, and with your recent interest in helping homeless street kids, well . . ."

Senator Chapman pumped Alastair's hand. "Getting that rabid foul old bitch out of the court system and into McKinnette's control on a medical adjournment, that was brilliant, Inspector."

Alastair smiled woodenly and jokingly asked if Kohler

SHADOWS IN THE WHITE CITY   283

and Chapman had had poor luck hunting along the river. He imagined they had escorted someone into the woods but had come back alone. He prayed it'd not been Christian.

Chapman talked as if among friends, a calm about him. "Too much rain this season out this way, everything swollen."

"Washes away the grime," commented Kohler, hefting the scoped rifle. Had Chapman wanted them dead, Nathan could have killed them from a hundred yards off.

Grime or crime, Alastair wondered. He also wondered at the shovels being carried by the three farmhands. Likely, they had come to bury all those identifying parts from hands to heads and teeth along with the personal effects of the second victim, as Mary Grace didn't have any. However, asking about this would not endear him to Chapman, and he really wanted Chapman to like him and Jane at the moment when he saw Jane's eyes and realized she was going to say more.

"How could you keep me outta the deal? You knew I wanted to be a part of this?" she persisted.

He took her aside and whispered, "If you want to get out of here alive, I suggest you follow my lead."

"I am I thought."

"If I negotiate a deal for you, and Chapman writes you a check, you will take it, too."

"Never. There I draw the line."

"To accomplish getting us both killed. We are both dead otherwise, Jane." He then returned to Chapman and Kohler, saying, "It was Christian's idea, the whole thing—getting the old crone committed."

"But you executed it, and here Nathan called you a hardnosed bastard who would not go along," countered Chapman. "I told Nathan, I said, 'He'll come round; time and money have a way of greasing the rustiest of skids.'"

Kohler nodded. "You did predict it, sir."

Chapman said in a near whisper to Alastair, "How about this chief of yours, Inspector? Never seen a man work so hard at kissing ass." He ended with a laugh.

"So who is the dead man that Mary fingered?" asked Ransom, pointing to the small man's corpse.

Kohler replied, "Your man . . . snitch of yours, Bosch."

"What? Are you insane?" he asked Kohler and then he moaned to the corpse in the barn. "*Ahhh* . . . Bosch . . ."

Jane felt the depth of his pained response.

"The old bitty was quite clear on *who* was butchering and eating the children," said Chapman, "and she named your man."

"It makes sense, Ransom," said Kohler. "Think of it. He knows not only the ins and outs and ups and downs of the homeless children, but he knows the workings of our department. In a sense, you yourself furnished him with information and—"

"But Bosch?" Ransom still could not believe it, and he imagined that the old wild woman, Mary, simply drew on the first notorious name leaping to mind, perhaps the only one she had known for any length of time in Chicago, Henry "Dot 'n' Carry" Bosch.

"A cripple like Bosch . . . you really think he was behind your granddaughter's death, Senator Chapman?" asked Ransom.

"Whataya mean, a cripple?"

"Bosch had a wooden leg."

"W-wooden leg?" The senator glared at Chief Kohler. "What's he talking about?"

Jane realized one of the missing parts of what hung beside Bloody Mary from the barn rafters had no peg leg.

Nathan said, "I—I was told your men picked up Bosch."

"At the address you provided, yes."

Kohler raised his gun and hand in a gesture of innocence. "By time I got here, he was unrecognizable. I assumed it Bosch."

Chapman looked Kohler hard in the eye, "Shut up, Kohler! You bloody well sent us to the wrong address, and you said nothing about a goddamn wooden leg!"

"I had no idea it wasn't the gimp! It was handled by *your*

men! If you'd allowed me to call in my fellows, they surely would've known to get the right man!"

"All right! All right!" countered Chapman. "We have Inspector Ransom now, and he obviously knows how to find this Bosch creature." Chapman turned to Alastair. "Come along, Inspector, up to the house. We'll have a cognac and consider the circumstances, and you may have an advance on your turning this Henry Bosch over to me."

"But who is it, then, you've skinned alive?" asked Jane.

"A street person; no one of consequence," replied the senator.

"Certainly no one who will be missed," agreed the chief.

"Come with me, Jane," Ransom told her.

Jane now did precisely as Alastair asked.

As they straggled behind, Jane asked Ransom who besides Bloody Mary had been butchered back at the stables. Behind them, they heard Senator Chapman's men bring to life a huge, steam-engine operated saw, and the piercing sounds it was making in the stables could mean only one thing. They were doing the finer work of feeding the rest of the body parts to the hogs. "Purchased that remarkable saw at the agricultural pavilion at the fair," Chapman proudly announced, keeping pace ahead of Alastair and Jane.

"You know as much as I do," whispered Alastair in Jane's ear. "I've no idea who stood in for Bosch."

"And do you believe for a moment Bosch is Leather Apron?"

"Not for a moment."

"Then you are a champion at charades?"

"I wish it were *all* a charade."

"We're not out of the woods yet," she cautioned.

"It's not the woods I fear. It's those two." He indicated Kohler and Chapman ahead of them.

"You were left with your weapons. It would appear they believed you back there. And frankly, you were quite convincing."

"I swear to you, Jane, I never seriously considered Mary

a part of the Vanishings, and I still don't. The kids' stories were built around her because she scared hell out of them."

"That's all?"

"That's all, until I can prove otherwise, yes." He felt a judicious lie at this point might just keep her alive. Ransom feared telling her of Bloody Mary's last admission to him, and he wondered if the old loon had died thinking that he'd used that information to turn her over to Chapman and Kohler. For now, he felt keeping old Mary's secret a kind of justice, the fact of her son, the man in the picture with the grim brood. Besides, if he were to share this information with Jane just now, she'd surely believe him a liar and a part of this carnage.

Better to let her believe as she did, that Mary was an innocent victim here, too, caught up for no better reason than the stories children told on the street.

Ransom and Jane got free of Chapman and Kohler as quickly as possible, Ransom given a timetable in which to return with Bosch, bound, gagged, and prepared for the slaughter. The coachman was well paid to keep silent, and Alastair imagined he had also been threatened that if any word of what he'd seen at the farmstead should get out, that he would be the next man flayed and filleted and fed to Chapman's prize-winning hogs. In fact, the bulk of their cognac visit was taken up by his showing them photos of each prize winner and rattling off the vital statistics of each hog and sow.

"What will you do now, Alastair?" she asked. "You've managed to implicate yourself in two murders back there by taking that check, and checks leave money trails."

"Not if I tear it up."

"Will you?" she asked, staring into his eyes, awaiting an answer.

"Will I?"

"Rip up a check for a fortune?"

"Imagine having that much to play with at the racetrack."

"Are you going to destroy the check or become a part of this bloody conspiracy?"

"I'm walking a sensitive tightrope here, Jane."

"What sensitive rope?"

"Suppose Christian is, like they say, part of this? Suppose he turned Mary over to them for a sum like this?"

She signed heavily and leaned back into the cushions. "Damn you, you're wrong. It wasn't Christian who did it. It had to've been McKinnette."

"We don't know how deep either of them're in, but from the outset, the senator has been throwing his money around."

"He's blinded by his hatred and desire for vengeance."

"He's fixed on one path, most certainly."

"An obsession. Suppose he does not get what he wants? Will he come after you, me, Gabby, anyone he can hurt?"

"There is little telling."

"And as you've pointed out, without a body in the possession of authorities, there is no crime."

"Hogs don't eat bones," he replied.

"You're not thinking of going back out there, are you?"

"Not right away, but when I do, it will be with a gunnysack. At which time, this untendered check becomes evidence."

Overhead, they heard the shaken coachman talking to himself, something about jumping the next ship or train out of the city.

"Perhaps we should take a clue from this fellow," Ransom suggested.

"Nonsense. It's not in your blood to run from a fight or a case."

"Jane, you know me too well."

"Well enough to know that if I'd gone out there to Chapman's funhouse with any other man, I'd be as dead as Bloody Mary right now, and no one would ever have known," she said, shivering a bit. "And I haven't even sufficiently thanked you."

"I'll take out thanks in this manner," he said and pressed his lips to hers, and they embraced to the lulling motion of the hansom cab, returning to Chicago by gaslight.

Ransom returned Jane to her home, angry with himself that he'd allowed her to go anywhere near Chapman's estate. It had taken all his powers of persuasion to convince Chapman and Kohler that she was harmless and would do as told, using such phrases as "a man who can't control his woman ain't no kinda man" and "she knows her place if she wants to eat and wear nice jewelry." Of course, Jane rankled at each such remark, but by then, she realized she must play her part to make it off the death farm alive.

They had gleaned that Chapman had to place his wife in a sanitarium, that she had collapsed under the strain of learning of her granddaughter's death, and that he had gotten his son and daughter-in-law out of the country, on a cruise to Europe for their health . . . all to plot and carry out his plan of vengeance.

Jane was glad to be home, met on the porch by Gabby; she held her daughter close. Ransom continued on, staring over his shoulder out the coach window at Jane and Gabby still locked in embrace.

After this ugly business, Ransom must, by every means at his disposal, turn up Leather Apron, the culprit behind the Vanishings—whether one man or many as Bloody Mary had indicated.

Alastair began searching his city, going to every location he thought plausible and mining every street snitch he knew in search of any news regarding Bosch and/or the lunatic the press called Leather Apron. As he did so, he garnered information that told him Bosch was already in hiding, that he somehow knew of the man who'd taken his place as the supposed guilty Leather Apron. It made Alastair wonder if Bosch himself had not set up the anonymous fellow now fed to Senator Harold Chapman's voracious hogs, sows, and piglets.

As luck would have it, Alastair turned up Samuel instead of Bosch, and they found a small, isolated area in a neighborhood park and talked. The boy was shaking the entire time, terrified. He had seen something.

"What is it, Sam?" asked Alastair. "You must tell me if it can save one life, you must."

"S-s-sir, yes . . . it's to do with Leather Apron. I've done like you said, kept my eyes and ears open."

"And you've seen something?"

"Heard something."

"What is it you heard?"

"Heard a homeless child tell another one where they could be fed."

"I don't follow you, son."

"No homeless who has been on the street invites another homeless for food. Homeless find food, they ain't sharing it with no one but their family."

"What about friends? They may've been friends."

"That's just it. She didn't know the other one."

"How can you be sure?"

"She introduced herself. Said her name was Alice . . . Alice Cadin, but it was really Audra pretendin', you see."

"That's impossible, Sam. Alice Cadin is the name of one of the dead girls."

"It's what Audra said, and Audra gave the other girl a piece of bread like . . . like a lure."

"Audra? The same as in Robin's band?" Alastair recalled that it'd been Audra who wanted to sacrifice young Sam to the Leather Aprons, the little manipulator.

"I followed 'em as far as I could, and it ended with screams, but I dared go no farther. Didn't see nothing, but I heard."

"Can you take me to this place?"

"You got your blue gun?"

"Always."

"All right. Then let's go."

"Brave lad. Lead on."

Samuel guided Alastair through several back alleyways, some so narrow his shoulders touched the clapboard houses on each side of him. They followed a winding, wending path below the raised platform of the electric train until finally it was clear that Sam was leading him toward the river where black, silent warehouses sat idle this time of night.

Sam stopped abruptly, saying, "This is as far as I went the other night."

"Why didn't you find me then? Why did you keep this to yourself?"

"I was afraid for one. Second, I tried but I couldn't find you. Third, I couldn't tell no one else."

"You're sure now it was the same Audra?"

"Yes."

"Wait here, Sam, and I'll go ahead . . . investigate, see if there's anything in the way of evidence."

Ransom inched forward in the deep shadow of the warehouse district. The smell of dead fish heads, the creeping skittering sound of wharf rats, and the glowing eyes of the occasional slinking cat added to the mix of whirring wind and tinkling ropes against mastheads. The river by day was alive with boat and ship traffic of all manner, delivering cargo of every sort to an insatiable, gluttonous city, but by night, the river and the wharf seemed a haunted world with ships whispering to one another, their rigging determining the strength of each voice. It was enough to make even a large man with both a gun and experience on his side quake deep within to think that Leather Apron could be awaiting him at every recessed doorway, every crevice and cranny that made up this black center of commerce.

The deeper he moved into the shadows of this place, the more he worried over Sam's safety behind him. The farther from the boy he got, the more he feared Sam's sudden disappearance, not of his own accord but as Leather Apron's next victim. If Leather Apron somehow knew of Danielle, then why not Samuel?

Given this fear for Sam, Ransom felt an overwhelming urge

to shout a challenge to the killer. *Show yourself and stand and face a man, and fight face-to-face, and to the death like a man.* But given this fiend's usual target—size, age, innocence—it was highly unlikely he'd stand and show himself.

Ransom wanted his hands on this fiend, and he wanted it tonight, now; Sam would have to fend for himself just as he had been doing long before Alastair had met him that day outside the grocery.

Alastair sniffed the air around a locked warehouse door and came away with an odor dissimilar to any he'd already swallowed here on the wharf, a smell branded in his mind since Senator Chapman's stables—blood, human blood.

Inspector Alastair Ransom stepped slowly back and read the warehouse sign almost invisible in the purple darkness here. An overcast sky, no stars, no moon conspired to hide the letters. When he made them out, they read OVERTON & HAMPSTEAD BOOKBINDERY AND STORAGE. The sign had fallen in disrepair, the lettering long since peeled away. It was one of a number of empty hulking, dead businesses that had come and gone, leaving its carcass—like some bone-picked pachyderm. This place proved large and sprawling along the city wharf.

While locked against entry by the unhappy owners, there must be several entry points. If homeless people could find a way in, so could Alastair. He motioned for Samuel somewhere in the gloom of a thick fog that'd swept in to engulf wharf and river. Somehow Sam saw his signal and joined him at the book warehouse. "Is this where the screams were coming from?"

"I—I—I think so, yes."

"OK, look, I suggest you get going." He paid the boy handsomely.

"Get going, sir?"

"Yeah, go back the same way we came and get outta here."

"I like police work, sir. I think I may be suited to it."

"That's well and good, but for now you're to go to a safe place."

"What's a safe place?"

Ransom gritted his teeth at the bit of wisdom. "Go to the shelter called Hull House, and tell no one about this."

"What're you going to do?" Sam asked.

"I'm going to find a way inside."

Sam breathed deeply and said, "I don't wanna seem no chicken around you, Inspector, and going off, leaving you alone is—"

"Is the wisest move at this point, so go!" He shooed Sam off this final time, and the boy disappeared into the gloom of night.

Alone, Ransom began searching for loose boards, broken windows, back doors, torn siding—anything that a killer might use to gain entry into the depths of the warehouse. With Sam gone, he could concentrate on burglarizing the place.

Ransom located a window at street level back of the warehouse, a window that had been broken. He instantly realized that whoever came and went at this portal must be slight of build, and he also knew he'd never fit, not without some renovation to the window. He'd brought a flint lighter of the sort used for lighting cigars and pipes, one he'd purchased at Sears Roebuck downtown, but he hesitated using it for light until certain he was alone and no one was inside.

So he felt about the windowsill with his bare hands in the pitch dark. The sill itself was old and worn and loose from years of rainwater and weather. Ransom grabbed hold of the loose frame in each hand. He then tore away the entire framework until nothing but stone and cement remained, along with a gaping hole large enough to accommodate Ransom's size. If anyone were inside and if Ransom had hoped to have surprise on his side, he could forget about it now.

Alastair eased himself down into the basement of the warehouse, this side of the building facing a paved road over which wagons traversed, and where men loaded and unloaded goods. His eyes came to street level as he dropped into the pit. It felt good to plant his feet firmly on the ground below, as it made him less susceptible to attack.

Ransom now used his flint lighter, and it was immediately refracted by the damp stone walls that seemed to bleed in the weak illumination. Ransom moved along, and as he did so, the light moved with him. Darkness filled the spaces behind Alastair just as light filled the spaces ahead. He was painfully aware that his own features and body stood outlined by the light like a man standing before a campfire. All that lay beyond him was a potential fright, a potential attack.

However, with the stillness so complete as it felt both outside him and deep within, Alastair guessed himself alone here . . . alone save for the source of the blood odor. He turned a corner and filled it with his light and all at once got the full shock of what he'd so fatefully come to find.

Rats.

A horde of them.

Feeding on something dead.

The industrious little beasts having created a kind of vertical bridge of one another's bodies so as to climb several feet up to their prize, the discarded remains of yet another child that had been carved on like a Thanksgiving turkey.

Ransom's boot sent rats flying, and he stomped and shouted and sent the rats skittering in every direction, leaving what appeared to be a bloody ham hock dangling from an overhead pipe. Little wonder he'd seen so many river rats gnawing and clawing their way in from the other side of the building.

"Nobody here but the dead," Ransom announced to himself just to hear the sound of his own voice, and just to break the spell of horror.

Alastair didn't know what to do; if he left to call for help, he must leave the body to the rats again, and he was not prepared to do that. He instead took off his coat and wrapped it about the body, and working with shaking hands, he unhooked the small body from a stevedore's tenterhook. He next wrapped his arms around what was left of the carcass. He refused to leave it alone again.

He went out through the front doors, unlatching them and kicking them open. He made his way out into the night air and for the first time since he could recall, he allowed himself a deep breath of oxygen. He made his way out toward the gaslit street, shouted down a cab. He then laid the precious cargo onto the cushion over the coachman's protests, and climbed in. "Cook County Morgue!" he shouted to the driver. "Now."

"With haste, yes sir!" the man replied.

"No . . . no rush. She's long dead."

"My God! It's the work of Leather Apron, isn't it, sir?"

"Aye . . . aye, it is that."

"Then he's still afoot, despite what the papers've said about it being that madwoman, Bloody Mary?"

"Afraid so."

The driver climbed back onto his seat and Ransom rode with the body, quietly speaking to the unknown victim. "This is probably the only time you've ever ridden in a hansom cab, and it's your hearse."

Ransom banged his cane on the top of the hansom cab, shouting for the driver to stop. He alighted from the cab at a police phone booth and made a call into the regional district headquarters, pressing the key designating murder. After a brief explanation, he was assured of twenty-four police officers in uniform, a paddy wagon, and all the equipment he might need to collect evidence on the scene.

"I'm to await the wagon here," he told the cabbie.

"But what am I to do with what's in me cab?" asked the driver.

"Continue on to Cook County and deliver it to Dr. Christian Fenger or his stand-in."

"Are you sure they won't take me for the killer? I hear rumors you killed a hackman once you believed to be a killer."

"That hackman was killed because he failed to follow orders!"

"Yes, sir . . . yes, indeed."

With that the cabman and the decaying body continued on for the morgue.

Out of the silent darkness and fog, a noisy police wagon arrived at the call booth. Ransom clambered aboard with his cane. Soon after, the police had cordoned off the book warehouse, Ransom giving them jobs to do—most canvassing the wharf as Chicago awoke and workers began filtering into the area and boats and wagons and people began their duties—Chicago stretching and awakening to dawn.

Difficult as it was, after hot coffee, Ransom returned to where he'd discovered the body. He asked the uniformed men remaining to fan out and search for anything whatsoever that looked out of order or out of place. The search for clues was on as light from outside began filtering through the dingy book repository. The row upon row of books collecting dust here gave silent testimony to the popularly held belief that the Threepenny Opera, the Lyceum stage, and sports events had made the bound book dead as diversions go.

Behan and Logan showed up, getting word of the discovery, and they were followed by Philo Keane who had come to take photographs. Soon after, Chief Kohler arrived to "take charge" and to "oversee" the investigation.

"Where is the body I'm to photograph?" asked Philo.

"You'll find her at the morgue."

"Sent off?"

"I sent her to the morgue, yes. You can photograph her there."

"Sure . . . sure, Alastair."

"You have any idea how long ago . . . that is when this butchery happened, Inspector?" asked Chief Kohler.

"About the same time as you and Chapman murdered that homeless fellow along with Bloody Mary is my guess."

"Hold your voice down!"

"My source heard her screams only last night. Sometime after that, the rats got to her, and I refused to allow them a single 'nother nibble. They'd got to the bone as it was. So I sent her off to Christian's care."

"So the work of Leather Apron continues," said Thom Carmichael, standing now behind them. "I'd like to hear your take on all this, Alastair, and about the mysterious disappearance of Bloody Mary and Dot 'n' Carry—Bosch."

Alastair took the reporter aside. "In time, Thom . . . in time."

A uniformed copper cried out from the second floor of the warehouse, "Up here! Up here!"

Everyone rushed the stairs and made their way to where the officer stood staring down at an obvious "living and sleeping area" for a number of homeless. Amid the usual debris of bedding and filth, there lay a horrid knife with a protective hilt and a curved blade like a pirate's dagger. Scattered pieces of flesh—small but noticeable—were also found about the dirty bedding, a ratty tick mattress, bits and pieces of a destroyed teddy bear, a top, marbles, ball 'n' jacks, a yo-yo, and a broken wooden doll, alongside scattered cigar and cigarette butts, ripped out pages of the *Herald* and the *Tribune*—stories about Leather Apron. A large part of the horrid odor proved to be filthy cans used for toilets.

"My God," cried out Ken Behan from a dark corner, his lantern light revealing a discarded leather apron, beside a small human skull denuded of all but a few stringy swatches of flesh.

"More than one person was using this area," said Ransom, his cane picking about the debris, "and that's not fish pieces we're looking at but cannibalized human flesh. This is the lair of the beast . . . or rather *beasts*."

"Then Leather Apron ought rather be called Leather Aprons?" asked Carmichael who'd stopped in his note-taking long enough to gasp.

"Philo, get this covered," said Ransom. "Take shots from—"

"Every angle, I know . . . I know if I can take the stench. Thanks for your concern." Keane lifted his camera and began firing off shots with his Night Hawk, a camera built for just such work.

Ransom gave a quick thought to how photography preserved the crime scene forever, or until the photos were destroyed or doctored. "Get us some paper bags, you fellows, and gather all this into the bags, and . . ." he took a moment to keep from getting ill. "A-and get those bags to Dr. Fenger at the morgue. If anyone can do *anything* with this mess, it'll be the coroner."

"You mean we gotta handle this shit?" asked one cop, pointing to the buckets.

"I'm speaking of the leftovers—the meat!"

"Yes, sir."

"Use gloves but get it done."

Ransom had no clue whatsoever whether Fenger could or could not learn anything from the meager human remains and bone, but he knew the teeth in a single skull would reveal approximate age as a child's teeth spoke volumes. It was one of the few truisms in nature.

Another shout, another discovery. Ransom followed the crowd and had to fight his way past others to see what the hullabaloo was over. When others parted for him, he saw that they had cornered an aged old rat, too slow-moving to get off in time. The sight brought back what Alastair had witnessed in the darkness below hours earlier. "Why is he hanging about this location, alone?" Ransom wondered aloud.

Logan pulled out his .38 and fired, killing the rat. The explosion of the gunshot in the empty warehouse resounded over the entire wharf just as the owners of the place arrived. Stopping Overton and Hamptead at the door, uniformed officers asked their business. The gunshot had caused every cop to drop and pull his weapon. Meanwhile, Alastair poked about where the rat had chosen to hover, and in a moment, he found a small chest amid the boxes.

He opened the small cedar chest and peered inside, others over his shoulder doing likewise. Doilies, knitted items, caps, mostly small, mostly children's items. As Alastair picked through the chest, Kohler said, "My God, the cretin has kept items from his victims, kept them as . . . as souvenirs of the murders."

The others gasped at this conclusion.

"It's worse than that, I fear," said Alastair, now lifting out baby booties, infant hats, and infant clothing. A set of old tintypes, old tins—pictures created from a process predating photography.

Philo, always the interested artist and historian of photography, automatically grabbed for the tins, as he wanted simply to handle the old metal depictions and to closely examine the features as well as the quality of the work. As an artist, he found the tintypes of boundless interest. But Ransom withheld one of the tins and held it up to the weak light, a depiction of a comely if hefty young woman with features burned into Alastair's brain. "It's her . . . it's her when she was Grace."

"What?" asked Philo.

Logan inched closer.

Behan swallowed hard.

Philo Keane stepped back and snapped a photo of what Ransom held in his hands.

Kohler erupted. "What in God's name does this mean, Ransom? Who the hell is Grace?"

Alastair dropped everything back into the cedar box and painfully got back to his feet, using his cane to steady himself. *How long since I've had sleep? How much of an attack on my sensibilities can I absorb?*

"Well, man! Spit it out!" ordered Kohler.

Ransom casually went toward a window and opened it, allowing in more air, and in the light, he produced the photo that Philo Keane had given him, the photo of an entire homeless family of five—mother, father, and three children. He held it up to the waiting, anxious group of detectives, cops, newsmen, and Philo.

"What're you saying, Ransom?" demanded Kohler.

"This is what Leather Apron looks like. Take a good look."

Every eye was focused on the desperate faces of the homeless family.

"Are you saying . . ." began Logan.

". . . that Leather Apron?" continued Behan.

". . . is not just *two* killers but a mother and a father?" asked Thom Carmichael.

"The knives . . . the many cuts that Dr. Fenger speaks of," said Philo, a realization coming over him. "There could be as many as five separate attackers?"

"It's a family affair, yes. And this is no chest of souvenirs of their victims, but souvenirs from the killer's childhood, maybe the old homestead."

"Family heirlooms," croaked Philo.

"Father, mother, and children?" asked Logan, eyes wide. "All murderous, all cannibals?"

"This is a helluva story," muttered Carmichael.

"Some story, and one of our own making." Ransom turned to the window and breathed in fresh air off the river. Morning sun had burned off all fog but a dampness remained in the air.

"Whataya mean one of our own making?" asked Kohler, pursuing him.

"Same as Stead means in his book?" asked Carmichael.

This alerted Ransom, and he faced Thom. "You've read William Stead's book?"

"I am perhaps the first to do so."

"Has it found a publisher?"

"It has."

"Good . . . good."

"What in blazes does a book have to do with all this?" shouted Kohler. "And who the devil is this woman in the tintype?"

The irony was lost on Kohler, that they stood in a grave-
yard of dead books amid a city full of illiterates, amid the
remains of this horror, only now learning that William
Stead's exhaustive exposé of the treatment of indigent and
homeless in Chicago, entitled *If Christ Came to Chicago*,
had been published. The question remained who *would* read
it, and who might care? Further irony lost on Nathan was the
subject of the ancient picture.

"I don't see that a book has anything to do with any of
this butchery," added Kohler in his ear. "And who the bloody
hell is this?" he demanded, pushing the old picture into
Ransom's face.

Ransom glared at Nathan. "We oft create our own monsters, Nathan—you among them!" He grabbed the tintype
and held it overhead, shouting, "It's Bloody Mary when she
was young! Now step off."

Nathan smiled. "Then that old witch indeed had something to do with the Vanishings after all."

Philo weighed in, asking, "Do you think this cannibalistic family was pushed to it by our ignoring them, Alastair,
until desperation and hunger drove them to . . . to cannibalizing children?"

"Throwaway children, yes. Nameless, faceless ones even
in death. Then came Anne Chapman and Alice Cadin, two
not homeless, two with names and faces."

"No one asked for this," countered Behan.

"Disposable children," added Ransom. "Until Chapman."

Philo snapped a photo of Ransom. He'd secretly begun to
compile a kind of photographic history of Alastair Ransom.
Some were photos of Alastair in various undercover dis-
guises, but this time Philo had caught in a moment of time
the rage on Ransom's face as he muttered through clenched
teeth, "Now we've got to hunt down and kill the monsters
we've spawned."

CHAPTER 18

Philo Keane did exactly as his good friend and police detective boss told him to do, and so he now stood over the remains of the unknown child being autopsied by Dr. Christian Fenger. Philo took pictures of the carved up body as Fenger and his most senior assistants worked to create an autopsy report. The coroner for the City of Chicago worked in what appeared weary fatigue, his findings corroborating all that Alastair had concluded regarding the number of suspects being perhaps as many as five, all with separate knives, a view that Fenger had early on suspected from the few clues left them. Once again, Christian proved a remarkable medical genius.

Philo also informed his good friend Dr. Fenger of the box of heirlooms discovered at the warehouse. He also explained the significance of Ransom's having seen Philo's photo of the homeless family—"A representation of desperation," Philo finished.

"What about Alastair?" asked the doctor, not looking up from his work.

"What about Alastair?" asked Philo.

"How is he holding up?"

"*Ahhh* . . . yes, well, he is the strongest man I know in all regards but *this* . . . well this had him reeling, I can tell you."

"I must see him and soon."

"To medicate him?"

"I need to *talk* to him."

"I suspect he is home by now, but most certainly unconscious."

"Thanks, Philo. I'll catch up with him."

"So what do you make of the latest victim?"

"Sixteen, maybe fifteen. Bit older than the others. Male . . . weight about—"

"Hold on! Male? Ransom believes her . . . *ahhh*, him . . . *ahhh*, it a female."

"It's rather impossible to tell when the chest and private parts are removed, now isn't it?" asked Fenger.

One of his assistants quietly said, "Trust us, Mr. Keane, we would know."

Fenger continued aloud dictating as another assistant took down his every word. "Ninety pounds, long blond hair—seemingly that of a girl's." He stopped to give Philo a nod. "Missing every appendage and major organ, excluding the brain. Bones show normal growth, no obvious disorders, multiple stab wounds and multiple carvings after death."

Alastair had indeed found his home and his bed; he calculated he had not had any sleep for thirty-six hours, and his last sleep had been disturbed at best. He showered, shaved, and went to bed, drawing the heavy burgundy curtains around his bedroom like a cloak. In the semi-dark, he struggled to find sleep, fitful of mind, feeling guilty at his humble comforts, knowing that a killing family in the manner of a coven of wolves continued to hunt its prey in Ransom's city.

His attempt at sleep was disturbed, jolted by his ringing phone, and he cursed his ever having got connected, as everyone called it. By the time he managed to roll over, climb from bed, and stagger to the phone near the door in the foyer, whoever was calling had given up. He imagined it to be Chief Kohler or Behan or Logan or someone else at the Des Plaines station house, but there was no telling; else it could be someone with the morgue, Christian himself, or Philo, or perhaps Jane or Gabby.

Just as he climbed back into bed, the phone again rang. Just as he got back to the phone, it stopped ringing, but it was replaced by the tinkle of the doorbell, followed by someone's knocking as he gathered a robe.

When he threw the door open, it was Jane staring back at him. She rushed in and past him, going for his bedroom. She'd never been in his home before, and so it took her a moment to locate the bedroom but she did. He followed her in and found her disrobing, saying, "I want you to make love to me, Alastair."

Saying nothing in return, he took her in his arms, his robe coming open. She reached round him with arms extended, kissing him passionately and with vigor. Between kisses, she said, "I so admire you, Alastair. I do . . . I do."

"What's brought this on?" he asked.

"I've realized what you've done."

"About what?"

"How Gabrielle is so happy and come into her own because you encouraged her to drop out of Northwestern and work under Christian Fenger, and to pursue what she finds of true interest and fascination—postmortem work of the sort left to the coroner."

"I did not take those actions. She did."

"You saw what was in her heart, and you encouraged her, and she is the love of my life, and I've never seen her more inspired," she replied. "She loves Christian and the work."

"He's intentionally kept her off the Leather Apron case, you know," he said, kissing Jane again. "Christian's fearful of losing her."

"Losing her how?"

"Should she see the worst cases before she's been prepared, before she's ready. Says the Vanishings case is the worst he has witnessed in all his years, and it's disturbed him to his core."

"As it must anyone. Look, Gabby knows what he's doing and why, and we've talked about this old-fashioned nonsense, this idea a woman doctor must be Molly-coddled."

"He's only got her best interest at heart."

"No, he's got his own best interest at heart!" she countered. "Gabby is a woman, and she's my daughter, and I tell you she can handle any medical job thrown at her, including a postmortem on a child."

"I believe it."

"And Fenger's just discovering it today."

"How so?"

"She's storming his office to tell him how she feels."

"Good for her."

"She's stronger than any of us knew, and one day she'll be the coroner for Chicago, and if not for Chicago then another major city."

"Good for her. Now kiss me again."

She did so. Their passion rose, and soon they were in his bed, a bed he had shared with no other woman, and Jane proved far more amorous than any woman he had ever lain with. Their lovemaking unfolded like a flower at first, growing in intensity, each lover picking up on clues from the other. Soon both aware of the other's needs, wants, desires, and their most sensitive areas, each playing to the escaping sounds and movements of the other until a kind of orchestrated dance evolved, a dance of bodies wrapped about one another.

Afterward, Ransom found the kind of sleep that had so long eluded him. He awoke eight hours later to find himself alone again, Jane gone, and for some moments, he wondered if it'd happened at all. An avid reader, he felt like the lead character in Hawthorne's *Young Goodman Brown*. Had his bride been there or not? Was Jane "his" or not? Or had it all been an amazing illusion, a trick of his addled, fatigued brain . . . or not?

But the confusion was settled when he smelled her presence yet in the room, along with other telling clues. The disarray of his bed for one, the tossed robe and nightshirt, not to mention his own deepest inner pleasure on reliving the moment as the odors of their lovemaking filled his nostrils.

"We make an excellent pair," she'd whispered in his ear, to which he scratched and replied, "And we make excellent chemistry together."

"Magical . . . electrical," she said to this.

He laughed. "Phrenologically phenomenal."

Now he heard someone coming through the door in the other room, and a peek told him she had returned with a sack filled with groceries. She went straight to the kitchen, believing him still asleep. He threw on his sleepwear and combed his thinning hair, looked critically, at himself in the mirror and wondered what Jane saw in him. He took a long moment to gauge his girth and his clumsy hands, as well as turning a jaundiced eye to every wrinkle, every smile line, every tooth in his head that remained. Then he got round to his ears, his less than penetrating eyes, his receding hairline, and the gray, and the thinness of it all. *Whatever does Jane see in me*, he wondered again even as he heard the crackle and snap of bacon, the smell wafting in to "wake" him.

Ransom and Jane spent a pleasant morning, but soon Alastair was busy pulling his team of investigators together to canvass Chicago for every hole in the city where a suspected family of cannibals might have set up shop anew, as obviously the book warehouse could no longer cloak such heinous activity. Ken Behan and Jedidiah Logan in turn called on their own network of snitches and connections with other police officers in locating the strange and deadly family. To help in the matter, Ransom had Philo Keane duplicate the photo he'd inadvertently taken—a representation of what the deadly family looked like. The number of stab wounds from different weapons was set at five, so they were looking for a family of five, all old enough to wield a knife. In the photo, the mother cradled an infant in her arms.

Ransom took a moment to visit Christian, to confront him about the fate of Bloody Mary along with some unknown who just happened to be mistaken for Bosch.

He caught Christian in his office. "I can't believe you turned over a madwoman to Chapman and Kohler."

"Hold on! I didn't turn the woman over to anyone."

"Don't hide behind your subordinates. It doesn't become you, Christian."

"Hold your voice down and think, Alastair. How long've you known me?"

"I'm not sure anymore that I do know you."

"I had second thoughts on the whole matter," said Christian. "Told Kohler I'm out, and he could expect no assistance from me."

"Are you saying—"

"I turned over no one to appease Senator Chapman's bloodlust. To that end, I *admitted* the woman to County."

"Then who released her to those butchers? McKinnette?"

"I don't know; someone who was paid well, I assume."

"Then you may want to find out who on your staff was bought off."

"I will handle it in-house."

"If you don't, I'll be back."

"You do that, Inspector."

"I will, Doctor."

"Where is she now? The madwoman?"

"Damn it, man, she and Bosch's stand-in are both *dead*. I do not exaggerate when calling Kohler and Chapman butchers equal to this Leather Apron team."

"My God." Fenger sunk into his chair as Ransom calmed down, found a seat, and related the scene out at Chapman's stables. Finally, Ransom asked, "Are you sure you had nothing to do with it?"

"Absolutely, Rance!"

"They thanked me, Christian! Kohler and Chapman actually thanked me in front of Jane for getting the woman out of the court system and into the asylum, and they even paid me for my part in it all."

"And you took the money?"

"I did! I had no bloody choice. I was in no position to take the high ground. I had Jane to think of."

"What in the name of God were you thinking, taking Jane out there?"

"Damn it, Christian, have you ever tried to control that woman?"

"Yes, yes, once or twice I've made the attempt."

Ransom looked long into his friend's eyes. He erupted in laughter over the famous doctor's last remark. Dr. Fenger laughed now.

People going by the office thought it odd how these two men could switch from shouting to laughter so quickly.

Still sitting, Ransom said, "No one will miss Bloody Mary, and we may never know who the other victim was."

"How will you proceed? Or rather, will you proceed against Chapman, Kohler?"

"I have no evidence beyond Jane, and I would not jeopardize her life."

"There is the coachman."

"Not bloody likely to ever see him again. He was paid well enough to be in Denver by now."

Inspector and surgeon sat in gloomy silence for a long moment.

"What'll you do now, Alastair? About the Vanishings . . . Leather Apron?"

Alastair shared the plan he was putting into operation.

Christian breathed deeply, giving thought to what Alastair proposed. "Have you given any thought to the tunnels below the fair?"

"Tunnels below the fair?"

"Talk to the architect of the fair, Daniel Hudson Burnham."

"I've read about him in the papers, yes, but—"

"I tell you, Alastair, the workers cleared away acres 'pon acres."

"I realize that, but still—"

"Land that was here is now over there, built out onto the lake even, and the fair builders wanted a lagoon, so they built a lagoon, you know. That takes a lot of subterranean work."

"I suppose you're right, now that you mention it . . ."

"The builders had to create some pylons for the permanent structures, and this means ever more subterranean work." Fenger leaned in over his desk.

"Then you're suggesting there are networks of tunnels connecting the museums?"

"No, I am not suggesting. I am telling you."

"How accessible are these passages?"

"Given the resourcefulness of this killer or killers, I suggest they could find a way in."

"Where is Burnham? Where can I find him?"

"He has a mansion on North Michigan Avenue, I believe. I've only met him at various affairs."

"He will have blueprints that'll include these areas below the Columbian Exposition pavilions?"

"He will know them inside and out. He is your guide, and if not, he will send you to his foreman. I suspect someone is in charge."

They parted in a handshake.

"Good luck, Alastair."

But luck failed Ransom.

It would not come.

Everything that could go wrong did.

Alastair had gone directly in search of the architect of Chicago's Columbian Exposition, a man in global demand now, only to learn that Daniel Burnham, with his major work completed, had gotten out of town, and in fact out of the country. With the fair of fairs in its waning days, its chief architect was aboard a Cunard cruise ship bound for Europe.

"A gift he gave himself," said his butler.

Ransom had to speak to others less knowledgeable about how the fair was built over the lake and what blueprints might exist. He wound up at the Cook County Building Inspector's Office, where they had no record of anything beyond the buildings at the fair, nothing whatsoever of a network of tunnels below the fair. He then tried the Chicago Public Library on Michigan Avenue, researching Burnham's baby, again without discovery.

Alastair was told by more than one official that it was not unusual for final "specs" and blueprints to be turned over years after the fact, and that there had been so many new buildings going up this year that what he sought might well be somewhere in-house but below a stack in someone's office.

For hours, he got the runaround.

During the day, he'd contacted Jane and Gabby by phone, insisting that if either heard anything from Audra, that he wanted to see her and talk to her. He did not go into why he wanted to talk to Audra.

He secretly wondered if Audra knew about the tunnels; if indeed, she knew every inch of the tunnels. He wondered if Audra was one of *them*—one of the Leather Apron gang. A child cannibal. Daughter trained to it. Sister who shared in the spoils—human spoils. The girl in the family photo, her hair matted and dirty, had been obscured, her face buried in a mother's apron. But she could be taken for Audra.

As night moved over Chicago with darkening clouds and a threat of storm, Alastair missed Bosch; he needed the little gimp to run down leads. Who had Ransom left to draw on? Samuel, but Sam had disappeared, likely terrified at what he and Ransom had discovered at the warehouse.

Reports from Behan and Logan turned up nothing new. Once again they stood at a dead end. The tunnels mentioned by Christian Fenger seemed the only avenue left. He debriefed the other two detectives on the possibility that the Leather Apron monsters might well be hiding out below the fair.

The three inspectors, Logan, Behan, and Ransom now took a cab to the Science and Industry exhibit, a centrally located permanent structure at the fair. They arrived at an hour when this enormous Greek-styled building was closing for the evening. Displaying their badges, the three Chicago plainclothes cops fanned out, each following a separate guide who took the detectives to separate areas of the sub-basement, each area cut off from the other at the point of entry.

Each inspector was on his own.

They had discussed bringing in whole search parties of uniformed police, but in the end, realizing that their plan was based entirely on smoke, they talked one another into doing the manly thing until which time as they actually turned up evidence that the Leather Apron family had in fact taken up residence here.

"For all we know, it's got too hot for 'em, and so they mighta moved on," suggested Ken Behan.

"They're homeless and without resources," Alastair replied to Ken.

"If they did shove off," replied Logan, "they did so afoot or by jumping onto a freight car."

Alastair had passed through marvels of modern technology, exhibits showcasing such amazing inventions as the steam engine and the McCormick Reaper, machines that revolutionized production and agriculture.

The guard who had ushered Ransom to his point of departure was given strict orders that if he did not return to this door within twenty minutes, he was to alert police and organize a search party—ostensibly for Alastair or his dead body. Behan and Logan made the same demand of their guides.

Most definitely, Christian Fenger knew what he'd been

talking about. Before Alastair lay a fluctuating chasm of darkness, a tunnel that seemingly led to Hades itself. It was at once in stark contrast to the brightly lit exhibits upstairs and in consort with them, for huge steam-driven machines had created these tunnels. "And you say it goes from here to the Natural History exhibit building?"

"It does, sir."

Working with the wick, his cane dangling on his forearm, Alastair lit the lantern he'd brought with him. It had a several-hour's-long wick and reservoir. Immediately on lighting the lamp, the odor of kerosene filled the small space here as light flooded the tunnel ahead of him.

"Nothing like announcing yourself," he muttered to the museum guard.

"Are you sure you want to make this trek alone, sir?"

"Why?" he asked. "Is there something in there to fear? What do you know of it, man?"

"I've not seen anything, no! But I've heard noises on occasion, noises I've taken for rats."

"Rats? Why'd it have to be rats. I hate rats, but tell me, how can rats've gotten down in here?"

"There are vents, and where there are vents—"

"Yes, yes, of course."

"One purpose of the tunnels is to take runoff as well."

"Runoff?"

"Water from the lake during bad weather, sir, so that any overflow is run away from the Midway and the pavilions."

"Aye . . . so no one at the fair should be inconvenienced. Wouldn't want anyone getting her Buster Browns wet."

"It's a complicated system, but it has to do with the creation of the lagoon."

"Of course, of course." Alastair again cursed the fact that the man most knowledgeable in all this was out of the country. He'd even tried to locate the man's assistant on the project and his foreman, but not too surprising everyone "responsible" for the fair had abandoned the city for some peace.

In a month or two, the fair would be shut down permanently.

"You will be careful, Inspector, as there is a storm brewing overhead," said the guard when they both heard rumblings of thunder.

"Who mans the gates on the locks controlling the water?" asked Ransom. "I certainly have no desire to drown down here."

"Actually, sir, no one mans the gates."

"What do you mean, no one—"

"The marvels of modern technology at work, sir."

"You mean, they open automatically when the lake rises to a certain level?"

"Aye, sir."

"I see." Ransom sighed heavily, turned and started down the tunnel he had chosen, the largest of the three, wondering if Behan and Logan were as well informed as he, and wondering if both or either would balk at this game when faced with the enormity of it all. "Look, those vents, are they large enough for a full-grown man to clamber down into?" he asked the guard where he turned for a final look out into the safe confines of the sub-basement.

"They are indeed, but wire mesh prevents—"

"And are there such vents in all three networks?"

"There are, sir."

"I see, then there well could be people living down here."

"If so, their eyes will have adjusted to the lack of light." The guard indicated the police lamp in Ransom's hand. "They'll know you're approaching well in advance."

He cut down the intensity of the lamp by controlling the window. "I'll not stumble about in pitch dark," he said and ambled down the subterranean corridor with its wet, earthen walls lathered as if sweating, breathing, reflecting the light. Ransom thought it looked like a lot of his nightmares, like he'd stepped into the maw of Hell itself. The floor here added to his disorientation as it was on a gradual incline that increased with each step.

The reflected lamplight off the stone floor glowed copper red and blood orange. *Perhaps I am on the path to Hell,* he thought.

Not far from Alastair another tunnel wall radiated off in another direction and in it Jedidiah Logan slowly descended. He too had heard the rumblings of an imminent storm out in the world overhead, as it reverberated underground, making him feel as if he were inside a drum or a human heart when his police lamp turned the walls a garish purple-red hue. *Silly,* he told himself. *Steady.*

For a long stretch of his search, his light held before him, Logan thought of how little he had upstairs in the world both at the office and at home. He felt an overwhelming loneliness creeping in with the dampness here, and he wondered if he were to die tonight, if anyone in Chicago would care, and further if anyone at all would recall his name or his face.

He'd had poor luck all his life with making friends of a lasting nature, especially with women. Yes, he was married but theirs was a childless marriage and a loveless one at that. He and Molly simply tolerated one another's existence in the cramped quarters of their small apartment. She took in washing, and he brought home a cop's salary. Not much to show for a life, he was thinking; then he thought how she'd give him hell if he came home with muck and grime on his pants or coat, and here he was faced with wading in brackish water that looked only deeper ahead. He saw no way around it, if he were to do a thorough job here. Else he could lie to Alastair and tell him he'd done the job, but Ransom was observant; he'd notice if he returned too clean. *Molly be damned,* he told himself and started into the ankle deep water, black and shiny as oil against his lamplight.

Two steps farther and he could not understand how the water had seeped through his shirt and coat at his abdomen. Out of nowhere came a thick wetness smelling of acrid copper, and it struck him that his stomach was in pain, aching.

His legs still continued ahead, but he felt a sudden faintness. At first, he thought it some sort of annoying stomach problem, but the immediate wetness, like pissing himself on a drunk, struck him as so odd as this was at his abdomen, while the wetness only increased. *Trouble* like a rupture. He held tight to the lantern like a lifeline with his right hand, while his left investigated the cause of the wetness. His left hand hit the strange hilt of a knife sticking from his gut, and this came as a surprise, like finding something completely out of place. He'd not heard it fly into him; he had not felt it slice through his coat, and a part of his mind refused to believe it'd happened.

It makes no sense, and yet it made all the sense, he thought, not realizing he'd gone to his knees, his legs having buckled.

Still Jedidiah held firm to the lantern. In fact, some mad notion inside his dying brain had his hands tearing at the lantern, ripping apart its metal casing to get at the kerosene screw nut, tear it open and with the flame taking on the fumes and kerosene licking the surface of the water around him, Logan covered himself in fire, choosing his death by fire, refusing to allow the dirty bastard who'd knifed him the pleasure of saying his blade had killed Jedidiah Logan.

Logan began screaming this but it was unintelligible by now, his clothing and body covered in licking flames. His burning form created a ball of light and fire that illuminated the grime-covered faces of his killers. Five pairs of eyes watched his body finally fall facedown, snuffing the flames in his fall. The broken lantern had wheeled away and once more the corridor was thrown into darkness.

Amid the pitch black crept people wading through the water toward Logan's body. The man who had wielded the knife, followed by a woman in rags, and she followed by three voracious children of varying ages. The woman and her children attacked Logan's remains, taking whatever clothing and jewelry that might be useful, ripping away burnt and useless clothing, finally getting down to the bare back and gleefully, as in a ritual of pleasure, all of them began stabbing repeatedly.

With Logan beyond dead, and with the initial excitement of the kill over, the cannibals began cutting away fleshy portions of Jedidiah Logan's corpse. Logan was the largest prey the family had ever brought down . . . so far.

Inspector Ken Behan had not gotten sixty yards down his tunnel when he decided to hell with it, that he was going no farther until he could bring a small army of men with him, and that what Alastair and Logan had decided with little to no input from him was in effect madness. Besides, he thought he'd heard something vibrating through the walls of his tunnel, sounds like those of a man crying out in pain.

In his head, he tried to understand how so muffled a sound could reverberate through rock walls here in the curiously damp, black hole he stood in. The damn lantern he had was threatening to go out as well. Some kind of malfunction. This alone seemed good enough excuse to return to the museum, *and why not?*

Behan thought of his wife and kids; imagined what their lives would be without him. He started back for the light at the end of the tunnel, the one that marked his entry.

As he neared the place where he had begun, he saw the guard looking down the corridor at him, and it made him feel as if he were in an endless, bottomless shaft that could turn into a labyrinth inside of which, if a man became lost, he might never surface. He panicked for a moment, thinking, what if the guard, for whatever reason, is going to close and lock that door against me?

He felt a clinging, clawing feeling in his chest, and his skin began to prickle, and his head felt fuzzy—dizzy as a midnight drunk, as if he might faint. *What if I were to faint here? Wake up with five beasties chomping away at my flesh?*

"Let me the hell outta here!" he shouted now, running

back toward the door and the guard, not caring if the museum man called him a coward or not.

Behan found himself rushing, tripping headlong down the shaft the way he'd come. The odor of sewage, earth, and mold still dizzying, filling his nostrils and brain, Behan fell headfirst into the light the other side of the door.

"Are you all right?" asked his guide, helping him to his feet.

"I . . . I must have a condition."

"Yes, and you left the lamp down in there. Shall I fetch it, Inspector?"

"You do that. I'm going for men and dogs."

"Whatever did you see, sir?"

"I . . . I'm not sure but there was movement, and I heard strange noises. *Someone* is down in there and it could be—"

"Not Leather Apron? Really?"

"We need a thorough search with a lot more men."

"Aye . . . if that is the rascal that you fellows are after, I agree one hundred percent."

"What about the lantern?" asked Behan, indicating the light some forty or so yards in.

"It's not my lantern," said the guard.

"Shut it up and lock the door, then," replied Behan, getting to his feet and going for the stairwell, shaken and wondering how his best friend, Logan, might be faring about now, and wondering too about Alastair Ransom's progress.

Alastair also heard the strange noise that Behan hadn't been able to decipher. Neither man could know it'd been the death throes of Jedidiah Logan, but Ransom's instincts were sharp enough to insist that he douse his light when he'd heard the bizarre sounds that had lazily wafted down the corridor toward him. He doused the light by dropping the door that acted as a gauge, allowing air into the glass and metal casing of the handheld lantern, a Chicago Police issue and regardless of its clumsiness, a wonderful improvement on earlier cop lights.

Now Alastair stood in near absolute darkness, but somewhere in the distance ahead of him, he saw some small light source. He imagined it one of the vents mentioned by the guard. How long ago had he had that conversation? A few minutes before? It felt like a week.

He checked his pocket watch to note how much time had elapsed, but even before popping the cover, he realized he'd not be able to read it in this blackness. So he moved on toward the light source ahead.

Ransom felt his way along, hand over hand, following the earthen walls that'd been cut out by men and machines. As a result, his hands became dirty and cold, but there was no help for it—except his cane. He began using his cane to tap his way along the side wall. Between his cane and the lantern, which he most certainly would need coming back, he realized his hands were literally full. If he must pull his gun at any time, he'd have to drop either the cane or the lantern, and he loved his cane.

These thoughts filled his mind as he continued down the now too quiet passage. If there were rats down here, why hadn't he heard rodent sounds? Not so much as a rodent peep—only that odd, all-too-human cry he'd earlier heard. He'd also heard muffled laughter and shouting that seemed to be filtering in from above at the fair, crowded to capacity.

The absence of a large rat population meant one of three things. The guard had exaggerated? The rats had run ahead of Ransom? Or had the rats run ahead of others lurking here?

Perhaps the most deadly animal scurrying about here was man and woman, and children born of them.

Another hundred yards and he found the source of weak light. Indeed a vent built into the wall on lakeside. He peered out through the mechanism to see only grim darkness outside, roiling, angry clouds out over the lake. The vent was a concrete bowl meant to fill up and spill into the tunnel should the lake rise over its banks, and indeed a metal mesh cover had been ripped away by human hands. Pranksters or monsters, he wondered, sizing up the vandalism. Getting out this way, especially with water rushing in, appeared unlikely and at best a difficult battle. He imagined a series of such vents filled to the brim could create a drowning pool where he stood.

A strange noise commanded his attention, and he wheeled, his wolf's-head cane raised to strike out at a rat scurrying toward him. The creature barely acknowledged him as a threat and moved to the grillwork and climbed out into the world.

"Smart fellow . . . knows when to walk away," Alastair said of the rat as his tail disappeared over the lip of the vent. "Perhaps smarter than I."

Cook County Morgue same time

"Where is he, Christian?" Jane had come to Cook County in a state of terror. She had not seen Alastair the entire day, and she sensed he was in trouble. Her daughter Gabrielle was with Dr. Fenger, the two of them doing an autopsy on an unidentified body found in the river. Fenger was determined to create as complete a description of the unknown victim as possible, regardless of the likelihood of the John Doe going off to Chicago's potter's field to be buried at city expense. Christian remained determined to keep Gabby Tewes away from the Leather Apron victims, and to do so, he kept her busy with more run-of-the-mill autopsies such as this.

When Gabby learned that Ransom had come to the hospital earlier in the day to see Christian, she joined Jane in pursuing Dr. Fenger over the matter of Alastair's whereabouts. It took some hard talk, but eventually Fenger told them of Alastair's interest in the passageways below the World's Fair.

"Why would he go there alone? Is he mad?" Jane asked.

"Well, as I understand it, he took Behan and Logan along with him. Besides, it's just a suspicion that may or may not come to—"

"But why not flood the area with an army of police?"

"Because a bloody army of police are moonlighting these days to control the crowds at the fair!"

"Alastair should have backup," said Gabby, "and I think I know how to get it."

Jane turned to her daughter, asking, "What've you in mind?"

"A call box near the fair. That is an automatic guarantee of twenty-four men and a wagon."

"But you need a key to open a call booth," countered Jane. "Don't you?"

"Mother, I know people on the force now." Gabby tore her medical frock away while going for the door.

"But what if Alastair is in no danger, and you call out a squad of cops for no reason?" asked Fenger.

"I am willing to take that chance," said Jane.

"And pay the fine?" he asked.

"And pay the fine, yes!"

"You might just anger Alastair. I suggest you two give this more thought!" Dr. Fenger shouted as they rushed out of the morgue for the nearest cab. "Damn," he cursed, tore off his medical frock and rushed out after them.

CHAPTER 19

Alastair pushed on through the black void, de-termined to gain as many footsteps in this underworld as possible before having to return to his starting point. In the semi-dark near the vent, he'd read his clock, opening it on its chime—the music being "Green Sleeves." The time read 8:44 P.M. Complete darkness in the storm outside only made the passageway he stood in blacker as he'd continued on.

Silence here proved complete save for the gay sounds of the fair overhead, noises filtering in through the same vents as the light. "Light . . . sound . . . OK . . . water not so good," he said to himself, trying to dispel the gloom. His own voice seemed the only warmth here, the only tie with a world outside of this place. If these tunnels were built for a purpose, he could not tell; he imagined they must've been useful during the winter months of preparation for the fair to move goods, lumber, and materials to work sites.

He had only thirteen minutes to be back at the sub-basement door. Having decided to keep the lantern turned off, he now held it in his cane hand, thus freeing up his gun hand, should he need it.

His eyes had grown more accustomed to the dark, and he could make out the shape of the walls as he moved through the passageway, going toward the next vent, where a smidge more light filtered into this dungeon.

The downward slope on the floor had steadily increased, and now he stood in water up to his ankles.

"What the hell else?" he asked of the problems he faced here. "Pour on the misery."

Ahead of him, he saw a slick shiny surface of what looked to be black ice. Not so, more water . . . deeper. Deep enough to have a current.

"Shit," he muttered. "Time to turn around. Nothing here to see."

Alastair was in midturn, prepared to go back the way he'd come, when something floating in the water caught his peripheral vision. At first he thought it trash, perhaps washed in from the drains, perhaps Thom Carmichael's *Herald*— *and a fitting place for it too*, he inwardly laughed.

He took a step toward leaving when something in his brain said, *No, that's not a newspaper floating there but clothing, a coat, perhaps.* He moved in for a closer look, and he relit the lantern, opening it full. The light created huge black swaths of darkness and shadow, the biggest being his own. It also illuminated the bloody clothing floating by from a secondary passageway.

Alastair waded into the water here, up to his thigh, and using his cane, he pulled in the clothing. It did not look like something long in the water, and in fact, it appeared a somewhat expensive tweed coat and there were snatches of linen from a shirt. As he examined the ripped coat, he smelled the blood even as his hands became painted with it. His reflex was to drop it but one hand had hit a hard metal object that pricked his finger—a badge.

Under the grim light, Alastair studied the badge number: CPD-1438. Jedidiah's badge, his coat, his bloodied shirt.

He immediately doused the light, and he carefully waded his way toward the direction from which the bloody clothes had drifted. The blood had been fresh, coming off in his hands. Whoever had killed Logan could not be far away.

Ransom knew he must proceed with great caution and haste at once.

Even the noise of wading through the water was too great, as it could alert someone waiting in the shadows ahead.

He recalled telling the guard to send for help after twenty minutes if he should not return by then. Time had already run beyond that, so someone would be alerted. He prayed backup was on the way.

More rats went past, swimming this time.

As Alastair continued on, the incline here was going up-hill, the water subsiding behind him as a result. Overhead, out in the larger world, he could hear claps of thunder that the humorist Mark Twain would call a real sock-dollopper! Nature's riotous calamity. Most certainly the clouds had burst.

Whoever was in the passageway ahead of him, they—*for there was whispering now*—must be aware of the storm overhead as well, and that the passages here could become a deathtrap if Lake Michigan swelled beyond her breakers. The resounding splash of waves slapping into the bowl-vents clearly announced this danger as a growing threat.

Ransom could not let whoever had killed Logan find their way to the nearest vent or to an open entryway into the museum exhibits. He must act quickly.

Another sound came to his ears as he inched closer to the whispering voices. It was the sound of feeding as of rabid animals devouring a carcass. Ransom feared the worst. The family he had been tracking all this time were here en masse, and they had descended on Logan, killed him many times over, and were now feeding on his remains like a pack of hyenas.

The thought infuriated Ransom almost as much as it ter-rified him.

He had come out of the water and feared that he could be seen by these rabid animals whose eyes surely, even super-naturally, worked more efficiently in pitch than in light, like the eyes of a pack of unholy dogs. He rested his cane against the wall, careful not to allow it to fall or clatter. He then took out his flint box lighter, and opening the lantern, he lit it.

Five pairs of eyes met his at once. They were some twenty yards off, the entire coven, all situated over Logan's nude, mutilated corpse, some off to the side, nursing hunks of flesh cut from Jedidiah's flanks and backside.

Ransom felt as if he'd gotten a glimpse into the last rung of Dante's Inferno, but there was not a moment to think. He hurled the lantern at the enemy, and it hit the woman hunched over Logan's flanks, its contents spilling over her and setting her aflame. Two of the children leapt back into shadow, while the oldest struggled to save its mother only to catch its own clothes afire.

The father hurled himself at Ransom, his huge knife extended like a lance, his mouth bloody with feeding on raw flesh. Ransom raised his blue gun and fired at the same instant the inhuman creature fell atop him, sending him into the water. Ransom went under with the dead weight of the man he'd shot threatening to drown him even in death, but in fact, the monster was yet alive, stabbing at him with the knife to the end. Just as the hyena-man had held on to the knife, Ransom had held firm to his weapon. The knife came down, tearing into Alastair's left shoulder, as the fiend was going for his heart. At the same time, Ransom fired twice more, and the second and third shot ended any movement in the madman. Only three bullets remained in his weapon.

Ransom clambered to his knees in the blackness, and he remained in the water when the woman and eldest child, sharing flames, leapt into the muddy sewage together to save themselves. Ransom aimed and fired, putting a bullet through the woman's brain when suddenly he was hit with a powerful blow to one leg where another child had stabbed him. The final child leapt on his chest and tore at his face with its knife, slashing wildly even as Ransom pounded the little hyena in the face with his gun.

Ransom sustained cuts to his cheek, forehead, leg, and the wound to his left shoulder. The three remaining fiends had regrouped somewhere in the black tunnel beyond the water's edge. It seemed, for the moment, that he owned the water and they owned dry ground. Where the infant might be, dead or alive, was anyone's guess. It flashed through Alastair's brain that one or more of the other may've succumbed to a liking for young human flesh just a little too much.

As the water began to rise, a chilling cold came over Ransom. He'd bled out badly at several of the wounds, particularly the one dealt him by the alpha wolf—the father. It flit through his mind that the cold in his bones could be the onset of trauma, that he could pass out at any moment, and this would leave him victim to the deadly children, and not one of them would show him any mercy whatsoever; in fact, if he passed out, they'd be feeding on his body for a long time. He was as good as dead, as good as Logan.

He gave a momentary thought to Behan. *Where in hell's Behan? Can I count on Ken? Or is he dead as well down here in this hellhole?*

He imagined Thom Carmichael's headline in the papers: THREE OF CPD'S FINEST FOUND DEAD BELOW THE FAIR. *How fitting . . .*

How will Philo Keane get through life without me, he wondered. Then he thought of the future he will have lost with Jane, of watching Gabby mature, marry and have a child of her own some day. But all such thoughts were dispelled when his instincts took hold on hearing the animals in the dark begin a slow-building keening, a kind of animal mantra, preparing to strike again.

The cane, he thought. *Need to get to my cane.*

He struggled to his feet, stumbled, weaved, his dizziness threatening to take him. But he made it to his cane, and he grabbed hold of it. The firmness of it, the solid shaft and silver handle gave him a grounding that filled him with a sense of something in this nightmare to hold on to. Still, his head swirled, his mind gyrated, and his ears rang out with a silent cry from his soul.

Somehow, Ransom fought off the disorientation and the inner turmoil that wanted to bring him down. He slowly gathered up every ounce of remaining strength and charged into the black, inky passageway where he could hear them but not see the remaining three beasts with long knives. The one who'd leapt into the water afire, while badly burned, had joined his siblings, one of whom had the long hair of a girl, Audra, he wondered. Ransom rushed in at the feral children screaming and madly swinging his cane, the deadly silver wolf's-head hoping to tear into the trio of vultures. At the same time, Ransom blindly fired his gun nonstop, hoping to further even the odds.

He saw winking deadly blades reflected by each gunshot flash, and he felt a glancing blow to the head where another knife struck out at him, then another cut him in the side, and a third jabbed him in the back as the whirlwind of maniacal children dodged his cane and survived his bullets and somehow got past him and were splashing down the tunnel in the water, *escaping.*

He wheeled and reloaded and fired and fired until his gun clicked empty again. Then he went to his knees again, the cane crumbling under his weight, and Alastair Ransom passed out, his blood running the incline and mingling with the two dead adult cannibals in the sewage.

Ransom's last thoughts were of Jane and Gabby and how much time and pleasure of their company he will have lost. *Dead here . . . cold and alone and dead,* he thought.

"I'm dying in this rat's nest," he muttered aloud in a final attempt to call out to Behan or anyone within hearing. Ransom then rolled over onto his back, his watch in his hand, thinking *One more thing to do before giving in . . . passing out . . .*

Alastair was unconscious when they found him, his rescuers locating him by the sound of chimes playing the old English tune "Green Sleeves." When Jane, Gabby, Behan, and

Fenger, and the uniforms got to him, they saw his watch had been opened and thrown toward dry ground.

And in fact the first uniformed police to locate him had followed Logan's original route because he'd heard the music, unsure what it meant. Jane, who'd heard the chimes before, had shouted, "It's him! It's Ransom!"

What they came across after the watch terrified Jane and Gabby, for at first what was left of Jed Logan, everyone took for what was left of Alastair Ransom. All this excitement happened before officers, led by a shaken Ken Behan, pushed ahead, finding Alastair bleeding out. These officers encircled Ransom's inert body half in, half out of the water, with lanterns, and Behan shouted back to the others, "Down here! It's Ransom! He's here!"

Behan had dropped to his knees there in the water, tearful, his nerves shot, seeing the big man bleeding and dying on top of having seen his partner, Logan, butchered like a ham on a spit. "Dr. Fenger! Come quick!"

Everyone getting a first look at Alastair assumed from the blood loss and his position that Ransom was dead, until Ken Behan, soaked and leaning in over Ransom, placed his hands on Alastair and felt life. He erupted with the news: "He's alive and breathing!"

Behan continued shouting for medical help. Other officers had held the civilians, Dr. Fenger, Jane, and Gabby back, but now they burst down the lantern-lit corridor to where Alastair lay soaked in blood and sewage in the rising water. Someone estimated that if he hadn't been found, that he'd've surely drowned in the next few minutes, proclaiming Behan a hero for having turned him over and having gotten his head out of the water when he did—all exaggerations Behan tried to deny. Others waded in and weighed in, the CPD closing ranks for one of their own, and together they heaved their huge cargo onto the dry floor.

Jane took in the fact that two other bodies floated in the water, both shabbily dressed adults, one woman, one man. She mentally reconstructed what had happened here, seeing that Fenger was doing likewise. She imagined how Alastair had been attacked by the dead couple in the water, and that just before he gave into his blood loss and faintness, Alastair had had presence of mind to open his chiming watch and toss it as far down the corridor as possible as a kind of beacon to others who might come in search of him.

With a great deal of disgust and outrage, Mike O'Malley and other officers worked the other bodies to dry ground, pronouncing both dead, the woman badly burned, gunshot wounds evident in both. The two dead people appeared a wretched pair indeed, from clothing to the lice crawling over them. In a moment, someone produced a huge curved knife with a hilt, the sort of thing one imagined pirates to use. "No telling what else we'll turn up from these two," said one officer.

A second held up a cleaver and said, "You think Ransom got the Leather Apron here?"

"Ransom always gets his man," said a third, and this seemed to settle the question.

"You're right. He got 'em," said Behan to the others. "Inspector Alastair Ransom's killed the Leather Aprons!"

A half-hearted cheer filled the underground passageway, but no one was ready yet to party, not with Ransom lying at their feet so near death.

"It'll have to be sorted out," said Dr. Christian Fenger who'd come behind the others, pushing cops out of his way, his medical bag in hand. From it, he snatched out surgical scissors and cut away at Ransom's clothing, searching for the worst of the wounds. "He's been stabbed multiple times, but I see no bullet wounds."

Fenger next ripped away at his pants-legs and found several wounds to the big man's legs, but none life-threatening in and of itself. He ripped away at his shirt and located a nasty wound to the left kidney area that would require surgery on his back, and another wound to his right side, not quite so deep. Fenger turned all attention to the worst of the knife wounds, the one to his shoulder, just above the heart.

He noted that Alastair's forehead and cheek had also sustained slashes and abrasions.

Jane had dropped to her knees on the other side of Ransom, while Gabby kneeled alongside Fenger, each wanting to help. They shared items out of Fenger's bag, tying off tourniquets, wrapping his lesser wounds as Fenger concentrated on the major problem.

"He's been stabbed at least seven, eight times, and he's got several cuts to the face," Jane informed Behan, who, hovering close, whispered that the lads wanted to know the prognosis.

"Will he live?" Behan persisted.

"If we can staunch this wound to the shoulder," Fenger assured him.

"And if we can keep out infection," added Jane. "The water's crawling with infectious disease organisms, no doubt." She realized she sounded like a doctor.

Behan looked into her eyes, silently pleading.

"I believe he's going to be all right," she tried to assure Behan. "None of this is your fault, Inspector."

"He's so still," said a tearful Gabby.

Jane added, "I've never seen him so white, not even when he was shot."

"He's lost a lot of blood," said Fenger. "Gone into shock, I'm afraid."

"Need to get him to a warm place."

Agitated, Fenger agreed. "A clean, well-lit, warm place, yes—my surgery."

A flash of light, repeated by another and another announced that Philo Keane had arrived. Philo somehow kept shooting even as he feared for Ransom's life.

Finished with their mending, Dr. Fenger and Jane began shouting for the men standing about to carry Alastair out.

"There's a waiting ambulance," said Fenger.

"No, please, use the police wagon," countered Philo, raising a few eyebrows, including Christian Fenger's.

"Why not use the medical wagon?" he asked.

"The last time Alastair was hurt, all he talked about afterward was fearing that he would die in the back of that meat wagon of yours, Christian."

Jane jumped in. "Philo's right, Christian. You really have to do something about it."

Fenger looked hurt but said nothing.

"It's more hearse than ambulance," Jane added, "and I inspected it and found it a hotbed of disease organisms!"

"Not to mention the stench," finished Philo Keane.

"We're not funded for anything better at the moment."

"Regardless, he goes in the police wagon."

"I suppose you two are the closest thing to kin he has, so whatever your wish, Mr. Keane, Dr. Francis."

This was enough for the cops who took Fenger at his word—that it would be Ransom's last wish to be kept out of the hands of Shanks and Gwinn. Six men lifted Ransom as they might a coffin, and this procession moved toward the entry point like so many pallbearers.

Christian pointed out that Ransom's cane lay nearby. The wolf's-head was stained red-ochre with blood. "His attackers felt the sting of his blow, and from the number of wounds all over his body, I'd say there were more than these two maniacs coming at him with knives."

Jane tried to imagine the life-and-death struggle down here. "He's got wounds to his legs that, if standing, he'd have taken from midgets or children."

"Compared to Logan, Ransom did damn well," said Gabby, turning heads. "I counted twenty-seven stab wounds on Logan's body before I gave up."

This silenced them as Jane lifted Ransom's cane and held firm to the walking stick. "Suppose Christian that you and Alastair were right—that there was an entire family of these cannibals down here?"

Fenger replied, "And so how many little monsters with ice picks and knives have escaped?"

"And what ages are the ones who got away?" Jane wondered aloud.

"Right now, we've got to get this man to my surgery and immediately."

"I think we've stopped the worst of the blood flow," she replied.

Gabby added, "He's strong. He'll pull through like before. Won't he?"

"Keep to your prayers, ladies," replied Fenger. "He's damn near bled to death."

Ransom made a good recovery, but a painful one. Fenger, fearing he'd become a morphine addict, controlled it personally, and on seeing Dr. McKinnette go near Ransom, he ran the man off with a proviso to the nurses at Cook County that no other physician be allowed near Ransom, especially Dr. Tewes and Dr. McKinnette. He made it clear that should it happen, people would lose their jobs.

However, he did allow personal friends visiting hours with his patient, so Jane Francis and Gabby were camped out at his bedside for days during his recovery. When he came back to himself, Gabby had gone home, but Jane had remained, and she now said to him, "This is getting to be an annoying habit with you."

After drinking a pitcher of water, Alastair asked, "What of Behan? Afraid I know Logan's fate. When I saw that pack of animals feeding on Jedidiah, I attacked."

"Ken's a hero—first to find you. Saved you from drowning in two feet of water and rising."

"Fool—they'd've given 'im a citation had he let me die!"

"As a matter of fact, you're both up for a citation—you for putting an end to Leather Apron and his gang, and Behan for bravery."

"Not all are caught, though, and it was no gang, but a family, the parents teaching their young'uns to be man-eaters."

"Yes, we few know the truth, but newspapers have it only as a gang. A bit less disturbing euphemism for the truth."

"Perhaps that's for the better."

"Better for whom?" she challenged.

"The merchants, the developers, the financiers, and politicians."

She sighed. "The public in general."

"Yes, what does it serve the public to know that in Chicago homeless are driven to cannibalism to survive?"

"A case of excessive aberrant, abhorrent behavior, and not an epidemic. Look, you've evidence the father was Bloody Mary's son. He came here, used her. Chicago did not spawn him. In fact, Gabby's learned he was born in London."

"Aye, home of the original Leather Apron."

"It came across the Atlantic along with disease and other vermin."

"It's him, all right. We'll have to post a letter to Inspector Heise, Scotland Yard."

"Look, you brought down the father and mother, Alastair. It's ended now. Those escaped children can't last long without their parents."

"Are they scouring the city for those three kids?"

"They are and in time, I'm sure, they'll be found as well."

"And the infant? What of the babe?"

"We may never know. Perhaps when the children are found, we can find out."

"Then what? What'll the grand state of Illinois, the County of Cook, and the City of Chicago do with those killer kids when they surface?"

"I can't say. Place them in an institution, I suspect. Work with them. They're feral children."

"Feral is the word, indeed. They have it in their heads now that the best meat is other kids—human flesh. That'll never change."

"Your job now is to get plenty of rest, get your health back."

"Those three, two boys and a girl, they were . . . Jane, they'd be better off today had I been able to finish 'em all."

"Alastair, you did everything humanly possible."

"I suppose . . . I suppose." Ransom still felt weak. "My greatest fear is for the homeless."

"The shelter children, yes, I know."

"Every child in Chicago remains in danger from those hyenas out there, wherever they are."

"Don't be naive, not you, Alastair. Our children have always been in danger from one kind of hyena or another, and after those murderous kids are caught, the homeless children will still be in danger from others."

"What do you propose?"

"We start up a fund-raiser. If the suffragettes can raise funds for their cause, then, by God, we can raise money for this cause."

"Whatever I can do, just tell me when and where."

Just then young Audra stood in the doorway. The young girl was shaking with tears, overcome by grief. Jane went to her and held her close. She broke down and began confessing nonstop. "They made me do it. If I didn't, Zoroaster—their father—he said they'd slice me up and eat me! So I did it. I did it!"

Jane rushed to Audra and hugged her. Ransom flashed back to what he knew of the girl's involvement. She procured for Leather Apron. Was one of them, even if that hadn't been her in that tunnel the night he'd killed the parents.

"Easy . . . easy, now, Audra!" Jane reassured her. "Whatever did you do that is so horrible?"

Ransom had eased from his bed, and Audra tried to pull away from Jane, fearful of Alastair, who asked, "Do you mean to say, Audra, that you led—lured—some of the children to Leather Apron?" It explained why most victims had not been in Aurdra's gang. She wouldn't willingly sacrifice her own, and Danielle's death may've been a warning to Audra to keep silent.

Audra fought to pull away, but Jane held her in a bear hug. She broke down completely, terrified of her fate, terrified of what Ransom might do to her—the man who had slain Zoroaster—and equally terrified of the three children of Zoroaster still at large.

"So this is how Anne Chapman, Alice Cadin, and even your friend Danny disappeared—by trusting you!" Ransom shouted. "Using their trust, your toothy smile and innocent looks."

"I had no choice! They'd kill me if I didn't do it!"

"Hell, who wouldn't follow her into a warehouse or into a bloody drainpipe?"

"Easy on her, Alastair! She's a victim here, too!" shouted Jane. "Can you imagine the terror she has lived through and the guilt?"

"I suppose not," replied Alastair, "since I'm not given to leading my friends to slaughter!"

"Bloody Mary made me do it! I didn't want to!" Audra's cries only increased.

Jane held her tight. "We're going to get you help, Audra. None of this was your fault. You're just a child, a frightened child."

"Have they contacted you, the other three Aprons?" demanded Alastair.

"No, no!" she blurted out, and between sobs, she added, "I—I came to f-find Miss F-Francis f-for help!"

"I'm going to get you admitted for observation," said Jane, "and we'll take one day at a time, Audra. All right? All right?"

"All right." Audra wiped her tears with a hanky Jane handed her. "Thank you, Miss Francis."

But as soon as Jane relaxed her hold on Audra, the child fled out and down the corridor, past people Jane shouted at to stop her. With the speed and agility of a sewer rat, Audra was out of the hospital in moments. Out front of the hospital, Jane gave chase, but it was no use. Audra had disappeared back into the streets. Jane scanned every direction. *Nothing*. She wondered if she'd ever see Audra again.

* * *

News of Audra's visit and her betrayal spread among all of
Jane's closest friends. Gabby, of course, took the news the
hardest, disbelieving. Alastair retold the story to Philo,
Christian, and to the man who purportedly saved his life
down in that black hole—Ken Behan—when he came to
visit at the hospital. Soon everyone in officialdom knew to
be on the lookout for this poor child, and in the meantime,
Jane remained angry at Alastair for frightening the child off
as he had. "You big . . . bear," she'd spoken her last to him as
she stormed away.

A few weeks later, Alastair had arrived home from the
hospital, and an hour into a nap, someone rang his doorbell.
He made his groggy way along on his cane to the door, and
when he opened it, he found Philo Keane and Dr. Christian
Fenger looking stern and grim on his doorstep.

"We have a matter to discuss," said Christian, "you and I,
Alastair, and I brought your best friend along to . . . well,
frankly, to keep you from killing me."

"Don't be ridiculous, Doctor. Come in, the both of you.
I'll put on water to boil, and we'll find some tea."

"That would be good."

Philo shot Alastair a look that only puzzled him.

Once everyone was seated with a cup of tea, the three old
friends stared from one to another, until Ransom said,
"Well, what's this about?"

"The good news, Ransom, is that those three feral children, the ones who got away, will never again feed on human flesh."

"Then they've been caught? Great! When . . . by
whom?"

"Not caught—killled."

"Killed? How? What happened? A manhunt uncovered
them, and they came out swinging, heh?"

"Not exactly."

"How did they die, then?"

"Kohler's involved."

"Kohler? Damn the man. He's taking credit for it all, isn't he? No public release of this information."

"Actually, no one else knows, and it's to stay that way."

"Christian, will you stop talking in cryptic code and tell me what the hell you're driving at?"

"It began with that girl Audra's confessing in your room. Seems she tried confessional at a church, but all she got from the priest was raped—according to her."

"Raped by a priest? Impossible."

Philo hadn't said a word.

"What's happened, Philo?"

"They got wind of Audra—Kohler and Chapman!" Christian blurted out.

Ransom digested this, his face bleeding white. "They got their hands on Audra, didn't they?"

"They made her talk, yes."

"Is she . . . is she alive?" He recalled Bloody Mary and Bosch's double.

Philo piped in. "They let her live."

"But she's no longer the same and never will be again," muttered Christian. "In fact, she is now a permanent resident at the asylum."

"Those bastards!" exploded Ransom. "They tortured her until her mind snapped, didn't they?"

"Not before she led them to the feral children," replied Christian.

Philo choked out, "That maniac Chapman made her watch as he fed those kids to . . . to . . ."

"Let me guess. Fed them alive to the senator's starved pigs."

"Only after skinning them alive." Dr. Fenger then tossed a small bundle tied with twine into Alastair's lap, causing him to spill his tea.

"What the hell? What is this?"

"Final payment. The two of them, Chapman and Kohler, insisted."

"Said you took a down payment to go after Leather Apron for the senator," Philo near whispered.

Ransom gritted his teeth. "I told you what happened, Christian, and Jane was in danger. I had no choice."

"Well, now, it would appear you are paid in full and the senator is happy, and Kohler is the richer for it, as are you."

"And you?" asked Alastair.

Fenger shook his head. "Not a dime."

"You have the joy of a clean conscious, then."

"Not that it will save me from my debts."

Ransom threw the bundle back at Fenger. "You told Kohler about Audra, didn't you?"

Fenger lifted the bundle and shook it at Ransom. "I have no idea in hell how that got out! Do you?" The accusation hung in the air.

Again the bundle was thrown to Ransom.

"Build that damn wing you want!" Ransom threw the money back at him.

"Give it to Jane for her plans for the homeless children!" shouted Fenger, tossing the stack of bills back.

"Are the two of you blind?" asked Philo. "Don't you see? This is Kohler's idea, all of it!"

"What're you talking about?" asked Fenger.

"Giving you, Christian, blood money to give to you, Alastair!" Philo shouted. "He wants to drive a wedge between you, a permanent one. And I am left to watch this pissing contest!"

"What're you suggesting, Philo?" Ransom's nostrils flared.

"I know he gave you the impression that Chapman was running things, but no, Nathan is and has been from the start."

"You mean he started this whole thing with Chapman in motion?" asked Fenger.

"When have you ever known Kohler to relinquish control? Either of you?"

Christian and Alastair looked across the chasm that

Kohler had created between them. Fenger finally said, "Philo's right. Giving this money to me to deliver to you . . . it's his design."

Alastair agreed. "Part of his goal from the outset."

Philo Keane felt as if he could breathe again. "That sounds a proper end to it—give the money to the fund Jane Francis has established for the homeless."

"Aye, a fitting end to it," Alastair poured himself another cup of tea, then raised his cup, and all three toasted this conclusion. Then Ransom asked, "Did they get the right murderous children? Tell me they didn't get it *wrong* this time."

"They were caught while sleeping, and their own knives were used on them," explained Christian.

"They were bred to it like animals by their own parents," said Philo.

Fenger added, "They were children turned into Frankenstein monsters."

"What justice is there in this end?" asked Ransom.

"Those children would've continued on, butchering other children, Rance—we all know that." Philo sipped the last of his spiked tea.

"They damn near killed you, Alastair," added Christian.

"Still . . . I was out there at those stables. I saw the kind of justice Chapman and Kohler meted out on Bloody Mary, an insane woman, and a complete other innocent man. I can't say any of this sits well with me."

"Still, you've got to take the money, Alastair." Fenger stood to leave.

"What're you now, Christian? Nathan's errand boy?"

Philo leapt to his feet and placed a firm hand against Alastair's chest, trying to calm him. "You two are allowing Kohler to win if you end like this."

Christian stopped at the door and looked deep into Ransom's eyes. "Until you lay the man low, Alastair, we all have him as a cross to bear, and we all have to work with him."

"That's it, isn't it, Christian? He holds your notes—bought up all your debts, hasn't he? Makes a mockery of your office as impartial coroner."

Christian's jaw twitched with the anger of this kind of information being shouted to the world where he stood at the open door. The two old friends held one another in a grim stare.

Philo determined to end this before more was said. He joined Christian at his side, shook Alastair's hand, and gave him a brief hug. "Don't you be led by Kohler, either of you! You are both better than that. Now we're going, Rance, and . . . and well . . . don't be a stranger. Come round to the studio, both of you. I have some of that whiskey left."

Ransom nodded and relaxed, bidding them good-bye and raising the money bundle overhead. He knew why Kohler had gotten his two best friends to bring the cash. Anyone else and he'd have shot them. This way, at some future date, Nathan Kohler might be able to use this blood money against him. He imagined that one of Nathan's spies was not too far from his door, closely watching everything. Unless he missed his guess, it'd be Henry Bosch.

A week later

More time had passed and Chicago returned to what most people termed "normal" and all commerce doubled and quadrupled daily, prices skyrocketing, and the homeless population, both adult and child, only increased, putting an even greater strain on the city shelters and jails. No one questioned the mystery of where Jane Francis's funds, or those of her brother, Dr. Tewes, had come from, and when asked, each was quick to reply, "A donor whose greatest wish was to remain anonymous."

Other than a program begun by a Dr. Jane Francis to find a home for every parentless child, and a roof for every homeless child, little had changed, despite the sheer terror of a story that was so horrendous that it would never see full play in the mainstream press. Word on the street had it that Inspector Alastair Ransom, with help from the deceased Jed Logan, and a heroic Ken Behan, had pretty much single-handedly taken on the entire family of beasts in their own lair and had wiped them out, one and all.

The legend of Beowulf *recounted.*

As for Audra, she could be found any day in the Cook County Asylum—seen daily by Gabby Tewes, and from time to time, Gabby's father, Dr. J. P. Tewes, whose phrenological exams, Audra looked forward to, although she could not voice this or any other fact. Another and final victim of the Leather Apron gang? Or Chapman and Kohler's inquisition?

As in all things he touched, no matter the twisted outcome, Alastair Ransom had landed on his feet. Most beat cops, firemen, and even most of the petty criminals and burglars and pickpockets had only more respect and greater fear of the Bear. But one man, Nathan Kohler, uneasy with all that Alastair knew of his true nature, lived now to destroy Inspector Ransom at all costs.